LETTERS TO SINGAPORE

LETTERS TO SINGAPORE

A novel by

Kelly Kaur

Stonehouse Publishing
www.stonehousepublishing.ca
Alberta, Canada

Stonehouse Publishing Inc. is an independent
publishing house, incorporated in 2014.

Cover design and layout by Anne Brown.
Printed in Canada

Stonehouse Publishing would like to thank and acknowledge
the support of the Alberta Government funding for the arts,
through the Alberta Media Fund.

Alberta◼
Government

National Library of Canada Cataloguing in Publication Data
Kelly Kaur
Letters to Singapore
Novel
ISBN 978-1-988754-39-0

To karma and kismet that brought me to beautiful Calgary

24 AUGUST 1985

Ten days in Calgary, dear Mummy.

Papa left today. We waited for one hour in the cold for the Taxiwallah to show up. We were outside Ramada Motel at Motel Village, where all the motels near the university are located. This was our temporary home in Calgary. Taxiwallah, Papa's new friend, had promised in his morning phone call he would arrive at 2 p.m. He never showed up. We panicked because Papa had to be at the airport to catch his flight, and it was getting late. Finally, Papa talked to the manager of Ramada Motel who called another taxi, and it arrived in ten minutes.

Then, it was time for Papa to leave. I stared at the yellow taxi in front of me. My tears made everything hazy. Papa stretched his right arm and tapped my back. I turned and put my arms around his neck.

He said, "Simran, you must be like a tiger now."

I nodded and remembered. When I was nine years old, I fell from a bicycle. I howled like a baby, but Papa picked me up, shook me by my shoulders and whispered, "Be a tiger, Simran. Be a tiger."

Our bones collided uncomfortably as I tried to stay longer in his embrace, but he pulled away, extended his left hand, and looked at his watch. He grabbed his suitcase and opened the back door of the taxi. I sensed he was worried about leaving me alone in Calgary, yet he was also exasperated I had disobeyed his orders and not gotten married to that man he had picked for me in Singapore—I had rejected all the arranged marriage suitors and begged to get a degree in Canada! Perhaps, it was not worry I sensed but regret he had given in to my rebellion.

My chest constricted with that thought. Maybe, I had made a terrible mistake in coming to Calgary, leaving everything safe and familiar behind. I wasn't feeling brave and rebellious in that moment. Papa's shoulders crumbled, and he blew his nose loudly into his tartan red handkerchief to hide his face. I was thankful he had even come with me to Calgary to make sure that I would be safe. I knew he didn't want me to leave Singapore at all.

"I am your papa," he declared that day when he came home with the flight tickets to Calgary. "As long as I am alive, I will take care of you."

How hard it must be for him to leave me alone in this strange country. My gruff papa barked his last words to me before he shut the taxi door. "Now get your degree and come back home immediately, Simran. Three years and no more."

I bowed my head and gazed at the road because I did not want Papa to see my tears. I had to be like a tiger! I couldn't swallow. I could no longer speak. I stood there, waved, and watched the taxi speed off but papa did not look back.

Just like that, I was alone. Totally alone in Calgary. I didn't feel that fearless anymore without my papa. Where the heck have I ended up, Mummy? What have I done? Twenty years old and alone, standing outside a motel, feeling the sharp chill of an autumn day in Calgary. Stupidly, I did not have a jacket. It was freezing, not the hot and humid thirty degrees Celsius of Singapore. It was ten degrees Celsius. I stared at the unsmiling, unfamiliar faces around me. People dressed in cozy jackets to wield off the icy fingers of the wind. Thoughts crowded my mind. Singapore. Calgary. Run away from an arranged marriage. Get a degree. Papa has left. I know no one. Conflicting contemplations.

Though as I shivered, a quivering feeling of euphoria slowly snaked from my belly to my throat. My eyes widened as I realized I had made it to the University of Calgary. To get a degree. Against all odds. The decider of my own destiny. What grand adventures would I experience? Sad but thrilled, I grabbed my suitcase and marched off in the direction of the University of Calgary. I knew it was about a fifteen-minute walk to my new dormitory room, and I needed to clear my head.

Suddenly, a yellow taxi screeched to a stop right in front of me. I jumped back from surprise. Wait. What? It was that bloody Taxiwallah that Papa had been waiting for to take him to the airport. That was the man we met when papa came with me ten days ago. When we arrived at the Calgary Airport, we went to the taxi stand and had gotten into this man's cab.

You see, Taxiwallah drove us from the airport to Motel Village close to the University of Calgary. He told us that there were about ten motels next to one another, and we could easily get one. Papa talked to him the whole way. Papa told him our whole family history and plans for the next ten days. So, Taxiwallah gave Papa his phone number and promised to show us around Calgary.

Papa asked him where the gurdwara in Calgary was.

Taxiwallah said, "Don't worry. I will take you."

He showed up two days later to take us to the Sikh temple in the southwest of Calgary. Then, Taxiwallah drove us to downtown Calgary and showed us the famous Calgary Tower and Bow River. Two new, unexpected friends! Papa made plans to meet him again the next day. Great—bonding with Taxiwallah. Papa was enthusiastic on the last evening together when we went to The Keg for dinner.

He put his hand on Taxiwallah's shoulder and on mine and declared to me, "Now you have someone who can help you when I am gone. Take care of my daughter."

Then, they both hugged each other like long-lost brothers.

So, here I was, Mummy. Papa had just left in the other taxi to go to the airport and here was Taxiwallah.

He jumped out of his taxi and said, "Sorry, sorry. Simran. I was stuck in a terrible traffic jam near the airport. Where is your papa?"

I glared at Taxiwallah and snarled, "You know he is gone. He left. You were late."

"Acha," he shook his head and smiled. "Ok. Ok. I'll take you to your dormitory. Come."

He grabbed my suitcase. I slid into his taxi in the front seat next to him. His taxi still had the pungent smell of stale cigarettes from the last few times I was in it. I cranked open the window to breathe the cold, crisp Calgary air. He glanced at me sideways while he re-assured me papa must have made it in time to catch his flight to Singapore.

Thankfully, it was only a five-minute drive, and we reached outside the seven-storey building of my new home—Kananaskis Hall—the building where my dormitory is in, Mummy, and he parked in the visitor's spot.

I jumped out of the taxi and said, "Thank you, Uncle. Goodbye."

"No, no," he said. "I'll come up with you and make sure that you are ok. Your papa told me to take good care of you."

What the hell. He would not leave. I put my hand up and waved him away. Nothing. He followed me into the front door of the building with my luggage in his right hand. I didn't know what to do.

"Ok, goodbye," I said. My smile froze like ice. "Ok. Go now. All good. Thanks."

"No, no. Let me make sure you are safe in your room."

I lunged to get my suitcase from his right hand. Taxiwallah laughed and waved me on. He walked past the elevator to the door next to it—the stairway. Taxiwallah followed a step behind me as I uncomfortably trudged up each flight of stairs. Third floor. I opened the stairway door and stepped into the common living area. I grabbed my suitcase from his hand, but he pushed me away from it with his other hand. He looked for my room number on the map next to the elevator and pointed down the wing on the left.

I stepped back and firmly shrieked, "Ok, Uncle, goodbye."

"No, no," Taxiwallah sneered. "Let's make sure the room is good for you."

I looked around the long empty hallway. Not a single soul. Trapped, I jiggled the lock and the handle of the door. I flung the door open and stood outside.

He said, "Ladies, first," and waved me in.

He shadowed my steps into the room, twirled around, and thumped the door shut. He tossed my suitcase on the single bed in the tiny room. Then, the bastard stepped up right to my face, firmly put his hands around my waist, pulled me close until his groin touched mine and his tobacco breath expelled on my face.

"Acha. Simran. Beautiful girl. Your papa told me to take care of you. I am here for you, anytime day or night. You can call me. Anytime. Come, I will take you to Banff. Your papa is gone. But don't worry. I am here. You won't be alone anymore."

I tasted bile in my mouth and whiffed putrid smoke and sweat. His leered at me like that villain in every Hindi movie we watched together, Mummy. Dirty old man. No wonder he came so late.

"Be like a tiger." I heard these words in my mind. Loudly and clearly.

With all my might, I pushed Taxiwallah off. He tumbled. I sprinted to the door, opened it, and jumped outside.

"Get lost!" I screamed. "Hello. Hello, anyone here?" I shouted. "Hello. Hello."

I kept shouting.

Taxiwallah stared at me and shook his head in disappointment. "Just like a sher. A tiger." He chuckled and handed me his card. "Never mind. Here is my phone number. Call me." He turned and walked away.

I jumped into the room, banged the door, dragged the chair, and leaned it against the doorknob. I threw his card into the dustbin. I picked up the phone and listened to the ringtone, which calmed me down. 999 to call the police, like in Singapore?

Shaken, I plunked on one of the two single beds; both had light green bedsheets and brown wooly blankets. Like a hospital room in Singapore. I glanced around the matchbox room—two single beds, two desks and chairs and two closets. On the wall opposite the door was a big rectangle window that looked out to a meandering walking path littered with brown leaves and bare brown branched trees. I stretched my legs out as far as they could reach and touched the other bed. My breathing restored itself to normalcy. With a sigh, I put my head down on the flat, squishy pillow and stared at the dirty, brown-streaked ceiling.

I know, Mummy. You must be thinking I have come to the dangerous jungle alone. I know. I know. I thought I was brave to come to Calgary by myself. Luckily, I watched all those Hindi movies with you. There was always a bad guy. Don't worry, Mummy. Remember what the Taxiwallah called me—sher? Exactly. Tiger. Let's see what else the jungle will bring. I am ready.

I am going to kill Taxiwallah if I ever see him again.

I miss you, Mummy.

Simran

10 SEPTEMBER 1985

Dear Simran,

I didn't get a chance to say goodbye to you in person. Actually, I was shocked to hear that you were going to Calgary to get your degree. One moment I had your wedding invitation, and the next, you were calling to say you were leaving.

How in hell did you get out of your arranged married situation? That must have been a miracle. For God's sakes, you showed me your wedding outfit that you have shoved in a suitcase under your bed. I can't even imagine sleeping with that overpriced wedding suit under your bed every day for three months. You must have had some nasty nightmares. How did you plot the perfect escape? Where the hell is Calgary? I would never have gone to some frozen, God forsaken country like Canada. I imagine you simply wanted to vamoose. Listen, I am dying to know the details.

Really, I am wondering why you are even trying to get a degree? Come on, Sim. You barely even passed your pre-university classes. Do you really want to get a degree, or did you run away to get your freedom? I have always had my freedom here in Singapore. Us Chinese are not as strict as you Indians. I always felt sorry for you— you lived in a prison of your family, your culture, your tradition. It never ended for you, did it? I couldn't believe that you could not even go out, go to parties, stay out late, travel…like I could. I guess I always had my freedom and took it for granted.

But we all have our crap to bear. While you always envied me about being free, you never knew the full story of my life. I started telling you about my mum. That one, I can't understand, lah.

She loves money and status. It was never enough for her to

have a husband who loved her. Can you believe that she had a great love story with my father? They met in college and married young. She didn't want to get an education. She didn't want children and was angry when she got pregnant not once, but twice. Of course, she blamed my father, but he was happy to have me and Steven.

My mum had big, unreal Singapore dreams. She yearned to be rich. She did not want to live in a boring three-bedroomed Housing and Development Board flat in Ang Mo Kio. She had no interest to be like all Singaporeans, housed in a boxed apartment stacked on top of each other in cookie cutter HDB blocks, right? She did not want to walk to the wet markets every morning, buy groceries, come home, cook, clean, and do laundry. She claimed that she was born to be in a mansion in Holland Village, with a fire-red Mercedes, and nannies and maids. Every day, I watched her turn into a screaming banshee.

Every day when I was growing up, I listened to her unhappy tirades. *You, ah. Don't be so stupid. You got hear me or not. Don't marry for love. Understand. Marry for money. Find a rich husband. Make money. Never enough. Don't live in a stupid HDB flat and watch stupid Chinese movies every day like me. Take bus everywhere. Buy clothes from Metro shopping centre, not Gucci. No escape, you know. No way out. Cannot go anywhere.*

Alamak. I can't get along with my mum. She is bitter and mean. Is this what unhappiness does to women? Is money more important than love? My father, well, he has become deaf and dumb. Every day, he comes home and goes directly into his bedroom to escape her screams and taunts. Bang. The door shuts. Nobody knows what goes on in our flats. Our lives compartmentalized like the flats we live in. Our secrets boxed in tiny spaces.

It's been a year since I've been back from Princeton. Back to Singapore. Back to family expectations and other people's hopes and dreams.

Are you coming back to Singapore? So much more to confess.

Tell me about Calgary. Is it even on the map?

Ciao,

Amy

25 SEPTEMBER 1985

Hello Simran,

You must be careful. All men will take advantage of you if you are not careful. I told your father about the Taxiwallah and he was very angry. He called him in Calgary but no answer. Acha, stay away from that man. You are doing the right thing. You threw him out of your room. You should have called 999, police. Good thing he left. It is not easy to be alone in a strange country. I told you not to go. Better for a girl to be married. Only father or husband can protect you. You gave up a thing when you ended your engagement. Such a nice boy. Good family. What is this education you want?

Alright. Never mind. It's your karma. Written in your stars. How is Calgary? Are you settling in? How do you feel? Now you are alone and free. Freedom is not easy. We are used to living together in Singapore and now you have no one. What to do? You must be strong. Pray every day. God will take care of you. That is the only solution. Check your suitcase. I put in a prayer book in English. Read one page a day. You can do it. Only Babaji can protect you. A hockey stick is useful too. Your father has one under his bed.

For me, it is difficult since you have been gone. I am alone. Broken family. Your brother is in the Singapore army now. We don't see him except when he can come home for the weekend. I miss him. Only happy when he comes back. Then, I make him his favourite food like roti, rajma and chicken curry. He is happy. Army food is bad. It is lonely and quiet without my children. All of you are gone. I know, Simran, you ran away from Singapore. You didn't want the life of a woman and to be married, right. Why does a woman need such a big degree? In the end, you still have to have a husband and children. You have gone so far away. All my life I take care of all my children. One by one, all of you are running away. Now I am old, no one is left to take care of me. Everyone escaped. No escape for me.

I saw Aunty Verma yesterday at the market. She was telling me about her daughter, Sunita. Do you remember her? The daughter was your age. Twenty years. Her family found her a nice family boy from Bombay. Arranged marriage. Not love marriage. They spent so much money on her wedding and dowry. Big wedding. Dinner at Shangri-La Hotel. Six months, her husband doesn't want to have sex with her. Sunita was very upset. One day, she came home early from work and she saw her husband in the bedroom. He was wearing her dress, high heels, and lipstick. What is happening to the world? It was big shock for everyone. They got a divorce. How? She could have kept quiet and stayed married. What's the harm?

Now, her husband has gone back to Bombay. Sunita is back in her family house. Back to square one. Spent all that money for a wedding for what? Everything is upside down in the world. I don't know what to say. Nowadays, getting married also difficult. The world out there is dishonest. My time, all was easy. I was sixteen years old and married off. No choice. No escape. Just take what comes.

To fill my loneliness since all my children have abandoned me, I am learning new songs to play on my waja. You always called my waja my little piano. My harmonium. I am getting good at hitting all the keys on it with my right hand and pushing the air in and out with the flap with my left hand. Still same. Every Wednesday is the ladies' group at the temple. All the ladies are fighting to see who will sing as the main singer. I smile at everyone and make sure I don't join in any ladies' fighting and gossip. Even singing God's songs is difficult. This is the life of a woman, wife, and mother. Cook, clean, take care of children, go to temple, keep husband happy. This is what you ran away from, right? I know everything.

Your father is same. He said he had a good time seeing new places and he said Calgary is very ulu. Quiet. No action. Dead place. Good. Better that way. Like that, it can be safe and sound for you.

Not like Dallas like we see on television where everyone is wild and doing drugs and sleeping around. What show is that? Dynasty?

Your papa told me he stood outside the office at the University of Calgary dormitory until the manager gave you a room to stay. He told me you had no place to stay because they lost your application. He was worried. He said he told the manager he won't leave until they give you a place to stay at the residence. Your papa sat outside the manager's office for three hours, right. The manager was scared of your father and promised to give you a room in Kananaskis Hall on the day papa had to leave. See. Otherwise, how?

You are lucky he went with you. It is not easy to let a daughter go to a foreign country and be alone. You could have been married instead of being in Calgary. I don't know how you escaped. Even your father was saying maybe it was a mistake to let you go. Ok. Never mind. In three years, you can come back and get married. There will be many Indian men who will be happy to marry a beautiful and educated girl like you.

Be strong. When girls are alone, they must be extra careful. Don't trust any men. Life is lonely here without you. I wish you are here with me in Singapore. Calgary is too far away.

Mummy

5 OCTOBER 1985

Hey Babi Betul,

Apa khabar? Semua bagus? How, lah? Are you missing our Singapore slang, already? For some reason, we called each other true pigs—babi betul. That makes me smile. How is Calgary, man? Can you believe I've heard about that place? You see, I was there five years ago with my hubby Gopal. Calgary is not that popular for us Asians. Never heard of it. People only know about Toronto or Vancouver. But Gopal and I heard about the spectacular mountains in the Rockies and flew to Calgary for a three-day holiday. Then, we drove to Vancouver. Oh, Simran. Calgary is a beautiful place.

So, you did it. You made the perfect escape from Singapore, lah. One minute you were getting married and the next, you cabut lagi. Good escape, my friend. I did not think in a million years that you would be able to escape from your arranged marriage. It is a miracle, right? Your father is a traditional man. Do you remember? You had to go straight home from classes and work. Even at twenty years old! Now, who is going to keep an eye on you?

I hope that you come back to Singapore. Singaporeans like to run away. They think that the world out there is better. Please, lah. I could never survive in such a freezing cold country like that. To be alone and away from my family. What for? Me, I love Singapore. Nice. Safe. Secure. Hot. Perfect. All Asians from all races. Let me tell you. You are going to miss all the food here. I just had satay and ketupat from Newton Circus Food Court. I am sure you are going miss the open-air hawker centres, my friend. Where will you go to get chicken rice for $2 from any outdoor food stall?

Things at home are hectic. The boys are one and two year old.

Add teaching long days every day and a husband who is going through some shit at work, I can barely keep up. Frankly, there are some days that I envy you. Your freedom. Your escape. Being responsible for only yourself. It's funny, isn't it. We yearn to find love. We want a husband. We die to be mothers. Then, we yearn to be alone. Still, my life is better than yours alone in Calgary, right? I have the perfect life.

Singapore, alamak, the only constant here is it is bloody hot. Thankfully, it rained the other day, an unexpected heavy downpour. I had my umbrella as I ran from my car to the school building. Useless. The wind blew all the spokes up. I was totally wet.

For some reason, I remembered when I used that umbrella to keep all of you in our English class study group, Shan, Maya, and Siti, at bay. Just like that, all of you conspired to attack me when I went to the toilet. I came out of the stall, and you all ran after me, caught me, and carried me across the canteen to the carpark. Then, you put me in the trunk of your car for the fun of it. Teachers behaving like kids. I think we all laughed till we peed in our pants. So stupid. Such silly days we had training to be teachers at the Institute of Education at Bukit Timah Road. Remember? Missing classes to go to A&W across the road. Girls becoming women. But you are terrible, Miss Simran. There will be payback, one day. I will have my umbrella ready.

Life goes on in Singapore! I am going for a hike to MacRitchie Reservoir this Saturday with work colleagues. Early dawn. We will walk for two hours in the jungled oasis, away from the buildings. I just love it there. So quiet. Then, like true Singaporeans, we will go have makan makan—yes, eat till we drop, at the nearby hawker centre. The next time you are back in Singapore, I'll take you with me for a hike. But I know you can't tahan the sun, you princess, as we say in Malay.

You will not believe who I ran into the other day. Remember Misha from our math class at the Institute of Education? Yes, that beautiful, dark-haired Punjabi girl. She is Miss Hoity Toity now. She hit the jackpot. Married to some rich thambi who is the Director of the Bank of India. No need to work. Just go shopping in Delhi and travel to London and Paris. Damn. This is the ultimate Singapore girl's dream. Just get married and relax, lagi. Maybe we got this idea of independence all wrong.

Sims, I miss you. I miss our weekly hangouts and chit chats. You had the best advice about everything for a girl who had no freedom. What a paradox. You always said you wanted more, bigger, better for your life. I hope that you find it in Canada. Enjoy your life in Calgary. I can't imagine how it must be for you from zero freedom to total freedom. Don't go too crazy on that. But tell me everything.

The one and only

Anita

10 OCTOBER 1985

Dear Amrit,

I hope you get this letter in time. Twenty-three years old, big sister. Happy birthday. Already a mummy to two daughters. I cannot believe it. Papa was my travel companion, right. It was strange and exciting. Really, I have never seen so many White people except on the TV Hollywood shows we watched when we were growing up. It felt strange, you know, to be the brown girl in a sea of white. In Singapore, we all just blended in, Chinese, Indian, Malay. I stand out here in Calgary.

When Papa and I reached Calgary, on the first day, we nearly got hit by a car. We were crossing the small street near the University of Calgary, and I looked the wrong way because Canadians drive on the right, not like in Singapore. But you won't believe how the drivers in Calgary are different. The driver, an old man, stopped his car and let us cross the road. Then, he waved at us. Not like in Singapore, where they would drive over you and kill you. The whole week I was puzzled about where to look when I crossed the streets. It's the small things about being in a new country that are challenging.

My university classes started. I figured out where to go on campus and saw many new faces in every class. In my German class, I met this guy, Marlon. Tall. White. Blonde hair. Blue eyes. He had two cute deep dimples on each cheek that were sexy. He sat next to me and talked to me in class. He asked me where I lived, and I told him I was five minutes away in the dormitories in Kananaskis Hall.

Guess what? Last Friday, late at night, the elevator door opened on the third floor at Kan Hall. I was watching TV in the common living room by myself. I was startled. He just showed up out of the blue.

I said, "What are you doing here?"

He said, "Let's study for our German test on Monday."

What? Strange man. But I was flattered. No Papa to kill this boy who just showed up, right? I went to my room down the hallway to get my books, and we sat at the study table next to the couches. Our session lasted minutes.

We only had a chance to practice, 'Wie gehts? Ich bin Sim," when he looked at his watch, jumped up and said, "Forget German. Let's go to a bar." What? "Hurry!"

I was confused. That's the problem. In Singapore, it would not be a possibility to go anywhere late at night with any man. Papa would kill me first, then the boy. What were the rules here? I had no time to think. I ran to my room, grabbed my purse and jacket, and the next thing I knew, Marlon sprinted to the bus stop across Kananaskis Hall, crossing University Drive. My brain cautioned me to stop following Marlon. I saw the bus come. He jumped on it. I should have stopped and turned back—gone back to my dorm. Instead, I ran like a madwoman and jumped on the moving bus.

Marlon smiled at me, and his dimples danced in joy. I sank into the seat and held on to the pole. I wasn't sure what I'd gotten myself into.

I stared at him. "Where are we going?" I asked nervously.

"Electric Avenue," he mumbled. "11ᵗʰ Ave."

It could have been Timbuktu. I had no idea about anything and anywhere in Calgary, and it was past nine p.m., late, dark, and cold. I clenched my hands and smiled awkwardly.

My racing mind realized I hadn't told any of the girls or my roommate at my dormitory where I was going. I was with a stranger—I didn't know Marlon that well. He could be an axe murderer. Worse still, as a newbie in the city, I didn't know my way around Calgary. Really, I knew no one. I caught a glimpse of my worried face in the window of the bus. What! I had barely combed my hair or put on any makeup. I looked like I was ready for bed, not for partying on this electric avenue he mentioned.

I apprehensively followed Marlon when he jumped off the bus and walked to an unfamiliar destination. The sign read, "Coconut Joe's," and we waited outside the bar for a long time in the freezing night to get in. Are these people mad? Standing in line in the cold? All new for me. What bar could I even go to in Singapore this late at night? The line shuffled forward, and we finally got inside the dimly lit bar. Marlon didn't say much to me. He talked to everyone else in the line and to people walking past. I shuffled and dug my hands into my coat pockets to stay warm and calm. Marlon didn't look that cute anymore.

Inside, the bar was crowded, noisy, reeked of smoke and alcohol. I pushed my way in blindly. I noticed everyone was White, and I felt out of place. I peered around in the dimness and didn't know what to do or where to go. You know me. The only bar I've been to in Singapore was the Raffles Bar. And that was a lounge! I stood in the middle of a crowd of intoxicated, dancing people and looked at Marlon to guide me.

Marlon whispered in my ear, "I'll be back. Enjoy yourself." What?

"Hey," I tried to grab his arm.

But the bastard left like a slippery snake.

My confused mind ran in circles. *Was this what a Canadian date was?*

I had zero experience to bank on.

Stranded in a bar alone, I snapped my fingers to the beat, pretending to fit in. I pushed my way to the bar, ordered a glass of Coke and stood awkwardly in the corner, smiling like an idiot, looking at the filthy floor, feeling petrified. Then, I heard a voice and glanced up. A young boy, who looked twelve—but he must have been at least eighteen, of course, to get into the bar—came up to me and mumbled drunkenly, "Oh, you are so beautiful. What's your name? Dim? Nim? Bim? Oh. Sim. Nice to meet you, Sim."

There I was, Amrit, already on my second date since my first date had apparently dumped me. This skinny, drunk, pimply boy was trying to pick me up. He babbled, hiccupped, and swayed back and forth, two bottles of beer in each hand. Strangely, I relaxed.

Maybe, it wasn't that bad. I was grateful for him because that Marlon was nowhere to be seen. This boy could be my knight in shining armour.

Mark, his name was Mark. He worked at McDonald's taking food orders. He was drunk as a skunk.

He leaned into me, repeating, "You are so beautiful, baby—Singapore? Where is that? China? You don't look Chinese."

I sighed. I didn't say much because it was loud and noisy. I closed my eyes, took a deep breath, opened my eyes, and watched the people grooving on the dance floor. I smiled at everything Mark said. He grabbed my arm and pulled me to the postage stamp dance floor. He screamed the lyrics to the song and pointed to me to emphasize words like "love" or "baby." Damn. I was here. What else was there to do but to point back and scream "love" and "baby" at Mark while he jumped up and down like a kangaroo. My first Calgary bar. Finally, Mark looked like he was going to collapse. He stumbled back to the corner.

"I have to leave, baby," Mark slurred. "Want to come home with me?"

I leaned into his ear and said, "My husband is here, and I have to find him."

"Oh, kinky lady." Mark shoved his phone number into my hand and stumbled out of the bar. I was tempted to leave with him. Now, I was alone in this crowd of madness, leaning against the wall, sipping on the melted ice cubes. I stared at my watch. Twelve midnight. No sign of Marlon.

Frankly, by then, I couldn't even remember what Marlon looked like anymore. I had only seen him a handful of times. Dimples. I looked for dimples. I circled the bar a few times, looking for a dimply man. It was more like I squeezed by the hundreds of people huddled in clumps, sloshing beer. No Marlon. What was I supposed to do? I didn't think I had enough money in my purse—maybe a five dollar note, not enough for any taxi fare. More people left the bar. I circled the bar five times.

Out of nowhere, I heard my name.

"Sim! Sim!" Marlon had magically appeared from nowhere.

"Hey, you want to leave?"

He smiled at me with his gorgeous dimples that danced innocently. I wanted to put my arms around his neck and strangle him. Relieved, I jumped up and staggered outside into the cool air. My heart pounded in confusion. I was at his mercy, it seemed. He stood on the side of the street and flagged down a taxi. I jumped in after him. *He better not think I was going home with him.* I sighed in relief when he told the taxi driver to drop me off first at the University of Calgary.

"You have any money?" He asked me.

I gave him my last five dollars.

"Where were you? You left me alone for four hours."

"Yeah?" he said. "Welcome to Calgary. I thought you were having a good time. I wanted to show you Canadian life."

"What were you doing?"

He tossed his head back and grinned. "I was selling drugs, man."

Drugs? In Singapore, we would be getting the death sentence! Drugs? And he took five dollars from me?

Thankfully, the taxi arrived at Kananaskis Hall. I jumped out of that taxi before it even fully stopped in front of Kananaskis Hall.

"See you in German class on Monday. Guten nacht!" Marlon's cheerful voice broke the silence of the night as I clumsily struggled to open the giant door of the building.

Safe. Alive. How do you say, "I'm going to kill you" in German?

So there, my sister. That was my exciting first and second date in Calgary. The taste of freedom. The price of independence. I remember all the times in Singapore when I couldn't go out at night, couldn't go out with boys, couldn't do anything we wanted because we all had to stay at home in prison, under the watchful eye of Papa. How I fantasized every night when I laid in my bed in Singapore about my first, romantic date.

Here I was, in the land of freedom and opportunity, and my unforgettable date in Calgary turned out to be with a drug dealer. Hahahahahahahaha. Thank God there's no death penalty here in Canada like there is in Singapore for drug trafficking. Don't tell Mummy and Papa. They will make me come home to Singapore immediately.

Have a wonderful birthday. Kisses to the babies.

Love you,

Simran

12 NOVEMBER 1985

Dear Anita,

I always meant to say sorry for stuffing you in the boot of my car while you tried to wield us off with your umbrella. Such foolish girls we were. Thank you for being a good sport.

You know, I was always jealous of you. You do have the perfect life. You married the great love of your life, Gopal. You both took off for a year and travelled the world. You came back to Singapore, have two beautiful boys, bought a fancy upgraded Housing Development Board flat, secured the perfect jobs as teacher and engineer, and live the ultimate Singapore dream.

Me? Here I am in Calgary. Yeah. It's a quiet city, compared to Singapore. Calgary is dead. It's cold. It's strange. I can't place myself yet here. I'm out of my comfort zone of my familiar Singapore. I miss my crowded, hot, humid, hustling, and bustling Singapore. Some days, I feel disconnected. I now wander between that land of familiarity I left and this new land of ice, snow, and possibility. I feel like a ghost, as I flit from one world to the other, constantly trying to carve a niche and to find a new place to meld into. It's a mind juggle to readjust to who I am. My life in Singapore was sharply outlined by family and tradition. My life in Calgary is slowly being redefined by shifting those traditional expectations. That's why a little freedom is a dangerous thing.

Everything in my life is an adjustment. Living in residence at Kananaskis Hall at the University of Calgary is the most unnatural feeling in the world. My Punjabi family's five-bedroomed flat had doors that I could not close or find sanctuary behind. This wild, strange building of floor upon floor has hallways and tiny rooms with people from all over Canada and the world. Some hodge podge laksa of lives intertwined. If you can guess my luck, I got the only all girls' floor of the dorms on 3rd floor Kananaskis—three hallways and sixty rooms of girls, girls and more girls. Gimme a break. Why couldn't I get the mixed wing floor? I could have been on the floor with two hallways of all boys and one hallway of girls. On the same floor. Imagine that exciting set up that would defy all my family's rules of no boys allowed near me. Sigh. All girls on 3rd Kananaskis Hall at the University of Calgary.

Have you ever seen dormitories at universities? I live in a tomb of a room—worse still, this room is for two people. Two identical beds, two desks and two closets, lined up on the left and the right. I thought Singapore flats were small. This is a matchbox room. At first, for one glorious week, I had that room to myself. I prayed that no one would occupy the other half. Then, I ran into a Chinese girl from Malaysia, Lin. She lived on the 6th floor. Obnoxious. Socially inept. Rude. Intel that I gathered from talking to her for ten minutes.

I couldn't stand her. Her ears perked up when she realized that I had no roommate. I felt a sinking feeling as soon as she said goodbye. She immediately ran to the Housing Manager of the dormitories, and one hour later, you got it, she was moving into the other half of my matchbox. What? I sank on my bed in despair and watched her unpack—she was one arm's length away from me and would not stop complaining about everything. She hated her roommate on 6th floor. Oh boy, I already knew that feeling. Do you think that there is God of Irony and Retaliation, and he has placed me in my Canadian version of hell?

The toilets? There is a big communal washroom with six toilet stalls and four shower stalls in each hallway. There are all girls on my floor, so that part is good. There is no kitchen. We buy food from the cafeteria. I miss a home with a kitchen and my own toilet. Every day is a new adventure.

Not ready to admit defeat by my accommodations, I decided to attend my first Canadian Rez party on campus—the famous Rez parties I had heard about from my fellow dormers. Every day, on my way back and forth from classes, I glanced excitedly at the posters pinned on the hallways announcing this big event. I didn't know many of the girls on the floor yet. I tried my best to cajole Lin to come with me; she sneered at me and shook her head. Oh, Lin! For the first time since she forced herself into my room, I would have gone with the devil herself.

As my dearest friend, I'm going to tell you something that you have to promise never to tell. All my life I dreamt of going to a real party. Wait till you hear what happened. I decided that I would grasp my beautiful new-found freedom and go to that party that I had imagined when I was confined and imprisoned in my room in Singapore with the door that I was never allowed to shut. Nobody could stop me now! At this Rez party, I would knock them dead. YES!

The evening finally arrived. Pumped and excited, I put on my pink blouse, my pink pants, my pink belt, my pink socks, my dainty pink shoes. I had pink hair-clips, pink earrings, pink bangles, and pink eyeshadow. My final glory—pink lipstick. As I stared at myself in the mirror, I felt...beautiful. Hot. Sexy.

Lin stared at me and murmured, "You look like cotton candy."

I glared at her. I wanted to strangle her, but I didn't want blood to mess my amazingness.

I looked at my watch, and it was ten o'clock, a time I was never ever allowed to go out anywhere in Singapore. I felt adrenaline rush through my veins. Defiance felt good as I started that long walk alone down the main floor of Kananaskis Hall, through the meandering corridor to the main cafeteria where they held the Rez parties for all resident dorm dwellers on campus. With each step, my feet felt like lead. My stomach churned bile. I heard the deafening sound of music.

I froze at the entrance of the cafeteria. The familiar long rows of tables and chairs were gone. It was an open space of mayhem, where hundreds of unrecognizable faces moved in some sort of frenzied giant masturbation dance, hopping up and down with their hands in front of them—in unison for a song they recognized but I had never heard in my life. I casually sauntered to the middle of the crowd and pretended to look cool—a pink virginal sacrifice, now that I think of it, Anita.

I peered in the darkness but couldn't recognize a single person. I could smell alcohol, and I had to dodge dancing drunks sloshing their beer onto my pinkness.

"Hey, Pinky," a disembodied voice shouted at me.

I waved, smiled, and pretended to be one of them. *Whoever that was.*

I reached the end of the jam-packed room and gyrated confidently in unison with the screaming voices shouting to *Money for nothing and chicks for free.* Yeah, yeah. I danced by myself. People were in clusters, swigging from bottles of beer. The floor was sticky and messy. I felt beer seep into my brand-new pink shoes.

Suddenly, someone grabbed my arm and pulled me into a dancing circle. Bobbing heads. Grabbing arms. Woot woot. Punched fists in the air. I couldn't recognize anyone in the group of dancers as the strobe lights were blinding.

My mind screamed. *I can do this. I can. Woot. Woot.*

I joined in the circle.

Then, the crowd went wild when a Starship song came on: *We built this city; we built this city on rock and roll.*

Everyone screamed at the top of their lungs. More beer spilled on my pretty pink blouse. I was now trapped in mesh of bodies, arms, squashed and tossed in the frenzy. The only one who was not drunk was me.

I froze. An intense wave of fear overcame me. I felt my cheeks wet with unexpected tears. Petrified. Alienated. I wasn't prepared for this party. I didn't know how to belong. Little lost Singaporean. I frantically disentangled myself from sticky, fervent arms grabbing and touching me all over.

The next thing I knew, I shoved everyone out of my way and ran out, all the way to my dorm room. The hallway was now littered with empty beer cans and meandering trails of barf. Anita, can you see it? Pink virgin in the valley of vomit! I fumbled with the lock of my dorm door. I kicked my shoes off and threw myself in my single bed on the right side of the room in the complete darkness, praying that Lin was dead asleep. Or dead.

Then, I heard a disembodied voice from the other side of the room sarcastically utter, "Back so soon, Cotton Candy?"

I stashed the pillow on my face to muffle my silent sobs. Enveloped in the smell of beer and sweat. I wept, feeling like a fool until I fell asleep. The next morning, I hurled my pink sacrificial outfit into the giant garbage can in the washroom.

Maybe I should have stayed in Singapore and married any rich husband my parents had picked for me. I question everything in my life. Welcome to Canada!

Anita, today, I envy your domestic bliss even more.

Miss you,

Simran

15 NOVEMBER 1985

Dear Mummy,

Don't worry. That Taxiwallah has completely disappeared. I miss you. I miss your dhal and roti. I miss your beautiful voice filling up the house with your prayers, singing and your loud harmonium. I never realized how lonely it is to be on my own here.

When I was in Singapore, being with family all the time drove me crazy. All the ups and downs. The expectations. Do this. Do that. Wear this. Don't wear that. But it had a funny sense of belonging that I did not realize until now. Here in Calgary, I am literally all alone. There is no this or that. Everything is in my hands to decide. I didn't realize how unprepared I am. Indian parents don't give their daughters any freedom or common sense. I am like a baby—day by day, I must learn the new rules on how to survive. New Western rules. They are so different from our Indian ways of life.

You always told me when I was growing up that if I held hands with boys, I would get pregnant. Mummy! I believed you for so many years. And, papa! He told you to tell me that if he ever saw me with a boy, he would cut the boy's legs off. Do you know how frightening that was for a young girl to hear? I believed his words, and I made sure that whenever I went out, I would look over my shoulder to make sure that papa was not following me. I still look here in Calgary.

Now, in Calgary, I am learning how to handle boys. I know you don't want to hear it, but I want you to know I have Indian common sense. There are so many boys around in the dormitories. There is this boy on the fourth floor. His name is Jake. He has a girlfriend, so I felt safe talking to him when I met him in the elevator.

Jake invited me to his room last week. He sat on his bed and asked me to sit next to him. I shook my head and sat on his desk.

He stared at me and without rhyme or reason said, "Sex is healthy for you."

I quickly answered, "Oh, thank you for the information. I come from a background where you have to be a virgin when you marry a man that your family picks for you."

He eyes widened. "That is a terrible idea. Do you like vegetables?"

"Of course," I said with a smile. "I love vegetables, especially bitter gourd!"

"Good," he said. "Sex is like vegetables. Both are good for you."

He looked surprised when I laughed at him.

"I am not that stupid," I told him. "I know the difference between healthy vegetables and hot sex!"

I giggled and said I was going to the grocery store to buy vegetables, especially cucumbers. I winked at him.

He didn't like that and muttered, "Hah!"

The next day, Jake phoned me and invited me to come up to his room for tea. I went up to the fourth floor, but he was not there in his dorm. Then, I heard his voice yell from the bathroom next to his room.

"Come! Come! Sim!" he yelled. "I need your help."

Worried, I ran to the bathroom, then stopped in my tracks and quickly looked up at the ceiling; there he was in the bathtub full of glorious bubbles. The idiot even had a cigar in his mouth. I burst out laughing at the ludicrous sight, and, boy, he got irritated.

"Why are you laughing," he demanded. "Isn't this what you want?"

I curtsied and walked out the bathroom door, chuckling, thinking of all your warnings about badmash men.

I shouted on my way out, "Thank you for the Canadian lessons on vegetables, sex and love, Jake. I'll let your girlfriend know how helpful you are."

I never went back to the fourth floor. Don't worry, Mummy. I am not that stupid. I know the games these boys want to play. At least I experience it for myself instead of you warning me. I believe you, now.

The funny thing is I frighten Canadian boys away easily without even trying because I always say to the boys, "If we have sex, we have to get married."

Then, I watch them run away. I am stuck in the world of Eastern values in the world of Western ideas. It is a confusing terrain for both me and the Canadian boys. I know I must learn to understand the ways of life in the West more before I can make different decisions.

Mummy, I feel lonely. I thought being away would be exciting, but my routine is boring. I get up. I eat. I go to classes. I come back. I have dinner. I go to bed. There is no family, familiar sounds, or familiar food. I talk to the girls on the floor, but they have their own cliques.

I am totally free. I am free, and I don't know what to do with my freedom anymore. When you yearn for freedom all your life, and you suddenly get it; it is a paradox. Complicated, Mummy. I know you will say *stay at home*, don't go out at night, and stay away from boys. Acha.

Mummy, thank you for secretly stashing away the almonds and cashews in my suitcase. They are delicious. But the packets of spices—aiyoh, they made my suitcase smell like curry, and I can't use them because we have no kitchen in the dormitories. There is just a cafeteria for us to buy our meals. I had to throw out your masala.

I thought about you last night. I can't imagine how you left India when you were sixteen-years old, sailed on a ship for three months with your mother-in-law and landed in Singapore to be the wife of a man you didn't even know and who was twelve years older than you. Did you miss your family like I do? But you had no choice except to go to a new place to be a wife. Me, I have every choice. We both left our countries to find a new world.

Don't worry about me, Mummy. I am strong like you, smart like you and brave like you.

I came to Calgary to get my degree so I will never have to depend on any man for my happiness and existence. I just miss your chicken curry and freshly made rotis. Love to Papa and Jay.

Love,

Simran

15 DECEMBER 1985

Dear Amy,

Where is Calgary, indeed? Frankly, I had no clue where I was heading to when I left Singapore. When I ended the engagement with Harjit, I knew I had to make the perfect escape from a life that had been predetermined by customs, culture and clans over centuries and karmic destinies that I had no say in. I felt suffocated. I felt trapped. I watched friends, cousins, and my sister all propelled into arranged marriages. Sure, some were happy, but I saw how some were married against their will. I asked myself if there was anything else for an Indian woman to do but to get married.

Amy, let me take you to my engagement day. On that day, my mother hustled me into her master bedroom, the one with the queen-sized bed. One length of the wall had built-in closets with full length mirrors on all six doors of the closets. At the foot of the bed, there was a tiny space between the bed and the wall. My eyes widened in horror as Harjit's mother, two sisters and six cousins entered the room. My sister and grandmother came in as well. There were thirteen of us in this sardine can. The older ladies plopped on the bed. Everyone was shoulder to shoulder in the room, standing awkwardly to make space.

Harjit's sisters Romita and Renu handed me some folded clothes to change into. I stepped out of the attached washroom, wearing a scratchy, silky red sari blouse and petticoat, feeling naked with my midriff exposed. I hugged my bare belly with my arms to hide the bulge. It was the 1st time in my life I was going to wear a sari, since no saris allowed for single ladies in my family. Everyone stared at me like meerkats. I hunched over and looked at my feet. I couldn't breathe. I couldn't think. I held back my tears as my sister smiled at me and nodded her head in encouragement.

Soon, the strangers' hands came out at me, tying voluptuous folds of deep burgundy silk sari round and round me, turning me like a puppet. I could smell their sweat and breath. They chatted and chuckled, like I was not even there. Harjit's sisters tucked the pleated folds of the sari into my petticoat at my belly. I recoiled at their clammy hands against my bare skin. More hands came at me from unknown and unnamed cousins. They rearranged the final part of the sari, the long palla that they draped over my bosom and hung over my left shoulder.

Startled, I caught my image in the closet mirror and saw this stranger—in a bold and beautiful deep burgundy silk sari with intricate gold thread designs. Unrecognizable. I wanted to unravel the sari and flee. I struggled to compose myself. It was awkward wearing a sari. I couldn't move. I felt encased in voluminous heavy silk. Trapped. The sweltering heat smothered me, and I moved to stand under the weak whirring fan hanging from the ceiling to stop the rivulets of sweat dripping on my face. My footsteps were constricted by the stiff, brand new silk sari.

The herd of women joyously beckoned me. "Simran, come here."

They pushed my shoulders down to sit at the edge of the foot of the bed. Brand new cosmetic sets emerged from plastic bags. Harjit's younger cousins, Leela and Guddi, applied make-up on me— bright blue eye shadow, garish streaks of red blush on each cheekbone, black, clumpy mascara, and fire red lipstick. The celebrating women were all giddy with delight, future female in-laws, oblivious to my angst. I caught a glance of myself in the mirror and recoiled. I looked like the Chinese opera singer ladies with their bright, exaggerated faces.

"Not so much," I weakly protested.

"No, no. Beautiful," the Harjit clan proclaimed.

My mother discreetly put her finger to her lip to advise me to be quiet. I had been warned. I looked down at the floor and assorted feet. My future mother-in-law opened a square, deep red jewelry box and showed the contents to my grandmother, mother, and sister for their approval. Everyone in the room cackled in delight as Harjit's mother and sisters shackled me with the cold, heavy 24 karat gold necklace, earrings and twelve bangles. I gasped at the ridiculous weight of these items. I peeked in the mirror and saw a caricature of me—in a silk sari with gaudy makeup and ornate jewelry.

I stifled a sob and shuddered. I drifted out of my body and floated up, up, up and looked down, down, down at this spectacle I had no say in. My mother and sister lifted me up by my elbows.

"Waawa, waaaa," the women in the room clucked in approval.

My mother placed the draped palla of the sari over my head, and I held the other side of it with my right hand. A cocooned-dressed-up-virginal-Indian-Barbie-doll.

My mother led me outside from the room to the living room of our apartment that was now brimming with people lining the perimeter of the walls. My cousin, Jatin, one year older than me, caught my eye and laughed at me.

I searched for sympathy; instead, as I walked past him, he leaned forward and whispered, "No choice but to be married off, lah!"

I was furious. Oh, no choice, indeed! I was trapped. I reached the sofa in the living room.

My mother gently put her hands on my shoulder to seat me down next to Harjit. She lovingly rearranged the sari over my head and placed my hands on my lap before she moved away.

As I sat next to my future husband on the sofa, he casually leaned into my ear and whispered, "I can't wait to fuck you."

At that precise moment, everyone in the room blurred, including my own mother who gestured at me to lower my gaze, to look down, be coy. I knew I wanted more than a man who smacked his lips and eyed me in contemptuous anticipation. I knew I wanted something different. I wanted more!

Do you remember our Junior College days? In those critical two years, I simply did not apply myself to my education. Do you know I never picked up a textbook at home? I barely passed any tests and bungled that crucial Higher School Education A Level exam—the one that would have gotten me into the National University of Singapore. I ended up with all D's.

All that went through my mind over and over when I was in junior college was, "Why bother to study and excel. You are just going to be married off."

The truth be told, I gave up at sixteen when the first marriage proposal came into my family from a thirty-year old man from the community. I had to decide at sixteen. I was terrified when my father asked me, and I ran out of the flat. I disappeared for three hours, walking aimlessly around the neighbourhood. Afraid to go home. The matter was dropped when my father saw my tears. I knew that it was a matter of time before I had to say yes.

I regret I did not study and pass my exams with all A's; I know I was more than capable of getting those grades in junior college. Do you know my secret dream was to get a law degree at the National University of Singapore? But I felt that my life was not in my hands. The only avenue for me was to accept an arranged marriage. I gave up. I flitted through life like a forlorn ghost, full of emptiness and sadness.

Amy, when you went away to Princeton University, I couldn't believe your luck. I wept jealously. As a Chinese woman, you did not have the same traditional expectations I have as an Indian woman. That must have been something that your great-grandmothers in China must have been subjected to—bound feet and arranged marriages. Your generation broke free from these outdated practices. Not mine. You have no idea what it feels like to have no say in my own choices. You never knew the pain and confusion I felt all those years in the canteen of our junior college, where I fell into depression. Somedays, I could not breathe. I never paid attention in any of my classes. It's a miracle I got a D, now I think about it.

That was then, Amy. Now, when you question my academic commitment and desire to get a degree, I say to you, *I do not need to hide my intelligence anymore. I can be curious. I am worthy of expanding my mind and ideas.*

No fear of arranged marriages for the moment.

I am in Calgary, and every single day, I enjoy the solitude and silence of being able to uncover my true self. To hear my innermost desires and thoughts. To speak my mind and to choose for myself. When I am in my English classes listening to the professor talk about great works of literature, like the heartbroken Miss Havisham in *Great Expectations* or about Virginia Woolf's *A Room of Her Own,* I feel an inner stirring within me. I feel motivated by the same quest for love and freedom by these women centuries ago. I am not the only one, it seems. Women have always fought to be independent. And when I glance at an image of myself in the mirror, I see the possibility of a bigger life and unlimited potential. I do not have to be the distressed bride adorned in silk and gold unless that is my choice. Getting an education at the University of Calgary is my way out. Calgary is my salvation.

Hah, Amy. When you ask me where the hell Calgary is, I say it is this peaceful little town at the foothills of the incredible mountains. There are barely 650,000 people here. There is one university, the University of Calgary. I live on campus, so I am ten minutes from most of my classes. It gets quiet at night, not like the maddening hustle and bustle of Singapore. And it is getting colder snow. I am slowly expanding my life to fit into this charming city. It's not your boisterous Princeton, ok. It's my haven.

By the way, you never told me the whole truth about your mother before. You hinted about her stubbornness and your clashes, but I never knew the truth. Frankly, I am stunned. I had no idea your mum was drawn by the web of glamour and wealth that the Singapore life sometimes offers to the few privileged ones. I always wondered about your boyfriend that you had at Princeton, the one you mentioned and sent me photographs of. Suddenly, you stopped saying anything about him when you returned to Singapore. It seemed Chin disappeared. Maybe now you can explain to me what really happened to your relationship with Chin when you were at Princeton.

The other night, I woke up in the middle of the night. I went out to the common living room outside the hallway. Thank God there was a kettle in the utility room. I made myself a bowl of instant noodles. I found Assam flavour Maggie Mee from the grocery store where I shop. God, it's true that we Singaporeans are food crazy. I miss Singapore food. I miss walking down my block of flats, making it to the nearby food stalls and indulging in satay, roti prata, nasi lemak, fried kway teow, wonton mee, roti johnny. I don't know where I can find any of these in Calgary.

No regrets, nonetheless. I can always find a cookbook and learn to cook Singapore food when I get a place with a kitchen, right? I'll explore the Chinatown here and look for familiar foods. Calgary is slowly growing on me. I found a place so peaceful and perfect for me to spread my wings. It's been a long time coming.

Sending you good vibes. Sending you photos of Calgary. The first one is my dormitory room in Kananaskis Hall. Yes, only half is my space. The other one is the arch that stretches from one side of the road to the other at the front of the University of Calgary.

Best wishes,

Sim

18 DECEMBER 1985

Sims,

I cannot believe what you are even telling me about Marlon, your drug dealer. So, you leave Singapore and in the first few months you are already doing all kinds of crazy things. If I tell Mummy and Papa, you will be on the next plane home. What a cheapskate drug dealer to take your last five dollars.

I'm jealous. You've escaped from this traditional life. You can do what you want now. Me, I was forced into this arranged marriage at twenty years old. How? Couldn't even say no. Everyone forced me to say yes. Look at me. Stuck with two babies at twenty-three.

So boring. Get up in the morning, take care of my crying babies all day.

Husband comes home in the evening and asks, "What did you cook for dinner today?" I want to strangle his neck. But his mother is watching me from the corner of the living room. She is always observing my every move. I put my dupatta on my head, and I look down on the grey ceramic floor. As a daughter-in-law, I can't say anything.

I just nod and say, "Yes ji; No ji."

I change smelly dirty diapers all day and night. And there you are in Calgary, Miss Freedom Butterfly.

This flat we live in is getting smaller and smaller. One room is for the Queen. She got the master bedroom, the one with attached bathroom. Yes. That is what I call my mother-in-law. She is a self-proclaimed Queen. What? One room is for me and Manjit. Soni and Roni share the other room. There is zero privacy in my life.

The Queen watches me all day.

"Did you clean the toilets?"

"Did you iron Manjit's shirts?"

"Did you, did you, did you?"

It never stops. Every morning I must touch her feet. It's our tradition, right. Show your reverence for your mother-in-law by bowing down and touching her feet with your fingers; then, touch your forehead to show respect. You laughed when mummy had to do that to Mamaji. Now it's my turn. It's funny how older women can make the younger women feel subservient. Once upon a time, the older women were the bullied ones.

Queen spends all day watching TV or going to the temple. Thank God. I get some peace, at least. I sit on the floor and play with kids. Do you know how boring it is to play with babies? When Soni and Roni finally fall asleep, there is still no break for me. I wash the clothes waiting for me in the bathroom. It's my only time for peace. I take the clothes that are soaking in the pail of soapy water. One by one, I scrub the shirts on the washboard and with a hand brush. I close my eyes and dream about Calgary. Cook, clean, wash, shit, carry babies. Sleep with husband. Repeat ad nauseam.

I dream about that teaching diploma from the teaching college here in Singapore. I had four months more to finish, and I would have been a teacher. All false promises. Everyone forced me to get married. I was not allowed to finish my studies. I don't understand how I could have no say in my own life. Nothing could happen the way I wanted for my own life. All lies. Everyone fed me lies. Now, I am just a baby factory. I don't understand why I couldn't make my own choices.

What is my life, Sim? When I go to Mummy and Papa's house, then I can fully breathe. Mummy makes me roti and aloo gobi. Jay plays with the girls. I sit on the sofa and stare out the window.

Mummy keeps talking nonstop. "This is life, Amrit. Be patient. You have a good husband. This is a woman's life. She gets married to a good man. She has children. She finds happiness in this life. My grandmother, my mother, and my life—we're wives and mothers."

I was fascinated by a bird perched on a branch outside on the

Angsana tree. How high did it fly to get there? To tell you the truth, sometimes, I daydream about Calgary. I looked at the photos you sent me of Bowness Park. I could see the snow. All white. No leaves on the tree. The river was frozen. In one of the photos, people skated on ice. How did they glide? It looked like a dream.

Oh, Sim, I want to touch snow and roll in it. It's my dream. I chuckled when I saw the snowman you and your friends made in Bowness Park. Carrot nose, ya? I stared at the strangers in the background in the photo and made-up stories about them. I giggled at your puffy black jacket, your bright red hat, your bulky gloves, and your scarf, which was the red dupatta from your engagement ceremony, right?

I couldn't even see your face. Cold, ya? How cold? You were smiling and throwing your hands up in the air. Manjit was in the bed next to me.

He saw the photo and said, "Is that Calgary? Where your sister is alone? Women should not be in strange countries on their own. Not proper."

I glared at him and turned away. I hid the photo in my drawer next to my bed between the pages of my diary that I can lock up.

You wanted photos of Soni and Roni. I took them to the playground downstairs from our block of flats. They love the swings. Soni is in a red dress and Roni is in yellow.

I'm tired and want to put my head down on the pillow and close my eyes, but I have to hang the clothes I washed out to dry on the bamboo poles and hoist them outside the windows before it is too dark.

Please don't marry Marlon.

Love,

Amrit

20 DECEMBER 1985

Dear Mummy,

I haven't heard from you. I am lonely, so I am writing to you, again. It makes me feel you are here, Mummy. It's quiet here today. Everyone has gone away for Christmas. There are only a few people left on residence, but everyone is going home to their family. Susan is going to Toronto. Maggie is driving to Edmonton. Sunny is going home to London. Even my annoying roommate, Lin, is going to Los Angeles to visit her friend.

I have nowhere to go, Mummy. Today, I walked around and realized I was the only one left in the seven-storey building. There are usually around 350 people in this building. I am alone. I didn't know Christmas was a big thing here. No one even knows that I'm in my room. I'm afraid to go to the common living room outside. I jump out of my skin when I hear a noise.

At night, I lock my door and put my desk across the door. I put the telephone on the chair next to me. 911 in Canada. Not 999. Don't worry. I have a big hammer under my bed. I bought it from K-Mart, a shopping store in Brentwood, two days ago.

Ok. Don't worry. I can do this. Let me tell you how I'm learning to survive in Calgary. In the first week I arrived, I had to figure out how to wash my clothes. There's a small laundry room between the elevator and the washroom. They are these two machines, a washing machine, and a dryer. A dryer? I have never seen a dryer in my life! Also, our washing machine in Singapore is half the size of the giant washing machine here. Our dryer in Singapore is the sun!

Really, I felt confused. I followed my Canadian dorm neighbour to watch her use the dryer.

Monica asked, "Why are you stalking me?"

"No," I said. "I just don't know how to use the dryer."

"What do you mean? How did you dry your clothes in Singapore?"

"Well," I said. "Easy. Natural Singapore sun power. We washed our clothes by hand. Very few of us had washing machines. We hung our clothes on 10-foot bamboo poles; then we leaned out the windows of our flats, and we put the poles into the round bamboo holders attached outside the windows way high up in the sky. The clothes dried naturally."

Monica stared at me in surprise. "What? I can't even imagine," she said. "Well, in this snow, you won't have that option. Come. Watch me. It is easy as pie."

I observed her carefully put in four coins. Push the buttons. Ok. Easy. Finally, after waiting and waiting for my turn, I got a chance to put my dirty clothes in the washing machines. I put my four coins into the coin dispenser. I put in some laundry detergent. I pushed some random buttons and waited. I heard the water rush into the machine. I forgot to ask Monica how long it would take, so I checked every fifteen minutes until I heard the final beep beep.

Now, what? I took all my clothes out of the washing machine and chucked them in the dryer. There was no one around for me to ask any questions, so I just put my coins in and pushed all the buttons until I heard the machine start. Exciting. First time ever no bamboo poles!

One hour later, I came to get my clothes. Wow. Dry. One hour. Not days like in Singapore. I took everything out of the dryer, carried the pile of clothes to my room, and tossed them all on my bed. Then I saw the only blue wool sweater I loved so much. We bought it at Metro. I remember how expensive it was. I picked it up and screamed. Shrunk. What? Now, it was the size for a two-year-old child. I held the sweater up to me. What happened? How could I be so stupid? How would I survive in Calgary on my own? My eyes welled with tears. I shoved my clothes onto the floor and jumped into my bed, pulled the blanket over my face and sobbed. There's so much to learn.

The next day, I woke up late in the afternoon. I glanced at the crumpled clothes on the floor and sighed. Now, I must go to Market Mall to buy a new sweater. I'm freezing. I'm wearing three t-shirts under my sweatshirt.

Merry Christmas. I will get chicken nuggets and fries from Mc-Donald's for my Christmas dinner. I hope they are open. If not, more Maggie Noodles. Maybe bread and cheese. Everything is closed on campus. It is a ghost town.

Love you, Mummy.

Sim

22 DECEMBER 1985

Hey Sim,

Merry Christmas, my friend. I haven't stopped laughing, imagining you in your virginal pink ensemble. What a sight, pandi. What were you thinking? That was the perfect outfit for meeting a potential arranged marriage suitor in Singapore, all sweet and innocent. I'm glad you threw that cotton candy out. For goodness sakes, go buy a sexy black dress!

You're not that same girl anymore. You can never be—from Singapore to Calgary. Different countries. Different landscapes. Different expectations. Can you ever be the same girl who was in Singapore just months ago? It will be a great reincarnation, Simran.

Gopal and I are taking our sons, Ravi and Ramesh, to Penang for our upcoming New Year break. I'm thrilled. I love quaint Penang. Shopping, temples, beaches. The kids will have fun. We're flying there and staying at a fancy hotel on the beach. You see, Gopal got a promotion at work. We are celebrating.

It's blistering here in Singapore—remember how the heat withered you? I can't imagine how cold it must be in Calgary. I am a true Singaporean. I detest the cold. 30 degrees Celsius here. On Sunday, Gopal, me, and the kids went to East Coast. Family outing. The beach was jam packed, as usual. We found a perfect spot under a tree, laid out our mat and had a delicious homemade picnic. The boys jumped with excitement. They made sandcastles, and we all swam in the warm water and laughed as we splashed each other. It was refreshing to dip into the water and get a break from the heat.

The day quickly turned into evening. A soothing cool breeze wafted, and the boys conked out on the mat. It was another gorgeous evening in Singapore. The sun slowly set in the horizon, past the bobbing ships. It was breezy and cool, like someone turned on a gentle fan. Gopal and I held hands and talked about everything and nothing.

"Hey, Gopal. What is latest about your father?" I asked him.

I've told you about Gopal's father, Appa. Appa has an unpredictable temper, and he treats his wife terribly. That's what Gopal has grown up with all his life. Gopal is afraid of his father. Really, Gopal doesn't know what to do. Oh, I feel sorry for Gopal's mum, Ammah.

Just listen to this story. Last week, Appa and Ammah went to the wet market five-minutes away from their flat. Gopal and I were with them, an outing, we thought. We were in front of the fresh vegetable stall. The next thing we knew, we heard Appa scream at Ammah.

Why? No reason. He didn't like the vegetables she had bought and had in her basket. Seriously. Just like that. Appa walked up to Ammah, looked in her basket and went berserk.

"Why did you buy brinjal? I don't want to eat it." Appa screamed at the top of his lungs.

Aiyoh. It was worse than a Tamil movie. Every single person in the market stared at us. It was painful and embarrassing. I grabbed the basket from Ammah and pulled her away from the old man. He screamed obscenities at her. Cursing, swearing, at the top of his lungs.

"Come, Ammah," I said. "Let's go home." We walked away, and I held Ammah's trembling arm.

Gopal tried to calm down his ranting and raving father. I walked in silence, squeezing Ammah's hand to comfort her. She rambled on in Tamil, looked down to hide the stream of tears, and stumbled all the way home.

There was no sense to what had happened. No logic. My heart ached for her. Apparently, this incident was a usual event in the house and outside. A battered wife. Nowhere to go. No escape. Just constant assaults by an unpredictable, angry man.

One hour later, Appa and Gopal came home, chatting and laughing, like nothing happened. Gila, lagi. Ammah fell silent and ran to appease her husband, a familiar pattern, it seemed.

That day, after the market scene, Gopal didn't want to talk about it. He said that was how it was for him as a child growing up every day. He didn't want to remember his painful past. Really, Gopal avoids talking about the relationship between his parents. I can sense the tension and see the unpredictable outbursts when we go for a visit. It worries me, especially when the children are there as well.

I let the matter of his father's temper drop, yet again, opting for the peace and beauty of the moment at East Coast beach. So, we stretched our legs on the mat, gazed at the ships so far out they resembled toy ships bobbing happily in the South China Sea. Around us, the tall palm trees gently swayed in the incoming breeze. The boys stirred, but we savoured every moment until they woke up and both jumped in my lap and hugged me. Perfect. Life is simply perfect.

Eh, your roomie Lin is quite the character. Just your luck to get a fellow Asian in Calgary when you left Singapore and the millions of Asians here. It's ironic you ran away and ended up in your own Little Singapore dorm room! Never mind. Enjoy your Christmas break; it's big in Canada, isn't it? I will gorge on satay and nasi lemak for you—your favourite, right?

Vanakam, girlfriend.

Anita

25 DECEMBER 1985

Dear Amrit,

Don't worry. I won't marry Marlon, the drug dealer. He dropped the German class and has disappeared, dimples, drugs and all. My first date in Calgary! In your letter, it seems your housekeeping and childrearing duties never end. You hated doing those chores when we were teenagers. Now, you must do it every single day. When we were teens, you told me your dream was to be a teacher and to travel the world. Maybe, one day, that can still be a possibility. At least you can come visit me in Calgary, right?

Ready for my next confession about life as a foreign student in Calgary? Don't tell Mummy or Papa. Don't tell anyone, ok? Promise. Mummy knows part of the story, but I want to tell you the rest. It's December 25. Merry Christmas. You may think I live a glamorous life in Calgary. The truth is that I'm completely alone in my room on the third floor. I'm the only one in the whole building. Three hundred and fifty people in Kananaskis Hall have left for the Christmas break. The neighbouring building, Rundle Hall, is vacant as well. There is no one here.

I had no idea that Canadians left for Christmas. I didn't know students went away for two weeks during the winter break. It never crossed my mind.

Frankly, I didn't know what to do. I was in a state of panic. I can't even lock myself in the safety of my dorm room. I have to leave my room to go to the common washroom in the hallway—use the toilet, take a shower, or watch TV in the common living room. I jump out of my skin when I hear a sound. I bought a hammer, so I carry it with me. There is no one I know I can call here. It's dark everywhere and the lights are off at night. I use my flashlight. It's better if no one knows I'm alone.

There is no food in the building because the cafeteria is shut down as well. Every afternoon, I walk to McDonald's, which is twenty minutes away. No matter what the weather, even in a snowstorm, I go out if I want to eat. It's freezing cold, like ants biting my face. My face is puffy, swollen and red. I wrap my scarf tightly around my face, to no avail.

At least McDonald's is familiar to me. I buy fish burger and fries and slowly eat my lunch, sitting by myself in the corner booth, looking out at the carpark. I look down and avoid people. Everyone looks the same. I am the only Brown girl sitting here in McDonald's. It feels odd to be the only one. It's not like in Singapore, where I felt I belonged. I felt safe and comfortable in Singapore. I feel out of place here. I look different. I sound different. I'm different. I just want to blend in.

Maybe tomorrow I will go to The Keg. That is a fancy restaurant next to McDonald's. But it is expensive. I can't spend money just like that. It's better if I go to Safeway, the grocery store and get some noodles, bread, and cheese. There is no kitchen in the dorm. There's a small fridge and a kettle. Ugh. Awful. No proper food. I am even tempted to call Taxiwallah. Mummy told you about Taxiwallah, right? Don't worry. I won't. It will be like inviting the devil. Just a moment of hopelessness. That's how desperate I feel.

Every day, I leave during the day, and I sneak back into my building, quietly. My instinct tells me when I come home, to make sure no one follows me or sees me. I quickly unlock the front door of the building; then I dash up three floors, sprint into my room, and lock the door. Damn, but I have to go to the toilet, which is four doors away from my room. I'm counting the days until the girls on the floor come home. I don't even know when people will be back.

One night, I felt overcome by utter loneliness and laid in my bed, praying, *Waheguru. Waheguru. Waheguru.* The hours ticked by slowly. I was about to leave my room to use the bathroom when I heard loud footsteps outside. What? I jumped up and put my ears to the door, listening.

My brain screamed *Run, run*, but I had no shoes or coat. Where would I run? I locked my door and listened. Yes. Footsteps.

There was a knock on my door. "Hey, Sim. Are you there?"

"Who's that?" I asked through the door.

"It's Charlie—Sunny's friend. Open the door."

What? Charlie? Why was he here? I had only met him four times when he came to visit Sunny. I was confused. He was Sunny's ex-boyfriend, as they were now just friends.

Charlie smiled at me and engulfed me in a loving hug. "I realized you are here on residence alone, so I came to take you home for dinner with my family."

Then, without warning, he leaned over and kissed me. I froze, not clear what was happening. I knew he broke up with Sunny four months ago. My brain warned me to jump back into my room and shut the door, but I didn't care anymore. I didn't want to be alone in that building.

I threw my arms around Charlie and sobbed. It was like a Hindi movie. I didn't ask any questions. I was relieved. One person in the whole of Calgary had come to save me. Charlie was here to take me to his family's house for Christmas. Waheguru. Waheguru. All that raced through my weary mind was I didn't have to be alone in the building tonight and could spend my first marvellous Christmas in Calgary with Charlie and his family.

It was spectacular. Everyone in Charlie's family welcomed me with open arms. They spoiled me with curry, roti, rice, turkey, mashed potatoes—the dishes were endless. I mixed and mingled, like a lost soul who just found some people alive. When Charlie dropped me off at Kananaskis Hall that evening, he kissed me passionately and said he would be back the next day. I skipped all the way back to my room, refusing to think too much. Charlie's mum had packed a Tupperware of chicken curry and rice, and I put it in the tiny empty fridge in the utility room. Tomorrow, I wouldn't need to go to McDonald's. I was weary of burgers and fries.

That night as I lay in bed, I wondered what Sunny would say

about me and Charlie when she came back from London. When I met Sunny, an Indian girl from London, who lived on the other wing of my floor, I felt hopeful. Maybe, we could be like family? Then, this incident happened. Last month, I had a terrible headache. I saw Sunny in the common TV room and told her I was in pain.

"I have aspirin," she said in her lovely British accent. "I'll get them for you."

What a kind girl. Sunny went to her room and came back with her bottle of aspirin. She gave me two tablets, and I swigged them back with some water. Relieved, I sat in the common living room with five other girls from the floor, watching TV.

Within ten minutes, I felt a strange, tightening sensation around my eyes. I ran to the washroom to look in the mirror. My eyes were now two narrow slits, and the area around them was red and puffy. Swollen—getting larger and larger. I didn't know what was happening. I felt icy-cold fear plunge through my veins. A crowd of girls from my floor gathered around me as I sat trembling on the couch.

One of the girls, Leah, said, "You should go to the hospital. Maybe we better call the ambulance?"

It was nine or ten p.m. at night. I couldn't see as my glasses couldn't fit over my bumpy eyes. I couldn't think. Why were my eyes swollen? Papa…can you help me? I stood up and sat down, not knowing what to do.

Leah said, "I called the ambulance."

I was in my pyjamas. I touched my eyes. They felt bumpy and protruded like limes.

The elevator door opened, and three medics came out to the floor. I stood up and gripped the back of the sofa, terrified.

One of the medics asked me to sit down, and he examined my eyes with a bright beam of flashlight. I blinked nervously.

"What's wrong? What's wrong?" I repeated.

"Are you allergic to anything?" the medic asked me.

I peered at him but could only see a shadowy face.

"No. I don't know," I shook my head and glanced around at the undistinguishable faces gathered around.

Nothing like this had ever happened to me. By now, my eyes were completely swollen shut, like slits. I couldn't even wear my glasses. I was almost blind.

"What's wrong? What's wrong?" I uttered in a high-pitched voice.

"Ma'am," the medic said. "We have to take you to the hospital."

"No," I whimpered. "I don't want to go. I don't want to."

I sobbed as the two medics loaded me onto a stretcher. The girls on the floor encircled the stretcher. There were many people around the stretcher. Lin brought me my purse and shoved it into my arms.

Sunny looked at me and said, "Oh no. I hope you'll be ok."

"Will anyone come with Simran to the hospital?" one of the medics asked.

All the girls moved away from the stretcher and shook their heads. Silence.

I heard a British accent say, "I have a midterm tomorrow."

Lin said, "Good luck. Hope you don't die."

I was flabbergasted. No one? I covered my head with my arms, as fear and disappointment engulfed me. My mind raced back and forth—every time I was sick in Singapore, Papa was always there. He took me on his scooter. He waited for me at the clinic. He came in to talk to the doctor. He tolerated my unsmiling face. I never realized how much I relied on him. Papa was always there.

The medics slid the stretcher with me on it into the back of the ambulance. My tears rolled down the sides of my cheeks, which made my swollen eyes worse. I peered anxiously inside the ominous space of the ambulance. The medics spoke to each other cheerfully while one of them put an I/V in my reluctant arm. Suddenly, the ambulance came to an abrupt stop. The medics rolled me out of the ambulance onto the stretcher and pushed it down the passageway into the basement of the hospital.

The medics hoisted me onto a narrow hospital bed and left without a word. I peered in the darkness at my tiny room defined by drab grey curtains around the bed. I tapped on the bed. I touched my swollen eyes. I tossed and turned. I caressed the tightness on my arm around the I/V site. Hours must have gone by before the curtain was rudely ripped open.

Finally, a doctor came in.

He declared, "You must be allergic to aspirin. Don't take aspirin ever again."

I sat up to ask a question. The doctor turned and left. I didn't know what the doctor meant. I had never ever had an allergy before. I sat up on the tiny bed, balancing my arm and the I/V. With my free hand, I held my glasses on my swollen face. What now? I watched people go past the gap in the curtain. Should I leave?

Hours later, a nurse marched in. Silently, she pulled the I/V out of my arm. She put her hand on my shoulder and said, "You can go home. You're ok now. The swelling is down."

The nurse left. I sat on the edge of my bed and rubbed the sore site on my arm. I gingerly caressed my eyes and the swelling felt less. I didn't have my winter coat. I didn't know how to get home. I stumbled through an endless maze of hallways until I saw large sliding doors. Hugging myself, I stepped outside the building; a cold blast of air hit my face. Even my nostril hairs froze. The heavy snow fell mercilessly and covered my glasses.

I wandered aimlessly outside the hospital and, thankfully, saw a line of taxis at the other end. I wrapped my arms around me to stay warm and calm myself. I must have looked like an escaped hospital inmate!

I was the first one in line at the taxi stand. Oh no. A surge of panic momentarily coursed through me as I thought about Taxiwallah. I opened the door of the first taxi and peered at the taxi driver, but my eyes felt tight and uncomfortable still. I shivered. I didn't care, anymore. I jumped into the back of the taxi. It was a friendly White guy who greeted me with a cheerful voice. He calmed me down with his touch of kindness. I gave him my destination and closed my eyes and leaned back.

I was grateful when the taxi arrived at Kananaskis Hall.

I paid the taxi driver and he said, "Take care, young lady. Keep warm."

I gratefully collapsed in my dorm bed, relieved to have survived the ordeal.

I heard Lin's disembodied voice yelp in the darkness, "Oh. You're still alive."

I wondered how long before I would have to kill her. Sunny did not even come by to check in on me. Little did she know that our paths would cross again.

Guess what? One week later, I got a bill from Foothills Hospital for $300 for the ambulance. I stared at the bill in confusion.

Being alone in a strange country is not as glamorous as it sounds, is it?

Wish you were here,

Simran

30 DECEMBER 1985

Hey Girlfriend,

Today, I was thinking of you. I wanted to wish you a Happy New Year. We are in Penang, as I mentioned in my last letter, staying at the fabulous Shangri-La's Rasa Sayang Resort and Spa. Gopal is with the boys. I am getting a massage in an hour and wanted to send you a quick note and drop it off at the reception desk.

The boys and I spent the day at the famous Snake Temple. I wasn't excited to see the snakes crawling around the grounds of the temple. I was horrified and jumpy, but the boys and Gopal thought it was fun following the slithering snakes.

So, I am sending you a picture of the boys with the snakes draped around their shoulders to wish you Happy New Year. I hope 1986 will be amazing for all of us.

Love from Penang,

Anita

27 JANUARY 1986

Hey Sim,

Oh my goodness. Your engagement sounds like a nightmare. What is wrong with you Indian people? It's so dramatic. If it were me, I would have walked out the door. I don't put up with that kind of bullshit. I'm lucky I'm not Indian like you.

Happy New Year to you. I had a wonderful New Year's Eve party. I met up with a group of alumni from my Princeton University days. We had a fancy party at Shangri-La Hotel. You should have seen us. All posh and stylish. Everyone wore the latest name brands from top to toe. Brand name everything. Gucci this and Gucci that. The food was to die for—a ten course Chinese dinner. Sharks' fin soup. Finest abalone. Chilli crabs. Fried rice and noodles and more. We were impressed by these meals prepared by the top chefs.

Now there's this guy, Henry. All the girls have their eyes on him because he's a rich Chinese tycoon. He's a little fat, short and bald guy. He's not my idea of Prince Charming, but well, other things make up for his shortcomings. His family owns many buildings on our prestigious Orchard Road downtown. Henry was at Princeton University three years before I was there, and we were there together when he was completing his final year. He never talked to me at Princeton. I noticed in New Jersey, Henry particularly liked blonde girls with blue eyes even though they were all taller than him. Hah, he was the eternal optimist, but deep pockets go a long way.

Anyways, at this New Year's Eve party, Henry talked to me all night. Everyone stared at us, especially the women. I smiled at them, giggled louder than I needed to, and coyly touched Henry's arm. I marked my territory. We reminisced about our Princeton days, and I teased him about his Barbie dolls.

Henry guffawed and said, "My family would disown me if they knew. So, I had my fill of beautiful American bombshells."

I looked at my watch and realized how late it was. An entourage of beautiful Asian girls hovered close by, waiting for a chance to replace me at Henry's table.

Henry held out his hand and said, "Are you ready to be driven home in your pumpkin coach?"

I nodded disinterestedly. "I can take a taxi."

Henry laughed and steered me to his red convertible Porsche. Red. It was a sexy car. I glanced back at all Henry's admirers who were left behind. I sensed they wanted to claw my eyes out. I leaned on Henry's arm and seductively whispered in his ear. I looked good in his Porsche. I hope he calls me because I'm perfect for him!

Please. Don't tell me you are now a literature maven because you've read those few books. I read them in my first-year English class at Princeton. I thought they were utterly boring. Of course, I got an A. What are you even going to do with an English degree? A teacher, right? It's the favourite Indian girl's job in Singapore. A nice safe job if they are allowed to work.

By the way, Calgary sounds like a bore. It must be some small town, all White, little house on the prairie, right? Is there even any theatre, opera, or ballet shows there? What are you going to do with the Rockies? Climb them? Are all the men cowboys?

Now in Princeton, we had the best of everything. Of course, New York was close by, and my friends and I would go there all the time to catch the best Broadway shows, theatre, jazz, museums, and top-notch restaurants. What do you actually do in Calgary?

My mother is leaving me alone a little now that I told her about Henry. You remember my mum and her fascination for rich men and expensive lifestyles, right? She is beyond excited.

Every single day, she asks me: *Did he call you? Are you going out? Play hard to get but not too hard, ok? His family is very rich, you know.*

I smile and nod my head. No use to argue with that one since she is happy with me, finally. More importantly, this Saturday I am having high tea with Henry. Raffles Hotel.

We Singaporeans can never escape from our love of our food. Everywhere we go, we only talk about Singapore food. Your Maggie Mee sounds atrocious. I hope you don't get too fat on it.

Ciao for now,

Amy

29 JAN 1986

My Dear Simran,

You can't just write to me about Charlie then disappear and give me no updates. Oh my God. What happened? I was sad to hear about your hospital visit. How? You wanted to be alone and now you are totally alone. There is no one there to help you. The last time you ended up in the hospital was the night before I got married. Do you remember? Me, you, and Mummy slept in my single bed in our room, and we laughed and joked all night. My last night in our house before I left for my husband's house.

We hugged each other, and you wept. You couldn't stop. And you gasped and choked. Next thing, you couldn't breathe and wheezed like a whistle. I ran to get Papa you couldn't breathe and gasped desperately for air. We all panicked.

Papa jumped out of bed, got dressed and took you to Toa Payoh Hospital on his scooter. You were gone for hours. We couldn't sleep till you came back. That day, you had your first asthma attack in your life. The doctor said it was stress and trauma.

That whole night you slept in my bed with me, and I could feel your wet tears on the back of my shoulders because you did not let me go. My tears fell silently as well. Tomorrow, I was going to leave the house forever. You were my best friend. We were always there for each other since we were young. You always had to go everywhere with me. Remember? I could not go anywhere unless you were my chaperone.

I know you didn't like taking on the role of my chaperone because you had to follow me everywhere I went. But you never said no because you knew I couldn't go if you did not go with me. So, you were dragged to my friends' parties, meetings, school outings and everywhere else I went. You knew no one. You sat in the corner and watched everyone, like a grandma. The youngest grandma, of course because everyone else was older than you.

I wish I could be there with you in Calgary. Can you imagine what we would do? Just be crazy. Travel. Go to the disco. Talk with boys. Dance. Just not have to worry who will see us or what will people say or worry that Papa will kill us. I hope my two daughters will be like us. Two good friends and sisters. I am too young to be stuck in this marriage I didn't want. Can you imagine Mummy a mother at sixteen? Me at twenty. What a bloody life.

My life here in Singapore? Well, I don't talk much with my husband Manjit. We're like two strangers, not husband and wife. We have nothing in common. He's an engineer and an old, boring fart. He has nothing to say. No conversation. No hello. Just like a dumb fool.

Last week, my friend Sunita told me a rumour Manjit had a Chinese girlfriend for two years, but he was forced to marry me. Nowadays, he is out to very late at night. He doesn't take me out anywhere. I don't know what to talk to him about. We only talked to each other once a week for two months on the phone. Then we got married. We had sex on our wedding night. Bam. Just like that. We only met twice at our house and at the temple at Silat Road for ten minutes on our own. Indian dating style.

These days, my darling husband is always busy and grumpy. At night, we sleep back-to-back. Only when he feels like, then he turns me over and roughly climbs on me. No romance. No tender love. No sweet words. No passionate kisses. He just grunts like an animal and it's over. I close my eyes and dream about Raffid. Remember, he was my classmate who liked me, but Papa said I could not talk to him? So, I drift away and smile until Manjit gets off me, snores and is in his own bloody world. Oh, to be a man. There is no satisfaction for me. I read an article in *Her World* magazine about how to pleasure a woman. I left the magazine on Manjit's bedside table, and he threw it out. I try to imagine what orgasms are but have no clue.

Why? Am I a baby factory? It seems so with Manjit.

Some nights, I hear Soni cry then Roni starts. I stumble into their room and sleep with them in their room. When they both go to sleep, I lie on the mattress on the floor and stare at the ceiling. I can see the shadows cast from the lights outside dancing on the walls in strange shapes. I can hear cars honking from the streets even though we are on the twelfth floor. It's surprisingly peaceful to be on my own without being bothered.

I don't think anyone knows if I'm dead or alive. I hear the usual—*Where is my daughter? Where is my daughter-in-law? Where is my wife? Where is my mother?*

I ask, "Where is Amrit?"

Or I say "Waheguru, Waheguru," like Mummy did all her life.

Is prayer the only salvation for lonely wives? I am a ghost, invisible.

One day, I will come to Calgary. We'll drive to Banff to that castle hotel you sent me a photo of. I will lie in the snow and move my arms and legs like you said—make a snow angel. I want to be a snow angel. We'll sit in the outdoor pool, and I will stretch both my hands out and catch the snowflakes. We'll drink martinis and eat potato chips. We'll sleep when we want to. We'll go anywhere we like. We'll wear any clothes we want. We'll be sisters of freedom. This time, you don't have to chaperone me because I won't behave.

I'm waiting for your next letter to tell me what happened. Don't take aspirin ever. Just take Panadol. I'm alone. You're alone. Those were the best days when we were younger, and you were my tail and went with me everywhere. Write to me soon.

Big sister,

Amrit

3 FEBRUARY 1986

Simran,

I put twenty dollars in the envelope so you can buy a new sweater. Why you cry? It's only a sweater. You will have a hundred more sweaters. I heard that the dryer in Canada will destroy everything. Try and see if you can wash all your clothes by hand and hang to dry in the washroom—can hang your sweater over the door. It's better like that the old-fashioned way.

Be strong. You are a brave girl. Go to the temple. God will protect you. You can meet people there. They will take care of you.

When you are afraid just close your eyes and say "Waheguru, Waheguru."

Say it a hundred times a day. It will give you peace of mind. It will make you strong. You don't need anyone. You just need yourself.

It is not easy to go to a new country. I remember. When I was sixteen, I travelled with your grandmother on the ship for three months. It was a new adventure because it was the first time I was travelling from one country to another.

The ship was full of people. Every morning, we cooked our own roti and dhal on a little Bunsen burner. At night, we slept on the thin mattress on the floor. It was cold at night when the wind blew from the open sea. I followed your grandmother everywhere. I put my dupatta on my head. I cannot look left or right. She was a very fierce lady. I touched her feet every morning like a good daughter-in-law must do. I followed her everywhere she went. I wasn't allowed to be alone even for one minute.

Your grandmother wore only white suits. She was a widow. Do

you know an Indian widow has to mourn for her husband for the rest of her life? She can't wear colourful clothes or make-up. In the olden days a widow had to walk into her dead husband's burning pyre and die with him. It was her duty. She was also considered bad luck. Your grandfather died when she was a young lady. He died in a car accident when he was only forty-five years old. She was a tough lady. She survived on her own with her children. I admired her strength and courage. Brave lady!

Your grandmother came to Delhi to bring me home to Singapore for your father. I only saw my future husband a few times from my window when he came to my neighbourhood to play hockey with the neighbour boys. He was very handsome and tall. Thin. On the spot, his mother asked my family for my hand in marriage.

My family grabbed the chance. We were a very poor family, living hand to mouth. They were rich Singapore people. I didn't want to get married and ran away the day before my marriage at the temple. But where could I go? In the end I came back in tears. I was scared to leave my mother, father, sisters and brother. But what to do. It was my karma. My family was penniless. Some days there was no food on the table. These Singapore people said no dowry necessary. I wanted to make life for my family easy. It was difficult for them to have so many daughters to marry. I hid my tears for days because I did not want to leave my family but my father heard me and hugged me every day.

There was no turning back and I left for Singapore at sixteen years old. When the ship arrived in Singapore, we were quarantined for one week before we could go home. I know how you feel, beti. It is not easy to leave your home and arrive in a strange country.

I felt confused when I arrived in Singapore. Singapore is different from Delhi. Chinese people. Malay people. Indian people. So many races. So many languages. My English was medium-ok. I finished my General Certificate of Education Ordinary level in India which was a big thing for a girl. I studied till I was sixteen. I was lucky my family let me go to school. I got very high marks and was top student in Hindi.

After the quarantine, we went to my new home in Singapore. We lived in this house on Race Course Road with so many rooms. Our bedroom was upstairs with your grandmother, Mamaji, who had her own bedroom.

I was alone in Singapore. I had no one. No family. No friends. I was a foreigner. I did my duty and followed your grandmother like a puppy. She was very strict but nice as well. As a young wife, I couldn't talk or do anything without her permission or your father's permission. It was double jail for me. Your father was worse. He had a hot temper and shouted if I did anything wrong. On the second day he screamed at me because the roti was cold. I knew I was in hell now.

Every day, I looked out the window on the second floor and saw food sellers with their carts selling kacang putih, ice kacang, mee siam, ice cream. This is all types of food from different races in Singapore I didn't know. I had never tasted many of them before. I looked at the long lines of people from one corner of the park to the other to buy the delicious food—how long did they have to wait?

In the evenings, Mamaji took me for a walk with her. I ran to the swings in the playground across the road. I jumped on one and swung it back and forth. I kicked my legs under the swing so that the swing got higher and higher.

Your grandmother sat on the bench and watched me. I often wondered what she was thinking of. High up on my swing, I clung to the chains and shut my eyes. The cool breeze touched my face. Soon I was flying in the air. Up, up, up. Nobody could touch me. My heart went thuck thuck thuck. Excitement. Freedom.

Next thing, I heard Mamaji's voice call me. "Kuldip, acha, challo."

It took me some time to realize she was talking to me. Did you know your grandmother changed my name from Kushi to Kuldip because she did not like my name? She gave me a nice new Sikh name. I didn't say anything. What for? No use.

I just say, "Acha, ji."

Like that. New country. New husband. New family. New name.

What can I do?

Listen, beti. Don't be afraid of anything. Stay strong. You are a brave girl to go from one country to another. You are an independent lady. You chose to go to Canada on your own free will.

When you are lonely just cry and let the tears come until no more tears. You have left your safe nest and now you are a free bird flying up in the air alone. Be like a man. Soon, you will come home and we will take care of you again.

We all miss you very much.

Mummy

6 FEBRUARY 1986

Amrit, Amrit,

Your letter made me reminisce about our childhood. I want to be your tail again. Those were the best days of my life. We went everywhere together. Yes, I admit I was irritated because I had no choice, but you also had no choice. Couldn't leave the house. *Come back at this time. Do this. Do that.* But when we were together, it was pure happiness. You always told me all your secrets. I know everything about you, man. I lived your life. From when I was ten years old, I was everyone's secret keeper.

You thought I didn't know about your Jesus Christ? I knew that if Papa knew, he would stop you from going. So I just sat quietly and became the collector of secrets, not only for you but also for Mummy. How many secrets have I kept for all of us?

That Christian group. Ya. I didn't know what the big attraction was. We went to the community centre and sat outside on chairs in a circle.

That man with the annoying Singapore voice screeched, "Jesus loves you all; He will save you, lah. He is the supreme, you know or not."

My god, he drove me crazy. I tuned out all the time. It was boring. Sometimes, I took a nap on the bench. But you looked happy, reading, discussing, singing songs, clapping. I thought, even though I was only thirteen, if you could be happy for two hours, it was better than nothing. You were lost in a world where you could do what you wanted. I was happy you didn't make me read the Bible. Thank God, lah.

Charlie? He seems like a nice guy. His family is from Mauritius.

They are all kinds of Indian mixed race. Every day, he came to my dormitory and took me to his family house. I was relieved not to be alone. He's in the Engineering department here. A perfect suitor, right? This is all new adventures for me. We held hands, kissed, went to movies, went to dinner. I never had the freedom to date or go out and be seen with a boy and not be killed by Papa. Here in Calgary, I was a free bird. It was intoxicating. I couldn't stop smiling.

Mostly, I was relieved not to be alone in the empty Kananaskis Hall. He took me to his house every day and introduced me to his family as his girlfriend. Wow. Girlfriend? He didn't ask me but who cared. Maybe this is the Canadian way of dating.

His family cooked similar Indian food like back home. Chicken curry. Roti. Dhal. It was delicious, not as good as Mummy's but better than Maggie Mee. I felt safe with Charlie. I relaxed. I stared at his handsome face. I agreed when he said we should be together all the time. This was like the love stories on television.

Deep down, I wasn't sure how to react or what to do in a situation like this. All I know is Charlie should marry me like we have to do back in Singapore. Get married. Get married. No sex. Be a virgin. That is the right Indian way. I mean, he's got some Indian blood in him. What's the problem?

But wait, my love affair was worse than a Hindi movie, Sis. Two weeks later, the evil British girl from my floor, Sunny, came back. Charlie went to the airport to pick her up by himself. He said he would tell her about us on the ride home. Finally, the elevator door opened and Charlie and Sunny stepped out. Where's my hug?

Sunny stormed out the door. She was weeping. She glared at me, pushed me by my shoulder, and ran straight to her room.

Charlie looked at me; tears rolled down his cheeks and he uttered, "Disaster. She will not accept me and you."

I watched in stunned silence. Charlie promised me they were exes and were over for six months. Now, Sunny, the one who tried to kill me with the aspirin, was having a fit in her room.

"I can't see you anymore," Charlie said. "She's my best friend. I can't do this to her."

I stepped back, bewildered. Love triangle. How did I get cast in this bloody Hindi movie?

I ran to Sunny's room and knocked on the door. "Hey, Sunny." No answer.

Charlie came up, banged on the door, and lovingly called her name. Guess what? The door opened and Charlie walked in.

I screamed into the gap of the door. "You are such bullshitters. Go to hell!"

Oh, that made me feel better. Frustrated, I put on my coat, went out in the cold winter evening and marched to McDonald's to order the largest serving of French fries possible.

What the hell is wrong with all these people? Maybe an arranged marriage was the best way to go. It's over. Drug dealer Marlon gone. Jake the vegetable lover, gone. Lying, cheating Charlie back to his ex. I suck at this dating game. What is love, anyways? Well, at least I had good food and company over the Christmas holidays instead of waiting to kill someone with my hammer while I lived stranded alone on the third floor of Kananaskis Hall.

Yes, I remember my first asthma attack. It was the night before your wedding, man. I fell apart. It was traumatic to watch you. I didn't understand why you had no say in your life. I laughed at all our jokes and, suddenly, the sobs emerged from the bottom of my soul. It was the first time I had felt pure grief. I couldn't bear seeing you leave to go to another house. I was heartbroken. I thought I was going to die that night. Couldn't breathe. That's what life feels like, sometimes. Just cannot breathe.

Eh, your husband is a difficult one to understand. He is a mama's boy. No balls. If he had a Chinese girlfriend, he should have had the guts to marry her instead of going with an Indian arranged marriage. I am sick of this usual story where a family forces their son to marry a girl of their choice. The boy says yes because he can't stand up to his family, but the boy does what he wants after he gets married, anyway. The poor girl gets into a life of prison because she is stuck in a loveless marriage and comes under the thumb of mother-in-law. Hmmm. Come to think about it, I've not heard of a girl who is forced to marry an innocent boy but continues to be with her previous forbidden lover. Have you? It's a man's world, isn't it?

I know you tried to say no. Remember that day?

I said to you, "Say something before it is too late."

You told Mummy and Papa that evening that you didn't want to marry Manjit. They said it was normal to be afraid. All girls should marry. He is a good boy. He is an engineer. He comes from a good family. Where would they find another boy for you? Blah blah blah, nonsense.

I remember your eyes were lifeless as you whispered, "See, I told you. It is not possible to have your own life."

I said, "Bullshit."

Why should you give up now? I think you should finish your teaching diploma. You only have a few months left, right? Maybe it is possible to be a wife, mother and live your dream? Be independent. When I come back to Singapore for a holiday, I will check for more information. See what we can do, ok.

I thought marriage would be so fun. Love. Hugging. Sex. Oh, sex. The forbidden word. The sin. On TV, it always looks glamorous. Maybe, try and make Manjit fall in love with you. Maybe, try and seduce him. You know, like the women do in the movies.

He is a boring old fart, though. It is hard to even have a conversation with him. He answers everything in one or two words. I tried to talk to him when I was in Singapore and gave up. He likes to stare at my breasts. One day, I am going to slap his face. Do you think his Chinese girlfriend finds him exciting? She must, right?

I checked about Banff Springs Hotel. It's expensive to stay there, but the photographs of the place are like a fairy tale. It's our castle. We must go. Never mind. I will save a little every month. I promise you when you come, we will rent a car, drive to Banff, stay at the Banff Springs Hotel and go crazy with Jesus, Waheguru, and snow angels.

Hugs to the little girls, Roni and Soni. I miss their cute little faces. Let's make sure they will be each other's tails as well and when they grow up, nobody will tell them what to do with their own lives.

Love you,

Your Tail, Simran.

25 FEBRUARY 1986

Dear Anita,

Snake Temple. Ugh. I am petrified of snakes. I wouldn't go there if God beckoned me. Your New Year sounds delightful, nonetheless. Mine was interesting, to say the least. Nothing worth writing about for now. Hey, I loved your photographs. The smiles on your sons' faces were joyfully contagious. I grinned to see how they proudly clasped those slithery snakes over their shoulders. Even Gopal looked at ease with the slimy critter. My family and I used to go to Penang all the time when I was in Singapore. It seems terribly far away now. Really, Penang is my favourite place in Malaysia. I wonder when I will go for a visit now.

Really, Anita, your life sounds idyllic. Beaches. Holidays. Holding hands in the sunset. I hope I meet a nice guy like Gopal. I'm jealous of all the adventures you've both had. Travelling for a year around the world together. Soulmates. Who does that, anymore? I want to have a husband just like Gopal. You lucky pig.

Come to think about it, you represent the heroines in the crazy love novels I used to read when I was in Singapore! You know, Harlequin romances. Every week, I went to my favourite second-hand bookstore in Serangoon Gardens. I would buy seven Harlequin books to devour, one for every night. I mean, each was fifty cents, and I got money (ten cents) back when I returned them. Love is cheap!

I swooned over the titles. *Catch a Dream. That Man Bryce. Heartbreaker. Castle of Temptation. Sweet is the Web.* I loveeeeeed these stories. The struggles. The challenges. The ups and downs. But love always triumphed in the end of these novels. The heroine always got her man. Just like you got Gopal.

Oh dear. I was sad to read about Ammah, your mother-in-law. I can't stand that kind of patriarchal bullshit. Where can women in Singapore go for help? Nowhere! Nowhere! It drives me crazy. In my literature classes, I am reading more and more about women trapped in unhappy situations. I took a class where the novels we studied are all by post-colonial writers. I sat on the edge of my seat in class and devoured every word by my fabulous Professor Mila. She brought these novels and the challenges of these women to life. It was as if she was talking about me. Yes. Literally. I did not know that there were women of colour like me who wrote about women of colour just like me.

Listen to this, Anita. Hey, your namesake: I'm drawn to writer, Anita Desai. She is an Indian novelist who writes about Indian women trapped in situations I am familiar with. The usual patriarchal crap where women fulfil their God-given obligations as wives. I am reading *Fire on the Mountain*. I can't put the book down. I can see and feel this woman's life—Nanda Kaul—as she thinks about her life as a wife and mother. *Fire on the Mountain*—it's the quiet, solid womanhood that hides the inner burning desires, just like in the lives of unhappy, stoic women.

Get it from the library or MPH bookstore if you can. I can't stop reading about stories that mirror the lives of Indian women. Then, I was drawn to this English woman, Mary Wollstonecraft. I decided to write my essay on her for a different English class. Just look at the title of the essay I picked for my essay: *A Vindication of the Rights of Woman*. This was written in 1792, and I am still seeing the same things that need to be done for women to be free. It's 1986, for Goodness 'sake.

These books are unleashing something in me: uncovering how women have been silenced and subjugated. Throw in the specific stories of Indian women's lives and how they are treated in *Fire on the Mountain*, and my mind is ablaze with questions and thoughts. No wonder people, and men, say a little learning is a dangerous thing. I know my grandmother, mother and sister, and your mother-in-law, Ammah, have not and will never read these books about women's lives. They will never question patriarchal oppression. They accept it. You have these ideas, Anita. You are an independent woman, right? You are a mother, wife, and teacher. You are a modern woman of the times.

I'm grasping to find a voice that deserves to be heard. What arranged marriage? Never again will I accept this idea if it is not what I want. My mother had no choice in the direction of her life. She fulfilled her role as dictated by others, to be shipped off as a wife at the tender age of sixteen. Maybe, just maybe, my sister has an opportunity to shift this perspective of a woman trapped in her duties as a wife and mother, especially if she has dreams to do more in her life. It's not too late, right?

I never knew about women in literature and history until I took a literature class with Professor Brown. I couldn't believe the struggles of Mary Wollstonecraft, one of the authors. I was enthralled. I researched, read, wrote, and handed in my essay about this intriguing woman one month before the due date. No kidding. I felt proud of myself.

Then, every day, I anxiously waited for the professor to return my essay. Nothing. I was too afraid to ask him, but I revelled in my own amazing content. I knew he would be impressed by my essay, for sure. It was two months later before I finally got the essay back. My heart thumped. I fidgeted in my seat until I held my essay. As soon as class was over, I bolted to my dormitory on campus, ten minutes away. I wanted a private moment of joy to celebrate.

I plopped on my bed, flipped the pages of my essay, and stared at the mark. My heart stopped beating. D. D? What? D for Donkey. How was this even remotely possible? I looked at the professor's comments—scribbled obscenities about how my ideas were reasonable but my writing was atrocious.

My eyes fixated on this sentence: *You will never get a university degree.*

My essay fell to the ground. I grabbed my coat and bag and stumbled back to the English department office. I glanced at my watch and remembered it was Professor Brown's office hour. I raced to the third floor. I took a deep breath and tiptoed to his door. It was slightly ajar. I gently knocked on his door even though I wanted to break it down and rush in.

Through the crack in the door, I saw Professor Brown hunched over in his chair at his desk.

He did not even look up, but I heard his voice say, *Go away. I am busy.*

I was astounded. Maybe, I misheard him. I looked at the posted timetable of his office hour on his door again. No. I was right. It was office hour, indeed!

"Professor Brown," I persisted in a loud voice. "Can I talk to you about my essay?"

Once again, without even looking up, Professor Brown hollered, *Go away.*

My feet felt like lead, and I pulled back my hand from his doorknob. I looked down the empty hallway and back to his posted office hours on the door. Confusion and trepidation set in. Have you ever heard of such shoddy treatment in all of your life? What do I do now, I thought? I can't imagine in Singapore if my teacher screamed at me like that. I felt helpless. I realized I still had lots to learn about Canadian life: how to write, how to survive in university.

What to do? Where to go next? I know in junior college, I got D's because I did not put any work into my assignments. But I turned things around at the Institute of Education. I mean, I have my teaching diploma, for God's sakes, and I got A's in all my English courses because of my hard work and passion. What could have happened to my writing to get an A in Singapore but a D in this Calgary class? My mind raced. I questioned my own competence but stepped to Professor Brown's door one more time. As I raised my hand to knock, the door slammed in my face with a resounding bang. I took a step back, aghast. I needed to talk to him and ask for help. For clarification. For guidance. For justification of this red scarlet D.

Baffled, I turned and left the department. I raced down the flight of stairs. I marched furiously in no clear direction. I tightened the grip on my backpack over my shoulder as it dawned on me it was freezing. I was underdressed for winter, as usual, and my insides felt as icy as the weather outside. Waves of panic engulfed me as questions raced through my mind.

Maybe, I can't write. What am I doing in Canada? I gave up everything to be here. A comfortable home. A great country. A marriage with a potentially good man. My identity. My culture. My language. My food. My father really couldn't afford to send me to Canada. I was a fraud. D. For dumb. Disaster.

Maybe this D was a sign I should go back to Singapore? I should pack my bags, get on the next plane, go home with my tail between my legs, and marry that man. My family would take care of me. I wouldn't need to write another essay and get punched in the gut with my incompetence. I wouldn't have to knock on professors' doors and beg for vindication.

As I berated myself, my footsteps led me across campus and towards Brentwood, a strip mall fifteen minutes away from the university. A small laundromat led to warmth of the mall. As I passed, I saw a tall man inside turn and face me. He wore a long black coat. The next thing I knew, the man held his coat open with both hands. Wait. He was naked under that coat! The man in the laundromat just flashed me!

I stared directly at the open coat. My eyes locked on his groin. My jaw dropped. Oh, glory. My body convulsed into giggles. No one else was around. Just lucky me.

It was the most ludicrous sight I had ever seen in my life in any country. Me pondering my failures while a stranger flashed me his glorious giant penis. Oh. Hah. A penis. How stupid it looked. You know, just hanging there. Wow. My first penis sighting. I tore my gaze from his exposed penis to his grinning face.

He waved at me. Naturally, I waved back—I don't know why. It felt like the polite thing to do, you know. I turned and scampered away.

This penis was a sign. It was a way of reminding me that the

D, the crazy prof, the flasher were all obstacles. I could walk away, gawk and be offended or I could face the obstacles head on.

Yup. The brain is a powerful thing. Just like that, right at that moment, I made my mind up. I had choices. I was not a helpless victim. Triumphant, I turned around, held my head up high, and purposefully marched back to the university. I headed straight to the Registrar's office in the main building. I filled in the forms and signed my name with a vengeance. Then, I dropped that bloody course.

Did you think I was going back to see Professor Brown? What for? Even in my infancy of being a brand-new Canadian student, my instinct told me there would be no positive outcome. I felt it in my gut. Though I loved that class, there were some battles that were not worth entering. Yes, Mary Wollstonecraft. I will fight for my education. I wasn't going to be painted by the brush of D—the Scarlett letter of that essay by that incompetent man.

Still that night, I cried in my pillow for all that money lost. I cried for my failure. I just cried. It seems I am doing a lot of crying in Calgary. Well, at least I saw my first Canadian penis. Hah.

Hugs,

Simran

9 MARCH 1986

Hello Simran,

This girl Sunny, who gave you aspirin and now wants her ex-boyfriend back, is a useless friend. And Charlie is a playboy. They deserve each other, lah. It is better that you are saved from this Hindi movie. You know what your problem is? You read too many Harlequin romances from that Serangoon Road bookstore. Always a fool for love.

Same with me and love. When we lived at home in Singapore, I couldn't wait to get married, be in love and find freedom. What a mistake. I'm out of the frying pan into the fire.

I see a big irony now that I'm married. In our father's house, at least, I had all of you. Papa was strict and controlling. Still, I realize he really loved me. Do you remember when he unexpectedly brought home three dresses for me. I was amazed. One was sky blue with tiny white flowers. One was forest green with yellow dots. One was fire red, like a matador's cape. They were all soft and silky. The blue one was my favourite. It had soft, see-through long sleeves and a Peter Pan collar. When I wore it, I felt like a princess.

I twirled and you clapped your hands and said, "Your Majesty," and curtsied.

We laughed hard, fell on the bed and sang "Like a Virgin," by Madonna. It was the perfect song for us virgins, right?

I know we couldn't go out anywhere we wanted or without you being my chaperone. No boys. No parties. No dates. But now I see things differently. In our father's house, I felt special. Mummy made my favourite brinjal dish and lady's fingers in masala with roti. She made whatever I wanted. I just had to ask. Papa took me everywhere on his scooter. To school, to the doctor, to my girlfriends' houses. Whether we wanted or not, he was there on his scooter to drive me anywhere.

Every year we went on holidays. We had little money. Still, Papa took us to Cameron Highlands, Penang and Genting Highlands for holidays. We were a team. Together. I always felt safe. A daughter is safe in her mother and father's house.

Now I feel like a stranger in my husband's house. I am an outsider. I feel uncomfortable. How can I explain? You know when you go to a new place and nothing fits? The chair is hard. The room is dark. The bathroom is weird. You feel you must tiptoe in a stranger's house. That is how I feel in my husband's house. It's not my house. I am a pariah. I cannot find a safe space to unwind. I'm on constant edge. I wait for the Queen or Manjit to command me to do something or the other.

No one prepared me to go from my father's house to my husband's house. Everything was chosen for me. All my decisions were out of my hands. If I could go back in time, I would say "no," louder. But I've lost my voice after one small attempt. I had no courage. No point. I wasn't allowed to say no. My duty was to get married and have a new life. But you know what? It is not a new life. It is a life that's not even mine. Sim, I'm trapped. I am suffocated.

I'm jealous of you. You were smart. You ran to Canada. I don't know how you got out of this trap. What did you do that I couldn't do? Even with your wedding outfit packed in a suitcase under your bed ready for July, the wedding cards ordered and ready to send out, and all your clothes, shoes, jewelry all bought, you dropped a bomb when you said no. I don't think anyone ever dared to say no to Papa. From where did you find that courage, Sim?

Me? I didn't see any other different way. I wanted love and marriage. I wanted to please everyone and do the right thing for them. But now I am trapped with a stranger. I have a mother-in-law from hell and two screaming brats. How is this life better for a wife?

Now that I am married, I don't know how to find a way out of this unhappy and complicated life. I still try to make everyone happy. Except me. I don't know how women who are forced into married lives find any joy. What do I have to do? Live like this until the children are grown and leave the house? Then what? I have to be a daughter, be a wife and be a mother. Those are my choices, it seems.

Yes. Can you see why I am jealous of you? Your life is easy. You do what you want. I think that you must be going crazy with no one watching you anymore. No Papa watching you. No Indian people asking your family when you will be getting married. No one checking on you. Suffocating your breath. Choking your freedom.

You have new adventures every day, ya. I imagine wearing skis and going down the mountain. How crazy is that. My adventure? Every week I go to visit Mummy and Papa. That is ironically the only time I can relax. Before I couldn't breathe in my father's house. Now, going there is relaxing. Life can be strange. Hey, Mummy and Papa are worried about you all alone. Also you are expensive and give them a lot of stress. It is a miracle you are in Calgary. I lie to them and say you are well-behaved there. It's payback for you being my chaperone.

I am lonely, Simran. That husband I sleep with every night is becoming more and more a stranger. No conversation. No hugs. No kisses. I have nothing in this marriage. I am a puppet in my husband's house.

Send me more photos. The mountains look like big breasts. The snow is like ice kacang. Looks fluffy but hard. Strange. I will dream about Banff. I will also put on skis. I will fly down the mountain. It looks very easy.

Write to me soon.

Amrit

10 MARCH 1986

Dear Amy,

Chasing the Singapore dream, eh? Money, men, and Mercedes. Well, I certainly hope that your Mr. Moneybags turns out to be your ticket to a posh condo on Orchard Road: the fancy cars, the diamond rings from Tiffany's, Chanel outfits, Givenchy handbags, Cartier shoes. Err, did I miss anything?

Frankly, I have never understood your hunger for overpriced name-brand material goods from Orchard Road. Really, how did it go? Was Mr. Princeton the savvy Singapore gentleman and you, his sweet Cinderella? That would be your perfect love story, eh? I remember when we in junior college, you said Princeton or nothing, not some third-rate university in Alabama. You primped and primed yourself for the picking. You gave me your strategies, right from the time we hung out in the canteen at junior college. In fact, you gave me a hard time about dressing like a slob and cautioned me that no one would marry me. Me—I'm too uninterested in name brands and more excited by big, sexy brains. Oh man, it takes too much effort to look pretty for a man.

Calgary, oh yes, the Cowboy town of the West. Don't be such a snob, Amy. And I did love *Little House on the Prairie*. But it's the mountains that excite me more than the prairies. I had heard about the Rockies in Calgary but never had a chance to go. A golden opportunity came up when I went to Singapore Students' Club dinner outing at the Ginger Beef. I met twenty new Singapore students studying at the University of Calgary. The group made many plans for different outings. One of them was a ski trip to Lake Louise. I snagged a seat in Balraj's car. I was one of the lucky four. Balraj was the driver and his best friend Siva was also coming with us. Jenny had arrived in Calgary a month ago and was renting a room in a house on University Drive across Kananaskis Hall. She was passenger four.

I couldn't wait to go to the Rockies. I see the silhouette and peaks of the mysterious mountains when I stand outside Kananaskis Hall and look west. Awesome. The fateful day in February finally arrived. At 6 a.m., I stumbled sleepily to the Kananaskis building carpark, the meeting point. Balraj and his friend Siva were dressed in full winter gear. I tugged at my waist length black wool coat and felt apprehensive. It was the only coat I had.

These Singapore boys were fun and cheeky. They had been in Calgary for four years—Calgary veterans! When they invited me, I could not say no. I hoped to learn more about surviving in Calgary from them. Also, I was eager to make more friends on campus. They talked my ear off while we were waiting for Jenny to show up. I mentally noted all the places in Calgary they suggested I visit. Balraj told me he and Siva were novice skiers. I had no clue what that meant. How hard could skiing be?

With Balraj in the driver's seat, Siva in the passenger's seat, I slithered into the back seat as soon as Jenny showed up. I felt comfortable with my new homies from Singapore. New friends and new adventures. These were people from Singapore and familiar tongues and places back home to talk about.

Frankly, I had no idea where we were heading to in Balraj's car. I had not ventured further than the northwest sector of Calgary. Balraj was a great tour guide, pointing out places as we drove on Highway 1 to Lake Louise. Once we got out of the city limits, it was a long two hours' drive to our destination. We drove past frozen fields. Siva pointed out the Morley Reservation, where native Indians had homes on their designated land. Then, I pointed at the sign, Kananaskis Provincial Park. That was the name of my dormitory building.

Glimmers of light shone on the highway, and Balraj shouted, "Canmore, next. That is a town in the Rocky Mountains, midway to

Lake Louise. Then, Banff. Then Lake Louise ski hill."

As we got closer to Canmore, I was mesmerized to see the landscape change in ways I couldn't even imagine. Massive frozen lakes on my right. Towering, bare trees lined the left side of the road, and their branches were weighed down by white icicles; a mysterious canopy cast shadows in the dimly lit morning. The foggy, shadowy peaks ahead silenced me. As the car meandered through the glacial landscape, I peered out the window covered in droplets of condensation and had to wipe the beaded drops of moisture with my gloved hand to gaze at the frozen whiteness outside. The stillness of the ice-covered expanse stretched further than I could see in the moving vehicle. It was the first time in my life I had witnessed the sheer beauty of the landscape of winter. What a contrast with the heat, humidity, and towering buildings in Singapore. Night and day. I was mesmerized by the spaciousness and expansiveness of this snowy terrain.

Balraj's voice broke my trance. He had read my mind.

He said, "Enjoy the view. No tall skyscrapers here or reclaimed land. Just God's playground."

When Balraj stopped the car at a lookout just before Canmore, I jumped out and stretched my arms as if to embrace the mountains ahead. I peeled my wet flimsy gloves off to photograph the mountains and the lake. Snap. Snap. I hopped from one foot to the other to stay warm in the minus fifteen degrees Celsius cold as my breath misted and the cold permeated the exposed skin on my neck. I stared silently at the majestic mountains that encircled me. The boys teased me as I looked like a clumsy ballerina darting from one spot to the other.

A strange sense of awe came over me. I approached the railing and leaned on it; my hands were cold from the icy metal. My cheeks trembled from the blast of air and excitement. I sensed a quavering in my chest. All the anxiety of the last few months whooshed away. A balance restored within, and the feeling of being an outsider diminished. I felt tranquility. Like I belonged. Here in this wide expanse of the wild and snow of the Rockies, I felt a profound connection with the land. Was this why I had, unconsciously, picked Calgary? Not Winnipeg. Not Vancouver.

"Hey, fellow Singaporeans. Come, lah!" Balraj, impatient, rushed us back into the car so we could get to Lake Louise before it got crowded.

A few hours later, we finally arrived at the ski hill in Lake Louise. When Balraj pulled into the massive car park, it was full. He found a spot far away from the ski lodge, and we groaned when we saw the ten-minute trek up to the main building. Frankly, I had no notion of what this skiing thing was except what I had seen on TV. We arrived at the main building, stepped out of the main lodge, and stood at the base of the ski hills that were ahead.

At this point, my eyes widened in disbelief.

I looked at the boys and said, "You want me to ski down that mountain?" It looked as tall as our twenty-five-storey block of flats in Singapore.

Jenny grabbed my arm. "No, no, no," she whimpered. "It is impossible to ski down that giant mountain! So scary, lah."

Balraj and Siva guffawed dismissively. "It's easy, lah. Just go and rent some skis. Any idiot can do this."

The icy fingers of panic twisted my heart. What had I gotten myself into this time? I had not asked enough questions or done any research. Skiing was not like a shopping expedition, I realized. I was unprepared. I had not brought my Ventolin for my asthma. The air was thin, and my breath became raspy. My nose felt raw and swollen from the biting cold. I looked around nervously and noticed that everyone was dressed in sleek ski suits, wore heavy gloves, thick toques, or balaclavas.

Me, I had my Wrangler jeans, a thin, flimsy green sweater, two-dollar gloves from K-Mart, a cute little red felt hat and the pièce de résistance, colourful blue, red, and green leg warmers over my jeans. I was quite the sight. Oh yes, and mirrored blue, red, and white sunglasses which I had picked up from the gas station in Calgary for five dollars to match those darn leg warmers. It didn't cross my Singapore mind that there was a proper way to dress for the

Canadian winter and to go skiing. I mean, what did I know about any of this?

We were now in the ski rental shop; Jenny looked equally apprehensive.

I grabbed Balraj's arm and said, "Maybe we should take ski lessons?"

"Don't be stupid," Balraj laughed. "See that baby hill?"

He pointed to a mid-sized hill on the far right.

"That is for babies. Just go up that Bunny Hill and go straight down. It's nothing. It's like going down a slide."

"How do I stop?" I asked.

"Oh," said Balraj. "You'll figure it out. It's damn easy. After the first time down, you will know how to stop. No big deal."

"Ok." Siva chirped. "No more wasting time. We are going to the very top. Enjoy yourselves. The Bunny Hill is that away. Bye!"

The two goons took off before I could protest. What? I thought they were going to help us, teach us, be with us. Jenny, who had only arrived a few months ago from Singapore, looked equally alarmed. We had each just spent a lot of money to rent all the equipment because the boys said we had to. Now what?

"Bloody Singaporeans!" Jenny said, "Come, lah. Let's try."

In irritation, we plopped on the crowded benches in the shop. We struggled to put on the heavy, giant ski boots. They felt like hard metal helmets with a tight opening that I had to slip my feet in. It didn't even fit naturally without contorting and shoving each foot in. Once my feet were in, the top of the boots cut into my shins. I stood up and stumbled. Jenny and I tottered outside.

Confused, I decided to put the skis on my boots, thinking it would be easier to move. Big mistake. I promptly and painfully landed on my behind, contorted amidst the twisted skis and poles. Now, I couldn't get up. Jenny tried to help me. Then she fell.

Our hoots of laughter and bewilderment made things more difficult. I unclasped my boots from the skis and finally stood up. What if I tried putting the skis on, again? I glided against my will, so I stabbed the snow with my poles to anchor myself. Petrified at the lack of control over my feet and skis, I couldn't figure out what to do and how to move. Being on these uncomfortable slippery skis was like gliding on butter. Snow. Skis. Mountains. Biting cold. Nothing was remotely familiar to me, and I felt stabs of anxiety. I hadn't even made it to the Bunny Hill yet.

Determined not to give up, Jenny and I headed to the nearby bunny hill, which was full of wee kids. Great! Perplexed about what to do, we hobbled sideways like crabs with skis and side stepped all the eager little kids on our way to the T-bar line. T-bar. Literally, it was an upside-down T. The long bar was attached to the rolling conveyor over our heads to pull skiers up to the top of the hill. I glanced up to the top of the Bunny Hill; it looked four storeys high like our block of flats in Singapore. The long bar of the T was the seat to put our bums on. This is what I had to do. Grab the T-bar, lean on the seat with another skier on the other side of the T facing up at the hill, and the conveyor belt would pull us up. Our legs and skis dangled until we got to the top of the hill, and we had to ski off the path of the conveyor belt.

My heart raced. Ok. No one to help. We stood there for twenty minutes, carefully watching and learning. Finally, Jenny and I had the courage to stand in line. We watched what everyone did and grabbed the T-bar when it was our turn. The T-bar whooshed us up the hill. I couldn't balance myself and clutched the middle bar. My feet on the skis were dangling in mid-air as the T-bar went up on the hill. Fear engulfed every pore. The T-bar reached the top of the hill at the designated get off point.

"Get off! Get off!" I heard people scream when the T-bar reached the exit point at the top of the bunny hill.

Jenny managed to slide off the T-bar and ski off to the side. Me, I was so agitated I felt hot tears haze my view as I collapsed in an unsightly heap, barely out of the way of the T bar and people skiing. Twisted in a pretzel with my poles not within my reach, my face met a rude awakening in the snow as I tasted cold, brittle shaved ice in my mouth.

I heard Jenny's voice, "Eh, are you ok?"

Trying to be oh so cool, I twisted my torso, unraveled my knee, and rearranged myself in a sitting position. Those mirrored glasses hid my tears. Ouch, ouch, ouch. I felt a stabbing pain in my knee. Jenny bent down and released the twisted skis from my feet. I didn't know her that well at all, but I was touched by her concern. The tears welled, and I realized that something was painfully wrong.

An older, blonde lady skied up to me. "I'm a nurse," she said. "I saw you fall. It didn't look good. I am going to get the medic, ok."

"Medic?" I whispered.

Jenny plopped on the snow next to me and howled. "First ski experience. First ride up the T-bar. First Bunny Hill. Fun, right."

"Go, Jenny. Go and try. I am stuck here. I'll be ok."

Jenny and I stared at the skiers effortlessly gliding and sliding their way around, like they belonged. Me, I felt like an alien in outer space. Frozen outer space. After fifteen minutes of waiting with me for the medic, Jenny finally decided to try a run downhill by herself. I watched her slide down the hill, sideways. She fell and picked herself up. She waved to me and continued in that fashion.

"Good for you, girl!" I yelled.

I became quite the spectacle, anyways. Curious children pointed at me and shouted at their parents in loud voices.

I heard them screech: "Look at her. What's happening? Why is she there?"

On my bum, I decided to inch myself down the busy bunny hill. First, I went sideways, trying to find a path that was the least occupied. One butt cheek at a time, with the skis and poles in my hands, awkwardly balanced. Medic. Maybe, they forgot about me. Good. I looked down the hill and saw that it would take me an hour or so to navigate myself butt cheek by butt cheek. People and children gleefully skied past me, so I maneuvered myself to the very edge of the hill, still quite the display and delight of the other skiers.

Then I saw him. The medic, I mean. He had a stretcher he pulled on ropes behind him. He must be the medic, right? I glanced at my watch. Forty-five minutes. That's how long I had been waiting and inching my way down. He was a blond man, maybe in his thirties, not bad looking, wearing a bright yellow jacket, with the word, "Medic" across. He stopped in front of me. A medic on skis and a stretcher on snow.

"What's wrong with you?" he asked.

"Uhhh, my knee. Listen, I think I am ok." I felt guilty.

"Get in the stretcher," he barked. "We'll get it checked when we get to the medic station."

Very rude, I thought. No love here. I looked at the very small, long cloth stretcher on the snow and reluctantly inched myself onto it. There was nowhere and nothing to hold onto once I got on. Then, Mr. Medic piled my two skis and poles and his two poles as well onto me as I grabbed them all in the crook of my arms. I was flabbergasted. How was I going to balance all the skis, poles, and myself on this narrow piece of stretcher that was sliding down the hill?

By now, I was the main attraction. Picture this: Brown girl on a stretcher on the Bunny Hill of white snow. I prayed for the ground to open and swallow me as I heard the children's mocking laughter.

With a jolt, the medic took off and my heart lunged out of my chest. He skied downhill with me on the stretcher behind him. I wanted to shrink from embarrassment. It was the most unnatural sensation in the world as I awkwardly struggled to balance. The next thing you know, ski, pole, pole, pole, ski, pole, Simran had all fallen off the damn stretcher. I froze on the snow, literally, as Mr. Medic continued skiing downhill, unaware that his patient was plopped in the middle of the Bunny Hill.

Assorted skiers shouted at the medic: "Hey, you dropped your patient!"

It took an agonizingly long time before the medic stopped, looked back, shook his head, and stomped up to me.

His face contorted in a red puffy ball, and he whispered, "You are making me look very bad!"

Stunned, I angrily retorted, "I'm making YOU look bad. You are doing that by yourself, Buddy. YOU are making ME look very bad."

"Get in the stretcher!" he barked.

"Over my dead body," I hollered. "There is no way in hell I am getting back in that stretcher. Go away. Leave me alone."

Who was I? What voice spoke from me? Where was that nice Indian girl from Singapore? His face was a sight to behold—red, bulbous, ready to explode!

He glared at me and said, "Fine. It's your choice." Angrily, the medic picked up his poles and skied off.

"Asshole!" I mouthed silently.

Some of the skiers who had encircled us applauded. Jenny awkwardly made her way to me, one step at a time, laughing so hard she couldn't speak. She plopped herself beside me, and I told her the incompetent medic had left me to die on the slope. Jenny fell back in the snow, overcome by more laughter.

"Eh. Are you ok, Sim?"

"Go, go, go! Don't waste your time with me. I'm fine," I insisted.

I decided I would sit there on the slope and enjoy the sight. Jenny agreed. At least it was her third time down the Bunny Hill. She struggled to stand and slowly glided down the slope, but she fell most of the time. I could see that she endeavoured to make the most of skiing, and I laughed as I watched her go. At least one of us was skiing.

Sitting there in the snow, I looked up to the sky and finally tuned in to my surroundings. I was so caught up in my skiing tragedy that I had not appreciated the towering trees around me and the glistening white peaks as far as my eye could see. The sky was designed in glorious hues of blue and grey, and the light snow gently twirled and descended. I was on a Bunny Hill amidst the Rocky Mountains. I was in the midst of Rockies on my bum, man!

I took in the vast hills around me. I peeled my flimsy wet gloves off and felt the gritty feel of the snow. All my life in Singapore, I tried to visualize snow. I gathered handfuls of snow and rolled them into misshapen balls, then tossed them, grinning when they fell apart. My cheeks tingled from the biting cold, and I tilted my face up to the sky to feel the sun's rays. It was odd to feel hot sun and cold ice at the same time. This beauty of snow was nothing like I had imagined.

I looked at the hubbub around me as skiers dodged me. I even waved at all the people who turned to take a second look at me. Some of them waved back. The nice nurse lady skied by and stopped to ask me if I was alright. I gave her the thumbs up. All this while, I made progress down the hill. Inch by inch, I found myself closer to the base of the hill. It was hard trying to look dignified as I knew I looked quite idiotic sitting on my bum, clutching my skis and poles, and slowly sliding down the Bunny Slope.

Something, a strange butterfly feeling flitted in my chest. I felt a strange sense of victory. I had conquered a mountain. I didn't die! I was a skier! Bum skier!

My knee throbbed like mad by the time I hit the bottom. Out of nowhere, the two Singaporean clowns appeared. They had heard about my stretcher fiasco from Jenny and had come to check if I was alive. I really didn't want to talk to them, but they pulled me up to my feet and carried my poles. Hah. Chivalry. Finally, we left the ski slope. After I returned the equipment, I hobbled past the medics' tent. I saw the man who left me to die on the mountain. I waved to him and blew him a kiss. His face turned red. Yeah, thanks, Mr. Medic.

I didn't say much to the two clowns from Singapore on the long ride home. I closed my eyes, and all I could see in my mind's eye was the Bunny Hill and the priceless looks of the other skiers. I felt the incessant throbbing of my sore butt cheeks and my swelling knee. Slowly, in the heat of the car, I thawed. I was relieved when we reached Kananaskis Hall hours later, and I limped my way back to my room; I thanked Jenny for being there for me.

"Well done, Singapore skier," Balraj said.

"Here's to the Olympics," continued the cheeky Siva.

Those Singapore boys! Truly, they had thrown me to the mercy of the mountains. I cursed them silently in filthy Singaporean curses. Bloody hell. Thank God for Jenny.

I was relieved when I got home and plopped myself into my bed.

Lin, my roommate, offered her pearls of wisdom. "Hah. You don't know how to ski. Why the hell did you go? Did you break your leg?"

I turned my back, put my pillow over my face and groaned. I really wanted to put that pillow over her face. If only I had known the truth about skiing.

The next morning when I woke up, my knee was swollen and throbbing. I hobbled out to the main lounge and called for a cab. I knew I had to go to Emergency. I knew it would take a long time. You see, I was a pro now. I had my coat, my shoes, my Alberta Health card, my credit card, and my homework, "The Road Not Taken," by Robert Frost. I did not say a word to anyone, especially to big mouth, Lin.

The taxi arrived. For someone trying to avoid a certain Taxi-wallah, taking taxis seemed to be my popular pastime. I chose a different cab company to be safe. I got to the hospital in ten minutes, but I sat in the waiting room for hours. There was an endless array of people always streaming in with every kind of injury. Some commiserated with me as we gazed at the sick people on the rows of sofas and chairs in the waiting room.

What a morbid and depressing place! There were patients covered in blood who clutched broken bones and moaned in pain. Some patients looked like they needed immediate help as they were wheeled into the rooms at the back. I felt guilty taking up space with my ridiculous ski expedition knee injury. When the nurse called my name, I limped into a large room with four curtained beds.

The doctor finally came in, and I pointed to my knee and boldly asked, "Doctor, tell me exactly what you think this is and what I have to do?"

The doctor laughed with me when I told him my story of falling off the stretcher on the ski hill.

He checked my knee carefully and said, "Skiing is a dangerous thing, young lady. People die from falling and hitting their heads. You are lucky it's not worse. It's an inflammation of your knee caused by the twist and fall. Ice it. Put a hot water bottle to it. Take aspirin. The swelling will go down in a week or two. No more skiing without lessons first," he warned.

I chuckled. "I won't be taking aspirin, Doctor. That should be in your notes. But yes. No more skiing for me."

I hobbled out of Foothills Hospital four long hours after I arrived, grateful I was alive. I headed to the taxi stand. I knew exactly where it was.

When I got in the taxi, I said to the driver, "Take me home to Kananaskis Hall, please."

I glanced at my homework: Frost's poem, and I felt compelled to utter the last lines meant for me: *Two roads diverged in a wood, and I—I took the one less traveled by, And that has made all the difference.*

How true! I was relieved to head back to my dorm and sleep. I even finished my Frost homework that night. I felt content despite my skiing misadventures. I hobbled everywhere for two weeks, waiting for the pain to diminish. Eventually, it did, with help from Tylenol. And guess what? I got an A in the Frost assignment.

You know, quiet Calgary is slowly growing on me. I am free to go where I want. On Saturdays, I love going to a trendy hub in Calgary, Kensington. I hang out at the Roasterie, a cool coffee hangout, drink Cafe Thursday, and happily sip my coffee and mocha with chocolate whipped cream. I sit in front of the cafe around the bench planters and watch people go by—no rush, no guilt, no stress, just blending in and feeling Calgarian, as bicycles, dogs and people wander by. All by myself.

Do you think it matters that you are in New Jersey, New York, Singapore, or Calgary if you feel like you belong? For me, all that matters is that feeling where my heart does not flutter in agitation, I don't have to keep looking at my watch or have to be somewhere that someone has commanded me to be. It's being there in the moment and enjoying the bliss. And in Calgary, I am.

I'll keep my fingers crossed for you and your rich boy. I know you crave wedding bells, an exotic honeymoon, and a spectacular show. I mean, what's love got to do with it if he's rich, right? Hah. You criticized me in our junior college days for being an Indian woman who was unable to get out of my patriarchal prison and loveless arranged marriage situation. I told you I would, one day. It's my turn now to say to you that marrying for money is a treacherous option you might regret. Be careful, my friend.

From the Singapore Olympic Skier,

Simran

25 MARCH 1986

Hey Anita,

Haven't heard back from you. What's up? What's happening? I am in class right now. Yes. New one. This professor is an incredibly wonderful man. He is White, six foot, bald and bearded. He likes to perch himself on the desk in front of class, his large frame hovering in friendly attendance. What a difference from the pompous ass who gave me a D. It's also a literature class covering Keats to Rossetti.

The only problem is I've learnt less about the poets but more about love, marriage, and divorce. You see, Proffy here loves to talk—mostly about himself. It's entertaining, and no one complains. He's excited because his wife is due to give birth anytime now. His second ex-wife. Wait, maybe his third. No. Second. Ok, let me get his story straight. Proffy's first son is twenty years old, and Proffy is going to have another baby with his second wife. Imagine that. A twenty-year gap between his kids. I can't imagine that happening in Singapore. Proffy confided in us that his first marriage was a disaster. His wife won't talk to him anymore, and the divorce was nasty. He advised us that it was cheaper to bury a wife than to divorce one.

Wait. The class is asking questions—no, not about literature but about his life.

They want to know if he sees his son. *No.*

Where did he meet his new wife? *At a bar.*

How many children does he want? *Two.*

How long was marriage one? *Twelve years.*

How long is marriage number two? *Two years and going.*

Will his twenty-year-old son meet the new baby? *He hopes so.*

Damn. This is very entertaining stuff. He's not like our Singapore teachers who are prim and proper. I like this prof. He is raw, human, and engaging.

As I write you this letter, enjoying the class but wishing I could actually learn about Keats and Rosetti, Proffy switched gears. Oh no. I wasn't paying attention. Wait. He picked me. I had to read a verse of Christina Rossetti's "Goblin Market" out loud in class. I froze. Panic set in. My voice trembled. I couldn't pronounce the words like a Canadian—just like a bloody Singaporean with my accent. I took a deep breath and slowed down. Proffy nodded and smiled at me, encouraging me with his gaze.

I wanted to run out of the class, but this time, I persisted. I felt it was my time to be heard in Calgary. I delved right into the poem. I stumbled a little. I struggled with the rhythm, but I didn't stop. Oh, my goodness. It was a delightful poem about sisters fighting against goblins and triumphing at the end. I could relate. It's about my sister and me. I'm overcoming my goblins of fear in this class. I did it. Relieved and proud, I sat down. Proffy beamed at me. It was like he knew that the poem was for me. I smiled back. He's a good man, Proffy.

I felt more confident, and when Jeff, from English class said he would take me to a real cowboy bar in Calgary after class, I accepted the offer. We drove to the southwest. I saw the giant sign, *Ranchman*. I was intrigued, got out of the car, and followed Jeff. As we approached the entrance, these two big White dudes wearing cowboy hats, giant belt buckles and pointed cowboy boots under their jeans stepped in front of me. Jeff kept walking, unaware.

One of the men said, *Fuck all Indian pass-able sidewalks.*

I froze. Then adrenaline kicked in. I sidestepped them and ran into the bar. My heart pounded so hard I thought I would collapse.

Jeff looked at me and said, "What's up?"

I shook my head, confused. "Nothing. Nothing."

Indian pass-able sidewalks. What did he mean? Did I hear correctly? I didn't want to say anything to Jeff in case he wanted to go out and confront the men. I tried to focus on the music. Luckily, it was so loud that Jeff gave up talking to me.

My thoughts drifted back. Indian? Like Native Indian? They thought I was Native? Indian like where and what? These sorts of thoughts kept going through my mind like a noisy locomotive. *Indian pass-able sidewalks.* Like sidewalks that Indians should not be allowed to walk on. Which Indians? All Indians? Native Indians? Me? Brown people? I couldn't stop analyzing that one sentence.

Finally, I said to Jeff, "I've got a headache. Let's go."

I ran out the door to Jeff's car. A sigh of relief. No one was stood outside. Not the two bastards. I didn't say anything to Jeff. Jeff is just a guy from class, and we chat about what we are not learning about Keats and Rosetti as we leave class. I didn't want to confide in him. I needed time alone. I forced a smile and said goodbye when he dropped me off at my dorm.

The whole night, my mind raced. Did the men not recognize that I was a Punjabi girl from Singapore? In Calgary, I heard that all brown people are East Indians. I didn't understand that. East?

Could these men not discern the different brown people? I can. South Indians. North Indians. Iranians. Egyptians, Mexicans, Native Indians. An endless list. How dare they clump me all together into one group of brown people with no delineation. Why can't Indians use the sidewalks? Why?

Was I simply the exotic woman that Jeff was curious about?

Is that why people kept asking, "Where are you from?"

I tossed and turned all night. I was a perpetual outsider, trying to find space in a white world. Maybe I was no different, myself. I mean, how often had I said that all white people looked the same?

The next day, I marched to Angela's room across mine and knocked on the door. Angela looked at me quizzically.

"Angela, tell me about your family."

Startled and delighted, she invited me into her room, gave me homemade biscotti from her jar, and spent an hour telling me stories about her family who came from Italy forty years ago. They had settled in Calgary. She told me about Italian food and family celebrations. She spoke in Italian and painted vivid details about her grandmother who loved to cook and go to church. I nodded, thinking how similar that was to my grandmother who was a brilliant cook and went to the temple every week in Singapore without fail. Similarities.

I left Angela's room feeling a little better. I had lumped all white people together. Now, I learned about Italians. About people. About being human. I promised to ask more questions and learn.

It was heartbreaking that those men had singled me out for being brown and for uttering those vile words about any human beings. I looked at the girls on my floor watching TV in the common living room on 3rd Kan, and I smiled at the beautiful variety of women from all backgrounds. I knew Kathy was Polish. Sharon was Jewish. Hilda was South African. Frankly, I knew nothing more about them. I promised myself I would ask each of them about their background so I could learn more about other beautiful races and cultures. Maybe, at the end of the day, sometimes we are outsiders, and sometimes we are insiders. It's a dance I am getting to understand a little better each day.

Oh, class is over. Next class, Proffy promised he would let us know more about the baby. He even promised us some photographs and cigars.

You know, I feel as a greenhorn—every day is a lesson in navigating a new feeling, a new sensation, a new adventure. It never ever crossed my mind that when I left Singapore, I would have to learn to live all over again. I never thought about race, colour, accents, outsider, insider, white, brown, black, yellow. It felt safe in Singapore for me. We grew up and mingled with Malays, Chinese, and Indians in our neighbourhoods and in school. In Singapore, there was a political push for racial harmony and equality. We all knew the strategy had its flaws. We knew there was internal racism in Singapore. I witnessed it myself. When I was sixteen, Teck Hwa told me I couldn't go to his house, and he was not allowed to befriend a "mangkali kui"—an Indian devil. Maybe, I was naive. I am adjusting. Exotic Singaporean let loose in Calgary. What will I end up becoming?

Oh, let me share my shopping expedition with you. I know you love shopping! I went to my favourite shopping centre in Calgary—Market Mall—last Sunday to shop for a new coat. I overheard some girls in class saying there was a sale. I wandered in and out of the shops at the mall, enjoying myself. I entered the boutique store the girls mentioned in class.

A big grin erupted on my face as I touched every coat on the rack, intrigued by the feel, length, colour, weight. I mean, how the heck do I pick the right coat? Then, my fingers caressed this long pink coat made from rabbit hair. It was a shimmery pale pink. I lifted the heavy coat from the rack, held it in front of me and stared at myself in the mirror. I smiled as I thought about the matching pink lipstick I had.

"Try it on," urged the friendly saleslady.

She took the coat and guided each arm into the sleeve. Oh, the coat felt warm, safe, and cozy. I snuggled my hands in the two giant pockets on either side. The length of my coat fell perfectly at my ankles. I couldn't tear my eyes away. Aaah, so pretty in pink.

I heard the saleslady say, "The best thing is this coat has been reduced from $500 to $100. Where can you buy a rabbit fur coat for $100? You'll regret it if you don't snap it up."

Wow. It sounded like a steal. People wear rabbit fur, right? Without further hesitation, I made my decision.

"No refund on sale items," the lady uttered as I paid for the coat.

A wave of panic swept through me for spending so much money, but the pink coat nestled in my shopping bag gave me a sense of being Canadian. I kept stroking it on the bus ride home. So soft. So comforting.

Hurry up, morning. I got dressed and gingerly put on my pink coat. On my way to class, I lingered in front of the glass doors of the buildings to catch an image of myself. Beautiful. I floated to class as I snuggled my hands in the pockets. When I reached the fully packed class, I decided to trot to the back of the class so everyone could admire my new coat. I saw many heads turn my way.

Then, class was over, and as I was leaving class, proud as a peacock in my elegant, ankle length, pink rabbit hair coat, the professor glanced up at me.

He said, "New coat?"

I nodded proudly.

"Very pink. Is it fur?"

"Rabbit fur," I confirmed.

"Rabbit fur? Well, you look like a lady of the night," he countered.

What? I was too stunned to say anything. I rushed out of class and ran to my dorm room while tears flowed down my cheeks.

Lin was lounging on her bed and stared at me with her mouth wide open. "Rabbit fur? Gross. How many rabbits did you kill to make that coat?"

I yanked off my pink coat and furiously shoved it to the back of my closet. I'm the bloody exotic, erotic, clueless outsider, aren't I? Hell, I will never wear that coat ever again. And no more pink!

Thank you for sitting with me in some of my classes. I hope to hear from you soon as I relish in your lovely life of comfort and cuteness. Want a pink coat?

Love

Simran

12 APRIL 1986

Hey Simran!

Your life is dramatic. You can't even go skiing without killing yourself. Even in Singapore, I always thought you attracted chaos. Are you sure you aren't inviting drama in because you enjoy it? The last time we spoke in Singapore, you were stuck in an unhappy engagement your family arranged. Then, you ran away to some strange city that no one has ever heard of. Now, you endanger yourself on alien ground. Maybe it is time to be normal, right?

I hate skiing. Which idiot would want to put skis on their feet and slide down the hill and freeze? It must be too cold to even be out in the middle of the mountains. It's a stupid sport, to say the least. Me, I like my shopping centres better. Air conditioned and safe. The only danger is fighting off fellow Singaporeans who want to buy your Givenchy dress.

My life is heaven. I went out with Henry, the eligible millionaire I was telling you about. It was divine. It was a fairy tale. He came in his white Mercedes Benz to pick me up. He came to the door and had a bouquet of red roses for me. My mum, of course, couldn't resist, and ran to the door to talk to him. I quickly introduced him to Mum and darted out before she started planning our wedding. I left Mum with a huge smile on her face and a dozen red roses in her arms.

"Oh, how many cars do you have?" I laughed and asked Henry.

He shrugged his shoulders and said, "Four, I think."

I thought, Right. *A million dollars and he has so many cars he can't remember. What a nice problem.*

I was wearing my new dress—everything Christian Dior, of

course, from top to toe. It cost me many paycheques, but never mind, I know it was worth it! My nails were painted a delicate mauve and complemented my pastel yellow dress perfectly. I planned well.

"You look gorgeous," Henry said.

In my mind, I thought, "I know. Hours of shopping, primping, and painting."

But I said, "Oh, thank you. Just the usual work stuff."

Good. I made an impression on him. It was important to do that.

"Is the Raffles Hotel for dinner ok?" he asked.

"Oh, whatever. I go there all the time. It's not bad," I whispered, nonchalant, looking cool, calm and collected, even though my palms were sweaty, and I was trying not to squirm in excitement at going to the posh hotel I couldn't afford.

Henry and I arrived at the hotel and the valet parked his car.

He escorted me to the Long Bar first. "Let's have drinks," he said.

I gingerly sidestepped the peanut shells on the floor—some tradition of eating peanuts and tossing the shells on the floor. Now my expensive shoes will have peanut shells under them. We hopped onto the stools at the bar counter, and I had—of course—a Singapore Sling. Overpriced but who cares. I wasn't paying. Henry had Anchor beer. I was annoyed he was dressed like a bum. Jeans and a blue short-sleeved shirt. Here I was in my splendour, but I caught a glimpse of the logo on his shirt—aahhh, Burberry. Ok. Forgiven.

Listen, Simran. You know how I love Raffles Hotel, right? It was time for me to show off my Singapore smarts. I chatted about Somerset Maugham, Herman Hesse and Rudyard Kipling staying here and walking the very grounds outside. Henry was impressed, like I knew he would be. I swept him back into the history of those days gone by, and Henry and I imagined the type of food they served at the hotel. British, we guessed.

The servers moved us to the dining room and elegance began. Finest china. Sparkling silverware. Henry ordered a bottle of champagne. Moet & Chandon, of course. My head spun with giddy delight as plate after plate appeared with the finest delicacies. The champagne added to that. Not Singapore food. Please. That's for the hawker centre. Winter black truffle. Kristal caviar. Porterhouse steak. White asparagus roasted with ponzu and honey. Pommes dauphine. Cherry blossom Chantilly. Exquisite.

We chatted about Princeton. Henry confided in me how he wished he could go back to New York and live there. But his family would never allow him to. We all know the Asian son must sacrifice his freedom as he carries the family name. He must do what the family demands. This was the fate for Henry. Our conversation was animated and charming. We did not realize how late it was.

Henry stared at me and whispered, "Maybe, we should get a room here for the night? I've had too much to drink. We can continue our conversations. I really want to get to know you…more."

I looked at him coyly and smiled. "I'll take a taxi home. And so will you."

Please. Did he think I was so easy to get? He must woo me some more. And more gifts.

Henry touched my arm and chuckled, "Of course, my dear."

He leaned in to kiss me goodbye, and it was, well, mediocre. I mean, he's not very handsome or tall, but I guess I could learn to tolerate him. I went home confident I had impressed Henry and would hear from him again. Better play my cards right.

Please, Sim, those two Singapore clowns you went skiing with belong to the circus. They were the most ungentlemanly men I have ever heard about. How can they take you skiing and just dump you there? You're lucky you didn't break your neck. Find some rich men in Calgary. I am sure they have rich cowboys or something.

I'll keep you posted about Henry.

Regards,

Amy

25 APRIL 1986

Dear Sim,

Things fall apart; the centre cannot hold; mere anarchy is loosed upon the world?

Do you remember your favourite line from Yeats' poem, *The Second Coming*? I know I haven't written in a long time. Sorry for the silence. Things fell apart—that is exactly what is happening to me now. I know you won't believe it, Simran, but I can't live this lie anymore. Brace yourself, Sim.

Simran, Gopal has been physically abusing me all these years. And I, like a fool, kept this dark secret to protect him and to protect my family. How shameful, right? When you would write to me about my perfect life and perfect love, I would literally throw up. I did everything I could to keep this secret hidden from everyone, even his family. I mean, no surprise he has followed in the footsteps of his father, Appa, who has abused his mother, Ammah, all his life. Do you remember the scene at the market when Appa hurled abuses at Ammah for no reason whatsoever? Sim, that is what my life has been the whole time.

When I was dating Gopal, I saw signs that concerned me. I would see his eyes flash in anger if I disagreed with him or his voice rise if I spoke up. Nothing I considered out of the ordinary. I put it down to Gopal having a bad temper. We didn't live together, so the tantrums were short-lived. When we travelled, he always had an excuse for his bad behaviour—tired, hungry, cranky. I tolerated this because he was wonderful as well. I was young. I figured that it was normal for someone to have bad days.

When Gopal and I got married, things became worse each day.

He might throw the plate of food at me because it was not hot enough. He would lock the bedroom door and not let me in if I came home ten minutes late. He would slam me against the wall and scream into my face if I answered him in a tone that he did not like.

Nothing much, right? Just usual husband wife stuff. I mean, he always apologized the next day and was so penitent that I let it go. I let it go. And I let it go. And I told everyone, including you, only about the good stuff. Which was all true. There was good stuff. That part was all true.

Do you remember the bruise you saw on my arm when I came over for your birthday? I told you I had fallen off the bed. Well, the truth is that time, I didn't feel like having sex with Gopal, so he grasped me and punched me in my arms so hard that the next day, the welts were bulbous and angry blue and black. Gopal cried when he saw the bruises, and he kissed them tenderly and apologized profusely. My heart melted for him. It's not his fault. Violence was all he saw growing up with his father and mother.

I thought, *maybe, I could help Gopal*. I kept silent. I mean, where is there to go for help, anyway? His parents couldn't help since there was abuse in that house as well. In fact, they were worse, and the abuse in that house had gone on for over forty years.

My parents always said, "Don't leave your husband. What will happen to your sons?"

I felt I would lose my job if I said anything, right? No social services in Singapore to go to. How would I survive? What if he took my kids? Better to stay and to be quiet. I acted carefree and happy in public, and I knew you never suspected, right? It was easy. I just told you what you wanted to hear. Harlequin Romance. Your favourite.

I can't even bear to tell you how things have escalated over the years. Always in the bedroom. Always in the darkness. Always when there was no one around. Wearing turtlenecks and long sleeves on the hottest days of the year, I became an expert in disguise. He became an expert in careful selection of times to abuse me. But I love him. Maybe, it's my fault. You know, I'm too modern of a woman. I tried to make him go see a therapist. No. You know Singaporeans. They don't believe in therapy. They will never tell their secrets to strangers. Who else will listen to him? Only me. So, I became his victim and his therapist.

Last month, Gopal punched me in my left jaw. Just like that. He said he did not like my tone of voice when I replied to him. This time, he did it in front of the children. First time. Before, no one saw. Now, the children saw him strike me and cried. I had to pick them both up, my mouth bleeding. I was shocked; he had broken my tooth. What the hell. Without warning, Gopal walked out. He was gone for two days. I didn't know where he was. Was he alive or dead?

On the second day, I called Gopal's parents and had to pretend to talk to them without saying anything. I found out he was not there. I had to go to the dentist to fix my tooth. My stomach churned. Then, just like that, Gopal showed up in the evening. He came through the door, hugged the kids, got me purple orchids, and went about life as usual. I was flabbergasted.

At night, after I had put the kids to bed, in the quiet of our room, I turned to him and asked him, "Where were you?"

He collapsed in my arms and sobbed. "I was going to kill myself," he said. "I love you so much. I'm sorry. It won't happen again. I promise. I slept in my car for two days. I made a terrible mistake. I will never do it again."

He laid in my arms all night and sobbed quietly like a broken animal. I stared at the shadows dancing on the ceiling.

How many years of this crap had I put up with to be the perfect wife? How good an actress will I continue to be to show the world my enviable life of love and devotion? Who trained me to give this Oscar performance?

Sim, you are the only one I am telling this secret to. It's only because you are far away, and I can hide through the medium of penmanship. It feels safe to write about it. Honestly, I am relieved I can tell one person about my duplicitous life. As far as the world is concerned, all is good in my life. I want the boys to have a stable and comfortable life. I mean, where is there to go in Singapore? How would I survive as a single mother? What if I can't have my children? These questions are too difficult to face. It is better not to rock the boat. Don't tell anyone, please.

Simran, I enjoy reading about you and your adventures. They take my mind off my life. I am sure it can't be that easy to transport yourself from Singapore to Calgary and try to survive as a new Canadian and as an outsider. When you were in the Institute of Education in Singapore, you won the top prize for the English literature class, didn't you? You got an A with distinction in all your classes.

I can't believe that the professor gave you a D and would not even talk to you about your grade. It must be that pompous "I am better than you Asian" mentality. How can you even question your accent? You were the best speaker here in all our classes. Don't let your differences corrode your true worth. Don't let your professor colonize you!

People don't realize how difficult it is for a foreigner to go abroad and to get an education. It's a double-edge sword. We are grateful for the opportunity to get a degree, but we pay a high cost in the sense of the word. It's an education in everything, isn't it?

Hang in there, Sim. Tell you more next time.

Love,

Anita

26 APRIL 1986

Dear Mummy,

You should have seen the smile of joy on my face when your twenty-dollar bill floated out of your letter for me to buy a new sweater. I went straight to Kmart in Brentwood Mall and got a soft, fuzzy, warm blue sweater which was on sale. I told everyone on my dorm floor my mummy bought this sweater for me. I promise not to shrink this one in the washing machine and dryer. Thank you, Mummy. I love you.

It was interesting to read about your life in Singapore, Mummy. All my life, I had a hard time imagining what it must have felt for you to come to a strange country when you were a young girl. Now I feel our stories are a little similar. I mean, at least I am twenty, but I feel like I am sixteen because I don't know anything about the rules of being alone in a new country like Canada.

Even the small things in Calgary make me question my perceptions. I was startled when I saw a fifty-year-old woman wearing short shorts. How was that possible? She was old to show so much skin. Indian women would never do that. This Canadian woman looked sexy and beautiful. Age is not a hindrance in the West. Some of you Indian women behave so old. As soon as you are married, you behave like grandmas. As soon as your children are adults, you behave like you are eighty years old.

Look at Mamaji. As soon as she became a widow at forty, she could only wear white for the rest of her life for the next forty years. No jewelry. No make-up. No colourful clothes. Just simple white Punjabi suits. As a girl, I thought it was strange that she could not wear other colours or fancy colours until I heard about the expectations for Indian widows. Then I felt angry at her that she could not be alive when it was her husband who was dead.

I don't understand this Indian custom that a widow must live her life quietly and in the background. It's not her fault that her husband died when he was fifty-years old. Why are Indian women controlled by society?

But I was puzzled why Mamaji also treated you badly. She controlled you like a child when she brought you from India. It hurt me to hear stories about how you had to follow her around all day like a puppy and do what she told you. For me, the worse injustice was when Mamaji changed your name. She changed the name that your father gave you at birth. You had no say in your destiny. Just like that. She controlled your history. I don't like these old customs and traditions, Mummy. Go to hell with these old-fashioned ideas. It's time to change them.

I often think of you when I am alone and lonely in Calgary, lying in my bed and looking out my window. The white snow on the trees and the sidewalks glistens like mirrors, slippery if you are not careful. Winter feels alien and strange to me. Winter looks lonely and bare. I wonder how you must have been in the prison of marriage: told what to do, when to eat, how to behave.

You know, Mum, despite the loneliness of winter, I love being here in Calgary. Nobody tells me what to do—not even you. The only thing I regret is that I can't cook. I know in Singapore I fought with you all the time.

You said, "No one will marry you if you don't know how to cook."

I replied, "Good. Better not to marry than be his slave. You can give him a gold can-opener for my dowry, and he will not starve."

Mummy, truth be told, I regret I did not watch you, learn from you and cook with you. But you irritated me. Always telling me how a girl should behave. *All boys want is sex. Don't do this. Don't do that.* You even opened the bathroom door when I was taking my bath if I were inside for too long. I couldn't breathe. I couldn't close any doors to shut out the world. Now, I am here in Calgary, and I have so many doors to close as I wish. Sometimes, it is quiet, and it is lonely. Still, I love it here. I can breathe.

I have fond memories of the same swing you swung on at six-teen. I miss the swing in Race Course Road. When we went to visit Mamaji, I ran out with Amrit, and we both swung as high as we could. I loved the feeling when my heart skipped out of my chest when the swing went higher and higher. My throat tightened with this fear that I would fall, but I never gave up. I flew in the sky, free as a bird.

Amrit was on the swing next to me, and we laughed noisily and without a care in the world. Sometimes, I closed my eyes and imag-ined you at sixteen on that very swing, going up, up, up to the sky. How happy you must have felt to be with the wind and the clouds in the sky, without your feet stuck in the earth and people holding you down. At that moment, I was you.

Mummy, there are no swings near the university. I haven't seen any. I will look for them when the snow finally melts, and the grass turns green. The leaves will come back on the trees, and the sun will beat down its blazing glory. I will find a swing, sit on it, and swing and swing until it all becomes fuzzy. I will swing until I no longer know where I am, in what country I am in, who I am, and whether it is you or me. We all should be free to swing and to go up, up, up.

I went shopping at Kmart the other day. I saw a cute, cuddly ted-dy bear. Perfect, I thought. I bought it. When I got home, I dressed it in the sweater I had shrunk in the dryer. Perfect. The right size. The bear looked happy in the sweater. I took a piece of paper and wrote, "Welcome to Canada! Eh!" I put this sign in the teddy bear's arms. I've named him Mr. Jolly Singh.

Here, I sent you a photo of the bear and the sweater. It was meant to be for him, not me.

I followed your advice. I washed my new sweater in the laun-dry room sink. After, I hung it to dry over the sink while the water dripped and dripped for days. Never mind. I didn't give up. It took many days for the sweater to be dry again. This time, it did not shrink. I felt proud.

Last night, I dreamt about your aloo prontha and dhai. Even

though I refused to learn to cook from you, I cherished every dish you made. You are a magician.

Love, love, love you,

Simran

10 MAY 1986

Anita,

What the hell, Anita?

I froze when I read your letter about Gopal abusing you all this time. For the last four years, I envied you and your great love story. Now, you tell me that it was a sham. How on earth did you conceal a deep, dark secret? You should have told me, my friend.

Are you the best actress in the world or simply good at living two distinct lives? I'm furious and sympathetic at the same time. For God's sakes, this is 1986, not like our mothers and grandmothers who had no voice or recourse.

It seems I was duped by Gopal like everyone else. Gopal treated you like a queen when we were all out together. Rushing to get you your drink. Finding you a chair. Staring lovingly into your eyes. Every time I left the two of you, I was happy for you and sad for me, envious I didn't have such a great love in my life.

I'm sorry you felt the need for deception: for your lies and for your abuse. And now you have two children. You told me about your in-laws and how Appa abused Ammah. You declared you would never tolerate that. It must have been overwhelming for you.

I'm puzzled. You have a loving family and always had the freedom to do what you wanted when you lived at home with your mum and dad. How did you fall into the trap? How do we women fall into the trap?

Anita, do you really think you can change Gopal? He looks like the son has followed in the steps of his abusive father. I fear the way his father has treated his mother is a warning of things to come for you.

What can be done? Hidden secrets and abuse. Can you convince him to get therapy, at least? Maybe, just maybe, that may get him on a better track.

What will you do? Please write to me. Tell me everything. I am upset, worried, angry, and stunned. It's a lot for you to bear. I'm here for you.

Love,

Sim

12 MAY 1986

Hello Amy,

I was amused to read your letter. I did a literary analysis on it, courtesy of the amazing skills that I'm learning in my literature classes. I see an interesting picture of the pursuit of the Singapore dream by the Singapore girl getting more frantic and desperate. Come on, girl! All those days in junior college in the canteen, you talked about how you were going to be a strong, independent woman. You wanted to be the woman who would take care of herself and pay her own way. What happened?

You seem mesmerized by Henry's wealth and what that can offer rather than the integrity of the man himself. Frankly, I am surprised. You have always had the opportunity to do whatever you want. Your parents never stood in the way of your choices. Has your mother's attitude towards money rubbed off on you more than you realized? Why not be with a man who makes you happy, not with his wallet?

In your letter, I learned about your friends, Christian Dior, Burberry, Raffles Hotel, Mercedes Benz. Did I miss anyone? Please, man. Ok. Maybe, I am underwhelmed because I don't really know what these brands mean or what they are really worth. Expensive, right? I know I can't afford any of them, nor do I crave them. Give me my Levi's jeans and t-shirts, and I feel like a million dollars.

Tell me, is your Singapore dream to be rich? Not just rich but stupid rich? I know my father struggled to buy our government subsidized Housing and Development flat in Ang Mo Kio, and I am not even sure how he affords to pay for my education here in Canada. He moved from renting one room in someone's flat with my mom, to a one-bedroom flat in Jalan Tenteram, to a three-bed-roomed flat in Toa Payoh, and to a five-bedroomed HDB flat in Ang Mo Kio. This is the Singapore dream for the average Singaporean, right? You have a degree from Princeton, for God's sake. You are a million dollars right there. You got an amazing job in the hotel industry. You have so much potential.

Oh dear. I see I have gone off track here, trying to convince you otherwise when you seem happy about this jackpot. Ok. Maybe, I should wish you nothing but the best and success in making Henry see how amazing you are, which you are. I hope that he will chase you all the way to the altar and change your life in ways many Singaporeans can only dream about—the instant jackpot of the uber rich Singaporean.

Don't worry. I won't be running after the Singapore clowns who took me skiing here in Calgary. The good news is that they are both leaving in June as they are done with their degrees here. They will go back to pursue their own Singapore dreams. The white-collar job and the girls their mummies have already picked out for them, the five-bedroomed apartments they apply for with their wives, then wait for until that flat becomes available one year later. Maybe, some can afford to buy the quarter million dollars private condominiums in Katong. We all have such different dreams, eh. Me, I just want my damn education.

I want to live my life on my own terms. If that means skiing down on a stretcher and falling off, so be it.

I really, really, really hope you and Henry find love and live happily ever after. That will be one grand wedding.

Ciao, kiddo

Simran

10 JUNE 1986

Dear Sim,

Please don't be angry with me. I am angry with myself for living this double life all this time. It is exhausting to keep up appearances, to appease everyone. To be happy all the time. To be afraid of the man you love. The unpredictability of my life has been this incredible burden I carry. I'm trying to hold the fragments of my life together, but things have become worse.

Last week, Gopal drove the boys and me home from Orchard Road. He picked us up in front of the shopping centre, Tang Plaza. When I got in the car, I felt something was amiss. Gopal's lips were pursed, and his eyes were blazing.

"Are you ok?" I gently asked him.

"Shut up," he screamed.

The boys in the back seat stiffened in fear. I turned around to distract them.

I tried to ignite a conversation with Gopal.

How are you? We enjoyed our movie. What shall we have for dinner?

He grabbed my arm and hollered, "Did you tell my mum about me?"

I pushed his hand away and said, "I didn't say much."

"Didn't say much? You said enough!"

Without warning, Gopal extended his right hand and struck me on my face. I bellowed in pain and shock.

"How dare you tell my mum about me?"

I tried to calm him down, but he turned red and shouted obscenities. Confused, the kids screamed. Gopal sped, but there was nowhere to go with the traffic on Orchard Road. Cars honked at him as he dangerously weaved in and out of traffic.

I touched his arm, "Please, please stop. The kids are terrified."

"This is all your fault," he screamed at the top of his lungs.

He drove erratically with one hand and hit me repeatedly with the other. Instinctively, I put my arms in front of me. The next thing I knew, he stopped the car at the traffic light, opened the door and ran headlong into ongoing traffic.

Horrified, I reacted in the moment. I jumped out the car and chased him through the traffic, leaving the kids in the car. It was a spur of the moment decision. I ran as fast as I could, dodging cars as the drivers honked. I caught Gopal stumbling 100 metres down Orchard Road, with onlookers lining the street. Bloody Singaporeans all watched. No one did anything. Just gaped at my life, the spectacle.

I grabbed Gopal's arm and pulled him back to the car, praying the whole way that the kids were in their car seats. It was a horrible decision to leave them in the car seats in the car, but I knew if I didn't get Gopal, he would not make it.

Gopal turned silent, a vacuous look on his face, and I shoved him into the passenger seat and drove off, shaking in fear, trying to calm the children down. It was the most bizarre sensation ever. One minute he was Gopal the beast, attacking me, and now, he quivered and sobbed in the car.

I drove back—everyone was silent. It was eerily disconcerting, as I focused on just getting us back home. I found a parking spot near our flat. I hustled everyone back into the flat. Gopal was a few steps behind me. I was relieved when I opened the door and walked into the flat. The boys were frightened and did not want to let go of me. I had to pry off their little hands and feed them and put them to bed. I didn't know what I would face when I went into my bedroom, where Gopal had entered an hour ago and shut the door.

When I entered our bedroom, Gopal was on the bed, staring at the door and me. I didn't know if he was going to hit me or hug me. Exhausted, I fell into bed and turned my back on him. After all these years, I simply had nothing left to give. I don't know what he said, and I pushed his arms off me.

In the morning, I felt calm. I went to Gopal who was at the kitchen table.

I stared at him and whispered, "Please leave for a few days."

He nodded. Back to his rational self, Gopal quietly left. I think that he went to his parents' house. I was not sure what was in store for us as a family, but I was relieved I didn't have to tell one more lie or hide one more bruise.

Now, it is time to dig deep and muster courage to live life without a husband, without a father and without abuse. It's going to be a long road.

Please forgive me for all my lies. I struggle to forgive myself. Distract me. Tell me more about your adventures in Calgary. I love hearing about them.

Love,

Anita

12 JUNE 1986

Hi Simran,

Come on, Simran. Nothing wrong with the Singaporean dream. Do I detect envy in your voice? Of course, any girl would love to be swept off her feet and be wooed by a man of means. Please, it's the foundation of the Harlequin romances you loved so much.

Do you know how expensive Singapore is becoming? We can barely afford our HDB flats, those matchboxes perched atop one another. The same life of the average Singaporean who lives in these overpriced government subsidized flats. We are used to the common corridors on every floor of our flats. People congregating in the void decks of the main floor of every block of flats, waiting for lifts that go up and down to our flats. Cars here are more expensive than a flat in Calgary, I bet.

To survive in Singapore, I work sixty hours or more a week. There's no such thing as a forty-hour week. Some Saturdays and Sundays are workdays as well. If I want to make it, I'd better give my soul to my company. No room for slacking off. After a long day, we get in our cars, buses, Mass Rapid Transit trains, squashed together to be transported back home, late at night, too late to have dinner with our family or spend time with anyone. Bone tired. That's my life. Work, work, work. I listen to my mother screech and go on about how unhappy she is. I watch my father disappear into the shadows.

So, what if I want that Singapore dream—to be rich, powerful, and beautiful? Money buys that dream. I could work 100 hours a week and would never get out of my parents' HDB flat. Henry is my way out. There are the poor, the make do's and the stupid rich. Even with my degree from Princeton and my stable job, I can only hope to move to a flat with one extra bedroom, if that.

Envy all you want to, but my Singapore dream is simple. Give me my Gucci, my Porsche, my house on Holland Road and my holidays in Paris. All of these were out of reach for me until I met Henry. The possibilities are astonishing. The alternative is depressing.

Well, the good news is I've spent a lot of time with Henry in the last month. He spoils me. I love it! He loves good food, and I mean, expensive, international chefs, top restaurants, and posh hotels kind of food. Why, the other week, we went to the top sushi place in Singapore. The bill was a staggering $1,000 for two. I didn't even know such places existed here. Then there is the best French restaurant. Best Italian. He has a taste for the best. I love it. I am getting used to the way that the top three per cent live, not the two-dollar chicken rice at the hawker centre. Please!

Next week, Henry is taking me on a weekend trip to Hong Kong. Just like that, for the weekend. First class all the way. It will be the first time we'll be spending the night together. I've had to play my cards oh so carefully. My mother is over the moon. Finally, she is proud of me for something. She never forgave me for falling in love with Chin in my last two years at Princeton. I knew I had found the perfect man for me in Chin. We even lived together, unbeknownst to my mother, of course.

Now, I live a life of glamour and poshness. It's beyond my wildest dreams. This is not the life of the HDB dweller. It's more than Chin could have ever given me. Can love conquer all? Who cares? I am sure I can "love" Henry.

Good luck with your noble notions of life. To each her own. You and your idealistic notions of a woman getting an education. In what? A degree in English. Hah. Yeah, good luck with that.

Well, let the games begin. I'll go for my Singapore dream, and you go for your Canadian dream. Let's see what happens.

I'll let you know about my Hong Kong escapade. First class, all the way.

Have fun with your homework. Hope you get an A in something.

All the best,

Amy

13 JUNE 1986

Hello Simran,

I got your letter. Why do you complain? As Mummy, it was my job to keep an eye on you when you were growing. You must behave in the proper way of an Indian girl. You never listen. Now you are alone in foreign country. You have to be strong. You have to pray. Call on God—Waheguru.

When you are sad, say this prayer over and over again. I promise you that you will forget all your troubles. Everything you want will come true. Do you remember? I have written out for you here. Ok, beti. This prayer is the Mool Mantar and the opening verse from the Guru Granth Sahib. These are words all Sikhs should know and is the philosophy of Sikhism, Simran. I copied from my book in Gurmukhi and English for you.

Ek Ong Kar	The One, Universal Creator
Sat Naam	Truth is His Name
Kartaa Purakh	The Primal Creative Being
Nirbhau Nirvair	Beyond Fear, Beyond Vengeance
Akaal Moorat	The Image of the Undying
Ajoonee Saibhang	Beyond Birth, Self-Existent
Gur Prasaad	By Guru's Grace
Jap!:	Repeat!:
Aad Sach	True in the primal beginning
Jugaad Sach	True throughout the ages
Hai Bhee Sach	True here and now
Nanak Hosee Bhee Sach	O Nanak, forever and ever True

Put this prayer on your desk next to your bear. Look at this every day and say this as many times as you can. You can also put in your purse and carry with you. Waheguru will keep you safe. He will also keep you safe from all these rascals. These boys, they only want sex. They see a young girl and they want to spoil her.

You have to be careful. Indian girls are not like western people. We are from a different culture. You have to be a virgin for your husband. You can't have sex with all boys. That is bad thing to do. That is why it is good to marry young so that you can be protected.

Your bear and sweater—acha, nice. Call him your husband. He will be there for you. Good girl. I am happy to hear how you washed your sweater. Washing machine and dryer destroy everything.

Canadian people are brave. They wear what they want. They don't care. No restriction. Western women are just like men. Not like Indian women who follow their husbands like tails.

Why are so many men in Calgary looking for sex? Better if you avoid them. Just go to class and come back. Better if you have girls around you. Men are not trustworthy. That is why here we keep you safe at home. No one there to do that. Maybe Mr. Jolly Bear can keep an eye on you. Lock your door. Don't let any man come into you room, ok? You should move somewhere where you can cook. With proper kitchen. It's not that hard. You can save money. You can be healthy. Try. It's not too late to be a good wife for the future.

I'm excited you are coming back soon for holidays. I'll show you how to cook easy things like dhal or make easy chicken dish. Make roti. Learn. You won't starve. You were very stubborn girl. Didn't want to learn to cook. Didn't want to wash clothes. Now you will regret. There is no escape from this duty for a girl.

Simran, it is lonely without you. The house is quiet. I pray, I practice my music and singing. I watch Hindi movies with Amitabh Bachchan and Shashi Kapoor actor. Your father is the same. Your sister is busy with her children. That is the life of a woman who is married.

Bring me some kidney beans. My friend told me the kidney beans there is fresh. Red one. Not black. Your father loves rajma.

Buy me also lipstick. Rose colour. Not too expensive.

Don't forget to say the prayer I sent you. Must say every day.

Mummy

14 JUNE 1986

Hello Simran,

It's been a long time since I wrote. Life is not easy. I'm exhausted at night when Soni and Roni go to bed. Too tired to even write a letter. There is so much to do. I don't think I am a wife. I am a maid. Cook. Clean. Take care of the Queen. Take care of the children. Take care of the husband. Who will take care of me? I'm getting fed up. Three years of marriage and already stuck in this prison. How come you are so lucky you escaped? I don't know why this is my luck. You always told me to say no. Don't get married. I was afraid. How? Mamaji was married at fourteen. Mummy at sixteen. All our cousins eighteen, nineteen, twenty.

Do you remember the night before Dolly's wedding? We were all having a big party. Women were dancing. Men were drinking whisky. Children were running round in circles. Dolly came into the hall and sobbed and shouted. Remember?

She said, "Papa, I don't want to marry tomorrow. Papa, please. Please. I don't want to marry."

Then, she fell onto the floor and sobbed. We all froze and stared at her. Shocked. She was only nineteen. So young. Innocent. Uncle came up to her. He bent down and gathered her long black hair and dragged her from one corner of the hall to the other.

"If you don't get married tomorrow, I will kill you."

Nobody said anything. We all quietly stared at her. Aunty pulled Dolly to her feet and took her to her room. The next morning, everything was normal like usual. Dolly looked like a real doll in her red sari and heavy make-up. Red, red lips. Blue eye shadow on her eyelids. Red rouge on her cheeks. Chumkas hanging from her ears.

Twelve fat, gold bangles on each arm. She changed from a girl the night before to a woman. Her face was blank. Her eyes were lifeless. She was silent on the happiest day of her life—her wedding. He, her husband, oh ya. He looked excited. He was fat, bald, and ugly. We stared at his big black mole the size of a five-cent coin on the right side of his neck. It had three thick strands of black hairs sticking out. His face could make babies cry. He was ten years older. He looked at Dolly, salivating, like he was going to eat her alive. Virgin sacrifice.

I saw what happened that night before the wedding and thought, "How to say no? Where to escape? Who will listen?"

Two months later, it was my turn. I married a stranger. I saved my virginity for twenty years and then gave it to a man I didn't know or love. I didn't realize there was an option for me. For Indian girls. But you. I don't know how you managed to run away from this hell.

Mummy has accepted her life. "Can't do this and can't do that. Eat this. Sit here. Wear this. Talk to this person. Cannot go here. Cannot have friends."

How come my life is so similar? I have no love or attention. No nothing. I don't think I can take this for fifty years.

Never mind. Time to forget. Tell me about your love life. Have you had sex? Are you saving your virginity? How does it feel to have a choice and to do whatever you want?

Manjit is home less and less. How the hell can he do this? I take care of his mother, his daughters and him when he is around. He comes back very late every night—meeting this client and meeting that client. Going to the gym. Hanging out with his friends. No time for me or his family. My blood boils.

One day, I am going to put my hands around his throat and strangle him. Ok. Don't panic. I watched this Hindi movie where the girl's life was like mine. In the Hindi movie, the girl was patient, loving, and oh, she prayed day and night. She never gave up. Even when her husband slapped her face, she prayed and prayed. Patience. Miracle. At the end of the movie, her husband, the goonda, who was out all the time drinking and womanizing and did not take care of her, changed his ways. Miracle. There. That is my solution. Maybe that's why mummy prayed morning, noon and night. Hah.

Here are pictures of Soni and Roni. They are building sandcastles together at East Coast beach. See. They are like you and me.

Love,

Amrit

12 AUGUST 1986

Hey Sim,

What the hell? You came to Singapore and called me the day before you left? Are you trying to avoid me? How was your visit back to Singapore? I bet you ate everything in sight like the usual starved Singaporean. I was hoping we could go for satay at the Satay Club. The next time, we better meet up.

On the phone call you asked me about my mum and the Chin saga. I couldn't say anything because Mum was standing right there, next to the phone in the living room. Eavesdropping. As usual. Pretending to read *The Straits Times*. Always like that—just watching and meddling in my life all the bloody time.

Chin. Ya. My boyfriend. Now I can tell you the true story. When my mother came to New Jersey to visit me at Princeton, she found out I was living with my boyfriend, Chin. She went berserk. And it was worse than World War three. Oh, she was ruthless about it. She spent two days interrogating Chin, then me. She found out that Chin was a village boy from a poor village in Medan, Indonesia. She saw how he lived in the apartment frugally and carefully.

Mum pointed out his torn sweater to me and his jeans that were frayed and falling apart. She kicked his shoes that were barely held together with her Gucci heels when she walked in the door. Each day, she reduced Chin to a mere object, unworthy and insignificant. The irony was I had not even noticed any of these things. I was simply in love and entranced by the first-time emotions that I felt in my belly and soul. I mean, this was true love.

In one week, my mother meticulously destroyed this altar of love I had built for Chin.

"Oh, you are going to move to a kampong in Medan."

"Got toilets there or not? Hmm."

"Where are you going to work with your Princeton degree?"

"Oh, you are going to bring him back to Singapore?"

"Stay where? In my house?"

"You are going to marry him and have children with this man?"

"What is his degree? History?"

"Oh. So what job is he even going to get?"

"Wait. He got a scholarship from the government, so he can't even leave Indonesia?"

"So how? Your love will pay the bills, huh?"

Every single moment of the day, my mother questioned me about things I had never considered. I mean, Chin and I had decided to spend our lives together. He was the gentlest Chinese man I had ever met. He listened to me when I was in my furious moods. He rubbed my feet at night when I was tired. He even learnt how to cook so I could enjoy candlelit dinners with him. Chin left the house on most days my mom was there, shrinking from her obvious disdain and clear desire to deprecate him. It didn't take a genius to figure out her agenda.

Finally, on that Thursday when Mum left, when the two of us went to the airport, she gave me an ultimatum:

"Amy, I married your father for love. What for? Look at me now. The love disappears very quickly, you know. And in its place, there is nothing left. At least, if your father had money, I could forget about the loneliness and disappointment of being stuck in the middle of the sky in Block 545, looking out the window and seeing broken dreams. You think what? I am going to let you waste my money. We spent over half a million dollars to send you to Princeton, you know. So, you can go live in a village in Medan? If you marry Chin, I will disown you. You will have to pay me back the money I spent on your education. You understand or not?"

I stared out of the cab at the bulbous clouds floating in the sky. I saw my world crumble around me, just eager for the cab to get to the airport so I could stop my mother's brittle voice. Maybe she was right? Could I really live in Medan? How on earth would I pay her back half a million dollars? I knew she would not let that go.

When we got to the airport, I stared at her vacuously. She was a dream destroyer. She had come to Princeton, and in one week, she had dismantled all my hopes and dreams with her Singapore sensibility. I stepped back when she tried to hug me. I turned and walked away.

Mum's last words that I heard were, "Go, lah. Go and marry a loser. See how."

When I got back to my place, Chin was waiting for me. He had made my favourite meal, spaghetti Bolognese, Caesar salad and French bread with olive oil and balsamic vinegar. We dimmed the lights, our shadows cast on the walls by the two lit, long, tapered red candles in the middle of the table. In our silence, we both knew that there was no future. Worse still, I knew that there was nothing I could do to be with the man I loved. The next day, Chin moved out when I was in classes. I never saw him again. I did nothing. I sat at the table, lit the remnants of the candles, and wept silently.

I never told you what happened to Chin. Now, you know. I have to play by my mother's rules, and I did not have the courage to choose otherwise. She is a woman whose bitterness has hardened her. Her dream has embittered her. I don't think about Chin much. I can't. Circumstances have conspired against me, so I have to live my mother's Singapore dream. Here I am. Here I am.

How was your trip back to Singapore after being away for a year? Every time I went back to Singapore on a visit from my breaks from Princeton, I felt like an outsider. Singapore felt alien. Strange. It always took me weeks to adjust; then, it was time to go back. Did you experience that?

I will tell you about Henry in the next letter. I am drained from remembering about Chin. I have not talked about Chin or thought about him for a year. I am feeling hollow inside.

Till the next letter,

Goodbye

Amy

9 SEPTEMBER 1986

Dear Mummy,

It was nice to see you for two weeks. It flew by. It was too hot for me. I can't take 30 degrees Celsius, anymore. Even before I left the house, I was covered in a river of sweat. So bloody hot. I am getting used to Calgary weather. Dry. Cool. Cold. Hot. Changes all the time.

When I was in Singapore, Papa was quiet. He didn't talk to me much, as usual. I felt he must be angry with me. I am too expensive and too stubborn. I felt bad for him. I know it can't be easy for him to let me go. A difficult situation to love me and let me go. That is why he must be angry. I know I disappoint him. Not like Amrit, his favourite. She does whatever he tells her to do. They can talk for hours. With me, we are like two walls—hard and silent.

Here in Calgary, I'm back to my university life. My life is simple. I get up at nine a.m. and go to the cafeteria to eat. The food here is rubbish. Toast and a cup of tea is $6. The food is bland. I miss my Singapore food. The other day, I stood in line at the cafeteria, and the menu option was pork chops. The young man in front of me had his pork chop with applesauce. I was shocked. Applesauce is for babies, right? Remember the Heinz baby food jars? I asked the cafeteria lady if I could have pork chop with tomato ketchup.

The young man turned to me and said, "You are going to have pork chop with ketchup?"

He looked disgusted at me.

I glared at him and said, "You are going to have pork chop with applesauce?"

I don't understand the Canadian food here at all.

You wanted to know what my schedule was like. I go for my 10 a.m. class. I have three classes. I am done around 5 p.m. I live so close to campus, so I can walk to my room and back again within ten minutes. Very convenient. It's like our block of flats in Singapore. Everything is five minutes away. I don't know that many people here. It's not so easy to make friends even after a year. I mean, I meet many people in my classes and on residence, but every time I meet some interesting people, it is time for them to leave Calgary. There are many international students like me, and they come and go.

I met some nice guys from Germany. One was Andy. He invited me to come visit him in Germany. He doesn't speak much English. The day we chatted was the day before he was leaving to go home. Then I met John from England. I really liked him. He told me he could not be with me because he liked me and had a girlfriend in London.

Ok. Don't get excited. I met this Punjabi boy from Kelowna, Balwant. Tall, skinny, dark, no turban. Actually, he frightened me. We were just friends, but he was very possessive. He called me three times a day and wanted to visit me all the time. I felt uncomfortable about him. He was too Indian for me. Last week, he came to my room at 8 p.m., and he came straight from the hospital. Can you imagine that? He was in a car accident in the morning and had crushed his ribs. He decided that he missed me and wanted to be with me. Crazy man.

I was stressed. I never gave him any wrong messages. I never sat close to him. What the hell. He sat for one hour on my bed. He couldn't move or breathe because his ribs were broken. Why the hell did he come to my room? I ignored him, hoping he would leave.

Luckily, my roommate, Lin, came back and said, "Get out. I want to change into my pyjamas."

His face turned red. He was shocked. I laughed because Lin is annoying and rude, but that day, I wanted to hug her for throwing him out. He had no choice and left. I was very uncomfortable with this guy. I stopped answering his calls or talking to him. Sometimes,

I see him on campus, and he walks towards me and calls me, but I just run. I hope the idiot gets the message. There is my Indian dream man, a crazy stalker. I'm sorry to dash your hopes, Mum.

What do I do in the evening? In the evening, I do my homework for my five classes. Very busy. Some days, I don't even talk to anyone. Some days, I hang out with some Singaporean people, but they only want to eat and complain. So boring. I met two Canadian girls, but they like to drink, smoke, and go out at night. One girl, Suzy, likes to pick up men from her class, at the bar, anywhere. She brings them to her room. She told me she had sex with these boys, a different one every week. I don't know what to think. A girl should be able to do what she wants, right? Why should girls behave differently than boys? Why can boys do what they want? Indian girls have to be a virgin until the day of marriage. Why? Good for Suzy!

I am confused about the idea of sex. Some days I wonder why a girl should have sex so easily if the boy treats her like a dog. Suzy told me that she fell in love with Samir, a Lebanese boy. He's very handsome, like a movie star. But wait. This boy, Samir, was very cunning.

He took her to his room and then he said, "Oh. Look what I found in my drawer. A condom. I didn't even know it was here. Should we use it?"

Idiot. She fell for his tricks. She had sex with him because she thought he was the special one after one week of dating. She is only eighteen and comes from a very small town two hours outside Calgary. As soon as she had sex with Samir, he stopped talking to her the very next day. I found her crying in the common living room.

"Are you ok?" I asked.

Suzy shook her head. She was broken hearted. She sat and waited for Samir. She stopped going to her classes so she could try and catch him coming out of his room. He won't even look at her or talk to her. Now, she goes the other way, and she sleeps with many other boys.

Believe me, it is easy to find boys to have sex with. It is like a drug here. Maybe, when people have so much freedom, they don't know what to do to find the middle ground. I feel sad for her when I see her because her eyes are dull, and her smile is gone. She really fell in love with Samir who is now sleeping with three other girls from Kananaskis Hall. And they all know about each other and don't care. Maybe, I'm the old-fashioned one?

Me, don't worry. I am not. I know Indian people are worried when their daughters go abroad because now the daughters are free to have sex. For Indian people, virginity is this precious, rare diamond. It must be preserved until wedding night. It's so bloody stupid. I am confused. So afraid to do anything. I can hear your voice and Papa's voice in my head. By the way, how do we check if the boy is a virgin on his wedding day, Mum?

The other day, Samir saw me in the library. He came to me and put his hand on my shoulder.

He said, "Hey, I wanted to talk to you all this time. I always see you on third floor of Kananaskis, but you never look my way."

Great, what did he want from me, I wondered? He is handsome. Tall, dark hair, two dimples on his cheeks. I looked away quickly because my heart jumped in excitement.

Samir continued, "Imagine this, Simran. I am rowing a boat in the middle of the ocean. It is burning hot, and I can't see where I'm going, and I am so exhausted. Then, a breeze comes from nowhere and blows on my face. It's refreshing. It's fresh. It's real. It's a lifesaver. It makes me alive again."

What? Is he a poet? I was puzzled by his story, but I listened curiously. He looked at me, put his right hand on my cheek and lifted my face to his.

"You, Simran, are like this breeze."

I brushed his hand away. Rubbish. When I realized what he was doing, I chuckled. It was the stupidest thing I had ever heard in my life. Must be a Lebanese movie. Irritating.

I looked into his eyes. "Samir, watch me. I'm the breeze, and I'm blowing away now…out of your life."

Samir's face turned red. He's not used to rejection. I walked away, and from that day, he has never talked to me ever again. Good. Did he think I was going to believe his bullshit? I learn something new every day. I am the refreshing breeze of life.

See, when we were in Singapore, I did listen to you when you said all men only want one thing. I hope that you are not right. I think that because I avoid asshole boys, they show up. I am being tested. Us girls have to be smart to survive.

Men! I don't know how you dealt with Papa all these years. I don't like how men treat women when they shout at them and bully them. You are a strong woman. I know what you have gone through. Still, you believe in marriage and that a woman needs a man. I know a woman needs an education and a job so she can take care of herself no matter what. I always wondered what you would do if Papa died or you left him. Where would you go? How would you survive?

I don't want to depend on a man for my existence. I don't know what the right way is to even find a husband. Indian way? Canadian way? I'm scared. When I have a daughter, I will give her all the freedom she wants. I will let her experience life fully. No restrictions. If I have a daughter and a son, both will be equal. Both will get an education. They will learn to find what they want to be happy. Travel the world, meet people, and have adventures. Go out. Have sex. I will never stand in their way.

I'm homesick sometimes. When I am in Singapore, I feel suffocated. Cannot breathe. When I am in Calgary, I feel aching loneliness. Two opposite ways. Where is the middle? I miss hugging you tight and putting my head on your chest and smelling your Gucci perfume and onion garlic hands. Comforting. Safe. I miss all of you.

I hope you like the lipsticks.

Love you, Mummy,

Simran

Hey Sistah,

I couldn't wait to rush over to your flat with my presents for Soni and Roni. They liked their soft toy Canadian bears. That was a special afternoon as we sat on the floor and played with Barbies and cars. I can't believe that they are babbling, walking and busy getting into all sorts of mischief. It made me smile to see how close they were. I loved that Soni always hugged Roni. Just like you and me.

Two weeks went by fast. I had first-hand experience of what you mean by Manjit being in his own world. That Sunday when I was at your house, the whole day, I could see he was disinterested in talking to any of us. He didn't ask me one question about Calgary. Odd. First, he read *The Straits Times* in his bedroom. Then, he came out to eat toast, eggs, and tea. Back to his room to watch sports. He was invisible. Non-existent. Like a zombie. I didn't see him spend time with his kids or you. Is this how he is every weekend?

I don't understand why he agreed to marry if he was not interested in having a relationship with you. I'm irritated. Did he marry you because he didn't have the balls to say no to his mother? These Indian boys and their bullshit! They are yes, yes, yes to society's expectations and want to keep their family's reputation. Who knows what they are really up to behind the facade? I understand better now when you say how lonely you are. It seems all of you live separate lives in that house. No interaction. No connection. No affection. Soni and Roni clung to you all day. I cried when I left your house that day.

When I arrived home, Mummy asked me what was wrong. I told her what I saw between you and Manjit. She said it is normal behaviour. This is marriage. This is usual. Once people have children, couples live different lives. I was disappointed in her explanation. Maybe I watched too many Hollywood movies and read too many of those damn Harlequin romances. I expect love and togetherness. Not being alone in a marriage.

And your mother-in-law? She is really something. I could sense that she did not like me hanging out at your house all day. You are right. Indeed, she is the Queen of England. She sat there while you made her lunch. Then, cha. Dinner. My god. Are you married to her? That is why I hate Indian marriages and in-laws. Buy one-get-one-free.

I am sorry, Amrit. I am sad to see you. Maybe, it's time to start doing something. I don't know. Talk to Manjit? Talk to Mummy and Papa. Talk to Manjit's mom. I know you can't get a job because the kids are young. Try and connect with Manjit. Maybe. Who knows what marriage and relationships are? We only saw Mummy and Papa. Papa was in charge. She did everything he wanted. Simple. We saw Hollywood movies where love was fun and exciting.

I told you about the men I met in Canada. It's not easy for me because I'm naive. I felt many of these men wanted sex. I spent my time avoiding them. I have not had sex because I am afraid. Confused. Do I get married first? Do I sleep with every boy I go out with? How do I know who is sincere? There are different values and expectations for a woman in the west. I only know the traditional Indian way.

I like my Canadian friends. I like the western way of choice and freedom. One of my friends, Gina, told me that women in Canada can do what they want. She insists that sex is a normal part of dating. Natural. When people are in love, sex is part of life. Nobody in Canada would expect to wait till marriage to have sex.

Then, my other friend, Sarah has a great love story. Her boyfriend Jim has been with her for two years. They live together. Not married. Imagine that. I like to watch them. They do everything together. They hold hands. They travel like married people. But not. Strange, right? People here in Canada date for many years before they marry. Some don't marry. I am surprised to see the choices. It never crossed my mind. It is our Indian way of life that has many rules. Must marry or else. What will I do, I wonder?

Amrit, is there a way out? Talk to you, soon.

Miss you,

Sim

SEPTEMBER 20, 1986

Hello Anita,

It was a short trip to Singapore, and it was heartwarming to spend a few hours with you. Thank you for taking me to my favourite hawker centre, Newton Circus. I indulged in all my Singapore food I missed. That mutton roti john, dipped in egg, pan fried and dipped in special tomato sauce was divine. I had forgotten all about it. And Indian mee goring—fried noodles. I was starved. I pigged out. There's something about Singapore food, right? Addictive and a distinct connector between all us Singaporeans, regardless of race and religion. Through food we speak the same language.

Hey, I am sorry to hear about your divorce. Not surprised. Best thing to do under the circumstances. You should slow down a bit on that dating thing. Take some time to heal. Get to know yourself. I was surprised when you told me that you had already hooked up with this British man, Phil. You have never been without a man, have you? Try it. It's not so bad.

Can you believe I've spent one year in Calgary? I love fall here, and it's my favourite season. The air is crisp, not too cold. The leaves turn yellow, then brown, and fall to the ground. I step on them to hear the crunch under my boots. Crackly. Crinkly. The trees line the streets, branches outstretched and bare. They're like giants with their many arms. It is a sight to behold. In the evenings, sometimes, the sunsets turn all shades of pink and red in the horizon. When I look to the west, I see the silhouette of the mountains far, far away. I stand still and stare. Takes my breath away. Calgary has a way of growing on me.

Can you believe how time flies? I have started a new round of university classes. New interesting characters I love, better than the ones in my literature books. I must tell you about Professor Heathcliff—remember *Wuthering Heights*? That's what we students call him. He is a beast of a man. This man is over six feet tall. His dark, wavy hair, parted in the middle, cascades down to his shoulders. His scraggly beard hangs to his chest. His lips are always placed in a menacing sneer. He teaches Shakespeare. Oh, what a passionate teacher. When he reads passages from King Lear, the class is silent—in awe of his deep, strong voice, resonating with the passion of King Lear who bemoans his fate in the scene where he rails against the elements. Mesmerizing.

When he handed my essay back in class last week, he said, "Here you are, Princess."

Startled, I glanced up at him, puzzled.

"Kaur means princess," he continued. He read my first and last name, again. "Simran Kaur. Princess."

Then he walked away. Ever since then, he calls me Princess. He is a character to behold. Forget about the characters in the novels and plays I read; he is Heathcliff from *Wuthering Heights*—dark, broody, unpredictable. The gossip in class is he was married to a math professor at the university. They have two kids. Divorced. It appears that this professor has an uncontrollable temper. Unpredictable. Oh, my professors fascinate me!

Things got interesting because Professor Heathcliff had a fascination for Ashley. She's a student in one of my classes. She is tall and has long curly red hair which descends to her waist, legs from here to infinity, a figure like an hourglass, deep green eyes, and a megawatt smile. Yup. You guessed it. Professor Heathcliff was in love with her. When we had a different class, not taught by him, he stood at the door outside staring in at Ashley. It was disconcerting, to say the least.

One day in class, I sat next to her. I saw Professor Heathcliff peering in through the glass inset on the door. I watched his eyes fixate on Ashley. Of course, we closed the door, like we did for every class. It didn't stop him. He stood there staring in the little window.

Every class, he came by and peered in. Ashley hides in the corner to avoid him. Even our professor for the class knows of this improper behaviour and told Heathcliff to leave.

Heathcliff screeched at him. "I collect Japanese swords, and I am not afraid to use them!"

That comment freaked out everyone in class, especially the class professor. Hmm. Ok. Now, everyone in class avoids him. Poor Ashley—she darts off after class. Can you blame her? Can you see how my eccentric and colourful professors are better than the characters in the novels I read?

For me, Singapore is getting dimmer and dimmer in my mind. On some nights, I dream about my school days when I was ten. There's one dream that recurs where I am in class at First Toa Payoh Primary School. I'm distracted by the red ladybird crawling on the bougainvillea bush outside the class window. I don't hear a word Mrs. Tan says. I wait for recess to catch this ladybird and put it in my matchbox. At recess, I run out and the ladybird is crawling on the leaf. I take the top of the matchbox and gently shove the ladybird into the bottom of the matchbox. I put a leaf in the box so that the ladybird will feel at home.

What thoughts of a ten-year-old? Imprisoning a poor little critter in a matchbox. How it must have felt when I closed the matchbox, and it crawled in it in the darkness. I don't know why these memories have emerged here in Calgary. Singaporean memories ebb and flow, tangling themselves in snow, bare trees, and sleet.

Anita, it was wonderful to meet your sons. They have grown up to be handsome boys. I hope they adjust to the back and forth of divorced life. Can you believe you are the first Singaporean couple I know who is divorced? What are people saying about your divorce? You know Singaporeans and gossip. Are you coping?

So much for my fairy-tale illusions about your life. No happily ever after. Let me know how things go.

Love

Simran

30 SEPTEMBER 1986

Hi Amy,

My time in Singapore felt short. I missed my family, and mostly spent time close to home. I didn't go out much. Too hot. Jet lagged. Next time, I will come for a month. I am glad we had a chance to talk over the phone. I wanted to know more about Henry. Too bad your mum was loitering. My father does that all the time.

Finally, I get a better sense of what happened between you and Chin. When you came back from Princeton, I was astonished you ended your relationship with Chin. I remember those letters from you—*this is the one*—you said. That must have been an impossible decision to make. You lost that sparkle in your eyes when you came back. Your letter explained a lot of things about how your mum ended your relationship with Chin.

I'm back in Calgary—year two—things are less scary. I have a better groove going. I understand my classes. I figured out the cafeteria and food. I know my way around to the malls and Kensington. However, my living arrangement needs a revamp. Soon. My roommate Lin is getting worse and worse. Just my luck to get stuck with a fellow Asian from Malaysia. She is from Kuala Lumpur. She is five foot nothing, heavy set. She has an atrocious bowl cut hair, with the fringe on her forehead and a rock and roll mane contoured to the nape of her neck. Jet black. Permanently scowling. I swear, that girl never smiles. She has zero social grace. She says the rudest and strangest things. She has no filter.

The other day, this guy Ron I met in class dropped by our room. I was out.

Lin opened the door, stared at Ron and said, "What?"

Ron answered, "Hey, Sim said to drop by for coffee. So here I am."

"Sim is out." Lin grunted.

"Oh, guess no coffee then," Ron answered.

Then Lin went to my shelf, grabbed my jar of Nescafe, went up to Ron and shoved it in his face.

"Here is your coffee."

Ron was stunned; he snatched the jar and left. Ron told me about Lin and the Nescafe the next day in class. We laughed, but I was unimpressed. Why would she give my coffee away? And yeah, I didn't get my Nescafe back from Ron, either.

Listen, I'm dying in the dorm room with Lin. Her socks, you won't believe it. Putrid, rotten eggs and sour milk smell.

I have told her over and over again, but she says, "No. You are wrong. The socks don't smell. It's your problem, not mine."

The room is tiny, and that disgusting stench has overtaken the room and my life. I'm desperately looking for a new room. I am on several waiting lists at the main office for a spare room. I bought some lemon-scented deodorizer, but it's not working. I'm dying in my half of my room. Really, nobody can prepare you for these experiences. I wonder what I did to attract this lunatic into my very little sanctuary. Really, universe, I need a break.

By the way, I hope Henry is your Prince Charming. Oh, it will be nice to marry him, eh. He certainly is your mum's dream boy.

Sending good wishes,

Sim

2 OCTOBER 1986

Dear Sim,

In your letter, you asked what people are saying about my divorce. Things are tough. You know it's not easy dealing with divorce with Indians and with Singaporeans. There's this expectation that you should stay married. Forever. It doesn't matter if you are right or wrong.

Our family is furious. "What will happen to you? To your kids?"

That is what everyone is saying to me. It's like a woman can't take care of herself.

Mostly, I feel peace. When I come home from work, I don't have this knot of fear in the pit of my stomach, not knowing if Gopal is going to throw a cup of hot tea at me. Or if he is going to hold me and cry. Worried if the boys will be caught in the crossfire. Now, it's calm. Serene. These are things I've forgotten about.

I've underestimated my own strength and power. But tongues are wagging. Remember Jass? Gopal's cousin? She won't talk to me anymore even though we went to school together. In fact, Gopal's whole family has disowned me. *It's my fault*, they say for destroying the family. *The children will suffer*. People expect me to sacrifice like some goddess.

Even worse, some of Gopal's family members found out I went to London to meet Phil, a new man in my life. Hey, I'm in love. To tell the truth, I've been chatting with Phil on the phone for six months. First, I did it for fun. International love. Safe. Far away. I connected with Phil while I was married but knew things were over with Gopal. I felt I connected with Phil in our conversations over the phone. He understood me and what I was going through with Gopal. We shared our secrets and lives over the past six months. He kept me sane amidst the brutality of Gopal. You know, Phil told me to get out, to leave.

I was overjoyed when Phil sent me a ticket to visit him in London when he found out Gopal had moved out. Guess what? Phil is ten years younger than me. Isn't that interesting? He teaches Chemistry at the university in London. When he made me that offer, for once, I jumped at the chance to be spontaneous and free. Maybe I could take care of myself for a change? I left the kids with Gopal and his family and didn't tell anyone where I was going. It was his week with them anyways.

I felt alive, after such a long time living in secrets and fear. I smiled at everyone and felt those long-forgotten butterflies in my belly. When arrived in London, Phil was at the airport with a giant bouquet of red roses. I ran into his arms and rested my head on his strong chest. I know—this sounds like your Harlequin romance, again, doesn't it? But it was true. I was living the romance with my British boy. He hugged me tight, and, oh, I felt desired. My knight in shining armour!

I had a fairy tale week in London. After all the abuse, I felt Phil treated me like the Queen of Singapore. I was spoilt with kindness and gentleness. We talked all day and night, about everything under the sun. And the nights, yes, they were passionate and exhilarating. Everything feels right with Phil. It is perfect. He is perfect.

At the end of my trip, Phil whispered in my ear. You won't believe it, but he's moving to Singapore. He had even applied for jobs to teach here before I came to London. He is doing all the right things to be with me. For once, a man is doing everything to be with me. With Gopal, I made sacrifice after sacrifice. Is this what it feels to have a man do everything for me? It's meant to be.

I enjoy hearing about your professors at the University of Calgary. What an assorted mix of goofballs and lovely personalities. I have to wonder what you are learning in class, Simran? Maybe it's you, attracting all the strange people and professors. In fact, do you remember at the Institute of Education, our lecturers? The one that you disliked—Professor Tay—he asked you to stay back and talk to him after class one day. If I'm right, he even asked you to quit teaching because you didn't seem interested in his class and lectures. Didn't he complain how you sat in the back of class with an apathetic look on your face, not listening to him?

Am I remembering right that you, Ms. Cheeky, loudly declared the reason for your boredom was he was guilty of boring you to death with his lectures? There was silence in the class. That look on Professor Tay's face that day was priceless, right? The battle lines were drawn that day, weren't they? To irritate him more, at the end of semester, you got an A in his class and won a literature prize as well.

I remember the prize award ceremony at the end of our program; you purposely went up to Professor Tay like the troublemaker you are to shake his hand and thank him for his wonderful classes. His face was crimson red when you fled giggling. See, professors can be challenging everywhere. Remember, Sim, you are strong and smart. In any country!

I have to say when I was travelling the world with Gopal, we enjoyed ourselves. South Africa, Canada, United States, Australia and New Zealand. But I can tell you one thing, we both were dying to get back home. We were relieved when we got back to Singapore. To feel at home. To be a Singaporean.

Simran, you look like you're on your way out. Are you? I imagine it must be confusing to have one foot in Singapore and the other in Canada. Is the pull of Canada stronger?

Anyways, my life is a mess. My poor children are upset. It will be a big adjustment for them. They spend one week with their dad and one week with me. It's tough dropping the kids off. Divorce is such an ugly thing. Gopal has moved in with his parents. As you can imagine, things are tense with me and Gopal. He tries to talk to me and wants me to take him back. I can't. I won't tolerate his abuse anymore. Also, there's Phil now.

Hey, when I was a schoolgirl, I caught ladybirds and put them in matchboxes too. Must be a Singapore thing.

Love,

Anita

5 OCTOBER 1986

Hey Simran,

You should move out. Your roommate is a lunatic. Smelly socks? Good grief. How can that not be a deal breaker? Living with my family is like living with roommates from hell. If I could afford it and it was acceptable, I would move out. No luck. Here in Singapore, I have to live with my family till I die. Family obligations or get married. Option one or two.

How to survive? I stay out as much as I can. I come home. I avoid my mum. Dad is in bed early as usual. I get up early. I go to work. Repeat. Lucky for me, I can do what I want and go where I want. Not like when you were in Singapore with your family. Prison.

I'm sure you're dying to know about Henry and our trip to Hong Kong. Ok. Imagine the best. First class on Singapore Airlines. Ritz-Carlton. The penthouse was breathtaking—with a jaw dropping view of the harbour. Chauffeur service. Wined and dined at the top restaurants, only accessible with the right name and wallet. It was a world I have never known. I loved it. I want this life.

Henry was the perfect gentleman. Since I had played hard to get for nine months, it was now time. Sex. Ya. Whatever. It was quite awful, really. It was wham, bang, thank you, ma'am. I was surprised. He plays a good game romancing. Did not see it coming. He climbed on me, and, what? He was done. Ten seconds. Then he rolled over and snored all night.

I turned to my right and looked at the view of the harbour in the early light of the night. The neon lights were garish, but they actually lulled me to sleep. I adore this life already. I'm fine with anything with Henry. The days were for me. I shopped at all the posh boutiques, courtesy of my lover. The nights were for him. Sex every night, of course. Five minutes, the most. Fair exchange.

When we got back to Singapore, Henry dropped me home. He leaned over and kissed my cheek.

"See you tomorrow," I whispered lovingly.

He nodded.

But I have not heard from him since. It's been a month of silence. No calls. He won't answer his phone. Won't return my calls. I have not said anything to my mom. She questions me every day. I lie to her. It's easier that way. I go through the motions of my day. I keep thinking of those lights of the harbour—so bright one day and, totally dim the next. Was I a fling?

I was having high tea at Raffles with my colleagues last Friday, and I saw him. Rather, I saw them. She was holding his arm, laughing oh so coyly. A whole head taller than him in high heels so flimsy she probably couldn't walk without holding on. Long, straight, black silky hair to her waist. Her waist was the size of my thigh. Was that the latest Chanel dress? Japanese? Korean? Bitch. He turned and caught a glimpse of me. Blank. No recognition. No acknowledgment. In that space of two seconds, he diminished me. Rendered me non-existent. Invisible.

At that precise moment, the only thing that I could think about was Chin. I'm lost. I've had a taste of a life I yearn for. To fall to the reality of everyday existence is unbearable. I bought a ticket to Medan today.

All my best,

Amy

6 OCTOBER 1986

Dear Sim,

You are right about what you saw when you came over to visit me. I am alone in this marriage. Last Thursday, I took the kids to Mummy and Papa's house. I told them to take care of them. I asked Papa if I could borrow his car. I decided after your last letter I would get some answers. Where was Manjit going after work? He told his mother that morning he had a meeting until 9 p.m. Really? Meeting? Again?

I drove to Manjit's office and parked my car across his building, turned off the engine and slid back in the seat. I had a clear view of his front door. I could see his car on the street seven spots in front of me, far left. I waited for an hour. Nothing. Was I a fool? I was stuck in the seat in the car, and I had to pee. Just when I was going to give up, I saw Manjit. I slid down even lower in my seat and peered at him. I even had binoculars. It looked like he was going home. Good. I put my key in the engine, getting ready to go when I saw a young Chinese woman walk up to Manjit's car and get into the passenger seat, but I couldn't see much because his car pulled out of the parking spot.

My heart jumped out of my chest. What if Manjit saw me? I put on my cap and put all my hair into it. He did not go that far. Five minutes later, he pulled in a nearby block of flats and HDB parking lot and parked his car. He and the girl got out of the car. She walked to him and hugged him. I parked in the spot for the garbage truck metres away. I peeped through my window. They were still hugging, now kissing. Manjit looked around to see if anyone was looking. I ducked. They held hands and walked to Block 126 and disappeared.

She probably lives there. I sat there in the car, numb, staring at the giant dumpster in front of me.

I sped back to our house—or was it Manjit's house. It never felt like my house. The Queen was out at some temple event. Perfect. I ran into the room. I pulled my suitcase from under the bed. I hurriedly packed all my jewelry—the ones Papa and Mummy gave me for my wedding. I shoved some clothes for me and the kids. Just threw everything in the suitcase. The tears fell as I walked out of that house and did not look back. Three years later and this was all I had from my husband's house—one suitcase to go.

Mummy and Papa were shocked when I walked in their house with my suitcase.

"What are you doing?" Mummy demanded.

I told them about Manjit and his mistress.

"This is normal ups and downs in a marriage. All men are like that. Give it a day then you can go back," Mum retorted.

I stared at her and spat, "I am tired. I didn't have an affair. What if I did? Do you think I would be forgiven? So only men can do what they want? This is the new world. Women don't have to accept being cheated on."

"Ok, go sleep." Papa hugged me and tried to calm me down. "Tomorrow, we can talk."

By now, I was furious. Like that. Usual. As a woman, I was the wrong one. I have to forgive. I have to forget. That bastard—I'm guessing that woman is the Chinese girlfriend he loves. So, he didn't have the guts to marry her, but he has the guts to cheat on me. What have I been doing for three years as his wife? An ornament? I sacrificed my life for tradition and culture, and Manjit got to have the best of both worlds.

Sim, where can I go? Do I go to my husband's house or my father's house? I go from one man to the other, right? No place is my house. Simran, I'm jealous of you. You're smart to run away to Canada. I don't know what will happen. I am worn-out. Why do Indian women have no power?

Listen. Go and sleep with anyone you want. Don't save your virginity for Prince Charming. Be like a man. Look at me. I do every-thing right and I still have no happiness. I live my life for everyone.

Love,

Amrit

8 OCTOBER 1986

Simran beti,

Did your sister tell you about what happened? She ran to our house the other day. She found out her husband is having mistress. It's normal. Men are like that. They go and wander but always come back to their proper wife and tradition. A wife needs her husband to take care of her. And if she has children, she must have a mother and a father for her children. Your father, how many women he had. I tried to stop him. I went to the witch doctor. Got magic spells. Tried everything. No matter what, he always came back to his family. Some men are like that. They think they can do whatever they want. Manjit also the same, isn't he?

Manjit will come back to Amrit and his daughters. A man is nothing without his family. This Chinese mistress, she is a cheap girl. His affair won't last. In Indian lives, marriage is important. A woman needs her husband. A divorcee here, nobody will respect her. They will look at her like an easy woman. All the other women will also keep away from a divorced woman, so she won't go after their husbands. This is our society and mentality. We cannot change this. It's been this way for women for generations.

I told your sister to pray. We took her to Silat Road temple. We did special prayer for her. Everything will be ok now. We will take her back to her husband's house soon. Let her cool down. You also be careful in Canada. Men are all the same everywhere. You listen carefully. Don't have sex with any boy in Canada. They will all run away. Come back and get married. The proper way. You also remember to say Waheguru every day.

You write to your sister immediately and tell her to go back. Tell her she cannot behave like this. Women have to listen and follow their husband and family.

Mummy

26 OCTOBER 1986

Dear Amrit,

I was impressed to read your letter about how you tailed Manjit and found him with his girlfriend. Your suspicions were confirmed that he is a two-timing cheater. Hey, you go, girl. You took control instead of sitting around crying. That bastard. If I see Manjit, I'm going to kick his ass. Coward asshole. I don't understand why he married you if he wanted to be with his girlfriend.

I know you're going through a hard time. You have to deal with everyone on your back. Mummy, Papa, Mother-in-law, husband, children. I wish I could tell you to only listen to yourself. What do you want to do? If it's me, I would be done. They can all go to hell. You can be alone, take care of the kids, and get a job. Hah. You don't need a man who keeps you as a slave.

I see how women in the west are different in their marriages. Here in Calgary, women are tough. Linda, in my class, she is on husband number two. She confided in me that things are not good in her marriage. Her husband is a doctor. She finds him controlling. He has no time for her, has a temper, and she suspects he is cheating on her. After three years of being married, she says she's fed up. She is frustrated because she gave up her job as a teacher to be with him.

Instead, as her husband wanted, Linda ran his medical practice, not living her own dreams or passion. She gave up everything for him. Now, she sees no way out of her unhappiness except to file for divorce. That's where I see western women being empowered. Linda won't even move out of their family home. In fact, she told her husband to get lost. She felt suffocated and wanted her freedom back. Easy, right? No need to worry about society, mother-in-law, family, children. Just come and go. Marry and divorce. No need to wait for others to decide. Linda shows me the possibility for women to have autonomy in their lives and marriages. I know it's not easy for Linda, but she's going for it!

There are values and ideas I question myself now. Sex and men. Ya. It's not easy for me. I'm stuck in an Indian and Canadian world. Am I the East or the West? I'm a virgin. Still. Afraid. I'm not sure what will happen in my life. I'm still looking for a man who will love me and expect we'll live happily forever. Here in Calgary, I meet men, but I don't know how to choose. I meet many uncommitted men who want to only have sex or have girlfriends already.

Coming from our background, I don't know how to find a boy-friend. How to act. What is right? What is wrong? Here, the men I meet are young and finding their own adventures. They don't want to get married. Nobody wants to get married at twenty. You know how we Indian people are. We are the opposite. We push marriage to keep traditional order and stability. Opposite worlds. What is my answer? Let's see what happens.

Amrit, I have another secret to tell you. I have a friend, Jenny from Singapore who I went skiing with once. Last week, we met up and made last-minute plans to go to the biggest shopping mall in the world. It is in Edmonton, a city three hours away from Calgary. It was an impromptu decision. We grabbed our backpacks and jumped on the city bus that took us to the Greyhound station in time to catch the 8 p.m. bus to Edmonton. Jenny and I giggled and chatted on the three-hour bus ride. I loved how I could do anything I wanted. Finally, we reached the Greyhound station in Edmonton around 11 p.m. Oh boy. It was dark and scary when we got off at the station. I grabbed Jenny's arm. Now, we didn't know what to do. We hadn't even booked any hotel or looked up any information about the city besides the shopping mall. We didn't think too much when we jumped on the bus in Calgary.

Jenny and I anxiously surveyed the station and debated about what to do. We were two foolish girls alone in a new city. We clutched each other's arms. From the other end of the station, two guys walked up to us.

"Where are you going, ladies? Can we help you?"

I kept quiet.

Jenny asked, "Where's the closest hotel and how do we get a taxi?"

They were two native men. One looked around our age. He introduced himself as Rob. Rob was taller than me, around six feet tall. His skin was light olive like mine. He was slim and gangly and had a shy demeanour as he kept looking down. The other man looked older. He was Mike, Rob's uncle. I guessed he was in his thirties and was short and stout. He wore his hair in braids. Jenny looked around for a taxi, but there was none. The station was now deserted, dark, and it appeared to be in the middle of nowhere.

Mike looked at us and said, "You can come stay at my apartment. Don't worry. I will go stay with my nephew Rob at his place."

I shook my head and thought, *Were they insane?*

I yanked Jenny's arm to leave, but Jenny, unexpectedly, said, "Ok."

I gripped her arm. I didn't understand why she said yes.

She brushed my hand away, looked at me and whispered, "Come, lah. It's ok."

The next thing you know, Jenny and I were ushered and seated in the back of Mike's car, driving in the dark, in a city we didn't know, going to God knows where. By now, fear engulfed every ounce of my being. We were in a car with strangers. I didn't utter a single word, as Jenny carried on a conversation with these two strangers about Singapore.

I looked out the window to memorize buildings and signs, but it was useless. It was pitch black. Finally, after forty agonizing minutes, the car arrived at this apartment building. I peered through the darkness and noted it was pretty run down. I reluctantly got out of the car, clutched my backpack, and glanced around. It looked like a rough and tough neighbourhood. There was a rowdy group of homeless people drinking alcohol near the entrance of the building. The smell of cigarettes and cannabis permeated the air.

Mike opened the front door of the building, and we followed him and Rob up a flight of stairs. Mike took us to his apartment on the third floor. He opened the door of the apartment and gently shoved us in. My throat was stuck with a lump.

"Welcome to my home," Mike boomed.

I looked around the sparse but clean apartment. My hands trembled as I looked back to see if anyone was in the corridor. No one.

I turned to Mike and uttered nervously, "I think we should go to a hotel."

Mike said, "Nonsense. You are my guests. Girls from Singapore."

Mike saw the worry in my eyes. "Oh. Don't worry, young ladies. Rob and I will go to his apartment a few blocks away. We will come tomorrow at eight a.m. to pick you up. We can go for breakfast. You can have this apartment to yourself. Make yourself at home and be sure to lock the door."

I stepped back, flabbergasted. I didn't know what to say. Jenny had a fake smile plastered on her face. It all happened so fast. We were trapped in this apartment in a city we did not know. There was no escape.

"Bye," Rob said, unexpectedly. "It's late. Get some sleep."

"There's tea in the cupboards and fruit in the fridge. Help yourselves," Mike said with a pat on my back before he walked out the front door with Rob.

What? They left? We watched Mike and Rob trudge down the stairs and slam the door shut. My body convulsed with my tears. You know how you do stupid things, and you realize that it is a terrible mistake, but it's too late?

I asked Jenny, "What if they come back with five men? We're dead. Why did you say yes? We should have not come here."

Jenny doubled over and sobbed like a child. "I don't know why…I didn't think…."

Honestly, we didn't know where we were. We peered out the window through the curtains and noticed the group of men out in front of the building had grown larger. The only way out of the apartment was to go past them. I rummaged the house for any clues. Nothing.

Address? There was no phone in the apartment.

I was furious at Jenny for agreeing to follow the men. We fell in each other's arms, in tears. We debated if we should go out in the dark or stay here in the apartment.

"I'm sorry," Jenny whimpered.

We made a plan and tried to calm down. We decided the best thing to do was to sleep at the front door with our backs against the front door. We went to the kitchen and opened all the drawers until we found a butcher's knife and a cleaver, one for each of us. We left our shoes on. We sank to the floor and settled in at the front door, hugging our backpacks for our dear lives.

The whole night, my eyes were wide open. Why did I do something so stupid? I watched the clock ticking on the wall and shadows bouncing off the walls. Minute by minute, I was on alert. Noise? Someone outside?

"Waheguru. Waheguru." I instinctively prayed.

I didn't sleep for one minute, listening to the gentle snores of Jenny sprawled on the floor. I touched the blade of my cleaver. Good. It was sharp. Finally, a streak of light shone through the blinds. I walked to the window and looked outside to figure out what to do. I wanted to leave. If we could call a cab. But how?

We jumped out of our skins when the front door shook with boisterous knocks. We looked through the peephole to see the smiling faces of Mike and Rob. It was 8 a.m. already.

"How was your night?" asked a cheerful Mike.

"Wonderful. It was wonderful," nodded Jenny.

By now, we were a little convinced that Mike and Rob were not going to kill us or sell us to a prostitution ring. We quickly got ready and followed them down to their car. The homeless men were still there, sprawled on the cold cement. In the daylight, they looked less scary.

Relieved, Jenny and I tumbled into the backseat of the car. In the day, we could see we were in the middle of two crisscrossing highways. Mike was in a good mood and chatted as he drove us to West Edmonton Mall. Jenny asked them questions on the forty-minute drive. Now, she was investigating them. *A little too late*, I thought. As I listened to their answers, I thought they seemed like decent men. They told us they worked in construction at the arena close by.

I was silent in my thoughts. I mean, who would give their apartment to two strangers for the night? Worse still, which idiots would go to a stranger's apartment in the middle of the night in a strange city? The men tried to convince us to stay one more day. I looked at Jenny. I was relieved when she said we had to go back for an exam. Mike convinced Jenny to give him her phone number. She winked at me to convince me it was a made-up number. The last thing I wanted was for the men to show up in Calgary.

Finally, the car came to a standstill in front of the glorious, giant West Edmonton Mall. I wanted the men to leave. They looked disappointed, to say the least. We were terrible to the hosts, weren't we? Not even a proper thank you.

I jumped out of the car first and ran into the entrance of the mall, trusting that Jenny would follow close behind. As soon as Jenny and I entered the safety of the anonymous crowd in the mall, we hugged each other. We looked out the door to see if the men had followed us in and were relieved when we saw their car head out to the main road.

Relieved, Jenny and I looked at the never-ending stores in front of us at West Edmonton Mall. Maybe, just maybe, we could salvage our trip and celebrate being alive by immersing in this moment and being in the safety of a crowd of people. I couldn't get into a shopping mindset but was happy to meander in and out of clothing stores, shoe stores, and jewelry stores that never seemed to end. It calmed me down. Questions raced through my mind. How were we still alive? This is something I would never do in Singapore, right?

Jenny and I stayed in the safety of the mall until it was time to catch our bus. We took a taxi from the mall to the Greyhound station and were relieved that Mike and Rob were not at the station. We never found out why they were there, anyways.

On the long ride back to Calgary, I stared out the window into the darkness of the night. The words, *Fuck all Indian pass-able side-*

walks came back to my mind. Those were the words uttered to me by two white men outside a bar in Calgary some time ago when I went there. I agonized over those words for a long time, feeling confused by why someone would say that. Why would I or any Indian be singled out for our race or colour?

This evening, as the bus sped home to Calgary on the highway, I leaned my head on the seat in front of me and said a silent thanks to these two native men who had treated us with startling kindness and probably saved us from a terrible situation that night. My feelings of self-reproach mingled with relief and ironic gratitude.

Jenny and I promised each other that we would never tell anyone what we did. I am sure I have seen Hollywood movies like this where the girls end up dead. Amrit, do not tell anyone. I will deny it.

Write soon.

Love you,

Simran

30 OCTOBER 1986

Dear Mummy,

Amrit told me what happened with her husband and how she left him. She did the right thing. She caught him with another woman. That Manjit is a jerk. He married Amrit to please his mother and continued to have his girlfriend on the side. This is a man with no balls. He just used people. He pretended to be a good Indian man, but he did what he wanted.

Men should not get away with their bad behaviour, anymore. Women should not be treated this way. How do you want Amrit to live her life? Prayers to any God will not fix her problems. Better to leave this bastard alone. You have all shoved her out of the house to marry. Now, open the door and let her back in. Go to hell with tradition and culture. Why do Indian people consider a woman a slut because she left her husband? What nonsense is this?

I pray to God that you and Papa will see the truth and be brave to accept the reality of this Indian bullshit. Don't throw your daughter into the snake pit. I wish Amrit could have finished her teaching certificate. Get a job. Work. An Indian woman must stand on her feet. Too bad she didn't get married to a nice man like Lina did. I know there are many good Indian men out there. She got a rotten coward.

Mummy, it is time to change the destiny of the next generation for Soni and Roni. Women are equal to men. Don't make them second class citizens, anymore.

Love,

Sim

10 NOVEMBER 1986

Simran, oh, Simran,

Are you crazy? First drug dealer Marlon. Now strange men in Edmonton. What are you doing? From complete prison to complete freedom. You are like a baby learning how to walk. You're insane. I'm worried about you. You are lucky those men did not do anything. No wonder in Singapore we were never allowed to go out and do what we want. Don't do more crazy things. Promise, ok?

I had a taste of freedom, too. Manjit was shocked when he came home and found that I had left with the kids. He came to Papa's house and knocked on the door. Mummy and Papa told him to come back next day when everyone was calm. I stayed in the bedroom. *Good.* I thought. *Let him have a taste of helplessness.* Now who is in control? Now who has to worry about everyone else? I went to bed and put the pillow over my face, covered my ears. I wanted some peace for just one night and everyone to leave me alone. I knew the shit would hit the ceiling.

The next day when I came out of the room, the show was ready to start. Manjit took the day off. This was the first time in three years he had done that. They sat in the living room, the court of justice, it seemed. His mother, the Queen, cried and clutched her heart, like she was going to die of a heart attack. Good drama, Queen. Mummy and Papa sat on the sofa looking guilty—for what, I don't know. Probably for raising a devil like me and not the good Indian girl who would jump into the fire with her husband. Meh kya kita? Queen and Manjit sang their protests about me walking out with the children loudly and in unison. Yah. What did Manjit do? Nothing. That's the problem.

When all of them saw me walk into the living room, their voices got louder and their eyes flashed. Look at them, ready to point fingers and blame me. Usual, right? It's always the girl's fault. I ignored them, walked to the kitchen and went to take my shower. I even made myself a cup of tea. The Indian drama was going on in full force.

Now, part two of the scene. Let's blame the parents. The Queen shouted at how an Indian girl can't behave like this and leave her husband. How could I steal the kids? By now, I was fresh and ready for battle. I sat in the single chair by myself. On my left, Mum and Papa. On the right, my useless husband and mother in-law. Start, lah. The games began. The Queen told me I had no right to leave. Mum and Papa said I had to listen to my husband. My husband was dumb. He said nothing and stared at the floor.

Papa asked Manjit, "How can you have another woman when you have wife and children?"

Manjit looked up and mumbled something inaudible. Sorry? I don't think so. Caught. Guilty. He never looked at me.

All the voices got louder. Everyone argued at the same time. Punjabi. English. Malay. My head exploded from the tension. I couldn't deal with it anymore.

I stood up and shouted, "I am not coming back. Go and live with your Chinese bitch."

I went into the room and slammed it hard. Enough. All of them sat there blaming me. All of them insisted I had to go back, I had to change, and I was wrong. I heard lots of shouting. By now, the kids were up. You should have been there. You would have enjoyed it. Me, I was numb. Then it was all quiet. I looked out of the room and Manjit and the Queen had left. What? How? I was sure I was going to be dragged home to prison.

Papa hugged me and said, "I told them to go. All calm down. Talk some other time." Ok. Now how? Let's see what happens. I don't know what to do. What would you do? When I left, I had no plans after that moment. I feel something different inside me. Some fire is lit.

You, Simran. No more tamasha. I won't tell Mummy and Papa about Edmonton. 100% you will be dragged home.

Love,

Amrit

13 NOVEMBER 1986

Dear Anita,

Phil, London, romance? My goodness. Please slow down, my friend. Wouldn't it be better to resolve the divorce with Gopal first before you rush into something foreign and new? Are you sure you didn't steal my Harlequin Romance books and read them all? You know, it wouldn't be bad to be on your own with your kids for a bit instead of rushing headlong into a long-distance, multi-cultural, he-moves-to-Singapore-thing.

Am I the only one seeing challenges here? I mean, when is Phil coming? Are you sponsoring him? Visa? Is he a serial killer? Aiyoh. Miss Anita. Pelahan, pelahan, lah. Also, what is happening with Gopal? How goes the divorce? I can only imagine what will happen when Gopal finds out about Phil. And the kids. Ok. My head hurts. I'm worried for you, my dear.

It's getting cold in Calgary. A fog descends on the bare tree outside the window of my room as I write. I can hear Lin snoring. Again. Still no luck in getting a new roommate or a new room. Now that it is starting to snow, the thought of moving out of residence is not something I can contemplate. I will try for a different place in residence. It's not a good time to move. You see, no one leaves till December, when fall semester is over.

It is getting challenging with Lin. She is morose. She has this sneer on her face all the time. She has no social cues. I worry about her, sometimes. Angela, who lives across our room had an interesting Lin moment yesterday.

Late last night, her roommate, Amanda, came to our room and said, "Come see this." Lin and I went over, puzzled. No one was in the room. Amanda pointed to the closet. Lin opened it, and there was Angela. Aah. The smell of alcohol hit my nose before I saw the silhouette in the darkness. Drunk as hell.

Angela's disembodied voice, high pitched, slurred whispered, "Shhh, the Enterprise is on its way."

She continued in gibberish for five minutes. Star Trek?

Lin retorted, "Angela, you are such a drunk. Stop drinking. Get out of the closet, stupid."

"Oh no. Shut up, Lin. Don't fight with a drunk trekkie," I thought. No luck.

Angela heard her and screamed, "Get out of my starship."

Lin went up to her and pulled her out of the closet. "Stop drinking. Go to bed. You are an alcoholic."

Now, there was a full-out war between Captain Kirk Angela and Idiot Lin. I pulled Lin by her arm, trying to get her off the starship-of-the-drunk-and-disorderly. Lin yelled at me. Angela jumped out of the closet, mumbling Star Trek shit and shoved Lin out of her room. Lin fell on her bum. I pulled Lin up and ran out when I saw Angela stumble our way. We dashed to our room.

That is exactly what happens with Lin every single time. She has no sense of boundaries and shutting up when she has to.

"Lin, what the hell?" I didn't know whether to laugh or cry.

Lin sat on her bed, took off her socks that smelled of sulphur and soiled baby diapers and threw them on my bed.

"That girl Angela is an alcoholic. And cuckoo, as well," Lin said.

"She's having fun, Lin," I countered.

Lin sneered at me and ignored me. Really, I live in a matchbox asylum. That girl is down to one friend—me—now, none. Help me. I can't babysit her. Tomorrow, I am going to beg the Residence Manager to move me.

However, the Star Trek fiasco was not over for the night.

Amanda stuck her head in our door and said, "Fuck off, Lin. You moron."

Then, we heard Angela scream in the hallway, looking for Lin. I quickly locked the door. Here I was, trapped between an intoxicated trekkie and a smelly Malaysian. The only thing to do was get in bed and put the pillow on my face to drown out everyone and everything, as usual. Oh, my exciting life with Lin.

Anita, let me tell you about my tall, handsome, sexy Professor Bryson from my Canadian literature class. All of us students and professors were at an English department party last Friday after class. A group of us stood in a circle. Professor Bryson looked a little unstable on his feet, holding a giant glass of beer in his right hand, slurping it down, hiccupping. Joe, standing next to me, held up six fingers, motioned his hand to his mouth, and pointed at Professor Bryson. Got it. Six beers. I nursed a glass of wine in my right hand, sipping it oh so slowly. I had my left arm tucked behind me, trying to look casual and trying to fit in the large circle of ten students and professors. Suddenly, this loud voice directed itself at me.

"Simran, I've known you for a year now. I didn't realize you had only one arm."

Startled, I looked at Professor Bryson who was pointing at me with his right hand while his left hand mercilessly sloshed the contents of his seventh beer. He looked genuinely concerned. Everyone stared at me, puzzled. Then, laughter erupted.

Amused, I pulled my arm out from my back and said, "See, Professor, I have two arms."

Relieved, Professor Bryson came up to me, slapped me on my supposedly missing arm and said, "Thank god, Simran. Best news ever."

I felt his sticky, beer paws on my bare arm and sighed. Suddenly, Professor Bryson wasn't that sexy anymore. Maybe, if I introduced him to Angela, the drunk trekkie who lived across my dorm room, they could be drinking buddies. Ah, it's ok. My professor is simply human.

Listen, I hope things go smoothly for you. Does Phil drink? Just wondering.

The girl with TWO arms,

Sim

14 NOVEMBER 1986

Dear Amy,

I felt your pain when I read how your boyfriend Henry disappeared after your dream trip to Hong Kong. Sorry to hear that, Amy. Sadly, I am not surprised to hear this about Henry. Let's face it. He's the rich tycoon, with the pick of all these girls in Singapore who are also looking for the quick and easy Singapore dream. Each one is younger and skinnier. Unless Henry is looking for the smart intelligent woman like you, as well. Is he? You did hint at a possible intellectual connection through your university connection. I mean, you are the whole package, right?

I thought in junior college you said you wanted to be with someone you could share ideas with, talk to—a man of ideas. Did YOU get the package or is settling for financial comfort enough? You know some of our especially rich Singapore men are notorious for their many mistresses on the sidelines. My neighbour in Singapore, Auntie Foo, is beautiful and smart. She's been married for twenty years. Her husband was the top banker in Singapore. He was also the top gambler under the table. He had mistress after mistress, each one younger than the other.

The frustrating kicker was that Auntie Foo knew about all of the mistresses and could do nothing about them. Or would not?

I asked her, "Auntie, how? How do you take it?"

She said, "Aiyoh. Never mind, lah. As long as he pays the bills and we have a good life, who cares. He can do what he wants, lah. I don't like sex, anyway. This way, I have a good life and he doesn't bother me. Good, right?"

I remember being stunned at her honesty. Her acceptance. She was willing to put up with infidelity as long as her needs were met. I wondered if that was what love and marriage was all about? As a young girl in Singapore, I was corrupted by all the Harlequin romances. Not anymore today. There must be more for women!

One day, about four years ago, I was at Ang Mo Kio Central, and I saw Mr. Foo. He was hand in hand with a girl young enough to be his daughter. She wore a short red cheongsam with a slit up to her right upper thigh. The dress hugged her skinny boyish figure and she had six-inch black and gold stilettos. The neckline plunged down her chest, but she had no breasts to show. Flat.

Her face looked like the Chinese wayang opera girl. Oh my god. Caked white powder. Two diagonal lines of red rouge on each cheek—she must have forgotten to contour and blend them in. Her lips were painted a fire bright red, but they did not match her dull red cheongsam. Her eye shadow was half bright blue and half glittery gold. Her straight black hair was cut in a bob round the nape of her neck, with her fringe to her eyebrows. Every single man, woman and child in Ang Mo Kio Central stopped to stare at her. She was so out of place in the crowd of Singaporeans wearing t-shirts, shorts, and slippers. Mr. Foo liked that very much and strutted like a peacock.

Auntie Foo told me later that this was Mr. Foo's latest mistress. He had picked her up from a bar in Johor Bahru, Malaysia, and brought her back to Singapore. That mistress had a five-year-old son back in Johor Bahru who lived with his grandmother. She was a single mother from the village. I was stunned at Mr. Foo's choice but more shocked that Auntie Foo knew all the details of this new mistress she was sharing with me. Maybe, she did care.

It was then I realized marriage was all about sex and power. Do men want intelligent women or pliant, obedient ones? And Mr. Foo—ugh. Forget about it. His thick round black spectacles framed his already round face, barely perched on his flat, non-existent nose. His lips always opened liked an "O". His skin pimply and pock-marked. But his voice, yes. Now, that was amazing. I loved it. Deep, resonant, British accented and well-spoken. I wondered about his attraction to the bargirl from Johor Bahru. Or should I even ask?

Don't be a Mrs. Foo. There are millions of people in Singapore. Surely, you will find a better match.

Write soon,

Simran

25 NOVEMBER 1986

Hello Simran,

You are right. Your sister is very bold to leave. Amrit left her husband's house. She doesn't want to go back to her married life. How like that? A woman needs a man. Especially if she has children. Who will marry a divorced woman? No one. Only in husband's house, a woman will get respect and safety.

I told Amrit to give her husband Manjit a chance. If she doesn't go back, she won't find any freedom in this house either. Worse in father's house. Back to childhood prison. She has to go back to her husband and manage her house there. There she can be a memsahib. Learn to take charge. Manjit won't marry that Chinese girl. She is only good for playing. Not marrying. He will change. Now he knows Amrit is strong and won't take his bekuash anymore. Love, love. What is love? That disappears. Only in the movies. Now is time to raise the children.

You have flown far away to Canada. Your eyes are open. You can see how people live differently. Do you think divorce is easy? How many White people are divorced? How many times they will marry? Tell your sister to go back to her husband. Tell her divorce is hard. Indian people don't divorce.

Get your degree and come back home. Sending you to Canada is expensive. Your father is stressed. You know how he works hard. He gets impatient from stress and work. Sometimes, he screams at everyone.

Simran, you study hard and come back. You want an education and we agreed to that. Finish your education and come back and get married. You must keep your promise now.

Ok, listen. The lipstick next time get dark rose. Last one too light. No, not nice. Like burgundy is better. Kidney beans very good. Cannot get that quality in Singapore. I pray for you every day. God give you good health and strong brains.

Mummy

Hey Sister,

I was impressed by your courage to leave your unfaithful husband. I can't believe you finally said no to the double standards of how it is acceptable for a man to cheat on his wife. I'm tired of how some women are mistreated in their marriages. I wonder what Manjit was thinking when he married you and kept seeing his girlfriend? When you left, you showed him he could not take you for granted anymore.

If it's me, I would not go back to an unhappy marriage and an unfaithful husband, but I know it's not that easy. Living in Mummy and Papa's house could also be hell. Don't you remember? It will be the same. "Can't go here. Can't do this."

Maybe the way for you to change the system is to do so from within your marriage. Go back home and establish new rules. Be in charge. Get a maid to help with the house and kids. Go and finish your diploma. Establish an authentic connection with your husband—no mistress! How? Do you think it is possible? Surely, you can't go back to the same crap that you have put up with for three years. I think it's time for a revolution.

As for me, don't worry. My Edmonton trip was a foolish misadventure. This is what crazy girls like me do. I promise I won't go to strange men's apartments anymore. What a close call. I am learning life lessons slowly. Thanks for keeping it a secret.

An interesting opportunity unfolded for me last week. I went to the nearby grocery store, Safeway, which was a fifteen-minute walk from my dormitory. I crossed the road and saw a sign for rent for a duplex across from Safeway. I ran home and called the number. I went back to meet the owner and to look at the duplex. The rent was $500. It was huge. It was bigger than our flat in Singapore. It had a rectangle living room three times the size of my dorm room. There was a dining room across from the beautiful kitchen. At the back of the duplex, there were two giant bedrooms. There was one glorious bathroom with a bathtub. The place was fully furnished. It was an instant home. I couldn't believe my luck. If I found a roommate, it would be the same price I was paying for half a room with smelly queen from Malaysia.

I vibrated with anticipation, dreaming about this palace I could live in. I ran back to residence and asked everyone I knew if they wanted to move. No. No. No. Only one person was interested. I couldn't let this dream house go. It was across from the grocery store, Safeway. In three minutes, I could get groceries and have tea and toast whenever I wanted. McDonald's was across as well. If I wanted to go to a fancy restaurant, I could go to The Keg, a Canadian steak house. That place was a three-minute walk from the duplex. Yes, I could see my favourite place from the duplex as well—Foothills Hospital!

I called the landlady back that night and took the duplex the next day. I knew it would be gone if I didn't.

Welcome to my new big, beautiful new house. I even found a roommate at the last minute. My roommate? Aiyoh. Waheguru. It's Lin.

I move in December. I'm lucky. I don't have to buy anything as it's fully furnished. I have a huge queen-sized bed in my bedroom and a dresser with a mirror. There is a washer and dryer, and no coins needed. It is luxury compared to the dorm room I shared with Lin. It's big enough to avoid smelly socks. You know, life is strange. I keep learning when you try to run away, life just follows you.

Tell me what happened with Manjit.

Love to Soni and Roni.

Simran

4 DECEMBER 1986

Hello Simran,

I don't want to talk about Henry. He's dead to me. I have included a newspaper clipping below. That bastard married the Japanese model, the one I saw him with at Raffles Hotel. Look at the happy couple. It was the wedding of the year in Singapore. All the bigwigs and who's who of Singapore attended. I wept when I saw the photos of lavish spreads, famous people, and the happy couples. The lucky bride dripped with diamonds. My mother went berserk when she read the news and saw the photograph. She blamed me for letting this opportunity slip through my hands. She said I should have seduced him. Trapped him. Promised him anything he wanted. Married him

Even my father who never speaks had to pipe up and tell my mom to stop. "This is her life, ok, not yours. Go and cry in your bed. Go dream about your billionaire."

Mom stomped off in a fit.

For the first time, I looked at my father in a different light. I hadn't thought about HIS disappointments and broken dreams. He had married my mother for love. How had the years embittered his hopes? Had she destroyed him through her constant nagging and thoughtless accusations about being a terrible husband? Was that what I had done to Chin as well? I was hit by the sudden realization I had destroyed my love with Chin because of my grandiose constructions of what ifs. It was perpetuated by my mother's disappointments about love. I should have embraced the harsh realities of the sweet possibilities of savouring that companionship with Chin instead of running away. Because of my mother's influence,

I had repelled the very person that could have been my salvation.

I'm in Medan in a hotel room as I write this letter. I found Chin's whereabouts through a mutual friend who lived in Singapore. I decided to take a chance of a lifetime and fly to Medan. Apprehensive and excited, I called Chin as soon as my plane landed at the airport in Medan. Nervous, I hung up twice. On the third attempt, I summoned my courage to speak to Chin.

"Hello? Hello?" I heard Chin's familiar voice that had comforted me on so many occasions in Princeton.

I clung to the handle of the phone, desperate to touch Chin and see him. I could hear his heavy breathing on the other side.

Then he whispered my name. "Amy? Is that you? Amy?"

"I love you, Chin. I love you then, now and still. I want to be with you." I rambled on about regrets, loss, and possibilities. He listened in silence.

Silence stretched for an eternity. I closed my eyes and willed him to speak, to come back. I held the phone tightly to my left ear to catch the uneven gasps on the other side. We breathed in unison, till our breathing was in sync. Clutching the right side of the filthy phone kiosk, I prayed.

"Amy," I heard Chin's broken voice. "It's too late, my love. I'm married. Please don't call me ever again."

And then, click. Disconnected. I desperately put more and more coins in the phone, dialling furiously. The rings went on in perpetuity. I leaned my head against the phone kiosk and felt hot tears wet the nape of my neck. What a bloody fool I am. Did I need to fly to Medan to be rejected and learn the truth? It never crossed my mind that Chin could have found someone new. Our mutual friend must not have known. Married? My love. Gone.

I sat on the bench next to the phone kiosk at the airport in Medan. In a haze, I watched people scurry around me. Saying goodbye. Hugging. Kissing. Moving. In some sort of direction. Some meaning to their existence. Lugging suitcases and holding hands. I looked at the last coin in my hand as it nestled in the concave of my palm. Cold. Hard. Hollow. Alone.

Bitter tears glazed my sight. I took a taxi to the romantic hotel in Medan I had booked for my glorious reunion with Chin. I flopped on the king-sized bed littered with rose petals I had requested. Emptiness and regret flowed through my veins.

There is no going back, is there? Tomorrow, I return to Singapore, to my lovelorn father and my embittered mother. The perfect ending for my loveless life.

Write later.

Amy

5 DECEMBER 1986

Hey Simran,

Are you sure you are getting a degree at that university? I laughed when I read about your missing arm. Sounds like you have an entertaining array of professors. Do you remember at junior college you were in love with your English teacher, Mr. Stoddard from London? Maybe, you've always held a fascination for professors and been a teacher's pet. I'm glad to see you've not changed too much.

Talking about British men, Phil, my new boyfriend from London has managed to get a job at the university here. He arrives next week. I am excited and apprehensive. After years of secrets and silence, I feel I can be myself and live my authentic life.

The only problem is there are casualties in my quest for freedom. My family is furious at me. My brother says I'm wrong to have a new boyfriend so soon. My mother advises me to make it work with Gopal for the sake of our children. On top of that, every day, at 7 p.m., Gopal calls me and cries like a baby on the phone, begging me to take him home. He promises he will change.

Gopal's parents won't speak to me. My sons are acting up and having a hard time adjusting to our separation. Most of our mutual friends have disowned me, including those that were my friends first. I ran into Gopal's cousin Vin at Cathay cinema two days ago. She simply walked right past me, clearly ignoring me when I called her name. What a slap in the face.

I'm conflicted. For a long time, I pretended to be happy. I went through the motions of life, living a farce. Being a daughter, a wife, a mother, a daughter-in-law, a good friend. It is numbing. It's time to discard all those masks. To live my authentic life means to disappoint many people. I have no doubts there will be more challenges when Phil arrives. I don't care. I long for a genuine embrace and a passionate kiss by someone who will treat me well.

Tell me more about you and your reinvented life in Calgary.

Love,

Anita

16 DECEMBER 1986

Dear Simran,

Are you crazy? You moved in with the girl you were trying to escape from. You ended up with Lin as your roommate. What the hell. I hope that Lin does not kill you in your sleep or the other way around. On the other hand, that house sounds big and beautiful. Maybe you are learning how to adapt.

As for me, I stayed with Mum and Papa for a week after the big confrontation with Manjit and the Queen. I didn't know what to do. Every hour, I changed my mind. Somehow, things felt different when I quietly observed my life objectively. I was a wife and a mother. I had rights and responsibilities. I deserved to find my place in my marriage.

You know, Simran, there's something strange about going back to your parents' house after you marry, what's more with kids. It didn't fit. Mummy and Papa were getting impatient with me. They treated me as a child, but I am not anymore. They worried about what people would say.

You know, the usual. "Stay home. Make sure no one sees you."

They were trying to make me invisible. Hidden. This is not what I want the rest of my life to be. I watched Mummy in the kitchen. I looked at my daughters crawling on the floor, playing with their Barbie dolls. I saw myself in the mirror. What is the life of a woman? It was time for me to decide!

That night, I went back to Manjit's house. Mummy and Papa were relieved. I can't even call Manjit's house my home, but I need to do something about that. I must make one for me and the girls. Manjit was shocked to see me. I wasn't sure if he was happy or disappointed. Now it felt different coming back to my husband's house. Manjit's mother hugged Soni and Roni and nodded at me. Things are going to be different. Let's see what happens.

Love,

Amrit

17 DECEMBER 1986

Dear Mummy,

One year ago at Christmas, I was scared, lonely and all alone in 3rd Kananaskis, my residence building at the University of Calgary. Everyone on residence had left for their Christmas holidays. I had been in Calgary for four months, and I had no idea about the customs and celebrations of Canadians here. Good news, Mummy. This time, one year later, I am not lost. As Amrit told you, I have moved into a huge house ten minutes away from the university. It is bigger than our flat in Singapore. I listened to your advice about having a kitchen and cooking. My rent is cheaper than what I had to pay for the dormitory room at Kananaskis hall. I only pay $250 a month. I have included photos of my palace. I love it.

I know how expensive it is for Papa to send me to Calgary. I save more money now. I cut corners. The grocery store is a five minutes' walk from my house. Now I buy bread, cheese, tea, fruits, vegetables, and milk. I never have to eat at the cafeteria anymore. You know I can't cook. Don't worry. I improvise. I eat toast and butter. I can make an omelet. I make rice and stir fry vegetables and put soy sauce in. I'm proud of myself.

Look at photo of my kitchen, Mummy. It is huge. Maybe I can learn to cook from my friends. I should have paid attention to your cooking. You are the best chef in the world. I missed my chance. Ok, Mummy, when I come for my holidays, I will be your student. Not too late to learn how to make chicken curry and gobi aloo from you. In return, I can show you how to make spaghetti, tomato sauce and Caesar salad. Yes, I open a jar of Prego sauce for the pasta, but I make it special by adding mushrooms and broccoli.

The next photograph is of my roommate, Lin, the grumpy Malaysian girl I was trying to escape from. This time, Lin is staying home for Christmas, so I'm not alone. But being alone doesn't worry me anymore. This house feels like a home. I have decorated my home with our family photographs. I got a Christmas tree from the store. You can see it in the corner of the dining room. It is an artificial tree and is as tall as me. I bought some Xmas ornaments from Kmart. I'm not sure what is the right way, but it looks good. Makes me feel like a true Canadian. Guess what. I even bought a present for Lin. I bought her a dozen white socks. I hope she likes them.

You know Lin wasn't my first choice as a roommate. I didn't want to move in with her at all. But life has a way of showing you what you need to learn. There are a few advantages to Lin. You will like this part because Lin doesn't drink, have parties or have any men come over. She is annoying but still better than nothing. Luckily, the place is big, so I don't even have to be in the same room as her. I think Lin loves me and hates me at the same time.

Last year, I had a last-minute invitation to Charlie's house when Charlie came by the dormitory and found me alone. He took me to his family home, and I ate delicious chicken curry, goat curry, spicy potatoes, rice, and roti. This year, for Christmas, my Canadian friend Julie is coming. Two days ago, she came by with a turkey and shoved it in the fridge to thaw. I can't wait for my first Canadian Christmas meal. Julie said she will come over and make us a meal of turkey, stuffing, mashed potatoes, gravy, cranberry sauce, buttered carrots, salad, buns, and pumpkin dessert. I know—I don't know what half of these things are and I am salivating.

When I think about it, in all our lives in Singapore, we have never even once turned on the oven. I heard that turkey tastes like chicken. Turkey? We never had turkey in Singapore, did we? First time ever. I will find out on Christmas Day.

December is cold here. The window in the living room is foggy, and there are icicles hanging on the bush outside. The ground is covered in snow as high as up to my knee. Here, when it snows, you have to shovel the sidewalks and giant trucks sweep the roads.

Still, everything is icy and slippery. It's different for my Canadian friends who grew up in Canada. They know how to survive winters. I still struggle and think I am in sunny Singapore. I don't dare to drive here, and they drive on the other side of the road. Every day, when I walk past the lampposts, I want to touch them with my bare hands or lick the snow off the post. Luckily, Julie laughed at me and warned me not to do something stupid like that or my tongue would be stuck to the metal. Thank God she told me.

Every day in Calgary, in the winter months, the snow feels different. Some days, it gets freezing cold and there is a wind chill, which makes the temperature drop to minus twenty or more. The weather news says exposed skin can freeze in one minute. I don't even know how I can go out. When you come from a different country with no snow, you don't understand the cold. You don't understand how to walk, how to dress, how to buy the right coat, gloves, toques, scarves and boots. It is confusing. I try to watch my Canadian friends and learn from them, but I am used to hot, hot, hot Singapore.

I'm thankful for my new place in Calgary. It feels cozy and peaceful. I look out the window, and the scenery is breathtaking. Look at the photo of the white snow outside my house. Can you believe it? It took time to adjust to life in Calgary as an outsider. I felt loneliness and fear when I was on my own last Christmas. I went through many challenges as a student to get good grades. I came across people who were mean and untrustworthy. But I also felt joy in my accomplishments and experienced unforgettable moments.

Happy New Year, Mummy. Soon, it will be 1987. Time is flying.

Love to all,

Simran

18 DECEMBER 1986

Dear Amy,

I imagined you at the airport in Medan, calling Chin, only to learn that he was married. I felt your sorrow and pain. You must have believed things would be different for you to fly all the way there. You gave it your best shot, and that counts for something. It's better to know the truth rather than keep wondering. It's time to permanently close that chapter and start new ones. I'm truly sorry, Amy.

I am the hopeful and eternal optimist when it comes to love. In fact, I met my dream boy. This is a boy my family would approve of. Not only would I come back to Singapore with my degree but also an Indian husband. Ravi is from Edmonton. He is finishing his fourth year in Engineering. Oh, what a successful combination we would be. And tall, dark and handsome to boot.

"Waaaah. An Engineer," I heard my family's happy echo in my head.

I met Ravi at the last International Students' party on campus, a month ago, even though he is as local and Canadian as you can get. I had not considered this option of a nice Indian boy before. A Canadian boy with Indian sensibilities. Or an Indian boy with Canadian sensibilities. I hit the jackpot. I secretly planned our wedding in my head since I was well-versed in the ways of Indian matrimony by now. I quizzed him about his family background. I asked about his prospects. I gazed into his eyes in loving acknowledgement of our perfect match. God sent!

Every day, Ravi picked me up from Craigie Hall at the University of Calgary. He drove me home so I would not have to walk the fifteen minutes in the freezing cold. I checked all the boxes in my head. I wondered if Mummy had kept that beautiful silk sari from my broken engagement in Singapore. Maybe, this time, I would relish wearing it for my engagement to darling Ravi.

What a nice Indian boy! Patient, charming, well-behaved. He understood me and my Indian boundaries. Last Friday, he came armed with red roses, sparkling wine and strawberry cheesecake. A lethal combination. Maybe he might propose to me. You know Indian marriage timing—as soon as possible. I giggled in nervous anticipation. I felt a stirring and attraction for Ravi. What would it feel like to make passionate love with him, after we were married, of course?

The evening unfolded well. Lin was out. We had the place to ourselves. The bubbles went to my head, and they released Ravi's inner demons and usual restraint. We gazed into each other's eyes. I wanted to remember this special moment of tenderness and loving embraces, but something felt off. Ravi kept asking me about my sweet spots.

Do virgins have sweet spots? I thought curiously.

I kissed him tenderly on his cheek when he raised my chin, our eyes locked in love. True Indian love, of course. Ravi whispered in my ear, while his hands began to urgently search for my breasts. He ripped my buttons off.

"Slow down," I urged. "Take it easy," I cautioned.

"I have slowed down for a month," he whispered in my ear while biting my earlobe.

I let go of my guard for a moment. What would it feel like to give in to my future husband? Desire. Affection. Tenderness. Gazing in each other's soul. Right?

Ravi's heavy panting distracted me. His hands took over with a brute strength I had not seen before. He pushed me down on the sofa and clambered over me. I could feel his penis unfurl—good job of burying it all these months!

You see, it's not that I want to die a virgin or anything. But this Ravi was a different version of my respectful Indian boy. Err, his panting and drunk slurring included a monologue about a belt, tying me up or was it down? A threesome. Or was it a foursome. Oh, and with men and women. It was at that precise moment that my dreams came tumbling down. I wasn't looking to join a sex cult! I just wanted a nice Indian husband.

I shoved Ravi off with all my strength, jumped off the couch and stared at the man writhing in some sexual ecstasy with his belt in his hand. Aiyoh. He didn't look that tall, dark, or handsome to me, anymore. My dreams dashed. How naive and clueless was I about the world of sex out there.

I heard Mummy's voice in my head, the one ingrained from when I was ten.

"If you hold hands with a boy, you can get pregnant."

If Papa saw me with this boy, he would cut his legs off. Thanks, Papa. All I knew was to get married. Not date. Not have sex. Not have many boyfriends. No wonder I had stopped talking to the other two men who were interested in me. I chose to focus on Ravi, my potential husband.

Here he was, my dreamboat turned nightmare. Belts, threesomes and swinging both ways. I was at a loss. How do I handle a horny, drunk Indian boy from hell? I was unprepared.

I prayed in my head, "Waheguru, Waheguru."

There is a God. Guess who walked in at the precise moment? Yes. My salvation. My best friend in the whole world. The woman who deserves a medal. Lin. We heard the front door jiggle and fling open.

Then, that beautiful screech. "Why is it so dark here?"

Click. The lights flooded the living room.

Lin looked at Ravi on the couch, assessed the situation and asked anyways, "What the hell is going on?"

Thank you, clueless goddess. Shocked, Ravi jumped up, rearranged his erect member, and clumsily put on his belt.

"I should go," he mumbled.

"Yes," Lin yelped, saving me the trouble.

Sadly, my husband dreams were dashed as Ravi raced to the door, grabbed his winter coat, and shoved his feet into his shoes. He ran straight to his car.

I convulsed in laughter, looked at Lin and said, "Come, I have cheesecake for you. Have a slice. Have two. Tell me about your day."

Lin's face lit up as she nodded. We settled in at the dining table. We polished off the cheesecake and the bubbly. I confided in her about Ravi and told her what she had walked into.

Lin burst out laughing. "Your future husband?"

I looked at my saviour with new respect.

"Tell me about you, Lin," I urged. I was drunk and happy enough to listen.

Lin cocked her head and appraised me before she relaxed. "I'm getting terrible marks in all six of my engineering courses," she declared.

And Lin did some impressive impersonations of her engineering professors. I hadn't put much thought to how difficult it must be for a woman in a male dominated engineering field. Lin's tears rolled down her cheeks as she worried about her future. I listened and reached out my hand and touched hers. Our eyes locked in mutual understanding. I could see Lin was doing her best to survive, just like me.

The evening ended with two women. One barely passing her courses and me, a Harlequin heroine with hopes for an Indian groom totally dashed. No belts. No writhing bodies. Lin and I got drunk on our one bottle of exquisite champagne! Baby Duck.

My goodness. Nothing prepares you for an X-rated life and love with a belt. Yes, it's over with Ravi.

Till the next time,

Simran

26 DECEMBER 1986

Dear Amrit,

I read your last letter with interest—you went back to Manjit and the Queen. No, I think you went back to make it your place. I get it. It's hard to survive in Singapore.

Can you believe I have completed three semesters of university in Calgary? I have more good days than tough days on my own here now. One thing I am learning about is how to date. I have no clue what the right way is, except what I watched on television shows. Here is one admirer I don't know what to do about. A tall Caucasian Canadian boy. He is husky, has intense blue eyes and two-inch blond spiky hair. Very different from Indian boys I have to marry one day. He is exotic.

Wait, his forehead is large. Oh, you know who he looks like— like that guy from *Addams Family*, the show we watched all the time. That one, with the big forehead. His name is Carl. I can't figure out how old he is. I am guessing he is ten years older, but he won't tell me. Does age matter?

I met him in my literature class. Here's the thing with him. He's kind of weird. I mean, he just follows me. After class yesterday, I went to Mac Hall to get lunch and, boom, he was standing in line behind me. Then, in the evening, I went home and boom, there were purple orchids in my mailbox. The problem is he is not much of a talker. Shy and bashful. I am unsure what to do. It's tiring initiating all the conversation while he stares at me.

Finally, Carl invited me over to his house for dinner. I heard mummy's voice in my head, but he had roommates, so I felt safe going. I mean, I don't know any cues. I was apprehensive, but Carl picked me up, took me to his house, made a dinner I had not tasted before—salmon, mashed potatoes, and bean salad. White wine. Chocolate cake for dessert. I enjoyed my Canadian experience. I was touched by how sweet he was. Unfortunately, I was bored. Not much conversation. He told me how beautiful I was—that was our one-way conversation.

The next week, he came to my house to watch TV with me. Mostly, he sat on the couch and stared at me. I tried my best to initiate a conversation. I asked questions. I told him about myself. Frankly, it was like an interrogation. Exhausted, I gave up and ushered him out with a polite goodbye.

When Carl left, Lin said, "Err. What's wrong with this guy? He's strange."

Oh my God. If weird Lin thinks Carl is strange, is there hope? Disappointing. How many more men do I have to date to find my Prince Charming? Back home, in our arranged marriage world, everything came ready to go—a husband, and a wedding. So far, in Calgary, my dating record is dismal. I have met strange men. Here is one more.

My Indian mentality went to "Why can't Carl be the right one? He's nice. He adores me. A marriage made in heaven."

That's when I realized that it was like you and Manjit. Manjit was the nice, quiet man, great on paper, but you had no opportunity to explore if there was a connection, to talk to him for more than a few hours, to enjoy each other's company and see if you were both compatible. Hmmm. Maybe I do understand western dating, after all. Investigative explorations for future husbands. The next day, I broke up with Carl. He was heartbroken. I was relieved. Hah. I'm happily single again.

Hey, guess what. It was Christmas yesterday. I couldn't wait to have Christmas dinner in my own house. The plan was for Julie to come over to make Christmas dinner for me and Lin, Canadian style. I had thawed the turkey as directed. I bought a bag of potatoes, can of cranberry sauce, salad, and pumpkin pie. Strange, right? Nothing was familiar to me from the meals we had in Singapore.

Julie called me at 2 p.m. Typical Julie, last minute procrastinator, she was still writing her final English essay that was already late, and she was getting an extension. I should have seen this coming.

"You have to make the turkey," she shrieked over the phone.

"Are you crazy?" I screamed on the phone.

"Do it! Write down the instructions. See you at 7 p.m."

I stared uncomfortably at the turkey that looked like a little baby. I had never touched giant poultry. Then, as instructed, I washed, patted it dry, added salt and pepper, and put it in the oven at 350 degrees Fahrenheit. You know Mummy never used our oven in Singapore to bake anything. She used it as a storage bin. I nervously stared into the glass window of the oven, peering in every ten minutes to make note of any changes to the turkey. Praying it would brown.

Lin sauntered out of her room every half hour. "Burn the turkey, yet? At least McDonald's is right across," she said.

I glared at her and resisted the swear words that were on the tip of my tongue.

Julie finally arrived at 6 p.m. Relieved, I handed her the apron. She took over turkey duties. On the dining table, I laid my first Christmas dinner spread. I felt proud as the Christmas tree lights glimmered and cast shadows on the table laden with the first time offerings Julie had conjured. Wow. It was better than the hell of last year.

Julie, Lin, and I sat at the dining table. Lin opened our favourite Baby Duck champagne and poured it into fancy white stemmed wine glasses. Julie carved the turkey and put delicious slices of white and dark meat on our plates. Oh, my goodness. It was the most delicious Xmas dinner, and I loved the cranberry sauce with every mouthful of juicy, tender turkey. Lin and I wanted more, so Julie did her part and cut the turkey in two. She let out a scream.

I jumped up in alarm. "What? What?"

Julie pulled out a bag of something from inside the cavity. It was a bag of turkey giblets and innards in a bag.

"What the hell," Julie screamed. "You were supposed to take that out!"

I looked at her and chuckled. "You expected me to put my hand up that turkey's butt? I don't think so."

Who knew there was a plastic bag up there? Thank God we had dinner before we discovered that bag!

Maybe, just maybe, after cooking Christmas dinner, I am a little more Canadian now.

Best turkey chef ever,

Love,

Simran

30 DECEMBER 1986

Hey Anita,

Last year, you sent me a letter from Penang, wishing me a happy New Year. It's my turn. 1987 will be amazing. A lot has happened to all of us in one year. You have reinvented yourself, punted Gopal to the curb, and have a new hero, Phil, who is on his way from London. Can you believe it?

Me? I am getting closer to my dream of getting a degree. Last year, I didn't even know if I would survive on my own on the third floor of Kananaskis Hall, my dorm building. Every single soul had left for their Christmas holidays. A lost soul.

Now, I am queen of my own castle on Uxbridge Drive N.W. Calgary. Happy New Year, my friend. I'm looking forward to the next chapter of our lives.

Love,

Simran

3 JANUARY 1987

Hi Simran,

Happy New Year. You are a real Calgarian now. How long do you have to be in a place to be legitimate? You seem to be more settled in, and your new place sounds nice. When Gopal and I drove through Calgary on our way to Vancouver, we loved the openness, the green, the space, the mountains. It was breathtaking.

Phil, my new boyfriend from London, finally arrived in Singapore on New Year's Eve. Symbolic, huh? He didn't find a place to stay. I ended up bringing him to my house. I don't know how Gopal found out but there was a knock on my door the next day. I was in the kitchen, so Phil opened the door and kaboom. Gopal punched Phil in the face. I ran to the door and Gopal was slurring his words and cursing. Gopal sobbed uncontrollably and shook with fury. Phil held on to his broken nose, shocked at the blood on his hand and shirt. Phil screamed at Gopal and kicked him, while clutching his own nose. It was mayhem.

One by one, the neighbours ran out of their houses to watch the bloody performance. The boys woke up, screaming. It was a Chinese opera wayang. All the men in my life are berserk.

I dragged Phil and the boys in, shut the door and gave Phil a wet towel and an ice pack. He moaned and groaned in pain. I left Phil and scooped the boys up to calm them. I put the exhausted boys back to bed. I felt numb and on automatic pilot. Once the boys settled, I heard a sound outside and opened the door. There he was— Gopal—still outside.

Gopal looked like a zombie. I felt pity for him. I pulled him up by his arms, took him down to the main floor of the block of flats, and stopped a taxi nearby to take him home. He clung to my arm, refusing to let go. I pried his fingers off and shoved him into the taxi. I gave the taxi driver Gopal's address and money for the fare. I stood on the side of the road and watched the taxi drive off. Alamak, Sim. I was exhausted. I started my New Year with a bang, indeed.

As soon as I walked in the door of my flat, the phone calls began. Gopal's mum and dad were on the other end screaming. I told them Gopal was on his way home in a taxi and to wait for him. Then my mum and dad called, shouting at me. They demanded to know why I let Phil come to the house when the boys were there. I hung up. I went into the bedroom and Phil shrieked at me about Gopal. I have opened Pandora's box.

Happy New Year to you, Sim. Things can change at the drop of a hat. I hope that your life is less dramatic than mine.

Keep you posted.

Anita

2 JANUARY 1987

Hello Simran,

It's good you have moved to a new house with a kitchen. The photographs of your new place are beautiful. Such a big house you have found at a good price. Well done. Next is for you to cook. It is easy. You must try tomorrow. Ok. Follow this. Go to the grocery store. Safeway, right? Buy the ingredients. Cut an onion, ginger, garlic and fry in a little vegetable oil. Put cauliflower pieces and chopped tomatoes. Throw a little salt, pepper some spices like haldi and masala. You can also put potato cubes if you like. Fry for ten minutes. Cover with a lid and let cook for fifteen minutes. Sprinkle some chopped cilantro over. Aloo Gobi recipe. Just like that and you can eat with rice. Or buy roti and eat with that. Easy right?

I have never eaten turkey in my life. You can make the same way like chicken curry but use turkey. Same as aloo gobi. Use chilli powder, haldi and masala. Fry some onions, ginger and garlic first till brown. Make turkey curry. Can also put potatoes if you want. Once you know the first steps then same for most dishes.

When I came to Singapore at sixteen years old, I didn't know how to cook. I learned. I watched your grandmother how she cooks. She made me cut onions, ginger, garlic and tomatoes. Here is one tip I learned. If you put onion skin on the top of your head with a hair-clip it will stop your eyes getting tears from the onions when you cut them. Try.

Your sister Amrit can cook now. No choice. She must learn. Once a girl is married, she has to feed her family. I give her my recipes. She follows them carefully. Her mother-in-law's cooking is not that good. Their cooking is different style from us. The secret is the spices. Here I go to Serangoon Road and ask the man at the spice shop to make fresh masala mixture. I pick all the right ingredients and the man at the shop grinds all fresh. I only go to that one store because his spices are the best. Next time you come we will go to that store. You can take special masala back to Calgary.

Good you are saving money. Your father is working extra to pay for everything. You know it is expensive. When we change from Singapore dollar to Canadian dollar it is too high. Listen to my advice. You must study hard, finish your degree and come home immediately.

It is better you stay with Malaysian girl. She understands your background. She is better safety. Don't bring boys home ok. Better not drink any alcohol. That is bad thing to do. Make sure you lock the door at night. Put double lock. You girls have to be careful when you are on your own.

I like your photo of the snow outside your house in Calgary. So much snow, my goodness. I saw snow in Kashmir when I was sixteen years old. It felt like soft cotton wool. It was cold and I shivered all night. It's better if you wear thick socks with your slippers. Put on a shawl that I packed in your suitcase. Better not to go out when it is cold.

New Year, new life. One more year and you will be back to Singapore. Your teaching degree was helpful. Give you one year off. Come back and start teaching. Good job and good pay in Singapore. You didn't need a degree from Calgary because teaching degree was enough. Never mind. Babaji will bless you and give you good life.

Love you,

Mummy

23 JANUARY 1987

Hey Simran,

I enjoyed reading about your turkey cooking lesson on Christmas day. I have never eaten turkey in my life. How? Was it good? I don't even know where to buy turkey in Singapore. Your friend Julie tricked you well to make the Christmas dinner. It was a good plan for her to come late.

You have more luck with the turkey instead of men. Poor Carl. I think he was in love with you, and you dumped him because he was boring. You are exotic. He must have liked your long black hair that flowed to your waist and your soft brown skin. Big beautiful brown eyes. Your cheeky smile. You are a new flavour for him. Maybe he thought you were a well-behaved and quiet Indian girl who would cook and clean for him. Hahahaha. No such luck with you. You are too independent and strong for any man. You will drive a man crazy.

It's better for a woman to be tough. For me, there is no escape. My life is following Mum's and I'm a boring housewife. I'm back now in the house with Manjit. Things feel different because I am more aware of things now. I am asking what an arranged marriage is. You put two strangers together and tell them to begin a life together. Just like that the man and woman must find a way to exist as husband and wife.

Some people are lucky, like Seema, Deepti and Usha, our cousins. They were matched with the right men. Their arranged marriages were happy. Successful. I talked to Seema last month and she told me how she is in love with her husband. She didn't know him before marriage. But after marriage they are together and Gurdip her husband adores her. They spend time together. He takes her everywhere. She said it was like they were dating during their marriage. And their sex life is good.

I'm disappointed why my marriage can't be like Seema and Gurdip's? Manjit and I are not compatible. You know I had no choice. Just for our family and reputation's sake, Manjit and I were put together. I don't know what to do at this point. There is no change in Manjit. He continues to go out till late at night. We have little communication. Last week, I asked him if he wanted to go back to his girlfriend. He said he loves her and was forced to marry me. Now he feels stuck because we have two children. He says he won't leave me because, *What will people say*? He told me that his mother will never allow him to marry his Chinese girlfriend because she is from a different race. His mother threatened to kill herself if Manjit did not marry an Indian girl. I see that he could not live his life by his choice. I felt sad for him. I felt sad for me. I feel sad for the children. We are all victims of this tradition. What to do?

Manjit's mother is an interesting lady. Her husband died ten years ago, and she fully relies on Manjit to take care of her since he is the only son. I understand her situation. I mean, when I think about it, what can Manjit's mother do? How can a widow with no education or job survive in Singapore? We are all stuck in life's expectations. Really, you are smart to escape this trap. I think the only way for a woman to survive is to be independent. Get an education. Get a job. Whether the man lives or dies, a woman can still carry on with her life. Not stuck like Mummy, Queen or me.

Sim, it is smart of you to get your degree. Be strong. Be independent. I am back to the grind to being trapped in this vicious cycle. I have to think about what to do. I have to come up with a plan.

Love,

Amrit

24 JANUARY 1987

Hi Simran,

Why are you attracting strange men in Calgary? That Ravi with his belt sounds like a creep. Maybe it is the men in Calgary. You should have gone away to somewhere more sophisticated, like New York or Boston. Your Lin amuses me. That is a love hate relationship, isn't it? Seems like she wants to be with you. At least you didn't waste the cheesecake.

I'm struggling with Henry using me, then marrying some young tramp. I'm heartbroken Chin is married, and there is no going back to my true love. My mother convinced me to pick money over love. I gambled with Henry and lost. I should have stood up to my mother and married Chin. But I did not have the guts. I lost everything!

Simran, I'm worried about my mum. She is getting worse. She started drinking. Openly. She always hid her brandy in coffee mugs, but I could smell the alcohol. When I get back from work, usually late, she is conked out on the couch, drunk. My father doesn't bother anymore. He stays in his room as usual. The house is in disarray. I pull Mum up, and she falls in my arms. She is heavy. Then, she stirs and starts a tirade. Cursing and swearing. Without fail, she complains bitterly about her life. She denigrates my father in a voice loud enough that dad can hear her in his room. No wonder he doesn't come out of his room. What has happened to all that love my parents once had? I'm tired of being caught in the middle and watching this marriage unravel.

Then, as I take her to her room, she starts on me. I struggle to get her into her bed.

"You…you, such a loser. Can't get a husband. Had a chance with

Henry and now how? What? Stay with your parents till you die, is it? Stupid."

Her words are like vicious daggers that destroy my confidence and hope. I sacrificed my love for her stupid materialistic dreams. Like a filial daughter, I followed her demands and fell for her emotional blackmail. I went after Henry, a man I didn't even like. My mum lived her dream of being wealthy vicariously through me, and I let her do it because I thought she was right. I listened to her because I wondered if she was right, that money could buy love.

I regret I didn't make my own decisions. When she came to New Jersey, she threatened to disown me if I stayed with Chin. She didn't approve of him. She used the money she had spent on me as a weapon to sabotage my relationship. I often wonder if I should have chosen Chin instead of my mum. Honestly, I didn't have the guts. I couldn't, because of our Asian views about our parents and the notion of filial piety. I accepted that mum knew best for me, and I owed her my obedience. It's ironic that although I was in the west when I was getting my degree at Princeton University and experiencing western ideas of independence and choice, in the end, I accepted our eastern values. It's the paradox of the foreign student who is caught up in two conflicting worlds.

I hate watching Mum lose her happiness, peace of mind and her identity. She let her mind run amok with notions that being wealthy means being happy. She believes that money buys happiness. I think that she fantasizes about her Singapore dream of living in a mansion in Singapore and driving a fancy Mercedes Benz—only affordable by the few elites in Singapore. I mean, who has millions of dollars to afford this Singapore lifestyle? Not us working peons, not even with our white-collar jobs.

I wonder who my mum is? I simply don't know anymore. I don't want to ask my father because he is trapped in his prison as well. He has checked out of this marriage. He's like a zombie who goes through the motions of life. I'm stuck in the middle of this unhappy home. Is this what the road to love ends up at? I am worried about Mum. She won't see a therapist—you know Singaporeans. How are they going to talk about their shame and pain to a stranger? Can't lose face, right. I don't know what to do.

Here I am in this fiasco. In the morning, I put on my professional mask. I have a great job. I run a department at work. I have a good working life. That degree from Princeton University was put to good use. Then, in the evening, I go home to secrets and lies. We wear masks, and we suffocate behind them. I worry about me at my mother's age. Will I also get the disease of unhappiness? My irony will be I gave up my love with Chin.

I hope that your love life picks up. Stop dating the losers, please. I guess you can come back to Singapore and have an arranged marriage, so you don't have to worry.

Best wishes,

Amy

1 FEBRUARY 1987

Dear Anita,

From your last letter, I see your life is turning into a British-Hindi movie filled with fistfights and dramatic overtures. There are so many players involved in this one. I worry about the boys. I worry about you. Wouldn't it be better for Phil to stay on his own rather than be in your house? We all need time to grieve. Time to heal. Time to move on. Go slow, girl. My mom always said to me, *Out of the frying pan into the fire.* Whatever you do, don't rush in and marry Phil.

Am I a real Calgarian? Good questions. What colour do you have to be? What country do you have to be born in? I have been thinking of the idea of immigration and belonging. My parents came from India and lived in Singapore all their lives. They made Singapore their final home. They love Singapore. I am a first-generation Singaporean. Born and bred.

Now in Calgary, I wonder where I belong? The country of birth or the country of choice? I didn't choose where I was born. Can I choose where I want to be? I meet people in Calgary who have come from all over the world. They love Calgary.

However, when I go to the immigration office down at the Harry Hays building in Calgary to renew my student visa, I feel fear. It is a place of dread. I am ushered into this large room. There are people from all over the world. People of all colours and races sit in hard-backed chairs in the waiting room. All of us clutch little pieces of paper with numbers on them, waiting to be summoned. No one engages in chit-chat. We sit and stare ahead. For some reason, I always feel like a guilty outsider.

That day, while I waited for my turn, I looked at the officers behind the counters; they were mostly White officers. I watched them. No smiles. No welcome. Loud. Impatient. It makes me feel awkward for being there. That afternoon, I cringed when the tall White male officer behind counter one raised his voice at the immigrant from Sudan who couldn't speak English well or understand what the officer was saying to him. The officer repeated his demands for a specific letter, loud enough that everyone else in the large waiting room could hear. Then, the officer exchanged annoyed glances with his colleagues on his right and left—some sort of mutual acknowledgement.

The poor young Sudanese man shook his head, dropped his bag of documents, and looked around for help. No one dared to step up. Why do people talk loudly and slowly in English to people of colour and to immigrants? All of us non-Canadians witnessed the spectacle as the officer scolded the young man for the missing letter and ordered him to come back. The Sudanese man looked apologetically at all of us and hung his head. I felt his embarrassment and distress.

That's how I feel whenever I go to the immigration office. Apologetic. Awkward. I don't want to upset any officer, or he or she could throw me out of the country. My turn was next.

I stumbled to the counter, and the unsmiling old White male officer in his fifties glared at me. I nervously pushed my documents under the partition. My throat constricted. I wanted to ask for more time, but fear silenced me. The officer noisily shuffled through my papers. His stamp angrily made its mark on my precious document. I didn't argue. I didn't look up. I bowed my head and grabbed the renewed visa. I knew about the immigration drill now. I took whenever and whatever time they added to my student visa. I knew to have all my documents ready. Extend visa. Pay money. No use arguing. Just keep paying.

Once I got the stamped document from the surly officer, I ran out of the immigration office at the Harry Hays building down in Chinatown. I stepped out of the building and could breathe again.

I went to the Chinese restaurant across the Harry Hays building and had chicken rice. A touch of back home to calm me down. I relaxed and released my pent-up anxiety as I stared at the stamped visa. Permission to stay in Calgary for a little more. Then, I saw that young Sudanese man in the parking lot. I sighed. I did not envy his return trip to the Harry Hays building. A nightmare.

That is what is interesting about being a foreigner in Calgary. I struggle to belong all the time. At the immigration office. In the classroom. It's exhausting. It's that notion of *they are better than me* that infuriates me. Ok. Take Professor Shit, as us students named him in our World Literature class. He's a first-class asshole. The man does not know any insightful information about world literature. It is obvious to all of us students. He can't even answer our questions about the texts picked for his own class. How embarrassing for him.

Here's the scoop of Professor Shit. Every Thursday, for four months, for our three-hour class, he wears this same Hawaiian shirt: purple, with large flowers. The middle button bursts at his gut. Naturally, the ringleaders in class came up with, "Sure happy it's Thursday" shirt. Got it? Shit.

For my last assignment in his class, I wrote an essay on Singapore literature. I picked Catherine Lim's, *The Serpent's Tooth*. I loved every moment researching our Singapore literature.

I thought, *yes, finally this is my comfort zone—Singapore. Not meadows, sheep, poorhouses, unhappy women, or Shakespeare. Here is literature from my country, my background, my world. I got this!*

That day in class, when I got my essay back, I stared at it for an eternity. Here we go, again! It brought back feelings of inadequacy and shame. The grade was a shocking C. I marched to Professor Shit's office and demanded to know why. He stared at me, guffawed, coughed and couldn't give me any clear reasons. For God's sakes, he knew nothing about Singapore literature.

"Please explain my C, Professor." I almost said Professor Shit.

Finally, he looked at me and said, "It's…it's…just that you don't write like us."

I stared at him. I felt hot tears burn my cheeks, and I didn't want him to see me cry. My second year. Getting A's in my other classes, and this bozo tells me there is a "me" and there is an "us". Once again, I was relegated to the role of an outsider.

I got up and walked out of Professor Shit's office, but something made me stop in my tracks. I turned back, walked to his desk, and put my essay on his desk.

"I am appealing this grade."

The look on the professor's face was priceless. His eyes bulged, and he coughed uncomfortably. He nodded his head. Enough was enough. Another shit to deal with, but this time, I was determined to stand up for us outsiders. Bring it on, Professor Shit. Show me what you know.

I look forward to your adventures with Phil.

Till the next letter,

Simran

3 FEBRUARY 1987

Dear Mummy,

You are a great chef, Mummy. I know you could transform this turkey into delicious turkey curry, but the way turkey is cooked here in Calgary is different. The Canadian way. They put the whole turkey in the oven for three hours or more. They bake it at 375 Fahrenheit. You have never baked anything in our oven at home. I did not want to learn how to cook when I was in Singapore because you warned me that no man would marry me if I could not cook. I liked the sound of that—to marry no one because I was a bad cook and wife.

The funny part about living with Lin is learning patience. I give and take, mostly take, it seems. Lin has terrible manners. She flings my bedroom door open without knocking. She lurks in the kitchen and listens when I am having a private conversation with my friend since the house phone is in the dining room. She insults my friends when they come over. I ignore her most of the time. I tried talking to her about these issues.

She stares at me, shrugs her shoulders, and says, "I don't care."

What is the answer to that? Maybe, this is good practice for a husband. Close one eye. Close one ear. Don't argue.

I wanted to work in Calgary so I could help to pay for my education. I found out how strict the laws are. If I am caught working, I will be thrown out of the country. The best I can do is spend as little as I can. I feel guilt. I must succeed. I must.

Miss you,

Simran

Dear Amrit,

I'm sorry to hear that Manjit made the choice to carry on with his mistress. I see you adapting to life as a wife and a mother. I admire the way you adjusted even though you had no say in your own marriage choice. I know you sacrificed your hopes and dreams to accept this married life. I can't imagine if the tables were turned, and you carried on an affair while married to Manjit. Now that is double standard. Men get away with murder.

I am angry to hear this, Amrit. I'll come back and you can live with me. That's the problem with how women are trapped in unhappy marriages. There is no way out, it seems. It's impossible to live on your own in Singapore because it's too expensive. It's hard to get a job that will pay the living expenses. Women follow everyone's expectations.

My Canadian friend Kathy lives alone. She moved out of her family's home when she was eighteen. Imagine that. She worked two jobs to pay her rent, food and even got a car. Now she is getting a loan to go to university. These are difficult things for a woman to do in Singapore, right?

I see different expectations for women in Indian marriages. I think we Indian women are like women in nineteenth century novels; I am reading *Jane Eyre*. Here is a heroine who struggles to be independent and yearns for love. She has no family or money but finds a job as a governess and survives. She has clear boundaries about marrying for love and leaves the man because he is married. Jane Eyre is a woman of action and courage.

Can you find a way? I know it won't be easy, but I can't bear for you to be stuck in a loveless marriage and relegated to the role of a governess for your children. The fact that you left Manjit for a few days and went back to Mummy and Papa's house to determine a course of action is the beginning sparks of change. You also decided to go back to Manjit and create a new direction for your marriage. That's doing something. You remind me of Jane Eyre and her strength to fight against injustice.

There are many versions for what an Indian woman can be. I met an older Indian woman in Calgary at a party I went to. I was drawn to her. She is fifty years old. Her name is Raj. She is a highly educated woman, with a Master's in Philosophy from McGill University. She picked a nice Indian man of her own choice at the age of thirty when everyone in India told her she was too old to marry. They have a good marriage. They left India shortly after that. She won't go back to India. She said once she had a taste of freedom and independence, she could not go to India where her in-laws expected her to be a good wife who stayed home and took care of her daughter and husband. Oh no. She became a Philosophy professor in Calgary.

Raj's daughter, who is eighteen, lives her life, carefree and uninhibited. She is a modern woman. Imagine that. If you can live your life for yourself, your daughters can choose how they want to live. That's what my education is showing me, that I can choose. You can choose. Your daughters can choose.

I met an unsuitable man from Ghana at an International Students' party on campus. Even though we were from different worlds, I fell for his flirtatious charm. Once I showed him my desire to be with him, he flipped. I showed up at his office. I waited for him. He became cold and distant, but enough to keep me coming back. I don't even know why I didn't walk away. Within a month, he changed his tactics. He was not very nice to me. He had no time for me. He was busy with his PhD studies in Geography. But he called me when he was bored. He wanted to meet me for lunch when he had time. Like a fool, I always showed up. This is the man I got attached to because I didn't understand how to date. The more he was unavailable, the more I was drawn to him. Stupid, right? I couldn't understand me, anymore. My friend Julie told me to dump him and leave. I couldn't.

One day last week, I went to Ben's office, but he was out. The door was open. I went in and sat down. I looked at the pile of papers on his desk and saw a blue aerogramme letter. It was open and placed on his desk. I picked it up and read it.

"Dear Ben…I love you. Thank you for the Bible and the ring. I accept your proposal. When you come back to Ghana in July, we shall get married."

Ben walked in and saw me with the letter in my hand. I crumpled it and threw it at his feet. I thought about you. I thought about Jane Eyre who refused to be with a man because he was married to someone else. So, this is the journey to finding love and a husband as an independent woman, eh. Finding love is not easy as I dreamed it would be. That night, I cried a little. I laughed a little. But it's ok. It's a journey to self. I'm figuring out men a little better now.

I wish I were back in Singapore, with you, talking to you in person, laughing, cursing, crying, and celebrating. Life can be confusing and lonely without a sister by my side.

Love,

Simran

7 FEBRUARY 1987

Hey Simran,

What a strange feeling to have to go to the immigration office at Harry Hays to get a visa to stay in Canada. You are the outsider! I love my Singapore. I will never leave this place where I know I belong. I am familiar with the land, and I adore the people here.

I felt your frustration about Professor Shit. There is this superior attitude by some people in the west that they are better writers and thinkers than us in the east. We saw that in our literature class with our visiting professor from Los Angeles. Do you remember Professor Alex Kennedy? He was frustrated at us, and it showed. He chastised us for being quiet in class and for not participating in discussions. He openly expressed his annoyance at our writing skills. How we all hated him for his arrogance. That was the best day when we heard that he quit and went back home.

It's like your Professor Shit and World Literature from a White man's perspective. I am glad you challenged your grade. Don't stop standing up for yourself. Hopefully, he realizes that just because you are from Singapore, it does not mean you are inferior in any way.

I have a headache every day. The Phil drama is now a Hindi movie. I have one weeping ex-husband to deal with. I have one confused British lover to acclimatize to Singapore life. The divorce proceedings have begun. Gopal is determined to fight every step of the way. Every day, there is an angry phone call from him. Drunk. Weeping. Shouting. Silent. I never know which Gopal will show up. I know Gopal is angry about Phil, and you are right; I should have waited for things to finalize before Phil moved in. I guess I'm learning about rules of love as well.

Also, between you and me, things with Phil are not as rosy as our one-week rendezvous was in London. His promised job teaching at Nanyang Technological University has become one course instead of three. Guess who pays rent and food? Yes. Me. Phil is younger, and he has not been around kids much. He is not coping well with the boys. And the boys feel the same conflict and are confused. Now, I play babysitter for all three of them. Oh man. My new love story is turning into a nightmare. I rushed things, and I regret it.

The only good thing about this love drama is sex is great! Much better than the play-dead-roll-over-no-reaction-Gopal. Like fucking a corpse. Why should I not have my needs met? This young one is well-equipped. He has the stamina to satisfy my cravings, finally. Our lovemaking is passionate and long. I have never had that many orgasms in one hour. Then, he holds me all night in his arms. Wow. One thing is right in my life. Finally, some bloody passion and excitement in the bedroom.

Ok, lah. Here's to international peace in our lives.

Later,

Anita

1 MARCH 1987

Dear Simran,

Wow, you are having many adventures with men in Calgary. I see that dating is not that easy. Now you have a chance to go shopping for a man. It's good you saw the letter. Saved you time and more heartache. You must follow your intuition. You must be alert and aware because there are no parents to check out if the man is good husband material. Even then, look at me. Maybe, if I had dated Manjit before I had to marry him, I would have found out the truth that he was in love with someone else. Enjoy your adventures and explorations. It's tough because you are learning the rules as you go along. At least you have choices.

I'm making changes in my life, slowly. You won't believe it, but I hired a maid the other day from the agency. I picked one from Indonesia. It is very expensive. I don't care. I borrowed some money from Papa and paid upfront for three months.

Then, I brought the maid home. I knew Manjit and the Queen could not argue. There is no turning back because the maid is hired on a one-year contract. I took a big step on my own. You should have seen the looks on both their faces.

Manjit asked angrily, "How can you make this decision to hire a maid? Who will pay her salary? You know I can't afford this extravagance."

"Oh yeah?" I said in a calm and quiet voice. "Do you think I am your maid? Cook and clean for you and your mother while you have an affair? Nothing is free. I will get a job to pay for this maid."

For the first time, Manjit was silenced. I could see his shocked look. What the hell?

Did he think he could bring a virgin from one family to be his slave in his house? I've been observing him. He's a coward. He can't make decisions. His mother controls him but she can't control me. I am glad she has a safe, comfortable home with us. I have no problem with that as long as she stays out of my life.

If Manjit wants to continue his outside tamasha, he can go ahead. I see how you live in Calgary. I learned from Mummy how she lived hers. I feel alive now and I am waking up to possibilities. I am going to take what is rightfully mine in this marriage.

Do you think I am like the Jane Eyre you were describing in your last letter? Why? I also found a job. I thought about how I could make this happen. I needed money to pay the maid. You won't believe it but uncle Sodhi hired me to work in his sports store. He put me in charge of the clothing department. I went to his store and begged him to give me a chance. At first, Uncle was reluctant. But his own daughter is in Jakarta and is treated badly by her husband and in-laws. He told me I was like his own daughter. He said women should be treated like Goddess Lakshmi. I was relieved when uncle agreed to hire me, and I told him he would not regret it.

He said, "I am already regretting it, beti. Everyone will talk. But I will handle it. Don't worry."

Manjit was shocked at my news and wanted me to quit my job. He wants me to stay at home and take care of the kids. Even Papa and Mummy are worried I will be out of the house all day. The Queen complained about how women should stay home with their children. I can't believe how annoyed everyone is. I ignore her. In fact, I listen to no one. I follow my instinct. It's been a long time since I've felt this happy.

While you are being educated at the university, I am being educated by the women in our family. Dear sweet Aunty Balwant went missing last week. Sixty years old and she walked out after forty years of marriage. Her family could not find her. Papa drove all around Singapore. He found her near Race Course Road, by the swings, just sitting on the swing and staring at the sky. You know how uncle Gurinder had one mistress after the other all these years while married to her? Aunty Balwant tolerated his infidelities all these years. It finally took a toll. Aunty was in terrible shape, so Papa took Aunty to Woodbridge Hospital. The doctors are keeping her there for two weeks. No one knows about this family secret. We have been sworn to secrecy. Don't say anything. Women are secrets, you know!

I couldn't stop thinking about Aunty Balwant all week. It reminded me of my Manjit and his mistress. Finally, on Saturday, I went to Woodbridge Hospital to visit aunty. There she was in a bare, tiny room, sitting on the narrow single bed with drab grey bedsheets. She stared blankly at the wall, murmuring. Her eyes were flat and lifeless. Her hair was uncombed and tangled. My God. She looked like a real madwoman. I sat on the bed, held her hand, and kept quiet. What is there to say? What does she not know?

In that half an hour of silence, I saw myself in this room in the future if my life were to remain the same for me. Sim, it was a room that would make you crazy if you were not already. A square room, twelve by twelve. White walls and white ceilings that had streaks of dirt and handprints all over parts of the walls around the door. The door had a tiny rectangle window at the top, the size of a foolscap paper, to avoid escape, I guess. Nothing else. No window to the outside world. It was depressing.

How can a man make a woman insane? Here she was trapped in prison. She had no voice left. She was alone. I gave aunty a tight hug. She didn't want me to leave, holding on to my right arm. I told her I would come back the next day. "Acha," she whispered.

I stepped out of the room and looked in the small window on the door after the nurse locked the door and left. Aunty was now crouched on the floor, leaning her head on the bed, her back to me. I swore I would not let that happen to me.

As I drove home, I made my decision. I was going to find a way out. You escaped to Calgary. Me, let's see. For now, I'm a working lady. I am lucky Uncle gave me a job. I will show Manjit, Mummy, Papa, Queen, and the whole damn world. I will make a new path for my daughters. No asylum for me, yaar.

For some reason, I remembered that day, just before you left Calgary, when you and I went to Mount Faber for an outing. We took the Singapore cable car, slowly floated high up in the sky over Keppel Harbour. I could see the beautiful dancing clouds. I could breathe. I was free. I felt like a bird. What a glorious day.

Maybe, I will save a little bit and come to Calgary one day. Banff Springs Hotel, here we come.

Love,

Amrit

3 MARCH 1987

Simran,

Try to save money by cooking. You can make one dish and eat for lunch and dinner. We Indian people don't use oven. That is western people way. We use the stove. My style is to cook everything fresh. Not keep in fridge for many days. It takes a long time to cook fresh Indian food. I spend all my time in the kitchen all my life. Sometimes I want pizza but your father wants Indian food only.

How is Lin? It is good you are learning to get along with your roommate. You are 100 per cent right that you must learn patience. It is good practice for husband too. Cook for her also. Never mind. Share. Food will bring you together. You don't know what life she has and that is why she behaves like that. Be good to her. She will change. It is your karma to be with her. Maybe in your previous life she helped you. It's your time now.

Pray also can. I pray all the time for all of you. You should go to temple in Calgary. You will find peace of mind there.

I hope your sister will be ok. She is becoming stubborn like you. You study hard and soon it will be time to come home to Singapore.

Stay safe and be happy. Pray.

Mummy

24 MARCH 1987

Dear Amy,

It must be tough for you to take care of your mum. I'm sorry to hear she has turned to alcohol to hide from her sorrow. You didn't speak much about her when we were in junior college together. I feel badly for her. She must be disappointed with her life's choices. I thought about her last night. I wondered what made her believe money would buy happiness. Your family has a comfortable life, but I guess she wanted a life of extravagance and wealth. She was drawn to that life that your billionaire Henry briefly offered. She failed to accept the downside of extreme wealth and how Henry used it to his advantage.

I think unhappy women try to find ways to escape from their despair. Maybe, your mum found hers in drinking—to forget. Deep down, I imagine most of us want a reprieve from the humdrum of life. I do hope that your mum can grapple with her demons and find a way out. My mum had an escape too. It wasn't money or alcohol but prayer. Mum spent all her life in duty and devotion to my father. She didn't have any freedom to pursue her dreams. Now that I think about it, I understand why she prayed all the time. When I was younger, I noticed that she would go into the little room she converted into a temple and spend hours reading the Adi Granth. Her eyes closed and her body rocked back and forth in a peaceful trance. She waved me away if I interrupted her. We all learnt to wait for Mummy to pray—not to ask for anything during her sacred times.

Now, when I think about it, I see that my mum carved a niche for herself to meditate and to escape from her oppression. A clever rebellion of sorts, one that was perfectly socially acceptable but personally gratifying.

Hey, I was close to calling the police the other day. You see, my bedroom shares a wall with the other duplex. Late in the night, I heard a horrifying noise through it. A woman was screaming in agony. There were continuous bangs against my wall. I jumped up and put my ear to the wall. A murder? I heard a man's muffled voice gasping. Was he beating her? This went on for a few nights. I thought of calling the police. By now, I was worried and didn't know what to do.

I watched out of the window to see if could get a glimpse of them during the day. Finally, I saw them. I hid and peered out the blinds. I saw a 300-pound, six-foot man holding hands with a 200 pound six-foot lady—both dressed in what seemed to be bus driver outfits. He walked her to the passenger side of the car, turned her around and passionately kissed her for an eternity on the side of the street. I gasped and jumped back.

"Why are you spying on the neighbours?" a curious voice asked.

Arrrggh. Lin. She caught me.

"Nothing. Just looking to see if it is snowing."

"Don't be stupid," Lin countered. "I hear them having sex all the time as well. I'm just not a busybody like you."

My jaw fell to the ground. How naive was I that even annoying Lin had figured out the neighbours' passionate lovemaking? Hmm. I am curious. Those sounds sound intriguing now. Passion unleashed. Bodies writhing. What would that feel like? The burly man got in the driver's seat and drove away. Relieved, I chuckled inwardly as I wondered what the neighbours would have done if they opened the door to the police banging. Oh man. Take care of your mum. We live in our own little world where disappointment and desires intersect.

Onward ho,

Simran

23 APRIL 1987

Hi Simran,

I don't think you should call the police on your neighbours. I assure you they're fine. Are you that clueless? Please watch more gritty shows in Calgary. Not stupid *Melrose Place*. I have to admit that my sexual experience with Chin was an eye-opener. Coming from an Asian family, I was sheltered and innocent about passion, lust and sexual satisfaction. Chin was a good teacher and a great lover. When we moved in together, sex was a big part of our relationship. Here's my advice to you. Stop waiting to be married to have sex. That is an old and outdated idea for a modern woman.

Once I let go of my inhibitions about my body and sex, I enjoyed our raw lovemaking. Really, where are bashful Asian girls like us supposed to learn? Certainly not on our censored television programs in Singapore. My mother was the last person I would ask. I was overcome by desire to be touched, licked, and loved without guilt. Boy was it amazing to have a man deep inside me. Your neighbours were good teachers about the power of orgasms. That's what good sex feels like. Chin was a beast in the bedroom. I admit that I was as well. I wasn't an Asian damsel but a wild, sexy lovemaking woman. It was empowering. You? Please. Don't save your virginity for your Indian man your parents will pick for you. What a waste. I bet your future husband won't be saving his virginity for you. And believe me, you don't want a greenhorn in bed, either. I have to say I miss sex.

I came home late last Monday and saw my mum standing at one of the large windows of our flat. You know our Singapore flats and the windows that span from the ceiling to halfway down the wall. I joined her and looked at the view. Mum stared vacantly at the wide expanse ahead of her. We are sixteen storeys high up in the sky in our flat. We can see the tops of giant angsana trees and the roads that crisscross in the far distance. The blue clouds and sky seem an arm's length away.

"What are you doing, Mum?" I startled her, but she didn't turn around.

"Look," Mum whispered. "Looks so peaceful out there. Maybe, I can fly like a bird. Be free."

I dragged her away from the window. "Come. Let's go have ice-kacang downstairs." She looked happy with my suggestion yet distracted. I took her to her favourite food stall across our block of flats. We ordered ice-kacang and rojak her favourites. I wanted to cheer her up. I worried about her. As we ate, Mum rambled on about handbags and shoes. She loves fancy shoes. She wants these overpriced, designer Manolo Blahnik shoes.

At the spur of the moment, I uttered, "I'll buy Manolo Blahnik shoes for you, Mum. This Saturday. Let's go to Orchard Road. Shopping."

Mum's face lit up, and she grinned from ear to ear. She chattered endlessly about what colour shoes she wanted. I admit I was relieved to see her perk up. Sim, I can't afford those damn shoes. They are stupidly expensive. But I felt compelled. I took Mum home, and she was cheerful and affectionate. She held my hand when we crossed the street and hugged me as we waited for the lift to take us up sixteen floors. When we got back home, Mum went straight to the kitchen, poured herself a large glass of Courvoisier, entered her bedroom and locked the door. I stood outside her door and put my ear to the door. Listening. I wasn't sure for what.

My father came out of his room. "What are you doing?" he asked me.

This house has become one of secret chambers. All of us locked in our little rooms, in our flat.

"Why have you let Mummy become like that?" I demanded of my father.

He stepped back and retorted, "Me? I stopped being able to reach that woman years ago."

"Why?" I demanded. "She is your wife. It is your duty."

"My duty?" My father rubbed his temple and his voice rose a pitch higher. "I loved your mum all these years. But that was not enough. She wanted more. And more. You know how expensive Singapore is or not? How much do you think it cost to send you to Princeton?"

I stared at my father, angry at him because I knew it was the truth. But I didn't want to hear the truth.

I held his right arm and squeezed it. "Maybe, I should not have spent your money, Papa."

I knew he could have bought us a bigger flat if he didn't have to pay for my tuition at Princeton.

My father's voice dropped, and he mumbled, "I love her, Amy. But not enough. Don't know why she is not happy with what we have. Like that, lah. Live in Singapore, like that. Got a HDB flat is rich, right?"

For the first time in many years, my father pulled me to him and hugged me. I felt him stifle a sob and his chest heaved against my face. Abruptly, he turned away and walked to his room and shut the door. I stood in the middle of my house of closed doors and disappointed people. In that middle between the two rooms that were only six feet away, I stood alone and wiped the trickle of tears that rolled down my cheeks.

I don't know what to do about my life. I've given up on love. Please, lah, *Melrose Place* is not the map to a successful love life. If I could turn back time, I would have stood up against my mum and picked Chin and given our love a chance to get stronger. Now, I have neither love nor money.

Go find yourself a lover, Sim.

Ciao,

Amy

24 APRIL 1987

Mummy,

Today I am tired, Mummy. I feel alone. I can't lie in bed with you and hug you, like I always did when I was in Singapore when I felt this way. It's cold outside. It's minus 30 degrees Celsius. Ok, in Singapore, it is 30 degrees. Count back to zero and count 30 more degrees. Can you even imagine? We had an unexpected snowstorm!

Today, this is how I get dressed. I put on leggings. I wore jeans over that. I put on two t-shirts under my sweater. I slipped on my Puma running shoes and a big, black winter jacket. Then, I put on a hat and thick scarf round my neck. I couldn't forget my gloves for my hands.

I opened the door and bam, the cold air hit my face. I put my head down and slowly walked to the university. The sidewalk was icy. It was like walking on ice cubes because the snow melted, then more snow fell and made the road polished and slippery. Also, because people walk on the sidewalk, it made everything even worse. What a lesson I never learnt because in Singapore, I only wore flip flops everywhere, rain or shine.

I made it to the end of the sidewalk from my house. There was a slope on that sidewalk where I had to cross the road. Without any warning, my feet lost grip. My body fell backwards, and I landed on my butt with a loud thud. Feeling helpless, I put my hands down to break my fall. Bad decision. I twisted my right hand. Stunned, I sat in the wet, hard ice for a few minutes and slowly turned to my left, went on my knees and used my left hand to push myself up.

A lady walking behind me saw me fall, quickly walked up to me and helped me up. She saw the tears in my eyes.

She held my shoulders. "Are you ok, young lady?"

She looked at my running shoes and shook her head. She said, "No wonder you fell. Your shoes are terrible. You need proper winter boots. Look at mine."

I looked down and saw she had sturdy black boots with long laces. She put up one foot and showed me the sole of her boots. They looked like tires.

"You need this grip. Your shoes are like skates. Don't you have winter boots?"

I shook my head. I had boots but they were stylish black boots—I didn't know there was a difference, and they had no grip. Now, I had spent my money. I thought by now, my running shoes were fine, made warmer with two pairs of socks. They seemed ok all this time. What is this winter? Coats, boots, hats, gloves, scarves. You had to know which ones fit which winter day. Just when I thought I knew it all, something new kicked me in the butt. In this case, a hard fall.

The lady held my elbow and helped me to cross the road.

She turned to go the other way and said goodbye. "For goodness' sake, buy proper boots! Don't kill yourself."

The lady left me petrified. I stared at the white expanse in front of me. The glistening sidewalks looked treacherous. I thought I should turn around and go home, but I did not want to miss my university classes. I took a deep breath and put one step in front of the other. I walked on the shiny ice like a Japanese geisha girl, gently bouncing from my left foot to the right.

By now, my pants were wet and my backside frozen. I couldn't see where I was going through my tears. The weather changes all the time. Some days, running shoes are fine. Some days, like today, it seemed not. How many shoes should I buy? Winter boots are expensive.

I finally reached Craigie Hall on campus. Relieved, I entered the building and hobbled to my classroom. The hallway was deserted. I saw a big sign on the door with red ink. *Class is Cancelled Today.* With my wrist throbbing, I shivered, and walked into the empty classroom. I sank into the chair, put my head in both my hands and wept. At that moment, I wanted to go home to Singapore.

After half an hour, there were no tears left. I looked outside the window and noticed the snow falling heavily. I trembled and held the desk to calm myself. What could I do? If I fell and hurt myself, who would even know? I couldn't stay on campus. There was no one to call. The sky was dark. I took a deep breath, went to the front door, pushed it open, and a strong blast of icy air hit me.

Slowly, step by step, I took small steps to walk home, afraid of falling and unsure about the icy sidewalks. It usually takes me fifteen minutes to get home. Today, it took me thirty-five minutes. My wet pants felt uncomfortable. How many types of snow days are there in Calgary? This time, I said "Waheguru" on each step and pretended you were walking next to me, Mummy.

When I reached my house, I flung open the front door, yanked my wet shoes and threw them at the closet at the entrance. Lin sat on the couch, watching TV.

Puzzled, she looked at me and said, "What's wrong with you? Why the hell did you go to university? Did you not hear that all classes are cancelled?"

I stood at the entrance, stared at her, restrained myself from rushing up to her and choking her fat neck. Without a word, I went straight to my bedroom and collapsed on the bed.

I am going to take Panadol and go to bed. It is hard writing with my hand. Thank you for being with me today, Mummy.

Love you,

Simran

25 APRIL 1987

Hey Anita,

It was distressing to read that Gopal continues to bother you even though you are separated. I know Indian men struggle with the concept of divorce in Singapore. Add to the fact you have a new British boyfriend, and you have a complex Hindi movie. You are a rebellious Indian woman. I can see the complications of navigating those traditional viewpoints with your modern ones. I agree women should have the choice to do what they want, but it is not as easy as it seems, right? You have incurred the wrath of your family, in-laws, narrow-minded friends, and others who label you as the one who broke the family up. Even domestic abuse is acceptable by some as long as the family unit remains intact. Oh, Anita, I am concerned about you and your boys. It can't be easy for them. It can't be easy for any of you.

Now you tell me that your imported boyfriend can't fend for himself financially in Singapore! It's not easy to survive in Singapore. You have a lot on your plate. The excitement of a new lover sounded more promising than the reality.

Ok. Fine. I am glad Phil is making you happy in the bedroom. I don't know what that means—you will have to educate me. I hope that he can make you happy in other areas of life as well. Now, you are supporting him financially. It seems complicated, doesn't it?

By the way, your gossip about your separation and Phil has travelled here to Calgary. I went to a Singaporean dinner party a few days ago. Faridah was there. She went to the Institute of Education with us in Singapore. Well, she told a large group of Singaporeans at the party about this woman from Singapore who threw her husband out and was shacking up with a younger British man. I almost fell out of my chair. What a small world. I tuned in to the conversation and did not say anything.

Faridah looked at me and said, "Hey, you know Anita, right?"

I shrugged and said, "How do you know about her?"

Faridah's sister works with Gopal. Alamak. It's not a good version, my friend. It's drearier. Everything is fuzzier, and you are the total villain. They clearly didn't know the part where Gopal abused you. I didn't want to say anything. You know how with Singaporeans, news travels fast. No escape, girl.

I said to the group of listeners and to Faridah, "Don't trust everything you hear, lah. You need to listen to both sides of the story."

Faridah countered with, "Alamak. This is not how Singapore women should behave. Destroy their family and shack up with an outsider. This is not acceptable. We are Asians who should behave better."

Yes. You can see the attitude of how women should act has not changed even with Faridah's exposure to the west. All I know is that Singapore gossip travels far and wide. I wonder what our friends and my family know about me. What news of me has spread to Singapore? Honestly, it's a headache to be controlled like that. How ridiculous.

I am facing some challenges with Professor Shit. How should I handle him? I asked my classmate, an older Canadian lady, for advice. Ann hates the professor. She complained she was learning nothing in class. She found him arrogant and ignorant. I listened carefully.

She said, "Go and see the Head of the Department. Talk to him about your marks."

At first, I recoiled. Go to the Head of Department? Me? What will I say? But, why not? What if I followed Ann's advice? Slowly, I walked to the Department of English's main office. My stomach churned. The secretary was not in. I saw that as a sign to leave but kept on going. I didn't even know who the head of the department was. I peered at the nameplate on the door: Dr. Sanders. I hesitated, but against my better judgement, I knocked loudly on his door.

"Come in," a tentative voice said. Dr. Sanders looked up and said, 'Yes? Do you have an appointment?"

"Oh. An appointment. No."

"Come back when you have one," he said. He looked busy and important. I felt uncomfortable and lost my nerve. I mean, what do I say to him? That Professor Shit hates me? I walked out of Dr. Sanders' office and sat outside in the reception area until the secretary returned. I debated whether I should I make an appointment to see Dr. Sanders next week. This was all new to me. I didn't know what I will say or what will happen. What if I make things worse?

Doubts went through my mind. Maybe, I am a bad writer. Maybe, I don't write like Canadians. Maybe, I won't get my degree.

That was enough self-doubt. I stepped up to the secretary and set up for an interview with Dr. Sanders for the next week.

That evening, to celebrate my rebellion, I went to a bar with Raj's daughter, Tanya. I was ready for some adventure. Imagine my surprise to see it was a wild, gritty punk bar in the beltline area of Calgary. Well, I have never been to somewhere this crazy. I giggled because I looked out of place in my brown cord pants and frilly brown blouse. I was the odd one out amidst the punk rockers, all dressed in black with multi-coloured hair and piercings on their noses, cheeks, and tongues. I guess Tanya left out the part about the type of bar she had picked. Nobody cared I was different. Some smiled at me. A few raised their beer bottles to me.

The adrenaline flowed through me, and I swigged a beer. I felt the loud beats of the music course through my veins. I sauntered to the tiny, crowded dance-floor and rocked my torso in unison with the dancers and the music. Tanya waved to me from the other corner of the dance-floor and gave me a thumbs up. I grinned from the exhilaration of being one with my fellow dancers. Out of the corner of my eye, I saw a plump White man inching his way to me, smiling. Silencing any judgmental voices in my head, I danced with the guy. I mean, I didn't have to marry him or anything. I just had to be in the moment of freedom and opportunity.

My new dancing friend was Steve. We danced till the lights flickered to signal closing time. Tanya ran up to me, ready to leave.

"What's your phone number?" Steve asked.

Hmm. I grabbed a piece of paper from my purse, wrote down my number, and handed it to Steve. I grinned all the way home.

Let me know how things go with Gopal and Phil.

Love,

Simran

3 MAY 1987

Dear Amrit,

That must have taken courage to go to Uncle and ask him for a job. You found a way out of your difficult situation of being stuck in an unhappy marriage. You took action to change your role from a wife to a working woman. It took one modern man like uncle to change your destiny. Yes. You are like Jane Eyre, the heroine in the novel who stood up against tradition and found a job as a governess. We both have rebellious blood flowing in us. We both want something different than only being a wife. You are brave to make a change within your married life. It shows me that it is never too late to ask for what you want.

When we were young, we talked about how the only way was for us was to marry men our family picked for us. We've been sheltered and protected all our life. It's hard to fight to change the same path that our grandmothers, mum, and aunts have faithfully followed by accepting marriage. There is always a way out, right? There are many women who work today. Now, you are one of these working women.

I was heartbroken to read about aunty's breakdown. I guess the only way out for her was madness. Isn't that an ironic way for her to be heard and to protest her unhappiness as an unhappy wife? The similarities are too close. I shudder when I think of you and your unfaithful husband, Manjit. For the past three years, I saw you go through the motions of life as a wife and mother. You sacrificed your hopes and dreams. I know you wished you could come to Calgary with me. But Amrit, it's never too late. In fact, you inspire me. You are making waves for your daughters too.

Amrit, there are struggles for freedom, even when I am here, free to pursue my education. I've had some brilliant professors. I have to say my favourites are the women professors who inspire me to pursue my dream. I've had fun and funny professors, some who amuse and motivate me, but there are some who ensnare, and I am unprepared. Look at this professor who teaches Literary Theory. It's an exciting, challenging, and tough class. On some days, I don't understand the complex ideas in class lectures, but I am determined to get a grasp of it.

Now, Professor Mayhew is an old man in his fifties. He is shorter than me and has a large paunch. Intrigued by his lecture one morning, I went up to him after class and asked when his office hour was. He was at the desk in front of the now empty class, looking down at his notes, lost in thought. He looked up at me. His face changed when his eyes locked mine, like he was seeing something other than a student. It was an odd look and made the hairs on my arm rise. Something shifted in that moment.

"Professor, I want to make an appointment to see you."

He mumbled, "2 p.m. Today. What's your name?" He stared at me and had a lopsided smile on his face.

"Simran," I said.

"Oh. To remember God."

I took a step back, stunned that he knew the meaning of my name. "See you at 2, Professor Mayhew."

I arrived at Professor Mayhew's office, and he asked me to shut the door. I sat in the chair across his desk.

He said, "I never noticed you before, Simran. How can I help you?"

"I didn't understand the points you made in class and wanted to know what else I could read," I said.

Well, Professor Mayhew put both his hands behind his head, leaned back, and talked endlessly—Derrida, him, his papers, his conferences—nothing made sense. I know because I kept looking at my watch, waiting for him to stop. I felt uneasy and wanted to leave. Frankly, he wasn't helping me to understand the lecture. I nodded my head, shifting to find a way to leave. Finally, Professor Mayhew paused to look at his watch.

Relieved, I took the chance to say, "I have a class in five minutes, Professor. Thank you."

"Come see me, tomorrow. Same time." I heard him say. It felt like a command.

"I'm busy," I stammered.

"I will expect you tomorrow," he stared at me.

I felt uncomfortable. Confused. He probably wanted to explain more about the class lecture. That's it. He wanted to help me. I didn't know what the right thing to do was. I nodded and left.

I can't wait to hear more about your life as a working woman. You are shifting things at home, aren't you? I can only imagine how annoyed Manjit must be.

Ok, I'll write soon.

Love always,

Simran

15 MAY 1987

Hi Amy,

You are right. I decided *not* to call the police on my neighbours when I heard the unusual sounds from their bedroom. I need an education in many things, especially on the joys of sex.

Well, Amy, guess what? Today, I received a surprise letter from Singapore. It was from Sudhir from our junior college days? Well, I had lost touch with him when I came to Calgary. He told me he got my address from YOU! I'm over the moon. How wonderful of you to reconnect us after all these years. Sudhir mentioned that meeting you at the movie theatre was unexpected as well. Good karma!

As you know, Sudhir was the first guy who told me he liked me. I was only seventeen. He was tall, dark, and handsome. Unfortunately, both our parents were strict, and dating was out of question. I was uneasy about breaking my family's rules, knowing full well I would be married off to a suitable boy of their choosing. We could only gaze at each other in the school canteen, young, foolish, love-lorn teens. What made everything complicated was we were from different Indian backgrounds. Race didn't bother me, but it sure mattered to my family. You remember teasing me about my Hindi movie love story in the college canteen, don't you?

In Sudhir's letter, he mentions going to Los Angeles on a holiday and wants to come to Calgary to meet me. He says he wants to ask me something. What can it be; my excited heart is bursting? How did he look, Amy? I lost touch with him because my family wasn't open to me meeting him. Finally, here in Calgary, we can be free— free to be together, free to speak and free to do whatever we want.

I have a grand plan for the five days that he will be in Calgary.

Of course, we will head to Banff and Lake Louise. We'll rent a car. I love to see new visitors' reactions to my beloved mountains. I want to spend time discovering Calgary with Sudhir. We'll hang out at Kensington where there are restaurants, cafes, and boutiques. Then we can wander off to the Bow River minutes away. Maybe we can even go dancing at a bar. I have done none of these with Sudhir in Singapore. I am giddy with anticipation; I feel like a seventeen-year-old again. Second chances?

How is work? I hope that you find time to take care of yourself as well. Can't be easy to be a parent to your parents. Have you considered leaving Singapore?

Love,

Simran

15 MAY 1987

Dear Simran,

Things are getting complicated. Gopal took the kids last weekend and did not bring them back on Sunday at 5 p.m. like he was supposed to. I called him over fifty times. No answer. I called his parents. No answer. I could hardly breathe. Phil grabbed my arm and rushed me to my car downstairs. We jumped in my car and sped like maniacs to Gopal's place, going through a few red lights, waiting for a police car to stop me. I didn't care about anything.

I arrived at Gopal's apartment block. I shoved the car keys in Phil's hands and ran up five flights of stairs. Gasping, I stood outside Gopal's flat and banged on the door with my fist. Five minutes. Six. Seven. Finally, Gopal opened the door and looked at me with this sneer on his face.

"Where are the kids?" I screamed.

He opened the door wider and pointed into the living room. The kids were huddled under a blanket, in their pyjamas, watching TV. I flung open the door, ran to the kids, trying to remain calm as they looked up at me with their little faces scrunched up in terror at all the commotion.

Gopal jumped to my side and whispered in my ear, "Bitch, I'm going to get you for breaking up our family."

I stood still; fear plummeted like a rock to my belly. It was my fault. Everything wrong was because of me. The kids were now trapped in this cycle of uncertainty. They lived in mayhem. I pretended to be cheery, so I spoke only to the kids in a loud, happy voice as I gathered them.

Outside the main door, I saw Phil was waiting for me. Damn.

I thought he would have waited downstairs in the parkade. Idiot. Gopal saw Phil and charged at him outside like a drunken buffalo. The kids screamed at the top of their lungs, and Gopal's parents ran out of their bedroom, shouting in Tamil. Without warning, Gopal hit Phil on the right side of his cheek, and a streak of blood dripped from Phil's mouth. Phil haphazardly swung his fists. Without thinking, I hurled myself between the two men. I felt random fists punch me. I shoved Phil towards the lift, herded the kids in and sighed in relief when the door of the lift shut.

When Phil, the kids and I got home, I looked at the blood, tears, fear, and fury I had created and felt deep remorse. Still, I had to put on my cheerful mask and get the kids to bed. They clung to my neck until they fell asleep in the darkness of their bedroom.

I tiptoed out, looked at Phil with an ice pack on his cheek and thought, *Alamak. What a bloody idiot.*

Good grief! This is the second time in a row that these men have punched each other and left a bloody trail for me to clean up. My life is a never-ending boxing ring. These men are juvenile idiots. Let me tell you, at that moment, I wished I could twitch my nose and blink my eyes and send Phil back to London. For sure, there will be no sex with this clown, Phil, tonight.

Hmmm. You were curious about sex. You're such an innocent one, aren't you? You're missing out on being caressed and kissed on every inch of your body while you lay back and enjoy the spasms of exhilaration in every nerve. Imagine having tender words whispered in your ear and your breasts fondled with both passion and fury. And finally, that forbidden moment when a man enters you. Believe me, it's a moment of sheer ecstasy and intimate connection between two lovers.

It's not about guilt or being forbidden by society and tradition. It's not just bang, bang, bang like it was with Gopal with no regard for my needs. All these years with Gopal, I didn't know any better because he was my one and only lover. My goodness. What have I been missing out on? For me, I feel alive and enjoy the intense pleasure I get from making love with Phil. For once in my life, I recognize I deserve to be pleasured as well. Hey, Sim, don't die without trying some raw, animal lovemaking!

Bloody Singaporeans and their gossip. I know that Faridah who is in Calgary. She was good friends with Gopal here. Her mouth is bigger than all of Singapore. She is one to talk. She has been married three times.

I thought my life would be peaceful. It's like a tsunami from hell.

Me,

Anita

17 MAY 1987

Simran,

Be careful. When it is cold and snowy, don't go out. You should wear three pairs of socks then your shoes will have better grip. You wanted to go away from family and safety. Now you have to be brave. Some days are difficult. Everyone has bad days. That is life. Don't give up. Be strong. Be like a man. Puma shoes are good. My friend's daughter wears it in Vancouver. How do people live in such cold places? I will never live there. Too cold. Ice. Snow. How like that? Better you finish your studies and come back to Singapore. No snow. You will be safe and comfortable.

That is bad your professor cancelled class and did not let you know. Next time better you call and check. Take a bus to school also can. Life is difficult for many generations. When I was a young girl, my family lived in Lahore. During partition all Hindus must move to India and all Muslims to Pakistan. It was a bad time. In our life, we don't know when the difficult moments come to us. My father told us to get on the train and go to Delhi. He couldn't come with us. I was a young girl. Violent times. My mother, sister, me and younger brother all rushed to the train station and jumped onto the train.

This side the train was going to Delhi full of Hindus. Other side, train was coming from Delhi, full of Muslims. We heard how sometimes the dakus killed everyone on the train. Bad time. No food on the train. Toilets all broken. Smelly. No place to sit. Everybody on the train didn't know if they will live or die. It was all in God's hands.

See, Simran. Life is not easy all over the world. Be strong. Pray to God to protect you. My family made it safely to Delhi. We don't know if our father will get out of Lahore. Next day there was a knock on the door—Bapuji had caught the last train out of Lahore. If he didn't jump on final train to Delhi that day and push his way in the crowd, he would be dead since no more trains were allowed to leave after that. He would have been killed. We all hugged him and cried with pure joy.

You must have a strong heart, Simran. Don't let snow or cancelled class bring you down. Accept it is life. You don't know what people's stories are. Remember, you have a safe house to live. You have family here in Singapore. You have opportunity to get a degree. Keep your head up, beti. Everything will be ok.

God will bless you.

Mummy

18 MAY 1987

Hey Simran,

You won't believe how good I am at doing my new job. Yesterday, Uncle Sodhi was happy with my initiative and hard work. I arranged all the account books in order. It was a mess. I collected them and organized them. I made an easy system of price tags for the clothing and sports items like tennis rackets. I showed the cashier how to keep track of what had been sold by collecting the price tags and cataloguing them. Uncle Sodhi was using old-fashioned ideas here in the shop. They were terrible. At the end of each day now, Uncle Sodhi can tabulate everything in a shorter time than before.

He patted me on the back and said, "Beti, what a good job. Well done."

I floated on cloud nine all day from being appreciated. I come up with new ideas in the shop all the time because I watch and observe. It's the simple things like putting stools in the change room for those who need to sit. It's courtesy when a customer comes in to offer help and suggestions. Before, Uncle Sodhi lost customers because the staff was not attentive. Now, I've suggested a protocol for all of us employees to say hello, ask questions and say thanks and goodbye. You know Singaporeans in stores, right; they can be rude. The other staff members told me they like my new way. I'm excited to do something useful and get paid for it. I never had a chance to work before I was married. Now, I get up in the morning, take the bus, and make decisions at work.

You know, women can do anything when they are given a chance. At home, I don't worry because Sumira, our maid, is amazing. She is the same age as me. I give her a list of what to do each day. The children are used to her and like being with her. I write down what to cook, when the children sleep, and how to play with them. It's easy because this is her job. She gets paid for doing those duties I did for free. I have great respect for her and treat her with kindness and care. She told me her stories of survival. She comes from a remote village outside of Jakarta in Indonesia. She had to leave her five-year-old son behind with her mother to come to Singapore to work. Her husband was a drunk who beat her all the time. Imagine this. She found the courage to throw out her useless, unemployed, alcoholic, wife beater husband.

Sumira laughed when she told me about how quickly he found a new woman and married her. She is relieved he has moved to a different village. The only way Sumira could survive was to come to Singapore as a maid. She sends all her money home to her mother and son to support them. She has to work in Singapore for three years without going back to Indonesia because she has to pay off her maid fees to her agency. Her son will be eight years old when she meets him again. What things do women have to do to survive in this world. We can always find a way out.

You won't believe this, but Manjit is treating me differently now. When I come home from work, he sits down and has dinner with me. He talks to me more and asks how my day was—before he would ignore me and go to his room when he came back at night.

The other day, I told him about my new ideas in the shop. He smiled at me and said, "You are a smart woman. Good job, Amrit."

I lit up. Then, I asked him about his day. He told me about his boss and the new project he was working on. I feel comfortable. This is beginning to feel like a marriage now. We communicate more and spend time together. Even the Queen doesn't bother me much, which makes things less stressful. I'm surprised that Manjit does not go out every night like he used to. I notice he is spending more time with his daughters. Soni and Roni adore him.

When Manjit comes home from work, he takes Soni and Roni to the playground in front of our block of flats. Sometimes, they all wait at the bus stop for me to come home. Today, I felt excited when

I looked out the window of the bus and saw all of them waiting for me. We all went home hand in hand. A delicious dinner of rice, fried chicken and vegetable stir fry was ready on the dining table, thanks to our maid, Sumari. I looked at how clean the house was and smiled. My life has changed. I don't have much to do around the house. I now have time to play with the kids and be with Manjit. This is how I imagined married life to be. Happy, carefree and united.

What is happening with your Professor Mayhew? I have a bad feeling. Why is he asking you to come to his office for no reason? You are an international student, and everyone knows you are alone there. People know you have no family. Can you get help from someone? Maybe you can talk to a woman professor? These men can smell your vulnerability. Better be careful.

Love,

Amrit

19 MAY 1987

Hello Simran,

Leave Singapore? Why would I want to? Do you think every Singaporean wants to go to the west? Forget it, man. I love Singapore. I feel I belong here. I can go anywhere I want. Safe. Clean. Green. People think that going to the U.S. or Canada is exciting. Really? Why go to a place that has violence, like New York? Everyone has a gun. And why go to Canada and freeze in the snow?

Please. In Singapore, I am the queen of my land. I speak with my Singapore tongue—so comfortable, right. No need for anyone to ask, "Where are you from?" I spent four years in Princeton, and it was enough. I was always an outsider everywhere but Singapore, you know. I will never leave Singapore, lah. Born here. Die here.

Hey, I took my mum shopping last Saturday. We went to Orchard Road as I had promised her. Mum smiled and chattered all morning. She carefully picked her black Chanel dress. She had her black Chanel handbag and matching pumps. She wore her favourite pearl necklace and earrings. She combed her hair into a fetching updo. I watched her put on her meticulous make-up. She applied her favourite pearl pink lipstick. She was ready for a fancy gala, I thought. Before we left the house, Mum asked me to take a few photographs of her in the living room. She stood in front of the window, pointing to the blue sky outside. She sat in the red velvet armchair in the living room and made me snap over a dozen photos. She giggled and her smiles genuinely sparkled. It was like she was a different woman.

My father came out of his room and stopped to take a double look at her. He complimented her. "You look extra beautiful today."

Mum beamed and touched his shoulder. She looked like a glamorous movie star. Finally, we left the flat, and we took a taxi to Orchard Road. We got out in front of our favourite shopping centre. Mum grabbed my arm and pulled me faster than I could walk. We went into every boutique. Mum touched every outfit and held it against her as she twirled in front of the mirror. She held up a stunning Chanel beaded silk gown. It was ivory-white with exquisite hand-sewn sequins and embellished flower designs on the front panel. It had a scooped neck and three-quarters sleeves. The silk satin dress was nipped at the waist and fell in a full skirt to the ankles.

"Try it, Mum," I urged.

Mum stepped out of the dressing room and the dress hugged her vivacious curves. I gasped. She looked like an angel. She twirled in the aisle and made me take more photographs of her. I will send you a photograph soon of Mum in this heavenly dress. Of course, we can't afford it, but Mum was happy to just try it and put it back on the hanger. Maybe, that was enough for her.

Finally, we reached the shoe department. I sat on the bench and let her meander through the staggering shoe display. The shop assistant came back to the bench with Mum's ten shoe boxes and planted them in a pile. I watched Mum take each pair out of the box, touch the leather, the strap and the heel and try each pair on. She lingered over these black suede pumps with a strap across and dainty three-inch heels. Gingerly, she slipped them on and paraded in front of the mirror. I cheered her on and applauded.

"This one?" I asked.

She shook her head, and she went to the gold, strappy high heeled pair next. She could barely balance herself on the delicate heels, and we both laughed and shook our heads. The wrinkles on her face disappeared, and I saw that forgotten dimple on her right cheek, next to her lips. A deep, dancing cleft emerged when mum opened this last box of shoes—Manolo Blahnik shoes.

Mum gasped when she held the red high heels with heel support at the back and a covered front over the toes with pleated fabric that delicately crisscrossed in an intricate design. They were blood red.

She sat there and caressed the soft velvety fabric and leather sole. Her fingers followed the contour of the heels. She turned the shoes over to check if they were size 7 and held her hand out to stop the assistant from helping her put the shoes on.

Next to me on the bench, I watched Mum gracefully guide one foot, then the next, into the Manolo Blahniks. A half-smile deepened on her right side and her cleft danced again. With both shoes on, Mum stood up, tall and straight and walked to the long mirror against the wall. We both stared at her feet. She turned to her right and her left. Looked over her shoulder at the back of the shoes. Then she stood with arms akimbo and stared at herself in the mirror.

"How, Ma?" I asked.

"So beautiful," she gasped. "Fits perfectly."

I looked at Mum in her red pumps and felt her delight. "You want, Mummy?" I asked.

She nodded her head and grinned in joy. She carefully took off those prized shoes, put them in the box and took them to the counter. I braced myself as I pulled my credit card out of my wallet. $945. I turned to see Mum smiling, happy that she did not have to put the shoes back on the shelf; they were hers. I paid for the shoes and carefully placed the bag in her hands.

Mum eagerly clutched the large bag with her precious Manolo Blahniks in them and said, "Let's go home, now."

When we arrived home, she immediately disappeared into her room—with her shoes, of course. Me, I sat alone on the jade green sofa in the living room in the dying light of dusk, with a faint breeze billowing from the opened windows of the flat and thought, "What would make ME as happy as Mum was with her designer shoes?"

Oh, karma, indeed. I ran into your teenage love, Sudhir, at Cathay cinema. He told me that the two of you had lost touch. I gave him your address. Maybe?

Tell me what unfolds.

Amy

29 MAY 1987

Dear Anita,

Aiyoh, my friend. Every time you write, it's another bloody fist fight between your ex-husband and boyfriend. It reminded me of our primary school days when we watched Muhammad Ali's boxing matches with his arch enemy, Joe Frazier. Have you considered having no men in your life for the time being instead of two duelling for you? Tell me the truth; are you enjoying having two men fight over you? Listen, I want you to be happy. You deserve love and peace in your life. The whole situation is complicated because you haven't resolved your divorce with Gopal. I don't know much about relationships, but I feel it takes time to end a marriage, doesn't it? Gopal doesn't want to let you go. He has too much to lose—you, the kids. Can't be easy for Phil to step into all this drama, either. Please give one relationship time to end and the other space to be nourished.

Ok. At least amidst the mayhem, you are having great sex with Phil. That was quite the sex education for me, reading about your intimate moments. You're right. I have no clue what good sex feels like. My mum warned me that all men only wanted sex. Nobody I know talks about sex. I like how women can enjoy sex, too. For some reason, I thought sex was a man's dominion. At least your secrets will guide me better than guessing from those sex scenes on television shows. Hmmm. Tell me more.

Do you remember my fiasco with Professor Shit who told me I couldn't write? Frankly, I'm tired of being underestimated as a foreign student. I made an appointment with the Head of English, Dr. Sanders, to talk about my concerns. On that fateful day, I sat outside his office, waiting for our appointment. I tried to still my anxiousness by going over points in my head. I looked up and saw Professor Shit walk into the main office to get his mail. He stopped in his tracks when he saw me. He smiled and waved. I smiled back. Oh no!

At that moment, Dr. Sanders opened the door, beckoned me in and saw Professor Shit and said, "How is Ann? See you both at dinner this Friday."

What? Sanders slid into his large, black chair. "What can I do for you?" he asked.

My brain raced. "*Think…think…they are having dinner this Friday. Be careful. You can't complain about Professor Shit.*"

I put on my sweetest smile and said, "I wanted to find out…err… about…" I looked up at the wall behind him and saw his framed degrees. "About…the Masters' Program," I finished lamely.

Dr. Sanders looked at me and nodded. "We love international students. Good plan, young lady."

I grinned in relief. He grabbed a calendar from his shelf and passed it to me. Then, he went into a wonderful explanation about the Master's in English program. I sat up, unexpectedly intrigued by this information. Hmm. I had no intention of doing a Master's in English, but Dr. Sanders had now piqued my interest. Wow. I could apply for a scholarship as well, it seemed. I sat back in my chair, Professor Shit now completely off my agenda. Why worry about that twit? The best revenge would be to think about more degrees and scholarships. I couldn't believe my luck. I shook Dr. Sanders' hand and left with the application package.

That evening, Steve from the Punk Club called me. Well, he asked me out.

Really, I wasn't that attracted to him, but I thought, "Hey, Sim. Why don't you play the dating game you have always been curious about and go practice with Steve?"

It was time for new discoveries, right? Steve arrived with a lovely bouquet of flowers. I was taken aback. I love roses and was touched by his gesture. We went to Nick's Pizza, which is across McMahon

Stadium, close to the University of Calgary. Ok. This part was familiar like the arranged marriage meetings I went through in Singapore. But this time, I was there by choice. I noticed Steve was shy and quiet and it was a chance to practice my conversation skills. This time, I didn't have to worry about having to marry him after one date, so, I sat back and had some fun. I had a glass of wine. I munched on delicious Hawaiian pizza and let the evening unfold. I drank more during the lull of silence, unconcerned about impressing him. I could be myself. Hmm. Was I getting the hang of Canadian dating? I felt free because I didn't have to go out with him ever again if I didn't want to. I impressed myself when Steve opened up during the evening and talked more to me. He was probably nervous or new to dating as well, right? Maybe, I am quite the charmer, after all?

The evening came to an end, and Steve drove me home. Well, it wasn't a date to remember, but I had a nice evening out. He leaned forward to hug me, and I put my hand out to shake his hand. It was priceless to see the look of surprise on his face. It's never too late to learn to date, is it? Look at me, establishing boundaries. I waved goodbye as he left.

Feeling proud of myself, I sauntered up to the front door, entered and noticed Lin was in the living room. She was sobbing. Oh no.

I sat next to her on the sofa, concerned. "Hey, what's up?"

Lin was inconsolable. I sat in silence for a few minutes. I touched her shoulder gently, and she grabbed me and buried her wet, snotty face on my right shoulder. Her gasping and sobbing heaved us both back and forth.

"Hey, Lin. What happened?" I whispered.

With a heart wrenching wail, she gasped, "I got all D's in my six Engineering courses for my midterm. I don't know if I can graduate and get a degree. I can't afford to repeat a semester. It's so much money. What will my family say?"

I held her in my arms and felt a wave of compassion for my roomie.

Lin's face was contorted with a fear that I was familiar with. That fear of not making it. That fear of losing everything. That fear of being a stranger in a new country, having given up everything to come to Calgary to get a degree. For that moment, we bonded. I tapped her shoulder gently, tried to calm her, let her talk, and nodded my head. I listened without judgement. Lin's sobs slowed down and became a little gasp and whimper as she explained her fear, sadness, and loneliness all these months.

Then, without warning, Lin lunged at me and hugged me like her long-lost friend. I sank in her embrace and held her tight. At that moment, I realized I was really her only friend. That is why she followed me from the dormitory to this rental house. Over these two years, I was familiar to her, coming from a similar Asian background. She had no other friends, but she tried her best to fit in a Canadian world. How could I be arrogant and critical of Lin?

I succumbed to her second wave of sorrow as she put her face on my shoulder and wiped more of her tears and snot on my sweatshirt. We sat there in silence for an eternity.

Eventually, she pulled herself together, shoved me away and said, "Where did you go? Out with another loser? That weirdo Steve?"

What? I laughed. Old Lin was back. I patted her head and said goodnight. It had been an intriguing and eye-opening day. I stumbled to my bedroom, sank in my bed, and slept like a baby. My education in Calgary is taking all shapes and forms.

Love,

Simran

29 MAY 1987

Dear Mummy,

It's spring now. Winter is over. I keep thinking how hard it is to understand the snow here. It keeps changing. One day it is beautiful, like cotton wool that floats down from the sky. The next day, it can be harsh so even my nostril hairs freeze. The cold air bites my skin and turns it red and patchy. My Canadian friend Julie says I should embrace winter. She downhill skis at the Lake Louise ski resort every week. I tried it once, and I ended up going down in a stretcher and falling off. I'll tell you more next time. She says I am ignorant of winter fun and survival because I didn't grow up with snow and ice. *Of course*, I said. *I grew up in 30 degrees, humid Singapore.* It's two different worlds sometimes. Never mind. I chose to come to Calgary, and I should try new things. It's a big difference for those of us who move to and live in new countries as adults. There's so much to learn. But that's ok, you know. That's what life is about!

You're right, Mummy. Next time, when there is a snowstorm in winter, I will turn on the radio or news to check about whether the university is closed like it was that day I went in. Really, I should learn to miss a class or two as well when the weather looks awful out there. It's not the end of the world.

Mummy, I had no idea about how your family escaped to Delhi from Lahore. How awful. I was shocked how Muslims and Hindus killed each other during the partition in India. I looked up some old newspapers at the University of Calgary's library. I was curious about other people's stories. I read how the passengers of some of the trains that arrived at the stations in Delhi or Lahore were killed by the anti-Muslims or anti-Hindus who ambushed the trains. It was a terrible massacre. I imagine you as a young girl and how you escaped on one of those bloody trains. No wonder you tell me to be careful. You have seen bloodshed and mayhem at a young age. You are brave, Mummy!

Here at the university, I found that not many students take courses in spring and summer. These students go back home, or they work to pay for their university courses. I am completing as many courses as I can in spring so I can finish my degree in a shorter time. The spring and summer classes go by fast. I figured a way to save money and time by two to four months each year. I have to admit it is beautiful in Calgary in spring and summer. No snow to worry about! I love going to classes, and the weather reminds me of Singapore.

I am now taking senior literature courses, but I am getting the hang of it. My grades have improved. I have wonderful professors for most of my classes. I get many A's in my classes. I see improvement in my essays, and I am not afraid to speak up in class anymore. I am a grown baby who is learning new steps in everything.

My friend Julie is taking me to a second-hand store on Sunday to buy winter boots for the upcoming winter. She told me winter stuff will be on clearance in spring, and it is a great time to stock up. I am going to get a sturdy pair of winter boots so I can walk on ice. No more shoes with three pairs of socks. I am getting more Canadian, aren't I?

Love,

Simran

30 MAY 1987

Hello, Amy,

I loved the shopping expedition you shared with your mum, Amy. What a special time together. I don't know what Manolo Blahnik shoes are, but I am fascinated by them now. I will look for them when I go to a shopping centre in Calgary. These shoes sound exquisite and expensive enough to pay for several months' rent and food in Calgary. Oh, that was kind of you to treat your mum to these shoes. She seems to have found pleasure in owning them. They sound as magical as Dorothy's red shoes from *The Wizard of Oz*. You have different lives perched in the sky in the block of flats in Ang Mo Kio. A small space of dreams. And now for your mum, red shoes to take her home.

Thank you for reconnecting me with my teenage sweetheart from Singapore—of all places, in Calgary! Yes, Sudhir showed up as promised; we had made plans on the phone. I didn't know what to expect when I waited for him at the airport that fateful day. What would it be like? After all, I hadn't seen him in years. I anxiously stared at the airport door in the arrival area of the Calgary airport. Finally, there he was in the flesh!

Sudhir was taller and thinner than I remembered. He hauled his lanky frame and oversized backpack and headed straight to me. He had a gorgeous wide smile plastered on his dark sunburnt skin. His white teeth flashed a boyish grin, just like I remember when I spied on him in the canteen in junior college. Oh, my heart skipped a beat. This time, there was no one or nothing in the way. He rushed to me and enveloped me with his bony arms, and my face hit his chest and the straps of his backpack.

I could not believe that we were finally together. Aaahh. The next thing you know, he bent down and kissed me on my lips.

"Do you know how long I have been waiting to do that?"

I looked up at him and said, "Four years, to be exact."

Right there in the middle of the arrival hall for visitors, Sudhir clasped me in his arms, and we melded in each other's torsos. There was nothing to say. Everything felt right. All the pent-up emotions and hidden feelings spilled over. Finally, I grabbed his arm and propelled him to the carpark where I had rented a car for his visit. He put his hand on my shoulder the whole drive home, leaning over to kiss my cheek at every traffic light.

"I missed you, Simran," he whispered.

A wave of emotions overcame me, unrecognizable but exciting. It was a comfortable sensation of being allowed…to have permission to be. It's hard to explain. I could be myself, and not be afraid.

I raised his hand to my lips and gently kissed it. "I'm glad you came! It's been a long time."

When we arrived at my place, we giggled like teenagers as we ran straight to my bedroom. Sudhir dropped his bags and we tumbled into bed. Strange sensation. To be free. To be able to explore. All those junior college day fantasies came to life as we lay in each other's arms. I leaned over and kissed his face—all over. He gently pulled my head to his and I felt his wet lips devour mine. Our hands explored each other, unrestrained. Without warning, my bedroom door flew open with a resounding bang. Was my father here? We looked up, and Lin stood there at the door, staring at us in bed.

"Oh. Wondering what all that noise was." She turned and walked away.

Flabbergasted, I looked at Sudhir, and we collapsed in uncontrollable laughter. He went to the door and shoved his bags against them. With a smile on his face, he came back and enveloped me in his arms.

For the next four days, Sudhir and I lived a fantasy. We were inseparable. Was this how being together with a man would be? Our days were free and easy. We went to Market Mall and strolled the shops hand in hand. Sudhir took me for dinner to The Keg, where we had a long romantic dinner and laughed about memories of teachers, friends, and stories from junior college. Our conversations were effortless. It was a chance to share our feelings and thoughts. I felt safe with Sudhir. There was a familiarity that I enjoyed from having a past and a background that was similar. He told me stories of his adventures during his National Service stint in Singapore and how he rose to the rank of captain so quickly.

Of course, we went to my favourite place, Banff, an hour away from Calgary. He wanted to drive, and I loved how he felt the same joy I did as we approached the Rocky Mountains. At the end of the day exploring the place, we found the bench by the river and watched the glorious sunset amidst the mountain peaks, his arms around me. My emotions raced—confused, happy, afraid, excited. It was four days of making up for four years of dreaming of being together.

On the last evening before he left, Sudhir and I went for dinner at the top of the Calgary Tower. Romantic. The restaurant gently rotated and offered us a view of beautiful Calgary. It was bittersweet to think he would be leaving the next day. As we toasted our glasses of champagne, Sudhir leaned forward.

"Sim. Shall we continue this magic when you come back to Singapore? I've always been in love with you since I was seventeen. You were my first love."

Is this what freedom feels like? Could I choose who I wanted to be with? I felt exhilarated as I nodded and clinked Sudhir's glass.

"Absolutely yes. Let's do it."

I squashed my feelings of dread; I was ready to defy my family if they would not allow me to marry a man who's not from my same race and religion. I have lived in the shadows of traditional expectations for too long. As I looked at Sudhir's smiling face, I knew there was no going back. By the time I dropped him off at the airport the next day, we had promised to write, call, wait for each other and give this relationship a chance. It wasn't goodbye at the Calgary airport that day. It was a moment of definite possibilities. A degree. A boyfriend. A future husband.

Things are amazing. I'm excited about coming back to Singapore.

Thank you for reconnecting us. Yes, you will be the bridesmaid. For sure.

Love,

Sim

3 JUNE 1987

Dear Amrit,

I'm proud of you and the brilliant ideas you have incorporated in Uncle Sodhi's sports shop. You are quite the businesswoman! I can see Manjit, Soni and Roni waiting for you at the bus stop in my mind's eye. I love that you are spending more time with Manjit and your daughters. That's what women should be, independent and strong. I bet that Manjit is looking at you as a partner instead of only as a wife. I think of your maid, Sumari. It can't be easy for her to leave her child and come to a new country and take care of other people's families. It takes courage and determination. She is doing what she must to survive.

You're right to be concerned about Professor Mayhew. He is the one who wants me to come to his office every day. I was curious what he really wanted. The next day, I showed up at his office and sat in the chair. Professor Mayhew sat across me. I remained silent. Then, unexpectedly, he asked me personal questions about my age and my life. I answered as vaguely as I could. Sensing my discomfort, he stopped, leaned back in his office chair and put his hands behind his head.

"When I was twenty, I went to India. I backpacked from one place to the other. In Hapur, I came across a famous astrologer in an ashram. Curious, I asked him to tell me my future. He told me that in my later years, I would meet a young woman who would change my life." He stared at me intensely as he spoke these words.

I shifted in my seat uncomfortably. He watched me with a half-smile on his face. I wasn't an idiot. I knew where he was going with this. The best thing for me to do was to act dumb. Say nothing.

I looked at my watch and declared, "I have to go."

Professor Mayhew stood up and walked me to his door. "See you tomorrow, same time."

What the hell! Ordering me to come. I didn't show up at Professor's Mayhew's office the next day. Later in the day, when I went to his class, Professor Mayhew handed me my graded essay as soon as I walked in. I turned to the last page, and I froze. An F. I struggled to keep my composure and bravely sat through the class even though I raged inside. What was happening? I knew my essay was not an F! Simply put, I needed this specific class to get my degree. There was no other option. As soon as class was over, I ran out of class and went outside Craigie Hall. It was a beautiful day. I needed to calm down. *Think! Think!*

At 2 p.m., I went to Professor Mayhew's office.

He said, "I knew you would show up at my office to meet me today."

I sat down in the chair and put my essay on his desk. He took it, turned to the last page, and changed the F to an A.

"I see," I thought silently. I stared at him as he smiled at me. My instinct warned me to be careful and say nothing.

Then, Professor Mayhew chatted like nothing happened. He mentioned Simone de Beauvoir and Jean Paul Sartre.

"I want you to read about them," he said in a low whisper.

My eyes wandered round the bookcases in his office. There were three overflowing bookcases behind his desk. I read the titles of each book on his shelf to calm my nerves. My face gave nothing away. I knew Beauvoir and Sartre entered a sexual relationship with no strings attached. In my first year, Professor Mila in our literature class discussed Beauvoir, and I loved what I read about Beauvoir. Yes, I admired Beauvoir for her views on sex and marriage. She was a woman ahead of her times. Aah. My dear Professor Mayhew was grooming me. Things fell into place for me. The narrow long, rectangular window behind him let some light into the musty room. I surreptitiously glanced at my watch, wondering when I could leave.

Every time I made a movement to leave, Professor Mayhew

started a new line of questioning. Had I read this book or that. Did I have any boyfriends? I said little. I felt uneasy but plastered an artificial smile on my face. You see, I had one more essay to hand in and had to write the final exam for his class. I now knew the consequences of not coming in every day to meet Professor Mayhew. Simply put, if I failed his course, I would not get my degree. I knew Professor Mayhew knew this juicy piece of information as well. He was the only one who taught this class every year. I knew I could not walk away, or thousands of dollars spent on my education so far would be lost.

Finally, I stood up, grimaced a smile and said goodbye.

"See you tomorrow," Professor Mayhew commanded.

I nodded. I thought about seeing the Head of the Department but changed my mind. What's the point? Was there a way out?

For one month, I went to see Professor Mayhew every day. I sat and he talked. By the second week, at his insistence, we begin meeting for lunch. Frankly, I was relieved to be in a public space instead of trapped in his musty office. He would buy an egg salad sandwich, cut into two, and share a Caesar salad. Same thing. Every time. And tea. It was a ritual.

At every meeting, I felt on pins and needles until I could leave. Sweaty palms. He was as old as Papa. His wrinkles were deep on his forehead. I felt repulsed when he put his hand on my shoulder or back. I was trapped in an old man's fantasy and power.

I remember Julie had mentioned to me once about a free therapist on campus for students. She suggested I could talk to him about any problems I faced, and it would be confidential. At our next lunch, I told Professor Mayhew I had made an appointment to see the therapist on campus. I watched him closely as he looked uncomfortable.

Oh yeah, buddy, I thought. *What do you think about me talking to a campus therapist about the abuse you're putting me through?*

He stared at me and said, "I wouldn't do that if I were you. The therapist will put everything you say on your record, and it will follow you everywhere when you graduate. Everyone will know."

Everyone will know what? I thought. Was he worried about my secrets or his?

Professor Mayhew looked straight in my eyes and repeated slowly, "You will talk only to me. Tell me everything. I won't tell anyone. You are safe with me."

It looks like I have another roadblock with Professor Mayhew. I have to find a way out, Amrit. I've come too far to let anyone stand in my way of getting my degree. I can't succumb. I can't lose. I toss and turn every night, but I won't let any man stop me when I've sacrificed everything to get here.

I'll tell you more in the next letter as things unfold. For now, you are my confidante. Our secret.

Love you,

Simran

6 JUNE 1987

Hello Simran,

My life is getting complicated. It looks like Phil is not handling the stress well. Gopal comes over every night and makes things worse. I'm caught in the middle. The kids are acting up. My goodness. I can't handle any of this conflict anymore.

On top of everything, Phil can't support himself or make ends meet. Looks like he has many debts that are catching up with him. Guess I didn't know much about him before letting him in my house. His mail has been coming to my house, and he left his Visa bill on the counter. I was stunned to see he owed $30,000. I looked at the interest rate and choked. How is he going to pay his VISA debt when he can't even pay me any money for food or rent? Love is waning fast. Frankly, I'm not feeling the same joy I did on that platform in London.

I had no choice, anymore. I made a difficult decision, and I ended things with Phil that evening. I can't deal with his money problems, the stress, and my ex-husband. Oh dear. Phil fell apart when I told him my decision; just then, my psycho ex-husband, Gopal, knocked on the door. Oh no. Too much drama and tension. I marched to the front door and there he was. He wept and begged me to take him back. No more boxing matches, I thought. I sent Gopal home by promising I would talk to him the next day. Then I went into my bedroom and Phil was sobbing. Oh my goodness. Phil begged me to give us another try. I told him I would talk to him the next day, although my mind is made up. This love triangle has turned into a nightmare.

Exhausted, I went to the kids' room. Ironically, they were the only ones not crying. I slept with them the whole night, peaceful for the time being. Hmm. I am questioning the value of a man in my life.

Phil begged me to change my mind, but I gave him a few days to pack and leave my house. The next day, he packed his belongings, but he broke down in the living room. Luckily, the kids were with Gopal, so it was just me and him. Phil declared his love for me. Alamak. It was more than I could bear. Out of concern, I asked him what he was going to do. He said he was moving into a hostel. I didn't want to know too much or be responsible for him anymore. I said my goodbye while he clung to me until I finally pried him off.

Oh, Simran, I was relieved when he left. You're right. I rushed into this one. Maybe, it's the fear I can't survive on my own? Maybe, I love being with a man? Maybe, I love the idea of love? I must admit it is liberating to make my own mistakes, as painful as they are. I'm still standing, no matter what these bozos do.

You know, I love the way you're handling your challenges with some of your professors. Standing up to them is part of your education, it seems. I know you won't give up. The only way out of predicaments is to face them head on. Nothing that an aspirin and courage can't handle. In your case, no aspirin, right? Keep to Tylenol to avoid those allergies.

I am glad you are enjoying dating, even Steve. Once you realize you can pick, choose, and discard, you won't feel trapped like you felt in an arranged marriage situation. Enjoy your freedom and choices; they come with consequences, as I am finding out myself.

Good luck and hugs,

Anita

Dear Amrit,

I have updates about Dr. Mayhew and didn't want to wait any longer to share with you. I didn't go to see the therapist at the University because I was concerned what could happen. I was close to the end of my degree, and I didn't want any complications. So I continued to meet Professor Mayhew every day, as he demanded. Every time I did not show up to meet him, he made sure I regretted it. He would pick on me and ask me difficult questions in class. If I could not answer the question, he would humiliate me. Even when I answered the question, he would challenge me. I understood his warnings well and kept silent.

When I went to meet Professor Mayhew in his office, he was a different person. He was not a professor then. He never said anything about how he treated me as a student.

One day, I had the guts to ask, "Why are you harsh to me in class?"

His eyes softened and he reached his hand across his table to me and said, "I don't want anyone to know. You are special. Only in this office we can show our true selves. This is our secret sacred space."

Internally, I struggled, but I kept a straight face. Who was he kidding? It was a place of hell for me. I knew I had to figure out a plan. Surely, he could see I had no feelings for him except as my professor. I knew I had never given him an opportunity to think otherwise. He was older than papa. I saw him as a father figure, for god's sakes. There was nothing about him I was attracted to. Quietly, I wondered how many times had he done this? I couldn't be his first.

I was trapped in his vicious game. Every day, I calculated my options. Do you remember Siti's grandfather, our neighbours when we were younger? When I was twelve years old, I would go over to play with Siti. Her grandfather would grab me and hold me tight. I shoved and kicked. I quickly figured out that when I screamed, he let me go. Then I stopped going over. Now, I desperately needed a Canadian plan. First, the final essay for this class was due soon. I worked hard on my final essay. I knew it was excellent. Of course, it was. It was about Simone Beauvoir.

Then, I tested him again. I did not meet him two days in a row. When I showed up to his class on Monday, he handed back my final essay. I knew without turning to the last page what my grade was.

He said, "See you at 2 p.m."

I nodded. When I showed up at Professor Mayhew's office, his face was cherry red, and his mouth was pursed into two straight lines. I could see the vein on his right temple throb, as he did when I disobeyed him last time. Calmly, I sat back in the chair to hear his angry ramblings. I barely listened to him, conspiring, instead, how to survive and pass his course. My explanations for my absence fell on his deaf ears. It was ok. Frankly, I relished goading him now that I knew his game plan. Before I left, Professor Mayhew changed my mark to an A. He had a way of writing the F so when he changed it, no one would see the difference because the F had curves that easily became an A.

I had no option but this: my plan was to wait for the exam and the final mark to be on my transcript. That is all I needed to survive this bloody man. I dared not rock the boat. I attended class, sat through his office lectures, and went to lunch with him as commanded. I prayed for my strength to last until the end of semester. I could do that. I must.

Then on Saturday, I saw Professor Mayhew and his family at Market Mall. Bizarre. He pretended he did not know me when we walked past each other.

I wished I could have run up to his wife and said, "Your husband is planning on blackmailing me to have sex with him."

I could end it there, in front of Le Chateau at Market Mall. But I didn't. I let him ignore me and walked past. I gazed at his wife and two daughters who were blissfully ignorant of the power he held over me each day at 2 p.m. in the afternoon.

Well, just as I thought it couldn't get any stranger, it did. The next day, when I met him in his office, he told me that he wanted me to go to his house for lunch and to meet his family. I stared him down, but I knew I would have to show up. It was two days before the final exam. I was too close to the end to rock the boat.

As ordered, I went to his house, which was across the university. Dr. Mayhew introduced me to his wife, Martha, and his two children, Sue, sixteen and Allie, fifteen. To my relief, he had also invited ten other students from class. I stood in the corner of the living room and watched him. He barely spoke to me, which made me feel relieved because I had no desire to have any contact with him. I showed up in his house only to pass his course. I constantly looked at my watch.

Professor Mayhew watched me. He saw me squirm.

I desperately wanted to leave after fifteen minutes, but he casually sauntered up to me, handed me a can of Coke, and fiercely whispered, "You can leave when I tell you to."

The whole time I was trapped in his house, Professor Mayhew scrutinized me without anyone knowing. I moved to the safety of a group of students and pretended to be engaged in conversation with them. Finally, after lunch, everyone left, one by one. Anxiously, I edged to the front door, and Dr. Mayhew came up to me, gave me an intimate smile and grabbed my hand to shake it, holding it longer than he should have.

He said loudly, "Good luck on your exam."

His wife Martha came up to me, gave me a warm hug and said, "Oh, yes. Thank you for coming, and best wishes for your exam. I'm sure Professor Mayhew here will be good to you."

Oh, if the poor lady only knew the whole truth. I bolted out the door and did not stop until I got to my house. I pulled out my Ventolin and took two deep puffs.

Calm down. Calm down. I said to myself.

In my room, I looked at my image in the mirror and was taken aback by the haunted face looking back at me. Thoughts raced through my mind.

Why me? Why the other ten students? Did we all have something to be concerned about? I wondered.

I did the only thing I knew. "Waheguru, Waheguru."

The next day, I sat through Professor Mayhew's final exam in class, refusing to look up at him, knowing his eyes were fixed on me.

Easy exam, you bastard. I got this! I thought as I furiously scribbled in the exam booklet.

When I handed the exam to Dr. Mayhew, he grasped my hand and squeezed it. He said, "All the best, Simran. I want you to take my class in Fall. I expect you will be there. Make sure you do, now. I will check my class list today."

It was a command. I knew that. I nodded. I went straight to the Registrar's office. I signed up for his 400-level class. Then, I patiently waited a week for my final marks from his current class to appear on my transcript. The moment I saw my grade, I ran to the Registrar's office, filled in the form, and with my hand shaking, handed it to the lady behind the counter. A big, wide smile of pure joy and relief emerged on my face. I did it. I dropped Professor Mayhew's upcoming class in the fall, which I didn't even need. Deep breath. Finally, I could breathe, again.

My phone at home rang for many days, and I refused to pick it up. Lin answered it, but there was always a click.

"Asshole," she screamed into the receiver each time. I gave her a hug, and she was confused. But it didn't matter. No more snares for me.

Amrit, it looks like I outsmarted the devil! I have ten more courses to take. I carefully checked that I could avoid Professor Mayhew at all costs and still get my degree. My prayers worked. I didn't see his name anywhere. He doesn't work in the spring or summer semesters. And if he does, I know I'll find a way out. Nothing and no one is going to stop me now.

Don't tell anyone. This is our secret. Burn this letter. I don't want to talk about this pig. Why do I bother reading all those literature books for my English degree if all I have to do is secretly meet with men to get ahead in life? My life is a Victorian novel.

I can breathe, again. And, yes, I got an A in his class, like I deserved to.

Always,

Simran

29 JUNE 1987

Simran,

Good girl. You are doing well in Calgary. You are taking many courses and finishing your degree quickly. Your snow in Calgary reminded me of my experience with snow also. When I was fifteen, just before my marriage, my father took me to Kashmir to visit Dal Lake. There are mountains and lakes there, like the photos you sent me of Lake Louise. Same. We took the train all the way. You know, I was my father's pet. His favourite. Just like your father took you to Calgary, Bapuji wanted to give me a special time with him before I got married and went to Singapore. I was excited to spend time with him. I loved my father so much.

I knew it was expensive and my father didn't have much money. My family had no money for my dowry. I knew he was sad to have me go so far away to Singapore after my marriage. He felt bad for me. I don't know how he took me to Kashmir. I heard my mother screaming at him in the night when she thought I was sleeping. She was hitting her head and crying.

Bapuji said, "Last time I can do something special for my beti. I will do it."

My mother's eyes were red in the morning. I kept quiet because I wanted to be with my father. The two of us took a taxi to the train station. We jumped on the train. I had the seat next to the window. I looked out at all the villages and different stations. I fell asleep on my father's shoulder. We ate the aloo pronthas that my mother had packed for us. At one station, Bapuji bought two hot masala chai. It was delicious.

Finally, the train arrived in Jammu and we took the bus to Kashmir. Long trip. Peaceful. I didn't mind. I was with Bapuji and he was smiling. We arrived in Kashmir in the morning. I jumped off the bus. I looked around me. White. High mountains. My father held my hand and we walked to the hotel across the bus station. We had a tiny room with two manjas. I felt happy. It was cold up there in the mountains. February was winter. I put on a sweater over my suit. I had two wool shawls to keep me warm.

For the first time in my life I saw snow. Bapuji took me outside the hotel room and all the trees around us were white. Looked like a postcard I once saw from England. I touched the snow on the branch of the tree. I put some in my hands. Frozen. It was like ice from the freezer. Soft. It melted and became cold water. My hands were frozen. Bapuji laughed. Together, we collected snow and felt it in our hands and threw it up in the air. It was like frozen cotton wool that quickly became water. We giggled together and went for a walk around the lake. Bapuji held my hand tight. I think Lake Louise must be like that. We had papri chaat at the roadside stall. More chai. Bapuji bought me some sweet treats also—sweet, delicious gulab jamun. Those were the best days of my life with Bapuji.

That night, in my hotel room in Kashmir, I was freezing. Bapuji went out and got a second blanket for me. He sat on the side of my bed and stroked my head. He sang my favourite Hindi song. Finally, I fell asleep. We drank hot chai in the morning. It was cold for me but I loved every moment with my father. When we got back to Delhi, I knew there was no escape from my marriage. I knew I had to leave, whether I wanted to or not. I had no choice. Bapuji cried so much when I left for Singapore that day after the wedding.

We held each other tightly and he whispered to me softly, "You will forever be my Kashmiri princess."

Bapuji died two years after I moved to Singapore. I never saw him after I left India. Only Kashmir was the best memory. I still dream of Kashmir and Bapuji.

How do you take the cold weather? It must be difficult. Singapore is much better, beti. Nice. Hot. Safe.

Ok. Never mind. Study hard. Pass your exams. Get your degree.

Soon you will be home.

We miss you.

Mummy

1 JULY 1987

Dear Simran,

So you have to move all the way to Calgary to have a romance with a Singaporean? I am glad you had a good time with your teenage sweetheart. This sounds promising. Now you will have someone to look forward to when you get back from Canada. I found it was difficult adjusting to life back in Singapore after I had been in the west. Hopefully, you can plan a grand wedding when you come back. Make sure you don't leave me out like you did for your arranged marriage engagement! Front row seats, this time.

Sim, I don't know what to do about my mum. She is getting more distant and reclusive. She locks herself in her room all day. I leave her alone. I wish I could get help, but I don't know what help to get or where from. You know Singapore. Here, the only place is Woodbridge Hospital, the 'mad people hospital', as we all call it. How would I get her to go? My father says to leave her alone. Is that where unhappy women go? To their bedrooms or the asylum? I'm fed up with taking care of everyone.

On a sad note, I have been going to Tan Tock Seng Hospital every Saturday to visit my cousin who has cancer. She is twenty-five years old, and she has thyroid cancer, stage 4. Things look bleak for her. We were close as kids and lost touch over the years. It is such a dreadful place. You can smell death as soon as you step into the ward. The walls are a drab grey. The beds are old and rickety. The windows seem to repel sunlight rather than allow any in. Lai Fung sits in her bed and stares out the window that looks to the parking lot. I don't know what to say to her. I try to talk about movies or gossip about family. She mostly listens. Her hair has fallen off from chemo treatments. The veins on her arms are bruised blue and black.

Why I mention this is every time I go to the hospital to visit Lai Fung, I see this tall White man in his hospital gown, walking up and down the hallway with his IV hooked up to a bag on a pole with wheels. He smiles at me every time I walk by him. That day, he stopped and said "hi." We chatted. Now, after I visit my cousin, I spend time with Gunther. He is the same age as me. He has this strong German accent and is from Stuttgart, now living here in Singapore with his father and sister. He has been here for one year. I am learning more about him each day as he gets treatment for his brain tumor. Imagine that—dealing with life and death at such a young age like my cousin. I must admit that I'm getting fond of him. Maybe, we could be together, I wonder.

Between my mum, cousin, and Gunther, it seems like life's challenges are bringing me down. For god's sake, give me good news about you and Sudhir to counter all this bleakness.

Amy

5 JULY 1987

Dear Simran,

You are a brave girl. I was worried to hear about your professor trying to trap you and take advantage of you. That is disgusting. You can't be the first student he's done this to. That is the problem. You are young and innocent. Fresh bait. It seems like no one can stop him. Thank God you outsmarted him by completing his course, getting an A and escaping his clutches. I'm sure he has moved on to his next victim. That bastard. Please come back as soon as you are done with your degree. It's too much for a young girl to bear this abuse.

I have a secret too. You cannot tell anyone. No one knows, only Sumari my maid. When I left Manjit and went home to Mummy and Papa, I found out that I was pregnant. It was bad timing. I was furious. Two kids and one more to come. I didn't want another child. My mother-in-law had been hinting non-stop that it was time for a son. No more daughters.

I looked at her and said, "You were someone's daughter. Why only sons?"

She glared at me and said, "That's our Indian way. We want sons to carry our name and take care of us when we are old."

I muttered, "Go to hell," under my breath.

I went to this doctor who could find out the sex of the baby at eight weeks. I went by myself. I didn't even tell Mummy. You see, this was an Indian doctor from India. He works here in Singapore under the table, illegally, of course. I found out about this doctor from our cousin Rekha. I went to her because when she had her fourth daughter, everyone, even her husband, gave her a terrible time.

When her visitors went to the hospital to visit Rekha and her baby, they said terrible things. They told her she was cursed. Bad luck. Couldn't have boys. A disappointment. A failure. She admitted she had a bad time after the birth with all the emotional stress. She told me she wished she had gone to see this Indian doctor to find out whether she was having a boy or girl.

I didn't say anything to Rekha, but I wrote down the doctor's name and found him on my own. I made an appointment to see him, and he did an ultrasound on me.

He looked at me and said, "No 100% guarantee, but it looks like a girl."

I was quiet. I didn't want any more children. How am I supposed to have one more girl? I thought of the Queen and the look on her face. Even Manjit had said he wanted a son. How could I disappoint everyone?

On the spot, I made my decision and said to the doctor, "I want an abortion."

He gave me the name of a different doctor in Singapore. I took the name and phone number and memorized it, but every time I picked up the phone, I couldn't do it. I couldn't dial the number.

One evening, I was having dinner with the Queen and Manjit. The Queen talked proudly about her youngest daughter who gave birth to a son a few months ago. She went on about how a baby boy was good izzat and reputation for the family. How women should carry a son for her family. I bit my tongue. I glanced up at Manjit, hoping he would say something. Nothing. He nodded his head in agreement.

"Yes, Ma. No, Ma." Then, he said, "No more girls for me. Time for a son."

Bloody hell. The next day, I picked up the phone and made an appointment for my abortion. I took my maid Sumari with me. I asked mummy to take care of the kids. She asked me why and where I was going. I said I was going for gynecological check-up for my bleeding.

Mummy said, "Ok. Go. Better check at once."

Sumari and I took a taxi to the hospital. I was scared and wanted to turn and run. What did this poor baby girl do to deserve this? At the waiting room, I heard the nurse call my name and I entered the small room. It was so dark. The instruments were all over the table on the side. It looked like a torture chamber. I stretched uncomfortably on the narrow bed and the nurse put one foot and the other in the metal stirrups.

My heart jumped furiously. I panicked and tried to move my foot out of the clamps, but they were stuck. The door opened with a bang. The doctor came in. An old Indian man. He had an angry look on his face. *Bloody hell. Did he think I like being trapped in my life?* I closed my eyes and tried to relax as I felt cold metal inserted in me. I stared at the ceiling to forget where I was and what I was doing.

The whole procedure felt like hours but in fifteen minutes, everything was done.

I heard the doctor's voice say, "Successfully aborted. Rest for one hour here before you leave. Don't come back here again. I won't do another one."

Then the doctor and the nurse left me in that depressing and suffocating room. I lay there, guilty and upset. I didn't look at the bin on the side. My torso was numb. My hands were clammy. I couldn't swallow. Just like that I had ended an innocent life. I told myself *it was a good thing, right*? Rather than bring her into the world to suffer. To be unwelcome. What have I done, Simran?

After an hour, my maid Sumari came into the room to get me. I didn't tell her anything. She's a smart lady. I'm sure she can guess.

I will never tell Manjit. No one. Only you.

When I got home to Mummy and Papa's house, I told Mummy I was not well. That I was feeling dizzy. She told me to sleep. Sumari took care of the kids. All these women helping me, and I just destroyed the life of one. When I went into Mummy's bedroom, I closed the door and put my head on the pillow. My body convulsed and I felt icy cold. My insides felt empty. Nothing in me. I felt hollow.

This is a difficult secret to keep. Please don't tell anyone. I know you can understand. I hope so. I think the life of a man is easier, don't you?

Love,

Amrit

6 JULY 1987

Anita, oh, Anita,

Congratulations! You gave Phil the boot. I mean, I don't blame you. It seemed like you picked up one more child to babysit. I do feel sorry for the poor bastard, though. He came all the way from Jolly old London for you. He gave up his job and family there, came to find true love with you, and you tossed him out like yesterday's newspaper. I'm surprised he did not run when he saw your complex situation with your ex-husband, Gopal.

Hey, Anita, perhaps now you will see that as a sign to take a break and resolve the Gopal issue before you embark on new liaisons? You need to be in a better space to assess what is best before you bring in a man, especially since you have kids involved. You are a beautiful and vivacious woman! You will find someone special one day. No rush, ok.

Do you remember Professor Shit who continues his terrorism on me? Let me tell you. I dedicated a lot of time to the second essay. He gave me a C. Then, I agonized over the final essay. C. I had nightmares about the final exam. C-. I ended up with a big fat C in his class. The lowest marks I have received in all the university classes I have taken.

I asked that older lady in class who disliked this professor. She read my essay and felt it was an A. When I told her I got a C, she was shocked.

"Go see the Head of Department and challenge the marks," she urged.

Oh yeah. That again. I knew I couldn't see Dr. Sanders, the Head. Hmm. I felt new fire in my belly. I wanted to fight one last time, so I went to see Professor Shit about my final grade in his class.

Well, he must have dementia because he said the exact same thing to me. "You don't write like us. You write like this," and he pointed to my final essay.

"Can you show me a specific part of my essay that is not 'us'?" I challenged him. "Everything. All of it. You." He waved aimlessly all over my essay to prove his point.

I wondered if Professor Shit even read my essay or if my marks were based on my name alone. You see, there were no checkmarks or comments on my essay—as clean as when I handed it in.

"What can I do?" I insisted. "What do you want me to do?" I persisted.

True to his name, Professor Shit shrugged his shoulders and said, "Just write like a Canadian."

I stood up, grabbed my essay from his hand, and left. I stood outside his office, pondering my next move when I saw the head, Dr. Sanders and Dr. Mayhew, another one of my professors, walk by me. Dr. Sanders nodded at me as he entered Professor Shit's office. Well, the boys' club reigns, yet again.

Sometimes, to win, I know I must walk away, like I've done before. This time, I have no regrets or tears—just a keener understanding. C for a new Canadian, eh.

Then I turned to face Dr. Mayhew who said, "See you at 2 p.m."

My afternoon meetings with Dr. Tony Mayhew are a story for another letter. I didn't reply. I turned and ran as fast as I could out of the building, past the giant arch of the university at the front entrance, and I stopped short in my tracks. I glanced at the black blobs of cloud threatening rain.

I faced the famous University of Calgary arch and gestured both my middle fingers at it.

"Fuck you all, Professor Assholes."

"Thanks for the men's club, Dr. Sanders."

"Go to hell, Professor Shit. I'll show you how to write like us!"

"Just a matter of time, you horny old bastard, Dr. Mayhew!"

I yelled my frustrations at the solid, proud arch, perched in the sky. No one was around. Just me. For some reason, that made me giggle and feel better. I thought about the sacrifices my father made for me to come to the University of Calgary to get a degree. How dare these men push me to the peripheries because I was a young foreign woman. Erotic? Exotic? Oh yeah? I'll show them. Watch me.

I'm sending you giant hugs. Stay single for the time-being, girl-friend. Time heals all wounds.

Lots of love,

Simran

1 AUGUST 1987

Mummy, Mummy, Mummy,

I loved how you spent that special time with your father in Kashmir before you married and went to Singapore. It reminds me of how Papa came to Calgary with me to make sure I was settled in on my own. Good fathers!

I am disappointed I am not coming back to Singapore. It was a difficult decision, but I decided to take courses so I can be done by April 1988. It means I won't have much longer to get my degree. I know all the ways to save money and time.

What I have found in Calgary is in spring and summer, most of the university students take a break. Some of my friends are done with their degrees and have moved back to where they came from all over Canada. Many of the people I know are international students and have gone back to Germany, London, and Spain. Now you know why I am taking as many courses as I need to be done quickly. I am lucky the University of Calgary gave me credits for my teaching diploma, which means I can complete my degree in three years. I am going as fast as I can.

I loved your description of Kashmir. Let me share my beautiful Calgary. It is the size of Singapore, except there are not as many people here as in Singapore. It is hard to get around Calgary without a car and the bus and train system are not very good. I decided to walk everywhere. For example, I walk from my house to Kensington in one hour. I go down the hill to the Bow River, and I walk on the path all the way to Kensington where there are restaurants, boutiques, and coffee shops. If I have to take a bus back, I jump on #9, and it takes me back to the university and close to home. I have to find my own way to be a part of Calgary.

You won't believe it, but I bought a bicycle for $25 at a garage sale last week. I got a helmet, too. Now, I have a choice to bike down the hill and along the river for as far as I feel like going. The Bow River flows from one end of the city to the other. I watch people float and canoe down the river on hot days in summer. Canadians love their sun! Everyone comes out in shorts and summer tops. The parks in Calgary are buzzing with people. I love the smells of food people barbeque in the outdoor pits. Mummy, you would love Calgary in the summer. I know you don't like snow or the cold.

What do I do in the evenings? Well, some days, I try to cook. But my favourite is to come home and make butter and toast and a steaming cup of tea. It's simple and fast. I relax on my sofa and watch TV. Sometimes, my friend Steve takes me to a movie, or we go for dinner. He takes me to north-east Calgary where there are Indian restaurants like in Singapore. I have chicken biryani and papri chaat. It makes me homesick.

In nine months, I will get my degree. Can you believe it? I made the best decision when I came to Calgary. There have been many ups and downs here, but I will have fulfilled my dream for a degree. I couldn't have done it without you and Papa. I am a lucky girl.

Love,

Sim

10 AUGUST 1987

Dear Amrit,

I wish I could have been there with you and given you a loving hug. I cried for you and the innocent baby girl. My heart is heavy. What a difficult and terrible decision. I am glad your maid Sumari was there for you. I feel your loneliness, my sister. Your husband should have been there to support you through this traumatic decision and time. Whatever has happened cannot be undone. If there are Indian doctors who disclose the gender of babies in-vitro, there is a demand for this service in a society that mostly values boys. You must gather more strength and find better ways for yourself in this life. We must find new directions for Soni and Roni, so they will not face the same challenges like us.

Let me get your mind off things and share my crazy adventures. I went to the Calgary Stampede in Calgary in July. It is the biggest outdoor show on earth. You would love it. It is world famous. Imagine this—chuck wagon races, rodeos, bulls, horses, cowboys, and cowgirls. The whole of the Stampede grounds are transformed into huge outdoor stages for concerts, inside auditoriums for fantastic dog shows, bars, wild, crazy rides, hundreds of vendors selling a fantastic array of food and a huge arena for the rodeo just to name a few. Think of the fun fairs in Singapore we attended as kids—now, this is 1,000 times larger and more exciting.

It was my first time going to the Calgary Stampede. "Yee-haw." That's what everyone says at the Stampede. I went with Lin and her church group friends. Yeah, I didn't know she joined a church. Ten of them were going and she asked me if I wanted to join them. I was thrilled and looked forward to being a part of the greatest outdoor show on earth.

That Sunday, the whole group met at the university, took the bus, then the train to the Stampede grounds. People on the bus and train wore western gear like jeans and cowboy shirts. Many had cowboy hats on. I was proud to wear my Wrangler jeans and Calgary t-shirt. I felt like a true Calgarian.

We paid our entrance fee, and my eyes widened in excitement to see crowds of people inside. It was a fiery hot day. We walked past food vendors, and I salivated looking at mini donuts, pineapple ice-cream, bratwursts and hot dogs, pizza—it was endless. Food was for later, we told each other.

The group decided to first go to the rides at the Stampede; we headed to the Midway with the crowds of noisy people. There was a giant Ferris wheel, bumper cars, caterpillars, rotating teacups and strawberries, haunted houses, flying airplanes and death-defying swings—the ride choices were endless. George from our group pointed to the Tilt-A-Ride sign. Let me explain it to you: two people sit in a cage. The ride moves like a merry go round, but at the same time, each cage also completely turns either backwards or forwards. That's not all. The cage makes sudden tilts to the left and the right.

I was teamed up with George. I nervously entered the narrow cage and sat on the small bench inside, barely enough for our two bums. The attendant checked our safety belts and gave us the thumbs up. Soon, the ride started. It moved up, up, up, like a Ferris wheel. Then the cage vigorously tilted up and up and made complete rotations backwards and forwards. I had no idea which way the cage would move, and my arms flew all over from the impact.

George screamed like a baby. Within seconds, everything from George's shirt pocket spilled out—his keys, his comb and all the coins he had. We laughed, and George flailed his hands, trying to catch his keys. I tried to help, but the movements of the cage were erratic and unpredictable. I laughed until suddenly one of those flying coins lodged in my throat. I choked. I couldn't breathe and desperately gasped for air. I could feel the coin trapped sideways in my throat, completely blocking my airway.

I did the only thing I knew. I shouted, "Waheguru, Waheguru," while coughing, spitting, and trying to pound my chest with both my fists while the cage continued to jerk and move around. There was no way to stop the ride. George had no clue what was happening as he was still screaming and couldn't hear me. I felt dizzy. Petrified. Confused.

It felt like an eternity, but a miracle happened. The coin suddenly dislodged and jumped out of my mouth. I coughed and hit my chest to make double sure. Wait. Wait. I could breathe again. I desperately gasped in air, with my hands over my mouth this time. The ride kept going and going, so I shut my bloody mouth and eyes and prayed for the death trap to come to a standstill.

Finally, the cage shuddered, slowed down, and came to a slow rocking stop. George calmed down and bent over the safety belt and desperately collected his bloody missing coins and keys. He had no clue what had happened to me. I was dazed and dizzy from the ride and from almost meeting God with this Christian group.

When I stepped out of the cage, I saw a big sign at the operator's booth that said, "*Remove all coins and loose items from your pockets.*"

Really? George? What the hell? Maybe it was a sign I should be a Christian. This time, God definitely showed up and saved my life.

I told Lin what happened, and she said, "Oh. I would have moved into your bedroom—it's larger than mine."

Sigh. Even I had to laugh.

Don't worry. Obviously, I'm still alive. I can still feel that cold, round coin in my throat and taste the metallic acidic taste. Holy cow! Can you see the headline?

"*Singaporean dies in freak Tilt a Whirl Ride accident at the 1987 Stampede in Calgary.*"

You know, come to think of it, my life is an adventure like the Calgary Stampede. It is full of rides that go up and down. Sometimes, things happen to me I could not even have imagined. What really matters is, at the end, I'm becoming a true cowgirl in Calgary. I land on my feet and carry on.

Just like you, sister. You are a survivor. You fall off, and you get back on as well. I am proud of you and your determination to face the world. Giddy up, Amrit!

Lots of love and still alive,

Simran

Dear Amy,

My fall term begins in a few weeks. Time has simply flown by. Your friend Gunther seems intriguing. Tell me more.

My long-distance love affair with Sudhir has been great. He calls me often and writes long letters. We talk about possibilities of how we can be together when I get back to Singapore. This is making my return to Singapore more real and electrifying. Sudhir is contemplating either staying in the Singapore army or changing gears and becoming a doctor. I can easily get back into teaching. We could get a Housing and Development Board flat and start our life together. What can be difficult, right? I am willing to stand up to my family and let them know I want to be with Sudhir, whatever his race or background. I don't see any issue with these old-fashioned notions, right? I am dying to come back to Singapore. I want to use my degree, be with a man I love, be close to my family, start my life—how promising it all is.

Calgary is glorious. Oh, how I will miss it. I love the way the skies change colour, especially in the evenings. Sometimes, the sky above the mountain peaks which hug the city in the west, transform into mystical reddish hues of sunset streaks that light the sky. Peaceful. Breathtaking. I will miss my bike rides by the Bow River and those sun-loving Calgarians who float in their rafts down the stream, soaking all the unpredictable summer rays until snow descends in winter.

My Calgarians love to walk the pathways with their adorable dogs in tow. Such a vibrant display of living. I truly love the groove. I'm not looking forward to the urgent honking of cars and buses in

Singapore or the crowds of Singaporeans descending upon shopping malls.

Of course, it is not a fair comparison. There is simply more space here in Calgary.

Later, gator,

Simran

10 SEPTEMBER 1987

Dear Simran,

Alamak. I can't believe your Professor Shit. I mean, what do you do? If there is no direction or help, then there is only power and control. Seems like you are at the mercy of wolves. I hope that the C- won't affect your overall grade in a negative way. These people don't realize what sacrifices and cost your family suffered through for you to go there. I hope that you never have to have him as a professor ever again.

Exciting news. I've met a wonderful man. Anders. I was at a bar in Singapore with my girlfriends a few weeks ago. He was by himself at the bar. He kept a close eye on us. Finally, he came up to me and asked me to dance. Well, we danced all night. I let go of my worries and had fun.

He's nothing like boring old Gopal or quiet, reserved Phil. He is a firecracker. A hot and handsome Swedish expatriate who travels back and forth from Stockholm for work. He is such a gentleman. He's rich. We have spent every single day ... and night...together. He lives in a condo in Tanglin.

I'm being spoilt! Anders takes me to the poshest restaurants in Singapore, which I did not even know existed. Last night, we went to this exquisite Japanese restaurant and drank copious amounts of sake. Sushi and sashimi kept appearing, fresh and delicate. The bill was over $1,000. It was the top Japanese restaurant in Singapore, and I can see why. It was fabulous. Anders is twenty years older than me, which is a good thing. I find him mature, smart, fun, and sexy. It helps that he loves Singapore as much as I do. He would love to stay here. Oh, how wonderful that would be, and he is nice to my sons, and they adore him.

Don't worry. I'm keeping this one hidden from Gopal. After the last incident with Phil, I've learnt my lesson. My boys are young enough and won't say anything, anyways. One evening, I was out with Anders, window-shopping at Tang's. Guess who we ran into? Bloody Phil. I thought that he had gone back home. Phil stared at me, distraught. He came up to talk to me, but I turned away and dragged Anders with me. What the hell is Phil still doing in Singapore? Anders asked me if I knew him. I shook my head. I, *really*, didn't want to delve into it. I don't need a love quadrangle—is there such a thing?

My divorce papers are proceeding painfully. Now Gopal doesn't want to pay for anything. I'm tired and I want it all to be done. No one in his family is speaking to me. Of course, everyone feels sorry for him. Where were they when Gopal was dragging me across the living room?

Me,

Anita

1 OCTOBER 1987

Dear Simran,

How are your new professors for your fall semester? I hope they are doing their job and teaching you. No drama. I am feeling better about life. Work is good. I get excited about getting up in the morning and going to Uncle's Sodhi's shop in High Street. I meet new customers every day. I have fun as a working woman. I'm not stuck at home. You know, I have the highest sales in the shop. Anyone who comes in as a customer becomes a challenge for me. I take it upon myself to sell them whatever they came into the shop to buy. My customers never leave empty-handed.

The other day, a nice-looking Indian man came in, a tourist from Goa. He smiled and talked to me as I helped him with his shopping. I was excited. At the end, he bought six tennis shirts from me. Of course—I'm the best. The whole day, I smiled because I felt good and useful. Powerful. Beautiful. All things I had forgotten being a young wife stuck at home and unappreciated by my own husband.

My dear husband, Manjit, is back to his old ways. He stays out late again. He must be back with that Chinese girlfriend of his. Well, I don't care anymore. I'm not going to follow him and spy on him anymore. If that is who he wants to be with, he can go to bloody hell. I'll live my own life from now on. I am lucky I can go to work and feel strong.

When I get home, I am busy. It's my time to be with the kids. The house is clean and neat, thanks to Sumari. The food is prepared. The Queen is the usual, lah. Blah blah blah. I just smile and nod my head. In my left ear and out my right.

I am excited for when you come back to Singapore. You can

make your own choices about Sudhir as well. Maybe you and I can get a place to rent and live our lives as free birds? And the girls, too, of course. We will get a maid. Don't need to wait around for Manjit and be the spare wife. I gave him many chances. Now, it's my time. Who says we have no choice? Women don't have to live their lives like slaves till they die.

Miss you,

Amrit

5 OCTOBER 1987

Simran,

Please do something about your sister. She is becoming too bold.
She started working at Uncle Sodhi's shop and doing a full-time job.
That is too much for a married woman. She should spend time with
her children. Soni and Roni are too young to be left. She can't leave
her husband like that. She should be around and handle the house.
Her mother-in-law is angry. Indian girls cannot behave like this.
They must be respectful and do their duty. Amrit won't listen to me.

I tell her "Stop your work nonsense."

She says, "No. I am not like you."

"What do you mean *like me*? I have good children and a good
husband."

Simran, you know everyone respects me. I keep family together.
Ya. That is a woman's job. To hold everyone together. Now Amrit
leaves the house. Then how? Go to work and other men look at her.

Amrit talks to other men. Not good. We are not like this. This is
our custom. Our culture. Cannot be so stubborn and bull-headed.
Ask her to come to her senses. Tell her to stop working and stay
home with her children. She doesn't need a maid. If she stops working, then she can save money. She is not making any money. She is
spending money. She has to take bus, buy clothes, buy lunch. How?
All adds up, right? What is this independence you all want?

When are you coming home, Simran? Finish in April then come
home immediately. Don't loiter anymore. Can come home and find
work. Teacher job here is always needed. No problem. You can get.
My friend daughter is also a teacher. She is making good money.
Come back and start your life again. Enough of Canada. That is a

western world. Different from us. We are Singapore world. Asian values. Your degree is expensive already. Your father is having hard time. Please come back and relieve the stress.

Ok. Study hard. Be good. Tell your sister to stop her nonsense. Book your ticket home.

Acha.

Mummy

1 NOVEMBER 1987

Dear Amy,

I got a phone call from Sudhir last night. He sounded tense and terse, not the usual loving man he was on the phone. He didn't even ask me how I was. He went straight to his unexpected news: he had applied for immigration to the U.S.—alone.

Stunned, I whispered, "Why?"

"I want to be free," he coldly replied.

Then I had to hear Sudhir drone on about how he wanted no encumbrances. He had applied for jobs in Los Angeles and had a few interviews. He was tired of Singapore and yearned for a fresh start in the west. I listened to his bullshit while my disembodied spirit floated to the ceiling. Why hadn't I seen this betrayal coming at all? Our phone conversations and letters spoke of plans for my return home to Singapore. We made grand plans and fantasized about our lives together in Singapore. I looked forward to leaving Calgary, romanticizing about the poetry of our lives and connections: our Singapore high school love reimagined in Calgary.

I put the receiver to my left ear, slumped against the bed, slid down, and crumpled on the floor. I went numb. So many questions raced through my mind. All this while, Sudhir had led me on while he planned his own path alone. Duplicitous. One minute he was in love with me, and the next, with Lady Liberty.

"Hey, Simran, say something," he pleaded over and over again.

The phone fell out of my hand, and I hung up. What the bloody hell. All my hopes and dreams crushed by a man who has no imagination or courage to be with me. I sat on the floor for what seemed like an eternity. The phone rang and rang. I stared at it. *What? What words could he possibly have for me except for those to assuage his guilt?* I refused to participate in his absolution.

I must have sat on the floor in my room for hours. Words and thoughts recycled themselves. Finally, in the stillness of the dark, I pulled myself up. Enough of the self-pity. The only thing important was to get my degree. No one, and I mean, no one, will stand in the way of that. Once I get that piece of paper, I will have redefined myself. I do not need this stupid man who betrayed me at the first opportunity. He is dead to me.

How is the mysterious Gunther? I'm sorry to hear of his brain tumour. That is difficult to know he may not live. Please be careful with your heart. I would hate to see you hurt again.

I hope all goes well for you.

Best wishes. Always,

Simran

3 NOVEMBER 1987

Dear Simran,

Thank you for your concern for my mum. I knew she struggled, but I didn't really know the depth of her pain. Last Thursday, I got home from work around 6 p.m. I had an exhausting day at work, and I couldn't wait to get home. As usual, I got off at my bus stop and headed to my block of flats. A large crowd of people had gathered around my block, and I impatiently weaved through the throng of people on my way to the lift.

I noticed people gawking and craning their necks to see something. What? There were little kids with their parents. The parents had wormed their way to the front of the crowd. I headed straight for the lift, when out of the corner of my eye, I saw a lady's pump shoe. Red. Familiar. I stopped short in my tracks. My heart fluttered. Anxiously, I shoved my way to the lone shoe, poised at the periphery of the crowd. I gasped in terror. Manolo Blahnik.

I lifted my gaze ten metres ahead and saw the object of the gawking. Someone had plunged to her death from my block of flats, splattered under a tarp. The other familiar red shoe lay next to the bloody tarp.

I went numb and leaned against the pillar, while people's voices rose around me.

"Eh, why?"

"Aiyoh. She jumped, you know."

"Don't know from how many storeys."

"Crushed. Her brains all over—look."

"How terrible—such a poor thing!"

On and on, the voices became a terrorizing cacophony of

squawks. I stared at the blood that had saturated the concrete pad around the tarp. My eyes were drawn to the thin trail of bright red blood that encircled the red shoe. I gazed at the lone shoe. It looked poignant on its own. The familiar red pleated fabric at the front of the pump had soaked the blood and taken on a glossy hue. It glistened in the dusky, cool evening.

The police and ambulance arrived. They shooed away the onlookers.

"Eh. Go home, lah," the policeman said to the gawkers.

"Why you want to see a dead body. Let her be in peace, can or not?"

Reluctantly, half the crowd muttered and turned away, continuing their narrative about the jumper.

The tall, young Chinese policeman came to me. "Miss, go home, ok."

I had not realized my cheeks were wet with tears.

"Do you know who?" I hoarsely whispered.

"No, lah. How to know. Woman in her 50's. Wearing those red shoes, lah."

He held my arm, "Miss, you ok or not?"

I had fallen to my knees. I turned around and saw my father running to me. He looked at the tarp and he stopped. In that instant, we both knew for sure.

The rest is simply a blur. Police. Ambulance. Identification. Going back to the flat. The door of her room locked. The policeman broke in, and as he flung the door wide open, I prayed that Mum would be at the window, looking down. Instead, there was a chair against the window. All the windows were wide open.

I stumbled to the window and looked down. I hoped Mum flew with the ease of a bird and released all her sorrows of life on that hard, cold pavement. How could people fling themselves out of high-rise windows and plunge to their deaths? What violence. Why Mummy? What did she think of when she jumped out the window from the safety of her room into the cruel world outside? Perhaps, for Mummy, it was the other way around. Cruel world. Safe death.

Simran, I can't stop crying. For my mother. Her pain. Her desperation. Her inability to find meaning in her complex life. My father's grief is inconsolable. I let him have his space, and he lets me have mine. In this empty void of pain and loss, maybe we can find meaning.

Sorry to hear you and Sudhir are no longer together. I am disappointed by his choices. Indeed, we have both lost someone we love in such unexpected ways.

Love,

Amy

4 NOVEMBER 1987

Simran beti,

I have bought you a plane ticket to fly home for December holidays. I went to the bank deposit box and took out the money I had saved for long time from sewing clothes for the neighbours. No one knows about my secret savings. I had just enough to buy you a plane ticket to Singapore. I asked my friend Meena who is a travel agent to help me to book the ticket. She handled everything for me.

I know you are coming home next year but you were crying badly on the phone last week. You were sad but wouldn't tell me why. I held the phone and listened to you crying for a long time. I felt your pain strongly, beti. It's not easy being alone in a foreign country without your family.

I think it will be good for you to come to Singapore and be with us for two weeks. We miss you. Get your sadness out so you can succeed when you go back to Calgary to finish your degree.

Don't worry about money. In life we all struggle to make money. We become slaves to it. I read the other day that when you spend money, more money will come to you. You are at the end of your degree and everything will be good now.

Beti, come after your final exams. We are here for you. If you have time, buy two lipsticks for me. Burgundy and hot pink. Your father likes Cadbury chocolates. The one with fruit and nut. Pistachio also can. Very fresh from Canada.

Everything will be ok.

Mummy

15 NOVEMBER 1987

Mummmmmmmmmmmmmy,

I got your plane ticket to come home for Christmas. BEST PRESENT EVER IN THE WORLD! I cried when I got your letter. You have no idea how much I wanted to come. I miss everyone. I am homesick and want to be with my family. I was worried about what I would do this December when everyone is away again. Now, I get to be with all of you.

I feel excited. Ok. I am going shopping tomorrow. I will buy Estée Lauder lipstick from The Bay tomorrow. I will get Cadbury chocolate, Papa's favourite fruit and nut.

Thank you, Mummy. Love you. See you soon.

Simran

2 DECEMBER 1987

Hey Anita,

I must admire—or is it envy—your catlike ability to land on your feet after each man adventure. Just when I thought you were taking a break, you have already found a replacement in Anders. Wow. Well, when I think about it, why shouldn't a beautiful and smart woman like you do what you want? You're showing me it can be a woman's world out there. I love it. Just be careful, ok. My fingers are crossed that your Swede is your salvation.

I still spend time with Steve, the man I met at the punk bar. He is a nice man, and he reminds me of my life when I was in Singapore and how I searched for way out of my restrictions. I understood him a little better when I met his parents the other day. They reminded me of Indian parents who struggle to let their children make their own choices.

Steve took me to his parents' house a few days ago. He had to pick up his wallet that he had left in his other jacket. I went into the house with him. I was immediately encircled by his parents. His mother bombarded me with questions, questions, questions.

"Where are you from?"

"What are you doing in Calgary?"

"Where is your family?"

"Are you a Christian?"

She seemed rankled with my answers.

His father then grilled me with more questions. He prowled and watched. Then he pounced.

"When are you going back?"

"How long have you been going out with Steve?"

"Where is Singapore? In China?"

"What do your parents do?"

"Do you pray to idols like Babar the Elephant?"

Hah. I stepped back from the onslaught. It was like an FBI interrogation. They were concerned, for sure. Steve didn't say anything to stop them. That was the longest fifteen minutes of my life. I smiled and answered their questions politely. Boy, that felt like an arranged marriage set-up.

Steve's parents looked relieved when I said I was leaving Calgary for good in April.

"Good," said his dad. "We don't need more foreigners here. You people from the third world countries come here and take our jobs."

"Well," I retorted. "Singapore is a first world country, and I have jobs lined up back home already."

So, they were worried I would steal their son. Somedays, it is tiring being the outsider, constantly judged and questioned.

I looked at Steve and asked, "Have you ever considered getting a job in Singapore?"

He laughed and said, "Yes. Yes, I have."

Anyway, none of them should worry. I'm leaving in April.

Love,

Simran

3 DECEMBER 1987

Dear Amy,

I am heartbroken for you. I stared at the photographs you had sent me of your mum and her red shoes. The photo of the red shoes was poignantly painful, as I imagined you seeing them that fateful evening when you came home from work. I wept for your mum's pain and the thought of how she could find no other way out.

That day of your mum's shopping expedition for those Manolo Blahniks will be an indelible memory of her happiness. You shared a special day with her, Amy. I know you will hold on to that recollection forever.

I know there are no words to soften your loss and agony; I am genuinely sorry. Please know I am here for you in any way that you need. Send me letters with stories and about your mum whenever you want. When we meet again, I would love to hear your memories about your mum or sit in silence with you—whatever you need.

Love,

Simran

4 DECEMBER 1987

Dear Amrit,

I'm sure you're not surprised that Mummy sent me a letter about your rebellion. Here is your list of crimes and how you must remedy them:

1. First, quit your job immediately. Only shameless women work.
2. Go back to being a full-time mom to your kids. Your children will suffer because of your absence in the house. They will grow up to be criminals.
3. Be good to your lord and master, your husband, Manjit, no matter how he treats you, even if he continues to have an affair. After all, men can do what they want. Do not question men. Simply accept.
4. Do your wifely duties because that is what good Indian women do.
5. Listen to whatever Mummy and Papa command you to do as an obedient daughter must. Do not answer back or disagree.
6. Come to your senses because you experienced a bout of temporary insanity. It's not too late. You can turn things around by complying with solid old-fashioned values.
7. Don't fight the system because these traditions and expectations have been in place for generations and generations. Don't you dare topple the system.
8. Being a mother and a wife are God-given duties. You will be blessed for eternity.
9. Don't think for yourself because women are not allowed to contemplate and to make decisions about important matters. This is a dangerous thing and can cause the downfall of society as we know

it.

10. Stop stirring up shit by being independent, speaking up, doing what you want, expressing your needs as a woman and trying to live your own passions. Abandon all dreams, immediately.

Ok. I made some of these commands up, but you get my gist, right? I don't think our parents, Manjit and his family know what to do with women like you and me.

It is ironic that mummy and papa have recruited me to pull off this feat. I mean, who the heck is going to listen to me. I am the biggest shit disturber to begin with. That is why I want an education and a degree. This is my passport to economic freedom and a chance to question and challenge anything I find "old-fashioned."

Amrit, you got a job after your arranged marriage and stood up to what was unacceptable to you. I admire your strength and courage.

I respect your rebellion, my dear sister. You are braver than me.

I know there will be challenges when I come back to Singapore. I want to live on my own and choose my own husband. You know, like I can here in Calgary where no one questions me or bothers me. Freedom feels fabulous. Is it possible to return to Singapore? Really, I am having a hard time thinking of coming back to Singapore for good.

Which ones of the ten rules are you going to follow, Amrit?

Love,

Simran

20 DECEMBER 1987

Hey Lin,

Here I am on the plane, heading back to Singapore for Christmas and New Year. Thank you for getting your friend George to drive me to the airport. It was an unexpected and thoughtful gesture. You are my family in Calgary. We've gone through many ups and downs together as foreign students. No one understands what it feels like to pursue my dreams, have my family sacrifice so much, and come to a new country to get a degree. I am grateful for being at the University of Calgary, and I know you are excited about your mechanical engineering degree. Our degrees have cost our families thousands and thousands of dollars. We're the lucky few foreign women who can achieve our dreams and goals.

I'm thinking of you as I write this, and I wanted to applaud you on your strength and courage as well. I have seen your loneliness and struggles to fit in. We've had our intriguing dynamics as roommates, but I count you as my friend and family. I regret not saying this more often. You are a future engineer, and I imagine in Malaysia, you'll be one of the most educated and accomplished women. When I come back, let's celebrate. It will be my treat.

I didn't think I would be this excited to go back to Singapore to visit my friends and family. My heart is thumping erratically. I am impatient, stuck in this airplane seat. How am I going to survive this long, long flight home? I have two countries I love, Singapore and Canada.

I am glad you will be with your friends over the holidays. I will bring back some dodol, dried sour plums, and Singapore spices, as requested. See you next year.

Happy New Year, Lin.

Simran

25 DECEMBER 1987

Dear Steve,

Merry Xmas to you and your family. I am sure you had a delicious turkey dinner, with all the trimmings. Do you know that I can make a fabulous turkey dinner as well? I'll tell you the story one day and how I left the bag of giblets in the turkey.

It's Christmas in Singapore today. Not in my house, though. We don't celebrate Christmas. I arrived in Singapore a few days ago. It's mayhem. It's wonderful. It's terrible. I'm confused by the barrage of emotions, like a bubbling cauldron from within me. Every morning, I go to my window of my bedroom, high up on the sixteenth floor of our block of flats. I see the green sprawl of a canopy of trees far below me.

I'm staggered every time I see how much higher my family's flat is than the tallest trees. My mind is confused at the green leaves. I vividly recall the thick white canopy of snow covering the ground of Calgary on the morning I left for the airport: rushing from the door into the car, trying to keep warm in the minus 20 Celsius. My breath fogged up the car window as I pressed my nose on the frost covered pane. Two landscapes. Different. Both now engrained in my psyche as home.

I stood by the window until I heard my mummy's voice call me to breakfast. Hot pronthas fresh off the tewa, seasoned with salt and pepper, my favourite. A bull's eye egg next to eat and a steaming mug of sickeningly sweet tea, laden with both sugar and condensed milk. I sputtered out the first syrupy sip of sweetness, but it slowly got familiar again. The sweetness was in perfect sync with the salty pepperiness of the prontha. I settled into the breakfast meal that gave me a sense I was home.

Then, a flash of Calgary seared my memory. That view out of my window. Three bare trees with outstretched branches. Touching tip to tip, laden with mounds of snow, a stunning tableau. And I felt this twitch in my belly, a sense of homesickness. Missing. Odd, right? Belonging to and missing two places at the same time. Here and missing there. There and missing here. A sensation I have never felt before. Wait. Maybe, I have imagined it. Like torn between two lovers. Possible?

Of course, being with my family is—I am struggling for a word here—is difficult. Every night, I cry into my pillow from the sheer relief of being with the familiar. Know what I mean? My mum wants me to book my ticket for April for as soon as I write my last exam. Papa doesn't say much, as usual. He asked me if there was enough money till April.

I looked at the worry lines on his brow. I never wanted to think about how Papa would get the money. Could he afford this? Too late, aren't I? It made me feel thoughtless and selfish. I simply blocked it all out. I'll pay him back when I get home to Singapore and work.

My sister Amrit is different. Hmmm. Bolder. Taller. Fiercer. I love it. She's more impatient about the bullshit she has to deal with at home. I spent a lovely day with her and my cute nieces. Her mother-in-law stayed in her room all day. I was happy about that. That woman complains about everything. What an unhappy woman, always picking on my sister. Well, the way new and improved Amrit is now, even those nagging complaints wouldn't bug her.

Amrit was impatient, even with me. I was amused.

"Stop asking me what I am going to do," she chided me when I pestered her about Manjit. "I'll know what to do when the time is right."

Wow, I thought to myself. *You go, girl.*

On this trip, I'm trying to find ways to reintegrate into Singapore when I return for good in April. I mean, I only have 120 days left in Calgary.

On my last trip to Harry Hays building, the immigration officer gave me my stamp only till April 25th, 1988. As usual, that morning, my palms felt moist and sticky, and my eyes darted around the room at Harry Hays, where us immigrants, you know, mostly people of colour, were exposed to the usual air of arrogance on the other side of the counter. There was no privacy for any of us, and everyone could watch and hear the interactions between the immigrant and the officer on the other side of the counter.

One after the other, those of us in line, were called to the counter to endure the barely polite voices of the officers who spoke a few decibels louder in case the immigrant did not understand what the officer was saying in English.

Then it was my turn. I felt a rush of relief to see I got a female officer. I was sure I'd get some sisterly compassion and kindness from her. But I felt a pang of fear nestle in my gullet when the officer didn't even look at me.

Instead, she surveyed my information in front of her and loudly announced, "You've been in Canada long enough. It's time for you to leave. Go back to where you came from."

The officer's voice boomed round the room, and I guiltily looked at the sympathetic faces of my fellow immigrants. They understood my distress.

"Wait," I pleaded. "Can I have two extra weeks to get rid of my furniture, pack my belongings, and get my final grades. You know, I need to tie up loose ends."

The hostile officer stared at me for a long time. She had a sneer on her face. I knew she had total and complete power.

Slowly, she enunciated the words again. "You've been in Canada long enough. It is time for you to leave. Go back."

I felt my throat constrict as I tried to hide the burning tears that rolled down my cheeks. The officer silenced me, and I, helplessly, watched her stamp my visa with the date, *leave or else*—I'm sure that was what it said.

I knew I had been given my official boot, like many other immigrants in this Harry Hays office would. We all cringed in front of these officers who decided who would get that coveted immigrant stamp. I just wanted two extra weeks.

So, here I am, in Singapore, and I have an expiry date to exit Canada on April 25, or else. When I get back to Calgary, I have my last semester to complete. I'd better have all my ducks in a row and leave by that date if I don't want to be apprehended and thrown in prison.

I hope your Christmas was great. How was Christmas with your family? Did they ask you a million questions about me? Tell them I'm back in Singapore. That should calm your parents' fears about you and me. We shall meet soon.

Here's to a wonderful New Year.

Regards,

Simran

2 JANUARY 1988

Dear Lin,

Happy 1988! For me, I had an intriguing New Year's party at my house. Mum, sister, Anita, Amy. You know these women, and I shared some of their adventures with you when I received their letters. New Year's Eve—here we were, all in my family's living room. My beautiful Singapore women—raw, alive, despondent, rebellious, stubborn, hopeful, exciting, passionate, and joyous—all emotions trickling, bubbling, and overflowing.

My mum made a spectacular dinner fit for queens. The table overflowed with her signature dishes. She made her special chicken curry, dhal, aloo goobi, chole, keema, dhai, biryani rice and hot, fresh chapattis. We sat around the dining table and ate with relish and gusto as the dishes appeared and were quickly replenished. Mum made sure no one starved. Being typical mum, she spent most of the time in the kitchen, her castle, with Amrit's helper, Sumari who helped her. Finally, Anita dragged Mum out to be with us while Sumari brought out gulab jamuns and kheer for dessert. And hot masala chai, of course.

Mum was overjoyed to have all of us women there.

She hugged me and announced, "Simran is the first one in this family to get a degree. She is a modern woman. Her husband will have to understand how to handle her. Not like me. A young sixteen-year-old who was put on a ship from India to Singapore. In my time, a woman must listen to her husband and follow his rules. There is no other way for a woman. All of us four sisters prayed for a man to marry us. We waited until one by one, we all got married. My luck was to leave my family in Delhi and come to Singapore. It's alright. It's our karma to go where we have to. Simran is too smart and too independent. Her sister, Amrit, is the same. Amrit will own her own sports shop one day. Just you wait and see. Both my daughters make me proud."

All the ladies clapped and cheered.

Anita said, "Aunty, women these days don't need a man to survive."

My mum shook her head and said, "No, it's better to have the protection and safety of a man."

My sister Amrit stood up and hugged Mum.

"Mummy, sometimes, no man can give that to a woman. Look at me. My husband is busy protecting another woman, his first girlfriend before he was forced to marry me."

My mum looked uncomfortable and kicked Amrit on her shin to shut her up. Instead, she kicked me by mistake, and I giggled and held Amrit's arm. Amrit understood my secret signal and waited until Mummy went to the kitchen.

Amrit said, "Ladies, out of all of you, I must be the last woman forced to have an arranged marriage. Some arranged marriages work out well. Mine did not. My husband does not love me or cherish me. The only reward is my two beautiful daughters, Soni and Roni. I will do everything to make sure they do not face my fate."

Mum came back to the table, and Amrit winked at us and said, "Here's to Mummy and her wonderful cooking. She is the best wife and mother in the world."

My good friend Amy, who recently lost her mum to suicide showed up. Amy did not want to come, but I persuaded her to, even for a little bit. Amy told all of us about that fateful day her mother committed suicide. We listened intently.

My mum wept and hugged Amy. "It's ok, Amy. Your mum is safe and happy in heaven."

Amy smiled and told us stories about her mum. Happy stories. We laughed and cried with Amy. Sad. Then Amy had a surprise for us. She had brought her mum's Manolo Blahnik shoes—the red ones. The ones that her mom has last worn. Gently, she took them out of her bag. We all fell silent. My mum took the red shoes and put them on a chair at the table—she was the sixth woman of honour at our table.

Mum said, "Amy, your mum Sophia is here with us."

Acknowledged. Heard. Celebrated. We all toasted a glass of bubbly to Amy's mum, Sophia. From invisible to visible. From unheard to heard. From the end to a new beginning. It was a meaningful night for all of us. When Amy left later that night, she had a heartfelt smile on her face: like a burden was lifted off her shoulders.

At the end of the night, Amy packed the red shoes in her bag and whispered, "Bye, Mummy. I love you."

My beautiful friend Anita came as well. Lucky for me, she was available as her new boyfriend, Anders the Swede, had left a few hours before our dinner date. She came straight from the airport, laden with expensive gifts from her generous boyfriend. We were impressed and envious. Prada wallet. Prada purse. Prada handbag. I think her Prada handbag would pay for one semester of our university fees in Calgary.

I prayed and prayed that my mum would not say anything, but I lost that battle.

"Anita," my mum said. "Why so stupid? $1,000 can feed many children at the boys' home, you know."

Anita laughed and said, "Aunty, my husband Gopal beat me for years, and I kept that painful secret. Boyfriend number two, Phil from London, had no money; I paid for everything for him. I got rid of both. So far, this one, Anders, seems to be the best. He adores me, and he spoils me. Finally, I found someone who is good to me. I deserve it, Aunty."

My mum went up to Anita and shook her hand. "In that case, congratulations. Well done. You enjoy your presents. The Prada handbag is the best one."

All of us laughed, and Amrit looked at mum and nodded. Maybe, my mum was slowly accepting the new ways of women's lives. Sumari came to clear the table. We made her join us and she giggled and touched Anita's bags.

Sumari said, "Waaaah. Beautiful bags. In Indonesia, can buy one for ten dollars. All fake. My husband also fake. He beat me. He has many girlfriends. I kick him out. Maybe one day I also can meet a man who will buy me a real Prada bag like this."

Anita stood up and picked up the Prada wallet. "Here, Sumari. You don't need a man. Take this wallet. It's for you. A present to remind you of our stories and time together. You did the right thing to get rid of your useless husband. We are brave and strong women."

Sumari stood there in shocked silence and clutched the Prada wallet to her heart. Tears rolled down her face. Mum, Amrit, Anita, Amy and I stood up, and we hugged one another.

It was a remarkable night.

It's my last few days in Singapore. I miss Calgary. I yearn to get back to Calgary, yet I am also dreading it terribly. I am counting down the last four months in Canada, and it's giving me terrible anxiety. It's like being rejected by a lover. Never mind. I am coming back to the arms of another lover, right, to Singapore? But they are both different.

You know, it's not that one is better than the other. It's not like I'm escaping from one unhappy country to another. They are both amazing, wonderful, beautiful. Maybe, I am irate because I don't have a real choice. I can't get a Canadian citizenship like that. I am only a guest. *Don't overstay your hospitality. Leave your money here. Take your opportunities. Now, get out.* It's about that feeling deep within I struggle with. The elusive, unknown lover that woos you much against your expectations. Who, then, is my true lover? Where lies my genuine passion? Anyways, it's all moot, isn't it? I'll be back soon to my final farewell days in Calgary.

I hope you are enjoying your time off in Calgary. I saw the forecast of snow and freezing cold. It was a white Christmas, for sure. Let me know if you want anything else from Singapore.

Have a wonderful new year.

Simran

20 JANUARY 1988

Dear Mummy,

I'm back to my last semester at the university. I still think about the wonderful dinner you cooked for me and my friends. The food was delicious. I think of you often these days. My trip to Singapore made me see things differently. Don't get me wrong, Mum. I love Singapore. But it was hot, and I found it difficult to adjust when I was there. I was relieved to come back to the cold and snow in Calgary. It felt like home. I missed my house too.

I think about all the women at the dinner party we had. We are all different, yet our lives have similar paths. I hope that Amrit can find a way. I admire the way she has the courage to stand up. It's not easy to do, Mummy. It's 1988. In 2008, Roni and Soni will be close to my age. What will their world be like as women?

Surely, they won't have arranged marriages? I am sure these young girls will be able to choose what they want to do with their lives. I hope they travel, get an education, and pick their own husbands. They should marry whomever they want from any background or race. I pray things will change for my young nieces.

Think of it. You were married at sixteen. Amrit was married at twenty. You had no choice. You accepted what was given to you. Still, you made the best of your lives, and I am proud of you, my beautiful Mummy. You left your family, country and everything in India and came to a new place, Singapore. You're my inspiration.

Love you,

Simran

23 JANUARY 1988

Dear Simran,

Thank you. You have no idea how healing it was to spend New Year's Eve with you and all those fabulous women. What goddesses. You were all patient and kind. You listened to my memories about my mum. You know what, telling you those stories created a new sense of appreciation of who my mum was. Who she had to be. Who she ended up being. I stopped paying attention to her as I got older. I was too busy rebelling and fighting. I know women want to be heard. I didn't agree with some of her ideas, but I realize that was ok, right?

I should still have loved my mum in spite of our differences, our flaws, our hopes, our dreams. What must she have been thinking in those moments when I could not see eye to eye with her? On New Year's Eve, together with your mum, sister, Anita, and you, I laid some of my grief to rest and replaced it with sweet memories.

It was nice to see you, Simran. You seemed…hmmm…different. Calgary has changed you, hasn't it? I felt something has shifted. You have an air of confidence about you that was intriguing. I'm sure your experiences in Calgary have made you stronger and bolder. I noticed how you watched and listened to all us women share our stories of heartache and triumph with deep intent.

Do you remember what you said to me when I left your house that evening?

You said, "Amy, as women, we need to create our own destinies as well. Look at all of us in this room today. I'm seeing how essential it is to grasp opportunities that come my way. Any opportunities."

I thought about your words for a long time. I need to do the same. I don't want to be as unhappy as my mum was and to see death as the way out. I want to find my own joy. You have forged your own path in life, haven't you? Calgary has changed you in good ways. You didn't even ask about Sudhir or run to see him when you were in Singapore. I love how you closed that chapter.

Enjoy your last months there, Sim. The good news is that when you come back to Singapore, it'll be a new period of readjustment. I struggled adjusting to life in Singapore after being in the west for so long. I found it tough getting used to our Singaporean work schedule—long days and six days a week. I suspect it'll be an extra layer for you as you move back home and fall back into the traditional demands of life. Your mum told me she and your dad have been looking for prospective suitors for you already.

Thank you, again, for that extraordinary evening.

Your friend,

Amy

1 FEBRUARY 1988

Dear Simran,

It was wonderful seeing you here in Singapore. I am excited to have you back soon. I'm glad Anders was away on New Year's Eve so I could spend that time with you and those fabulous women. What a night. I can't believe it. Our lives as women are complex. There we were, Sikh, Tamil, Indonesian and Chinese women, and yet, our inner desires are in sync. We all want love. We all want to be heard. We all want to be defined by our own worth. We want to be visible.

Sim, I left your family home that night feeling invigorated. What a great way to start the new year. Our paths have all have meandered differently, haven't they? Look at how we are defined by our labels. By the way, I love your mum. What an amazing cook. She must have spent hours getting those Indian dishes prepared. I know how long it takes me just to make chicken curry. She showed true compassion when she put Amy's mum—Sophia's—shoes on the chair at the dining table. Who would have even thought about doing that? It was a heart wrenching and beautiful moment to honour Sophia.

You always said that your mum turns into a sixteen-year-old when she is happy and can be her true self. I detected a sort of innocence and joy that brimmed over in her mannerisms. I laughed out loud when I saw her kick you by mistake, not wanting your sister to disclose her family secrets. There's still that guarded traditional stance that comes through. The way she carries herself is enviable. She showed her incredible figure in that beautiful deep pink sari with flowers embroidered all over. I chuckled at her six gold bangles on each arm that clanged all night. I told her I loved her matching gold necklace and earrings—elegant rubies. There you were in your jeans and t-shirt while your mum was dressed to the nines even though she had to cook all those dishes.

Your mum epitomizes the traditional order—her long, black hair coiffed in a bun at the nape of her neck. Of course, she had her favourite rose lipstick you mentioned she wanted you to get from Calgary. What a beauty. That was an important night for your mum as well, as she saw us younger girls finding our way through a world much different from hers. She never had that freedom most of us have today. I keep thinking how she was married off at sixteen!

And your sister. Wow. What's with that? I sensed an awakening of sorts. I mean, I don't know her well, just what you have told me, but there is a composure I can recognize. She was excited about her job at your uncle's sports store. She proudly told me she was the top salesperson in the store and was getting a promotion. Imagine that. She went straight from school to a new husband's house. She had no chance to establish her sense of identity or self. Look at her now. Through her persistence, she rose to the occasion and is fighting for her voice. By the way, she is the spitting image of your mum. Such a beauty.

Do you know what was interesting? I married Gopal, a man I chose on my own volition. Amrit had an arranged marriage, and she had no say. We both have two children each. I left my abusive husband, and she has a cheating husband. What is fascinating is the parallel courses of our lives. I am grateful I can choose my way out. It's not easy, but it's possible. I hope Amrit can find a path as well. We don't have to accept what life dishes out to us. That night was a novel waiting to be written about us women. Right?

Me? Well, you know. Indian drama continues. Oh, pardon me. Indian Swedish drama. My hot, handsome, rich boyfriend—are you ready—is already married. That was my New Year's Day gift. A phone call from the Mrs.

I walked in through my front door from Tang's, a successful shopping expedition. Darling Anders had given me quite the generous gift card to buy whatever I wanted to make up for his absence. My arms were laden with the perfect Chanel outfit from top to toe, including the most beautiful silver clutch purse I had ever seen when the phone shrilled. I dropped the boxes and bags on the couch and ran to the phone.

It was an unfamiliar woman's voice but a recognizable accent. I frowned in confusion.

"Sit down," the voice commanded me. "Stay away from my husband," she cautioned.

"Anders?" I whispered. "He's married?"

"Yes. Anders. Let me warn you: he has affairs all the time, but he always comes back to me. He tells me about all you stupid women," her voice crackled over the phone.

"Is Anders with you in Stockholm right now?" My voice rose to a crescendo.

She laughed and said, "Is that what the bastard told you? No. He's in London, with his other mistress, Helena. He's juggling the two of you at the moment. You poor dear."

"I didn't know Anders was married! I never would have been with him." My voice fell to a whisper.

Anders' wife was briefly sympathetic, saying, "I know. I know. That's his game. I hope you haven't fallen in love with him. Easy when he flashes all that money. I found your number in his briefcase. Stay away, you stupid young girl. I've been married to him for twenty years, and we have three beautiful children. Don't think you can lure him away from me. No one has succeeded all these years. Listen carefully. He's mine."

I hung up. Married? It never crossed my mind. I stared at my bags from my shopping indulgence. Return them, tomorrow? Yeah, right. Fuck it. I went to my room and put on that stupidly overpriced short, sexy black dress, slipped into the silver high heels and carried that matching little purse. I stared at the woman staring back at me in the mirror. Damn. I looked like a million bucks. Saying goodbye to love in Chanel is bittersweet. With a sigh, I hung all my gifts from the cheating Swede in my cupboard. I thought about your sister Amrit and her cheating husband, Manjit, and felt a pang of sadness for her. Rejection is hard to bear. Listen, I am no one's second choice. Like hell I was going to return anything Anders bought me.

Yes. Another one bites the dust, Simran. But that's ok. I can meet more men. I can choose, again. Remember how your mum told us that a widow or a divorced Indian woman was ostracized and rejected—a taboo. Hell, yeah. Not me. I am going out tomorrow night in my hot new ensemble. I don't live by anyone's judgement of me. Screw those double standards. Come to think of it, I'll miss my shopping sprees more than I miss Anders.

Good luck with those essays. Those will be the last few ones you have to write before you come back to the Singapore dream.

Love,

Anita

20 FEBRUARY 1988

Dear Amy,

New Year's Eve, indeed, was a special night. Your mum's red shoes will always mean something for me. I think all women should own a pair of red shoes. Like Dorothy from the Wizard of Oz, right? Magical. I am going to get a pair this weekend. Maybe, I'll get red winter boots? That will be handy in the snow.

I have a secret to share with you. I haven't told my family, yet. A month ago, I applied for the Master's in English program. It had been on my mind after Dr. Sanders mentioned it to me. I did it on a whim. It was just for fun, you know. Well, yesterday I received this official looking letter. My hands trembled, and I tore open the letter.

Inside, there was my letter of acceptance into the Master of Arts in English program at the University of Calgary. The letter fell from my trembling hands. I felt both joy and red-hot fear. The program would start in September 1988. The joy gushed because I never imagined I could soar higher than I already had when I walked out of a near arranged marriage to get a degree. Now that I am at the end of my first degree, could I even think of getting a Master's in English?

I fell silent and sank into my armchair. I felt fired up by the possibility of getting an additional degree. I thought about my challenges with a few professors here. But there were other wonderful, inspiring professors who filled my mind with incredible information and knowledge. I handled those jerks who stood in my way. In the end, I wasn't intimidated. I would choose my courses wisely. I would get help to improve my writing. I would talk to my professors and interview them. I wasn't that gullible girl from three years ago who got a D in her first course and wanted to leave. All these emotions and more flooded my thoughts.

I know I will disappoint many people if I don't go back to Singapore. If I stay in Calgary, Mum will be heartbroken. But if I leave, I will be brokenhearted. In the quiet evening, I stared out the large bay window, watched the heavy snow fall furiously blanketing the reluctant ground, and wondered what I had gotten myself into.

Love and best wishes,

Simran

22 FEBRUARY 1988

Dear Anita,

Oh dear. Another one bites the dust. I'm sorry to hear that Anders is married and lied to you. You're right. It made me think of my sister, Amrit, and her cheating husband. I know how hurt my sister is. Now, Anders' wife is an intriguing woman, isn't she? She has accepted her husband's indiscretions, yet she still tracks his mistresses down. Is it love or money? I marvel at what women tolerate and the choices they make to be happy, or in some cases, unhappy.

I love your attitude about bouncing back from your search for love. I am impressed by your resilience. Do you remember Steve, the man I met at the punk bar? We spend time together, and it is a curious experience for me to understand the concept of dating in the west. At the end of the day, Steve and I share similar values about life. Even our families are alike in their expectations and love for their children. That's what connects all human beings, no matter our different races and backgrounds. But do I feel any sparks? Do I even need a man? Hmmm.

Keep on going, Anita.

Hugs and love,

Simran

1 MARCH 1988

Dear Simran,

I'm counting the days till you come home. I felt light as a cloud when you were back. It was wonderful to be with you, to not wear a mask and to laugh again. There was something different about you. You were confident and happy. I can see Calgary has changed you. I laughed when I remembered all your escapades and adventures— some crazy ones. But everything seemed to have made you into this stronger person, not that scared young girl at her own engagement, where everyone dressed her like a doll and pushed her to her future husband.

I loved hearing your stories when you were here. I think of your friend Linda who divorced her husband and got her own house to live with her two sons. She got a job, and her husband paid her money for the children, right? I like this concept.

As I told you when you were here, Manjit went back to his old ways and his old love. It's ok. I understand. Like me, he tried to make a way with us. I can't change him, and I don't want to anymore. My job isn't to be a business partner to my husband. I can't imagine the rest of life complaining about my husband's girlfriend. Unlike most Indian wives who have to accept infidelity, I'm not willing to close an eye to this behaviour. I listened to the stories of all the women in Mummy's house on New Year's Eve and I felt courage rise inside me. I mean if my maid Sumari left Indonesia and her son behind to come to Singapore to work, why can't I work to support my children? At least, I can go to Mummy and Papa's house and decide what to do after that.

This time, it will be a final exit. I won't be going back to Manjit anymore. I've decided—I will be the first one in this family to get a divorce. You are the first one to get a degree. We are first in everything, Simran. We will set the way for my daughters, so they won't suffer the lack of options we had. We fought for our rights and freedom. You did right when you left the country to get a degree. That is power. I will check if I can complete my education from where I was forced to stop when I got married. If not, never mind. I will start from scratch. I'm excited thinking about it. You inspired me, Simran.

Let everyone at the temple look at me and feel sorry when I get divorced. I'll walk with my head held high and feel joy and freedom. It's better than the looks of pity from those who know my husband has another woman. I won't be lonely when I'm taking care of my children and being a working woman. Maybe, maybe one day, I can have my own sports shop. Anything is possible, right?

On the day I got married, I looked forward to a happy life of love and being a good wife. When I gave birth to my children, I looked forward to being a great mother. The best part is I did not choose my own husband or when I was ready to have my kids. Everyone else decided for me. I was a robot. I lived my life on automatic mode. You rebelled. You said no. You lived your life on possibilities and adventures.

Ok. I've decided. It's my turn now. Watch out, world!

See you soon,

Amrit

10 MARCH 1988

Simran beti,

Just few weeks more and you will be coming home. You don't know how I have been counting the days. It's been three years. When you left, I cried and cried non-stop for many days and nights. I felt like my right arm had been cut off. When you have children, you will understand. I sacrificed everything for you. But I wanted you to have your dream. I know you didn't want to marry. Do you know how many suitors you had? One after the other. But you are a stubborn girl. You said no to the doctor, the lawyer, the businessman, the accountant, the millionaire. You threw them all in the dustbin. Come back now and you will have your degree. At least one part of your life will be settled. We will find a nice boy for you.

Your sister wants a divorce from Manjit. She packed her bags and came back home again with Roni and Soni. Please come back and knock some sense into her. This is not our tradition to divorce. We can talk through all problems and pray to Babaji. Everything will be fine again. It is the ups and downs of marriage. Indian women should never divorce. I'm not worried. Amrit can take a holiday here with us and go back to her husband in a few days.

It is time to start next chapter of your life, Simran. Soon you will be back to Singapore and our lives will be back to usual.

Buy Estée Lauder lipsticks. Try to get the latest colour.

I pray every day for your success, good health and wealth.

Pyar,

Mummy

Dear Amrit,

You are taking a bold step to divorce Manjit. I love it! You're right. You'll be the first one in the family to do so. I'm sure Mummy and Papa will try to convince you to go back to Manjit. What do you think? Will you be able to tolerate all the nagging at home? You'll learn to ignore what people say. Hey, you should talk to Anita. She divorced her husband Gopal. She'll give you some useful tips. You could start a women's divorce club.

I've had the most wonderful experience here in Calgary. Do you know Calgary held the 1988 Winter Olympics in Calgary from 7 to 22 February? I was a volunteer, Amrit. Lin and I went together, and we worked at the media room at the University of Calgary.

My task as a volunteer was a blast. I was a telephone operator for the athletes who lived on residence. When one of them called, I would transfer their calls. I had a chance to practice my German as well. Eins, zwei, drei. That's German for 1, 2 and 3. Hahahahahaha.

The best part of being a volunteer was I attended many of the events for free. For the first time in my life, I attended the opening and closing ceremonies at the Olympics. Oh, the lights, the fireworks, the cheers. The memories will forever be etched in my mind. All the volunteers got free winter coats, pants, gloves, and hats. I felt like a true Canadian in my snazzy winter gear.

I had never heard of winter sports since there is no winter in Singapore. Now, I had front row seats as I learnt about winter sports at the Olympics. So there I was, watching the underdog, Eddie the Eagle from England, come in dead last in ski jumping. He became famous for being the first Brit to take part in Olympic ski jumping since 1928.

That evening, I stood with thousands of spectators at the base of Canada Olympic Park on the day of the ski jumping competition. The crowd went wild—cheering and clapping—when Eddie jumped off the top ski hill and soared in the air. Eddie did not give up on his dreams. He wasn't the best in the world, but in his own mind, he believed in himself. I could relate to his desire to keep on trying his best. Never give up. I am Eddie the Eagle, jumping off the top of the mountain and flying in the air to get my degree.

I can't believe my fun days in Calgary are coming to an end. How lucky am I to be a part of Calgary history and the winter Olympics? Oh, wait. How could I forget the Jamaican bobsled team? You know Jamaica has no snow or bobsled team, right? These four Jamaicans decided to represent their country by going down the track in a bobsled. Look at the photographs I sent you of the team in their sled. You should have heard the rousing cheers of the crowd, even when the team came in last. Everyone at the Olympics supported the Jamaicans who proved anything was possible. I felt their passion—I was one of them. Like me, they were the outsiders who found a way in to belong and win the hearts of the world.

It was freezing right up to the Olympics, but I was one of the Calgarians warm and cozy in my full winter gear. So this is how Calgarians go out in winter; they are dressed properly. Trust me to learn about winter survival in my last few months in Calgary.

Oh, that's not all. I went to parties with athletes from all over the world. A group of us volunteers went to the bars on Electric Avenue, and we danced, drank, and talked to everyone from all over the world. It was a party every day during the two weeks. Do you remember that first time when I went to Coconut Joe's with my drug dealer friend Marlon? How scared was I. Not this time! I was in charge. I stood in the middle of the dance floor, jumped, and danced like a party animal. I said hi to everyone. I even looked around to see if Marlon was selling drugs that day. No luck.

Aaah, I will never forget these two weeks of the best party time in Calgary to celebrate my last few months in Calgary. The Calgary

Olympics is forever ingrained in my heart. I will keep that teal winter coat, and maybe one day, my child will wear it.

Let's be like Eddie the Eagle from Great Britain and the Jamaican Bobsled team. They made the impossible possible because they took a chance and had the courage to fail. That's no different than our lives. We have to jump off mountains and slide down icy tracks. We can do it!

Love,

Simran

27 MARCH 1988

Hey Simran,

I was taken aback when I read your letter. Do I sense rebellion again? You got accepted into the Master's program! That is interesting. I thought the plan was for you to complete your Bachelor of Arts at the University of Calgary and to come home to Singapore immediately?

You know, I spoke to your mum that New Year's Eve, and you have no idea how much she is looking forward to having you home. She loves you and misses you. She told me how hard it was to let you go by yourself to a new country. She worried about you all the time. She took me to her bedroom and showed me all your letters, which she kept in a red box on her dresser. She said when she missed you, she would read those letters again and again. You are fortunate to have a special relationship with your mum. I hugged your mum and told her you were a lucky daughter.

My mum and I didn't write to each other when I was away in Princeton. We barely spoke and became strangers in our absence and distance. I envy the close relationship you have with your beautiful mum. I can't bear to think of your mum's pain and disappointment when you don't come back. Think carefully. Are you being selfish and making a terrible mistake by staying in Calgary? How much education do you need?

For me, overcoming grief is confusing. I go through different stages. I get angry at what my mum did. I sob uncontrollably. Then I make peace with her and life. One hour later, I rant and rave at everything and everyone. Then it starts over again, a rollercoaster of emotions that make her absence impossible to accept. I am not sure how long these emotions will last. I reluctantly cleaned out her closet the other day. I stood in front of it, lingered over and caressed every item. I buried my face in her dresses and let my tears mingle with her essence. I could only sort a few items a day as each dress brought an onslaught of memories. I held that black Chanel dress she wore when we went shopping for her red pair of shoes. I pulled out the photograph I had taken of her that special day when she smiled, chatted, and held my hand. I folded the dress and put it in a box with the matching shoes and handbag. I put the photographs in. I went to my room and put the box under my bed. That way, she will always be with me.

My father, oh that poor man. He has shut down. There is no dialogue or conversations. He copes by pretending nothing happened.

I asked him questions about Mum, wanting to keep her alive in the house at least. He just shook his head. Before he left the room, he said, "Amy. Please. Let the dead lie in peace."

Silenced by my father's comment, I remembered how my mother always complained about feeling like a ghost. She said no one could see her. She felt unloved and unappreciated. I regret I didn't spend more time with Mum. I often came home from work and went straight to my room and shut the door. That's exactly what my father does to me now.

The irony is my mum is really a ghost now. She haunts me all the time. I see her in every corner of the flat. Sometimes, I stand by the window where she plunged to her death. I stare out the window as far as my eyes can see. What did Mum see? What did she think? Did she change her mind halfway down and regret her choice? It makes me second guess all my choices as a woman. I am afraid, Simran. Afraid of love. Afraid of life. Afraid of death. I've witnessed the downfall of love and the pain of loss, and the complexities overwhelm me.

Am I a ghost as well? Do I flit through life, unable to take chances anymore? I mean, why would I be drawn to Gunther, the German man I met at the hospital, who has a brain tumour—am I drawn to death because that is the safety of knowing loss? I've decided to stop seeing him. I need to live, not linger in the shadows of death anymore.

I want to ask my mum, "Why? Why, Mummy? Why did you kill yourself?"

I need to find my answers. Death cannot be the only way out.

Think carefully about your decision. I feel your mother's pain.

Sincerely,

Amy

28 MARCH 1988

Dear Amrit,

Why is everyone banking on me to save them? I can barely take care of myself. I feel an incredible pressure to please everyone but myself. I am torn about what to do. Calgary has penetrated my heart and mind. This is the place where I became my true self. A woman of my own. The highs and lows of my life unfolded here. Alone. I did it myself. If I go back to Singapore, who will I be?

The truth is, I am not sure how not to hurt all of you. I'm sorry. I know you and Mummy need me, but I have many dreams left to pursue. Should I accept the spot in the Master's of English program here at the University of Calgary? It's a dream come true for me, Amrit. I can do what I want and be my authentic self. I can make my own decisions and live my own life. Isn't it time to make my own mistakes? I can't live life for Mummy, Papa, you—and the whole damn world.

Being in Calgary has transformed impossibilities into real dreams. A Masters! Who in our family even has a degree? Not because the women didn't have the smarts to do so but because they were simply not allowed.

I am struggling to make everyone else but me happy. Can you try to understand my excitement… to be free? To mold my own life. I know you are worried that Papa can't afford to pay for me anymore. If I accept this spot, I will get a scholarship that will pay my way.

I didn't plan this or know this would happen. If I don't come back to Singapore, I think I may be disowned, right?

Love you, Simran

15 APRIL 1988

Simran,

Your father and I are relieved your degree is over. You have done such a good job and have great success. You are a strong girl. Congratulations on your degree, beti. You're the first girl in this family with such high education. No need for more education anymore. One degree is enough. Why do women need more? You're not a Canadian. You're a Singapore Punjabi girl, ok? I talked to your friend Amy and to your sister already. I smell a rat!

We know you must leave Calgary by April 25. We are waiting for you. It's time to come home. This is not the proper behaviour for a girl at your age. You are older now. No more twenty years old. You can't be alone in a strange country like that. Sooner or later, girls have to marry. They can't live like men alone by themselves in a strange country. You have completed your B.A. It cost us thousands and thousands of dollars. We supported you through thick and thin. We suffered a lot for your success.

Now you must come home and give back to the family. How can you survive without family? Your sister is going through a rough time. She needs your help. I need you to come and complete our family. I cannot take your absence anymore. My heart was broken, beti, for three years when you left for Calgary. Come and fix my broken heart and loneliness. We all need you.

Your father said if you don't buy the ticket, he will show up in Calgary and bring you home. He knows his way around Calgary. We will expect you home. We know the plane from Calgary usually arrives in Singapore 11 p.m. We will be waiting at the Singapore airport to bring you home where you belong.

Listen, pack your bags. There will be no more money after April. We have done our duty as your parents more than we needed to. It's time to start your proper life in Singapore like before you left for Calgary. Your time in Calgary is over.

Come home.

Mummy

16 APRIL 1988

Dear Amy,

Your letter made me reconsider my decision to stay in Calgary and get my Master's degree. You forced me to reevaluate my mum's feelings and sacrifices. I felt your pain about your regrets about losing your mum. Then, letters from my mum and sister warned me against rebelling. I'm engulfed by waves of panic, sadness, anticipation, dread—I never know which one will come to the forefront each day when I pack my bags and give away my belongings.

I empathize with your regret over the loss of your mum. I imagine it will be a permanent void in your heart. Don't be a ghost, Amy. You know how in Singapore the Chinese celebrate the Hungry Ghosts Festival in August, right? I thought about your feelings and think you'll have to honour it for your mum since this day is earmarked for lost and homeless wandering ghosts. Perhaps, you can find a symbolic way for you and your mum and give her this proper ritual send off to the world beyond?

Growing up in Singapore, I always wondered about all the burning joss sticks, paper money and offerings of food and drinks in front of my neighbours' houses for the wandering ghosts. When I come back to Singapore, we could hold a special ceremony for your mum. After the ritual offerings, we can take lotus shaped lanterns and set them afloat in the rivers to float out to the seas. I know this gesture symbolically guides lost souls to the peaceful afterlife. Your mum will like that, won't she?

We are all misplaced souls, aren't we? I feel like a lost ghost for sure at this crossroad of my life. You say you are a ghost. Your mum is certainly one. I think we need to banish our ghosts and our past and carve new ways to be content in the flesh.

I have begun my farewell tour of Calgary. I met my friend Raj and her daughter Tanya, the wonderful East Indian friends of mine who live downtown. They made me lasagna and Caesar salad, teasing me I would get too much Indian food when I returned home to Singapore. I told them about my graduate school acceptance and my final decision to go back to Singapore.

Raj looked at me and said, "Once a ship has sailed, there's no going back. You have to keep moving on through the storms of life. You can't go back to your old harbour, assuming it's even there waiting for you."

Tanya, her daughter countered, "I could never go back to that Indian tradition and expectations you told me about. Isn't it suffocating? Why would anyone marry a man picked for them? Even when you buy a car, you test drive it first, right?"

I laughed at them and said, "Raj, you understand the old ways since you grew up in Delhi and followed the traditional path. Tanya, you lived only in the west all your life, so you don't have to pick any side. I am stuck in the middle of both worlds, between the east and the west. Maybe I can take the best of both worlds back to Singapore and be happy."

Tanya stuck her tongue out at me and countered, "Or you could be crushed by the worst of both the east and the west. Ok, listen. Don't even send me your wedding invitation if you have an arranged marriage. I saw you dancing in that punk bar like the wild child and rebel you truly are. Remember that ridiculous smile on your face? What are you going to do now when you are controlled and restrained back in Singapore?"

I shook my head and changed the subject. I didn't want to confront any more life revelations. I wanted peace and quiet. On my way home, I stopped at the University of Calgary. I felt hot tears on my cheeks. Craigie Hall. The library. MacEwan Hall. Jack Simpson gym. Kananaskis Hall. I lingered at every bench and saw that young, naive twenty-year old who explored these grounds and charted her history in the nooks and crannies of the university. I carved my initials on the rock in front of MacEwan Hall, looking around cautiously to make sure I didn't get hauled away by security guards. Once done, I ran my finger over S and K. I smiled at its permanence.

I met Steve for our final lunch outing. We went to Nick's Pizza, a fitting goodbye spot. He was pensive and quiet.

"Maybe I'll come to Singapore," Steve said.

"You're welcome anytime, Steve," I said.

"No. I'll get a job in Singapore and come be with you," Steve smiled.

I nodded, and then imagined how my father and mother would have a fit if Steve appeared; they would surely lock me in my bedroom.

I giggled and said, "I'm sure my parents will give you a welcome just like the one your parents gave me. 100 questions and all."

Steve drove me around Calgary that day so I could say goodbye to my favourite jaunts. I had my last Cafe Thursday at the Roasterie in Kensington. We took a short walk along the Bow River, and I threw pebbles in the river, making secret wishes with each toss. I waved at the Calgary Tower and the Stampede grounds. Every part of Calgary touched my heart as I quietly acknowledged its lessons for me—the real education I had garnered from all these places, not just the paper degree I had earned.

That evening, I showed Lin my one-way ticket home to Singapore. She smiled and said she couldn't wait to get her one-way ticket home in four months. I admired her determination and resolve to leave Calgary permanently.

"You don't want to stay in Calgary?" I asked.

"Are you kidding me?" she said. "I miss my family, my food, my country, everything. I love Calgary, but Calgary is a temporary home for me, like it is for you."

I nodded, although deep down, I pondered over the idea of temporary. Is it that easy to be a fleeting traveller? Unexpectedly, Lin handed me a little box. I was startled and slowly unwrapped it. Nestled in the box lay a Calgary keychain in the shape of a cowboy hat. It was perfect! I hugged Lin. Inwardly, I chuckled, recalling the smelly socks, the sullen Lin, and the crazy comments—now all captured in the symbolic keychain. Ah, life and its twists and turns.

As you can see, Amy, I am slowly but surely disengaging and tearing myself from my home in Calgary. The goodbyes are more difficult than I imagined them to be. I don't think I'll come back to Calgary once I leave. This place is seared in my heart, but I have no choice. Immigration visas, money, family, tradition, expectations… goodness, the never-ending list propels me to the airport on April 25, 1988. If only I could choose!

I am conflicted when I say, "See you soon, Amy."

Lots of love,

Simran

25 APRIL 1988

Hello Mummy, Papa and Amrit,

I went to the Calgary airport today. I packed my bags with the last few things I owned. I gave everything else—from books to furniture—to my friends. I didn't want to get a ride with anyone because I knew it would be too painful to say goodbye, so I took a taxi to the airport.

When I arrived at the departure hall of the Calgary airport, I entered the building and walked to the glass windows. I gazed at the airplanes slowly taxiing in and out on the busy runaways. Where was each plane going to? Who was leaving, and who was returning? I felt a strong pull, unable to look away or move from my spot.

Slowly, I pulled out my letter of acceptance for the Master's program from my handbag. I read it again, and my heart swelled with pride. I had been accepted into the program despite the moments where I thought I would not make it or get the grades I needed. I succeeded even when I had a few professors who didn't believe in me. What no one knows is I accepted the offer four days ago. I walked into Dr. Sanders' office at the Department of English and gave him my signed acceptance. In return, he gave me a signed letter that confirmed my spot and my scholarship. He stood up and shook my hand with a big smile on his face.

"Congratulations, Simran, well done." Dr. Sanders happily beamed.

I put the letter away and pulled out my new extended visa from my passport. You see, I went back to Harry Hays immigration office last Friday. I had all my paperwork ready. I handed the immigration officer my signed letter of acceptance into the Master's program.

This time, the immigration officer behind the counter smiled at me, congratulated me, and stamped my visa for two years. I thanked him for his warm welcome and grinned happily. This time, I wasn't scared or looking like a lost soul. This time, I was in charge: I looked like I belonged in Calgary.

I pulled myself from the window and slowly walked to the Air Canada ticket counter. When I reached the counter, I asked the agent for an extension to travel at a later date on my airline ticket meant for that day.

"No problem, Simran," said the friendly lady at the counter. "Guess you're not going back to Singapore today, eh?"

I shook my head, feeling clearer and stronger about my decision each minute. The agent rebooked my ticket for a holiday in December now. All it took was a rebooking fee! With my suitcases in tow, I turned and walked out of the airport to the taxi stand outside.

This time, I felt like a Calgarian, not a lost and scared foreigner. I took the taxi to Motel Village and checked into the same motel Papa and I had stayed in three years ago. Tomorrow, I will find a place to stay—maybe even the Kananaskis Hall dorms at the University of Calgary. Who knows? I can choose.

Everything flowed smoothly today and helped me to make my mind up to stay in Calgary. It was my plan to come home to Singapore today even though I had my acceptance and visa confirmed. I tried my best to leave, but I couldn't get on the plane back to Singapore.

Mummy, Papa, Amrit, I decided to follow my heart and my dreams. I'm sorry to disappoint all of you. I know you're upset and angry I've made this decision on my own and disobeyed your wishes.

Please understand my desire to complete my Master of Arts degree. It feels like the right thing to do. I must live my dream and follow my passion. I really tried my best to leave today, but my steps and my heart took me back to Calgary. This is my destiny, and I will live my life with no more regrets.

I feel joy, peace, and hope. Even though I miss all of you, I know

I've made the best decision for me.
 I'm home in Calgary.

Love,

Simran

THE END

ABOUT THE AUTHOR

Kelly Kaur grew up in Singapore, came to Calgary to get her degrees at the University of Calgary, and stayed longer than she thought she would.

Kelly's works have appeared internationally in Singapore, Canada, the United States, Malaysia, Berlin, Prague, Australia, Zimbabwe, and the United Kingdom.

Her short story, *The Kitchen is Her Home,* was nominated for the Pushcart Prize XLVII. Her poem, *The Justice of Death,* was awarded Honourable Mention in the Creators of Justice Literary Awards, International Human Rights Art Festival (New York). She was selected for the Ulyanovsk UNESCO's The Only Question Project: 40 international writers share their questions and answers about writing. Also, her poem, *Women Rising Up,* is in a travelling exhibition in six museums in the North Dakota Human Rights Arts Festival from January to November 2022.

Her poem, *A Singaporean's Love Affair*, is going to the moon—twice. It will be sent on the Nova Collection of the Lunar Codex—Nova-C mission (June 2022) and the Polaris Collection—Griffin mission (Fall 2023) which archives and preserves the work of contemporary creative artists on lunar time capsules launched via parnters of NASA's Artemis program.

Kelly lives in **Calgary**, Alberta. Kelly was recently awarded a Canada Council for the Arts Research and Creation grant for her second book, *Stories in the Sky*.

ACKNOWLEDGEMENTS

Thank you to Aritha van Herk, my marvellous mentor, who inspired me, encouraged me, listened to me, and always made time for me—no matter where she was in the world.

Many thanks to Stonehouse Publishing and their wonderful team. I appreciated Netta Johnson's, Anne Brown's and Lisa Murphy Lamb's guidance, support, and brilliance. Thank you, Lisa, for believing in my women and their secret stories. You patiently and carefully gave me direction and encouragement every step of the way.

My sincere appreciation to the Writers Guild of Alberta and Alexandra Writers Centre Society for starting me off on an exciting journey.

I will always love and be inspired by Singapore and all my family, friends and memories there.

I am grateful for my daughter, Tegan Asha Post, who made me promise never to say no; my son, David Post, for his encouragement; and Nina Kuckreja, DP Dean Bedi, Mummy Asha Kumari, and Papa Hardip Singh Bedi for always being my life's foundation. Because of all of you, I can fly to the moon and live my dreams infinitely.